COLD WICKED
LIES

COLD WICKED
LIES

Toni Anderson

For fellow author Jenn Stark
High Priestess and guiding light. Friend and inspiration.
Pure Magic!

CHAPTER ONE

TJ SLIPPED OUT of the tunnel and into the woods he'd spent his whole life exploring, carefully avoiding the cameras he'd helped set up a decade earlier. For years, staying safe, staying off the grid had been the only thing that mattered to his family. Then the heartbreaking and unexpected loss of his mother in the spring had taught him that no matter how carefully they planned and protected themselves, there was no guarantee of survival. And, however much they tried to avoid it, the world, with all its inherent danger, was coming for them.

This quiet remote region of Washington State was drawing commercial loggers and environmental protesters, and the threat of conflict that had always seemed so compelling yet abstract in the past was now becoming a tangible reality. TJ didn't want conflict, but he was prepared. Only one problem...

His breath froze on a rough exhale, forming a cloud that rose up to join the mist shrouding the treetops. A stick cracked under his boot, and a deer snapped up its head, startled, then bounced away, crashing through the thick scrub. TJ cursed himself for not paying attention to where he was putting his feet. Distraction was dangerous.

He didn't want to be seen by anyone except the person he'd come to meet. Couldn't risk being found out. Not yet.

1

Wasn't ready to give her up, even though his dad would flail him alive if he found out what TJ had been up to all summer.

Through the woods and down the steep-sided gully to the almost dried up stream bed that marked the edge of Harrison property. TJ glanced up at the sign warning trespassers to keep away or risk being shot. It was no idle threat.

He stepped over the narrow trickle of water—a small act of rebellion. He wasn't supposed to leave Harrison land. Not without permission from his father.

TJ didn't doubt his father's love, but the man was overprotective. At eighteen, TJ was old enough to make his own choices.

He climbed the opposite bank with a silent tread, his heart skipping a beat as he thought about the girl he'd come to meet. He held his breath as he crested the top of the rise and looked down the steep wooded hillside.

He slowly drew the icy air into his lungs as his mind grappled with disappointment. She wasn't there.

He frowned. He was twenty minutes late because he hadn't been able to get away without someone seeing him. Had she given up on him?

Every Wednesday for months they'd secretly met up and spent a morning together—hiking his favorite trails, spotting wildlife. They'd even snuck away to the movies once when his father had gone into the city. It had been the first time TJ had ever been to a cinema, and it had been overwhelming—not the noise or the scents or the giant screen, but the feel of Kayla's lips beneath his. The sweet taste of her. It was the first time he'd kissed a girl, and it turned out kissing Kayla was addictive.

He wanted to see her so he could kiss her again.

Where was she? He couldn't call her. He didn't carry a cell phone—even if the government didn't track a person's whereabouts with them, they were useless in these mountains.

TJ made his way carefully through the deep green conifers, keeping to the shadows. Maybe that's what Kayla was doing, staying concealed until he showed himself.

There were more people than ever roaming these remote mountains. The numbers had exploded in May when some Canadian told everyone he'd seen a Sasquatch in the old growth forest north of here—where the loggers were supposedly headed next.

TJ didn't want the trees cut down, but his dad had told him to keep out of it. To not draw any attention to their compound or the people who lived quietly inside.

TJ forced himself not to hurry, scanning the surroundings for anyone else on the mountain. He didn't want to be punished and confined if someone from home spotted him. He didn't want to be banned from ever seeing Kayla again.

TJ reached the tree where they'd arranged to meet—a massive, damaged Douglas-fir that had escaped the logger's axe and saved this section of the forest. It was home to a breeding pair of rare Northern Spotted Owls. The environmentalists had scored a major victory for their cause when the endangered birds had been discovered.

The owls were the reason he and Kayla had met. They'd both come to watch the baby birds test out their fledgling wings and had ended up spying on one another as well. She'd been sketching the first time he'd seen her, long hair constantly falling across one side of her face.

More than six months of weekly meetings later, and TJ desperately wished he could see her for more than a few short hours each week. He wanted to be with her constantly. Soon, the snow would be too deep for even these stolen moments—the first big dump was late this year, and TJ took it as a sign of approval of their relationship from up above.

He swallowed the lump of frustrated longing that mixed with the familiar excitement in his blood. He leaned against the big, old, fat tree, the rough bark pressing into his spine. The angry chatter of squirrels and call of mountain birds floated on the cool, sharp air.

He'd been toying with leaving home, joining Kayla in her fight to protect the forest and creatures living within it. She had a tent, and he had a little money put aside. He knew she was traveling with a friend, but they could make it work. His family had money—cash and gold—buried in locations none of the others knew about. He could take a little, enough to live on. It was his as much as it was his father's.

But his dad had warned him that the end of days was getting closer, and they had to be ready to defend themselves. TJ clenched his jaw. What about Kayla? Who'd protect her?

TJ wouldn't leave her to die, not when he could offer her safety. He didn't care what the others said about not accepting strays into their fold. His mother had been letting in strangers for as long as TJ could remember. Most were distant relatives, and they all had to promise to contribute and abide by his father's rules. His parents had never turned anyone away. Why should TJ have to turn away the one person he cared about besides his father?

Assuming Kayla wanted to come with him…

He shoved his hands in his pockets and hunched his shoulders. If she didn't want to live in the compound, would she wait in her camp for him until spring? Would she be okay?

Or would she be forced to move on to a place where he'd never find her again?

The idea of losing her was like a sledgehammer to his chest.

Should he abandon the only home he'd ever known, the only security they had from the upcoming apocalypse? Maybe. Maybe for this girl—who'd never survive without him. *If* she wanted him to join her…

He glanced down the mountain, wondering if she'd already left and he'd missed her. A tiny flash of red caught his eye. He took a step forward. Then another. Kayla had a red wool cap that exact shade… Had she dropped it?

She was never late. Had she come and gone and maybe left a note with the hat, knowing he'd find it?

He moved faster, careful of the roots and loose rocks, the uneven footing. When he reached the hat, he saw it was simply that, a wooly hat with no note attached. He picked it up, confused.

It looked similar to the one Kayla usually wore, but he didn't spend a lot of time looking at her hat when her face was so close.

He looked around and caught sight of an object that looked unnatural and out of place in the shadows of the woods.

His feet moved him in that direction, a moment of prescience flowing over him as he dodged around the wide skirts of a western hemlock. This was bad. He knew it was bad even before the shape elongated into a human arm. The rest of the person came into view as he moved closer. His mouth crumbled to dust, and his throat constricted so tightly the air became trapped in his lungs.

Don't look, don't look!

But his brain demanded answers.

"Kayla?"

The body of a young woman wearing hiking boots, unzipped jeans, and a green t-shirt that had been lifted to reveal a naked breast lay in the dirt and pine needles. Her coat was discarded a few feet away. She looked cold. The thought rattled around his shattered brain like a loose piece of bone.

A mop of dark hair covered the woman's features, and her face was turned away from him. She was the same size as Kayla. His Kayla.

Tears swam in his eyes, and he took another step closer, knowing he should check for a pulse, even though he didn't want to cross the line from denial to truth.

He didn't want to touch her.

He didn't want to see her face.

Didn't want it to be true.

He crouched beside the body and couldn't resist pulling the t-shirt down over the girl's chest, out of respect. His fingers shook as he noticed cuts and abrasions on her torso and on her neck and face.

He forced himself to press his fingers to the side of her throat where her pulse usually fluttered shyly against fragile flesh. Her skin felt inert and alien, not warm and soft or vibrant the way Kayla usually felt when he touched her. He withdrew his fingers quickly, rubbing them on the side of his jeans as a horrified wave of repulsion raced over his shoulders, up his nape and scalp, into his throat which burned.

He recognized the t-shirt, but he still couldn't bring himself to move the dark hair off her face and see her beautiful features clouded in death. His hand hovered over her forehead.

The snap of a twig warned him he was not alone.

"What have you done? Get away from her!"

TJ looked up into the angry eyes of a US Fish & Wildlife officer. It was only as the officer started to grapple with his holster for his weapon that TJ realized how this would look.

No way was he going to prison for something he hadn't done, not when the world was going to end soon. He'd be trapped in a system where he would surely die. He whipped out his own 9mm handgun and pointed it at the surprised law enforcement officer.

"You've got it wrong. I found her like this." TJ's voice came out guttural and harsh.

"Sure, kid." The wildlife officer's upper lip curled. "Why don't you put the gun away, and we'll talk about it."

But TJ saw the truth in the man's eyes. He was already convinced TJ had killed Kayla. TJ started backing away through the branches of the trees.

"Don't follow me," TJ warned, then turned and sprinted, faster than a mule deer, dodging through the trees up the slope. This time he didn't worry about his footing or being quiet. If he was caught, he'd die in jail, and no one would ever believe he'd found Kayla already gone.

Tears half-blinded him. It had to be Kayla. Who else would be up here? He squeezed the woolen cap he still held in his hands, realizing he still carried it with him.

Shit.

His throat wanted to close, but he forced his mouth wide to gulp down oxygen he needed to get back to the compound. To safety. He tossed the hat away and, with it, the hope of a future with the woman he'd fallen in love with.

The wildlife officer shouted behind him. TJ leapt the stream and made it up the opposite bank, sliding on the icy ground a couple of times before launching himself over the top.

"Stop! Federal Wildlife Officer. Stop! You goddamn sonofabitch."

TJ didn't slow. The Feds would lock him up and throw away the key without ever giving him the chance to defend himself. Who was ever gonna believe an outsider like him?

No one, that's who.

He ran to the only safety he'd ever known, chest bellowing, making no effort to hide from the cameras this time, in fact, making damn sure whoever was on guard duty could see him and hear him coming and open the main goddamned door.

A hundred yards from the entrance, TJ heard the squeal of steel hinges in desperate need of some WD40.

"Hold it right there!" the wildlife officer behind him screamed.

TJ heard the sound of a bullet striking the reinforced steel of the main entrance at the same time he felt the sting of a ricochet across his cheek. Another inch, and he'd have been blinded. He launched himself through the door as one of the guards returned fire.

"Don't!" TJ wheezed. "Don't shoot. He's a Fed."

The sound of the high-power rifle cut through the air, and TJ knew it was already too late. There was no way the guard would miss at this range.

They'd been preparing for the revolution his whole life. TJ had just brought it to the door.

CHAPTER TWO

S UPERVISORY SPECIAL AGENT Charlotte Blood hurried off the giant C-17 military transport plane, dragging her small suitcase along behind her. The leader of the Hostage Rescue Team raised a brow, apparently amused by the fact her luggage had wheels.

She rolled her eyes and ignored him.

The only thing Charlotte cared about was resolving this situation without any further loss of life.

The Section Chief of the Crisis Negotiation Unit had made her the Negotiations Commander for this case, something she'd either thank him for or curse him for later, depending on the outcome. She was grateful for the opportunity to prove her abilities. Three of her stellar colleagues from CNU had already arrived on scene, and another Bureau negotiator was flying in from San Francisco in the morning. Hopefully, they could recruit a local to pad out the numbers and also give them access to pertinent information only a resident would know.

Ideally, this siege would be over sooner rather than later, but the Feds had learned the hard way that rushing things tended to lead to more lethal outcomes. With Thanksgiving just over and the holidays on the horizon, there would be some people desperate to end this as soon as possible so they could get home to their families to celebrate. She wanted to make sure everyone had that opportunity while justice was still served.

It was dark out already, and the area was dimly lit to disguise their arrival at this secret military base in northern Washington State. Broadcasting the arrival of the Hostage Rescue Team on local or national news media might inflame the situation, and that was the last thing anyone needed.

At the bottom of the plane's steps, she scanned the hangar and spotted a man waiting beside a black SUV that had its doors and rear cargo hatch wide open.

Their "local" contact was from the closest Resident Agency, which was still a hundred miles from this remote part of the state.

"Any updates?" she asked, introducing herself when she got close enough.

"Not since the director told us you were on your way." The agent showed her his credentials. Devon Truman. He was movie star handsome with obsidian eyes, pitch-black hair and tanned-looking skin. If he had language skills, then she bet undercover operations had already marked him for possible future assignments.

He took her suitcase and stowed it in the back. "I have to grab some equipment for the Incident Commander. I'll be a couple of minutes."

He smiled, and her ovaries started high fiving as she watched him walk away. No wedding band. Heartbreak handsome. Maybe there'd be an upside to this assignment.

She zipped her black down coat up to her chin, trying to ignore the sting of cold across the tips of her ears and nose. She wore fleece-lined leggings, sturdy boots, and silk underwear of the unsexy variety. When she'd discovered their destination, she'd packed more of the same.

This wasn't her first rodeo in this part of the world. She'd spent several weeks on and off this year, talking the Freemen down from their latest version of insurrection.

Agent Truman was speaking with one of the HRT guys. He pointed in the direction of several large boxes, which he and some of the other men started hauling in the direction of the SUV.

Charlotte caught the gaze of the HRT Gold section leader again. Payne Novak. He sent her a smirk before turning away to continue orchestrating the unloading of tons of equipment HRT needed to function.

And yet, he found her having a suitcase with wheels amusing.

The Tactical Commander and Negotiation Commander both worked with the Incident Commander to form the "Triad of Control," which meant Charlotte was about to spend quality time with Payne-in-the-ass-Novak. *Great.*

Though they'd never directly interacted, she'd ascertained from the frequent stares and frowns he sent in her direction that, for some reason, he didn't approve of her. She didn't have time for territorial or macho nonsense and hoped he could handle working with a woman as an equal.

Charlotte climbed into the front passenger seat of the SUV and waited for Agent Truman to finish packing the gear. Then he got in and turned on the ignition.

She'd be lying if she said she wasn't looking forward to spending a little alone time with Agent Hottie—maybe figure out if the guy was spoken for, or single and looking for love.

At thirty-two, after putting relationships on hold in favor of her career, she'd finally figured she was going to have to be more proactive when it came to dating. She wasn't in college anymore and most of the likable, straight, single men had already been snapped up. Agent Truman fitted the exact image she had of her perfect future partner. Polite, educated, cultured. Someone who'd comfortably fit behind the wheel of the family SUV with two kids and a dog strapped in the back. Someone who looked gorgeous enough to lick all over and virile enough to return the favor.

A sharp tap on the window almost had her heart levitating from her chest.

Supervisory Special Agent Payne Novak stared at her through the fogged-up glass.

She buzzed it down a few inches.

"I'm riding with you so you can update us both concurrently and save time. Unlock the door." Novak directed his comments to Truman.

He climbed in, and Charlotte's mood sank. She buzzed the window back up and stared out through the frosted glass.

It was probably a smart idea. Didn't mean she had to like his bulldozer attitude.

"What can you tell us about the situation? Any updates?" Novak asked.

Truman replied, "It's a mess. Federal Wildlife Officer name of Bob Jones was shot dead on private land that edges Colville National Forest. He'd previously radioed in to say he'd discovered the body of a young woman and was in pursuit of a suspect. He was shot, presumably by the suspect or members of a survivalist group who own the land and compound where the suspect lives. Sheriff and other wildlife officers went up there to assist FWO Jones, but a gun battle ensued, and now they can't get near the place to retrieve his body. Another deputy was also injured and is in serious condition in the hospital. Sheriff contacted us in Spokane, and we called Seattle, who called HQ. The director intervened. Everyone was told to stand down until the cavalry arrived."

The cavalry. The Tactical Operations arm of the FBI. CIRG. The Critical Incident Response Group—of which the Crisis Negotiation Unit formed a co-equal branch with the Hostage Rescue Team.

"How did the woman die?" Charlotte asked.

Truman shook his head. "We don't know yet. Agents from my Resident Agency are helping to process the scene. Medical Examiner arrived about thirty minutes ago."

"Her body is still there?" Charlotte asked in surprise.

"Director told our SAC not to let the locals touch a thing. I guess he's feeling antsy."

Charlotte didn't blame him. This incident shared aspects of two of the Bureau's biggest failures, Waco and Ruby Ridge. "Can you take me to the location where the body is? I'd like to view her before the ME moves her if possible."

"That's not your job," Novak stated firmly from the backseat.

She turned to face him. His close-cropped dark blond hair was hidden beneath a black knit cap, but his icy brows were clearly visible and met in a disapproving frown. Charlotte raised an eyebrow back, a little incredulous at Novak's audacity, but she held onto her patience. "SSA Novak, the Incident Commander hasn't arrived yet. My team is setting up the Negotiation Center and working to establish initial communications with the people on Eagle Mountain. In the meantime, I'd like to check out where this all started to get a handle on what exactly occurred so we can resolve this without anyone else getting hurt."

Charlotte held the steely glare in those blue-green eyes and gritted her teeth in an effort to be polite. "We can drop you off first if you need to supervise your people."

Truman glanced uneasily from her to Novak and back again.

"Actually, no." Novak flashed her a grim look. "A quick reconnoiter isn't a bad idea."

Irritation snaked along her nerves. "Are you sure you have the time, SSA Novak?"

"Sure. What are we waiting for?" Novak asked impatiently.

"I thought you'd want HRT to follow me to the ranch where we are basing operations," said Truman.

Novak glanced over his shoulder at his team. "Give me the GPS coordinates, and I'll let them know. They'll find it. Let's go."

Charlotte blew out a long breath and prayed for patience. "Yippee-kai-yay," she murmured under her breath, earning the tiny uptick of Agent Truman's rather excellent lips.

"Motherfucker." Came the rejoinder from the backseat.

"Indeed," said Charlotte.

PAYNE NOVAK LEANED forward in his seat, impatient to get on with things. It was killing him that a fellow federal law enforcement official was lying out in the dirt, exposed to the elements and abandoned like trash. No man left behind was a mantra he'd lived by since his Green Beret days. He swallowed, trying to loosen the tightness in his throat, thinking of another soldier on another hillside on the other side of the world. He had no intention of repeating that mission fail.

A short recon wasn't a terrible idea as long as it didn't stop him getting his men into position before dawn. As HRT's Tactical Commander on the ground, his job was assessing the threat, preparing for the threat, and developing action plans to eliminate the threat.

But from a personal standpoint, he also needed to get FWO Jones's body back to his loved ones as quickly as possible.

Maybe the negotiators could talk the leaders of this compound into a truce and giving up its shooters, but Novak doubted it. This sweet-looking blonde didn't seem the type to play hardball with killers. She looked like the type to bake cupcakes, hold hands, and kiss booboos.

Novak had seen the petite agent at several incidents since the summer, always smiling and joking with her colleagues. She glanced over her shoulder, and her blue eyes narrowed with unspoken criticism.

For some reason she didn't like him.

He smiled back.

He didn't care.

Special Agent Truman drove fast, obviously aware of the tension that filled the atmosphere like CS gas, and smart enough not to open his mouth and inhale.

Charlotte Blood was the Negotiations Commander for this incident, which meant Novak had to deal with her whether she liked him or not. Until the overall Incident Commander was on scene, Novak and Blood were running this shit show. Novak's immediate boss was out of the country doing something classified with the US Naval Special Warfare Development Group. Probably taking down a high value target in some remote part of the Middle East. If Novak fucked this up, he'd never hear the end of it.

The Hostage Rescue Teams were tight-knit groups. Same as the negotiators. Theoretically, they were all on the same side, and they shared objectives, up to a point. Ending the siege. Protecting the innocent. They simply had wildly different ideas about how to go about that.

"Do you have any experience with murder investigations?" The bite in SSA Blood's tone was unmistakable and something he only ever heard when she addressed him. She was sweet as pie to everyone else.

"Not a lot." He leaned back against the leather seat and glanced out the window. He'd served two years as a street agent where he'd learned about the law enforcement side of the agency, but he hadn't found it nearly as rewarding as his current role of kicking down doors and taking out terrorists. "I was on the violent criminal apprehension squad in Miami before I joined HRT."

Marking time until he could apply for selection. That had been five years ago. His rise through the ranks had more to do with his military know-how than his law enforcement skills.

"Of course, you were," she muttered under her breath.

Novak saw Truman flash a look of surprise in SSA Blood's direction, probably at her acidic tone, but he didn't say anything. Smart man.

"I suppose you *are* highly experienced—with murder investigations?" He hadn't meant it to come out snide, but it did. Her shoulders stiffened.

"I ran multiple murder investigations in three different field offices. We made arrests in all but two of the cases, which are still ongoing."

It didn't surprise him that she kept track of old cases.

"Just keep out of the Medical Examiner's way and don't contaminate the scene," she instructed.

"I am a qualified FBI agent, SSA Blood. Not some bum they picked up off the streets."

"We all know the Bureau wanted you for your tactical skills and experience, not your investigative prowess."

Was she seriously suggesting that he hadn't reached the same standards as other applicants when he had, in fact, far exceeded them? "Are you questioning my abilities, SSA Blood?"

"Only your experience at murder scenes and in peaceful resolutions, SSA Novak."

That rankled. "HRT is the tip of the spear. We're not paid to hold hands."

"Nor are the negotiators."

He opened his mouth to argue, but she didn't let him.

"You know the FBI is mandated to pursue negotiations as far as possible while lives are not at risk."

"Of course, I know that." Novak crossed his arms over his chest and stared at the back of Charlotte Blood's annoying head. She obviously considered him a freaking idiot. When she could solve complex algebra equations after a week with no sleep and running the equivalent of four marathons in full kit, they'd talk.

CHAPTER THREE

N OVAK SAT SILENTLY in the back seat, trying to ignore his irritating coworker. Long roads snaked through barren desert before climbing into rocky foothills and then higher, passing through steep banks covered in swathes of thick forest. It took forty minutes before they reached the valley closest to the incident and the small town of Eagle Creek. Flakes of snow rode the breeze, a warning that the weather could turn at any moment. They needed to get that downed officer to his family before the snow buried him until spring.

Truman pointed out the ranch where they were basing their operations. They left the convoy of HRT vehicles, who'd caught up twenty minutes ago, behind them. It took another ten minutes to reach a gravel logging road, another ten minutes of teeth rattling misery to get to a police cordon, and a string of emergency vehicles stretched out along the side of the road.

Truman pulled up beside an ambulance. The field agent had called ahead on the sat phone to arrange for someone to meet them and guide them to the scene. Truman pointed out the side window with obvious relief. "That's Agent Fontaine over there. She'll take you up to where they found the female victim. I'll figure out somewhere to turn around and wait for you here."

Charlotte Blood sent the agent a *butter-wouldn't-melt* smile.

Ha. So that's why she was pissed he'd tagged along. She'd wanted to hit on pretty-boy Truman, and Novak had ruined her dating plans. Well, tough.

He got out of the SUV and glanced around with a frown. A crowd of people, including the media, were being held back at one end of the dirt road. Law enforcement needed to secure the entire mountain and make sure no one went wandering where they weren't authorized. That wouldn't be an easy assignment.

Hell of a lot of local police activity too. Too many eyes and ears for his liking. Too many loose lips and potential wannabe heroes and victims getting in the line of fire if the men in the compound decided to make a break for it before HRT were embedded and firmly in control.

Novak switched his attention to their guide. Agent Fontaine had long dark hair tied back into a no-nonsense ponytail and smiling red lips. Her eyes lit up a little when they caught sight of him. Some women had a thing for body armor and thigh holsters.

Not his erstwhile Negotiations Commander, though. Nor his ex-wife, come to that. She hadn't even bothered to tell him she was leaving him for another man. He'd simply arrived home from a long overseas deployment to an empty house with a note on the kitchen counter telling him how much he owed her to cover utilities.

He pushed the thoughts out of his brain.

Charlotte Blood's mouth bent upside-down as she noticed Fontaine's reaction to him. Novak stood a little taller and possibly puffed out his chest. Not because he wanted to flirt with Agent Fontaine, but because annoying Charlotte Blood amused the crap out of him, especially since she considered him such a bozo.

"SSA Payne Novak." He introduced himself as he shook hands with Fontaine. "This is SSA Charlotte Blood."

Agent Fontaine barked out a surprised laugh. "Blood and Payne. Perfect. You guys should be partners and get your own TV show."

He and Charlotte locked gazes, her eyes reflecting the exact same horror he felt.

"Ha. Right," SSA Blood said between gritted teeth. "Please, call me Charlotte."

"And you can call *me* Payne." Novak gave Fontaine his best smile.

"Funny," Charlotte muttered. "That's what I always call you."

He let go of Fontaine's hand and raised a brow at his fellow commander. "I thought you were supposed to be the diplomat?"

Charlotte sighed. "You're right. It was a cheap shot. I apologize. Any idea who the victim is, or where she came from, Agent Fontaine?"

Agent Fontaine glanced at Charlotte then back to him. No doubt about it, she was interested in more than his weapon's holster. Not that he got involved with co-workers, especially junior ones—but he wasn't a regular field agent, and Fontaine lived on the other side of the country. A temporary hookup with no emotional entanglements wouldn't be completely out of the question if she was genuinely interested in checking out his equipment. Not that he had time to take advantage of such an opportunity should it arise. Probably just as well.

Fontaine lowered her gaze back to Charlotte. "We think she was part of a group of environmentalists and conservationists who are camped over in that direction." Fontaine pointed east. "One of the sheriff's deputies believes he recognizes her from a protest, but we haven't confirmed her identity yet. The FBI Director told Sheriff Lasalle to leave everything to the FBI, but we haven't had time or manpower to interview people there yet. Deputies are recording the identity of anyone who leaves."

"What are they protesting?" Novak took in the thick forests that surrounded them and knew the answer before she spoke. "Logging."

Charlotte glanced at him in surprise.

Yeah, SSA Blood, I have a couple of brain cells inside this thick skull.

"Let's go." Charlotte waved Agent Fontaine ahead of them, and Novak let her go next with him bringing up the rear. Outside the bright lights of police vehicles, it was pitch black—the sort of dark where you had to hold your hands out in front so you didn't walk into a tree. His eyes would adjust in time, but the others were impatient. They turned on their flashlights and trudged up the steep, uneven path.

"There are several groups who've joined together including, more recently, a small contingent of Bigfoot enthusiasts who are investigating a credible sighting," Fontaine said, straight-faced.

Novak shook his head to clear the ringing. *Credible* sighting…? "You're saying the victim believed in Bigfoot?"

Fontaine cleared her throat. "Not necessarily. Most activists here are protesting forest destruction because of rare birds and mammal habitat, but…well, it's possible, and I didn't want you going into the situation blind."

Great.

Charlotte Blood said nothing as they carried on up the hillside. He found his gaze following the sway of his colleague's ass as she hiked in front of him. She wore skintight, black leggings over slim legs and no-nonsense boots to tramp over the uneven ground. Unfortunately, it wasn't Agent Fontaine's ass he was ogling, it was the irritating Charlotte Blood.

Whatever.

His animal brain had observed and now his civilized one could ignore the fact that the negotiator hid a fit body beneath that frosty exterior.

A twig snapped, and they all paused as he shone his flashlight into the woods.

A six-pronged buck stared back at him, the retinas of his eyes reflecting eerily in the beam. Not Bigfoot.

He laughed at himself and took another step. His foot caught on a root, and he went down hard, taking SSA Blood with him. He managed to wrap one hand around her thighs to cushion some of the impact, but he weighed two-hundred pounds not counting equipment. His face landed against the softness of her ass, and they lay in frozen shock for a fraught nanosecond.

"I am so goddamn sorry. Are you all right?" He rolled away but not before the sensation of her form was imprinted on his from the waist up.

She twisted onto her back, glaring at him, and then scrambled to her feet, dusting off his touch like he had lice. "I'm fine."

"You do need to watch your step around here. It is treacherous in places." Agent Fontaine's voice carried a hint of amusement.

Great. He was never a klutz. He was supposed to be an elite fricking warrior. "I tripped on a tree root."

"Well, maybe you should pull out your night-vision goggles so you can see where you're going?" Charlotte snapped.

Did she think he'd done it on purpose?

The two female agents started striding up the hill again.

"It was an accident," he bit out.

"Of course, it was." Charlotte glared back at him.

He swore. Charlotte Blood thought he'd deliberately tackled her to the ground like some boneheaded defenseman. She really had a low opinion of him.

A soft rustle of leaves drew Novak's attention back to the woods. The hair on the back of his nape suddenly stood on end, and he couldn't shake the sensation he was being watched.

Part of him wanted to go searching out whatever was giving him the heebie-jeebies, but as he glanced toward the others who were rapidly disappearing, he didn't want to leave them unprotected—even though they were both professional law enforcement agents who would kick his ass if he suggested anything as sexist as him watching out for them. He jogged to catch up. Charlotte looked back and paused reluctantly to wait for him.

"We're almost there," said Fontaine.

Charlotte pointed down the slope to distant flickers of light through the forest. "Is that where the environmentalists are camped?"

Fontaine nodded. "It's about half a mile straight down the hill. Loggers had planned to come into this part of the old growth forest this past summer and harvest the biggest trees but were forced to abandon the idea when some endangered birds were found nesting here. Protesters are convinced that the minute they leave, the logging company will come in regardless."

Novak pressed his lips together in distaste. The idea of anyone cutting down these majestic trees left a bitter tang in his mouth. Not that his personal feelings mattered. Retrieving the body of the dead wildlife officer, protecting the innocent and federal property was his job. Upholding the law was the reason he was here.

Still, he liked trees. They didn't talk back.

"You seem to know a lot about the situation," Charlotte observed to the other woman.

Fontaine flashed a modest smile. "I'm interested in conservation. My first degree was in Biological Sciences, and I have a soft spot for the great outdoors."

"Well, the loggers are going to have to postpone any activities on this mountain until we sort this out." Charlotte spoke confidently.

"You think that could have been a motive?" Agent Fontaine asked.

"To stop the logging? Seems extreme." Charlotte frowned.

Novak's mood soured. He'd seen all sorts of reasons for death. Most of them were extreme. Standing around speculating solved nothing. "Let's move it, people."

"We were waiting for you to catch up." Charlotte glared at him like he was slow on the uptake.

He huffed out a laugh. "You think I have trouble keeping up?"

"Keeping it up?" The look she gave him told him she was

riling his ass and yet his ass still got riled.

"Funny. Ha, ha." Heat seared his cheeks.

"Ready?" Charlotte sent him a pleased-with-herself smile and continued up the trail after Fontaine.

She was probably the most annoying female he'd had the displeasure of working with. This assignment was going to be purgatory.

"I was looking at something in the trees," he said, giving in to the need to defend himself.

"What was it?" she queried.

Now he felt even more a fool. "Probably another deer." He cleared his throat. Although he was sure there had been something else out there, lurking, but he wasn't about to say that out loud.

Bigfoot for fuck's sake.

"Come on. Let's catch up with Fontaine. We don't want to lose her," Charlotte said impatiently.

He gritted his teeth. Right now, he wouldn't care a single iota if he lost Charlotte, and another negotiator took over command. In fact, that would be just fine with him.

Another five minutes, and they saw the first indication they were in the right place. Sheriff's deputies were staked out at various points along yellow crime scene tape that cordoned off a large area.

A guy took their names, and they signed into the log, putting paper booties over their footwear, before ducking under the tape.

Up ahead, the area was well lit with portable lights. Novak spotted a group of people near the body of a young woman and immediately sobered. This was no place for petty differences or dueling personalities.

A middle-aged man crouched beside the body. He looked up at their approach. "SSA Blood?"

Charlotte nodded vigorously. "Yes, sir. Sorry to keep you waiting out in the cold. We got here as soon as we could." She glanced at Novak as if he'd been the one holding them back, and he wanted to roll his eyes. "This is SSA Novak. My colleague from HRT."

The ME nodded. "I haven't been here that long myself. We're about to move the young woman into the body bag. Perhaps you can assist?" He directed the comment at Novak, and Charlotte bristled.

Being needed for his brawn was hardly a compliment. He sincerely doubted anyone would appreciate his Mensa IQ, not when there were bodies to move.

Novak scanned the nearby area before stuffing his cold weather gloves into a pocket and pulling on the latex gloves someone handed him. He approached the dead girl from her left side. A long gash covered the right side of her face. Her clothes had been interfered with. Coat removed—assuming she'd been wearing one, although she'd be foolish not to. Her jeans zipper was undone.

"She could have fallen against that tree trunk. Cracked her skull." Novak pointed toward the nearby trunk, which was stained with something that might be blood.

The ME looked impressed. "Good eyes. That was my first thought."

"Can you tell if she was assaulted?" Charlotte asked the ME.

"First glance suggests it's possible, but it could also have been an accident. Until I get her on the table and then run some tests, it's hard to say. She might have been attempting to relieve her bladder, tripped, and bashed her head on that tree as SSA Novak suggested."

"It is easy to trip in these woods," Charlotte said tightly.

Novak narrowed his gaze at her.

"Okay, let's move her. Carefully now."

Novak grasped the vic's arm and helped four other men place her gently into the body bag. He gritted his teeth at the noise the zipper made as they closed it up. He'd heard it before, in field hospitals in the desert. That final, incongruous death knell.

He looked up to find Charlotte Blood watching him, her expression, for once, sympathetic. He brought the shutters down.

He didn't need Charlotte Blood feeling sorry for him. He didn't need anyone feeling sorry for him, period.

He removed his gloves and tossed them to an assistant who was collecting trash. The crime scene had been trampled. Good luck with the evidence people getting anything useful out of this war zone.

"Where's the compound?" he asked Fontaine as the others got on with the grim task of trying to identify the young woman and establishing how she died.

"Quarter of a mile that way, other side of a small creek." Fontaine moved away from the others, pointing west.

There were clumps of snow in some of the hollows. Not enough to accumulate on the ground but enough to remind them all that winter was on her way. She was late this year. Novak bet they'd usually be knee deep in the white stuff by now.

Fontaine walked another ten yards uphill and then swung her flashlight toward yellow and red markers laid out on the ground about eight feet apart. "Here's what we believe to be our UNSUB's tracks along with those of FWO Jones." She pulled lip balm from her pocket and rolled some on to protect against the cold.

"When the sheriff's deputies arrived, they didn't preserve the crime scene as well as they should have, but we managed to take photographs and a cast of one decent footprint from the UNSUB, but the ground is hard and rocky in most places, so we didn't find as much as we'd hoped. We lost the tracks farther in."

"One of our negotiators is former British SAS. He's really good at tracking if we want him to come up here tomorrow and see what he can determine?" Charlotte Blood followed them closely, probably worried Novak might wander off and get lost.

"British SAS?" Fontaine asked with interest.

"He had to renounce his British citizenship to join the FBI, but he still has the cute accent." Charlotte smiled.

Novak knew Max Hawthorne. Guy was a solid agent, but Novak had been a Warrant Officer in the Green Berets. He had some skills. He started in the direction of the compound.

"We should head back." Charlotte raised her voice like he was a kid who wasn't paying attention.

"I want to take a quick look." He didn't stop moving, eyes scanning the ground with his flashlight, but he could tell from the stride length that the UNSUB in question was moving at a flat-out run. Tracks were easy to follow when you knew where people were headed. After the initial zig zag through the trees, the UNSUB bore straight west.

Agent Fontaine added markers to each new print he indicated.

Novak reached the steep banks of a small creek. There were enough trees to provide cover between him and the building, so he wasn't too worried about becoming a target. Still, he kept the light beam low to the ground and out to one side.

He scanned up and down the creek bed, then crouched. "Same footprints here but headed toward the direction where we found the girl." He pointed at a faint indentation in the dry mud. "The footprints are about the same age, and he's walking this time, not running."

Was he trying to show off? Proving to these agents he was as good a tracker as Max Hawthorne? Probably. He shook his head in self-disgust.

He glanced through the trees. He was so close to where the fallen officer lay, he couldn't resist the pull to go even closer. Memories of being forced to leave behind the body of one of his men after an overwhelming number of hostiles had lit up his platoon ate at his mind. He'd managed to persuade command to go back with reinforcements the next day but, by then, the body of Sergeant Frankie Duke had been taken and desecrated by the enemy. They'd never recovered his remains. Never given his grieving family the closure they needed by providing a body to bury.

Nausea gripped his gut, and he took two long, deliberate breaths through his nose to stop himself outwardly reacting. He stared at the ground again, searching for the calm focus he needed to do his job.

There were other footprints too, not many, but some. Novak didn't know if they belonged to law enforcement personnel, people from the compound, tree huggers, or random hikers.

He carried on, cautiously. Fontaine and Blood followed behind, but they were both getting a little antsy about the proximity to the compound.

Now he was here, he may as well take a look and try to figure out the best and fastest method for retrieving FWO Jones.

"Novak," Charlotte hissed as he hit the rise of the opposite bank of the creek.

He put his hand up for silence and, miracle of miracles, she did as requested.

There was that prickly feeling at the back of his neck again. Different than before but still very much a warning. The "No Trespassing" sign served as an additional caution.

A couple of sheriff's deputies started to approach them from the south. Much too late, in his estimation. It proved that the area was not secure, and the people inside may already have slipped away. Novak let Fontaine deal with the cops. He couldn't see anything through the dense thicket of trees. No lights at all, but that wasn't surprising. He pulled a pair of night vision goggles out of a webbed pocket.

"Keep it down," Novak instructed when the deputies got close enough to strike up a conversation with the other agents.

Charlotte glared at him.

He didn't care.

He put on the goggles and stared into the green-tinged night. A dead man lay out in that darkness somewhere, murdered while doing his job. And the assholes inside the fortified bunker wouldn't even let them retrieve his body? What the hell was with that?

No man left behind.

Not this time.

The subtle whir of something mechanical caught his attention. A camera. Pointed in his direction. Sonofabitch.

"Did you know they have surveillance cameras in these woods?" asked Novak, removing the night vision goggles so the others' flashlights didn't blind him.

"What?" Charlotte took a step toward him.

"What the hell?" One of the deputies rushed forward.

Novak pointed to the small gray box fifteen feet up in the tree. The deputy immediately pulled his weapon and took aim, but Novak pushed his arm back toward the ground.

"What do you think you're doing?"

"Getting rid of it!"

"Keep your weapon holstered. The FBI is in charge now. Unless your life or someone else's is in imminent danger, keep your gun in its holster and your mouth zipped."

The deputy blustered, but Novak ignored him and strode away. Charlotte came with him, and they both stared into the darkness toward the compound.

The local sheriff's deputies were bullish and trigger happy. Novak understood that—hell, he was the same when the need arose. He understood what it was like to be pissed and want to get revenge on someone who'd shot at you or injured one of your own. But that wasn't the most important thing at stake in this moment.

These survivalists were amped up, prepared to defend themselves from tactical assault. With nothing to lose, they would shoot at anything or anyone they considered a threat. How could he convince them he was unarmed and the only thing he was interested in—this time—was retrieving the dead man's remains?

Maybe they wouldn't shoot the female agents, but Novak

wouldn't take that chance. The only way the people entrenched here would believe for sure someone was unarmed was if they were stark naked.

Novak stilled, not liking the idea that lodged in his brain. But if the roles were reversed, this was the only way he'd trust someone wasn't carrying a firearm.

He moved out to a place between two trees and heard the whir of a second camera following him. Both were now pointed at him. The people inside the compound were actively watching him.

"Novak…" Charlotte hissed.

"Stay behind cover."

She muttered "Neanderthal," but he ignored her.

He took off his basic equipment vest, then his fleece jacket, and undid the black tactical shirt, and the long-sleeved t-shirt he wore beneath. Tossed it in a pile behind him.

"What are you doing?" Charlotte asked, clearly aghast.

"I'm stripping."

"Stripping?"

"Taking off my clothes."

"I know what stripping means," Charlotte snapped and damn if that didn't have a grin pulling at his lips.

Next came his weapon's holster, which really made him feel naked. He slowly placed his SIG Sauer on the ground on top of the clothes, making a show of it. Then his knife, and spare ammo, making sure they saw him remove his backup Glock-22 from his ankle holster.

Then he took off his thermal undershirt, and the icy air stung his flesh like killer bees. He bent over and removed his boots, along with the paper booties and socks, tossing them in the growing pile.

Below zero with the added lash of a razor-sharp wind—it was so cold he could barely breathe.

"SSA Novak, I don't know what you think you are doing but—" Charlotte's voice rose sharply, but she stopped talking as he shucked his long underwear. He tossed them behind him and heard a strangled exclamation.

He held up his hands in the age-old sign of surrender, looking over his shoulder at the other SSA who was open-mouthed and trying hard to keep her eyes north of his waist. Just as well, considering the temperature.

"I'm going to retrieve the body of FWO Jones while not presenting a threat to the safety of the people inside that compound. Everyone, stay back, keep your weapons out of your hands and do not make a move that will get me killed." His voice rang out through the quiet of the night, then he added softly to Charlotte and Agent Fontaine, "You might want to close your eyes."

He slowly turned a complete three-hundred-sixty degrees in front of the cameras to prove there was nothing taped to his back. He picked up his flashlight and very deliberately turned it on, so it shone over his body and onto the ground in front of him. He was lit up like a naked-human Christmas tree, freezing his damn balls off.

Yippee-kai-yay, motherfucker. Time to party.

CHAPTER FOUR

"WHAT'S THIS JOKER doing?" Malcolm Resnick rose from his seat in front of the monitors.

TJ wasn't a fan of his uncle under the best of circumstances. The man had wanted to throw him to the wolves earlier—despite the fact it was one of Malcolm's buddies who'd pulled the trigger and killed the man who'd been chasing him.

His uncle hadn't lived with them that long. One of his mother's four brothers, Malcolm had turned up for the first time in March.

"Looks like he's taking his clothes off." One of the other men sitting in the surveillance room sniggered.

This mess was all TJ's fault. He should have stayed and explained the situation to the lawman. Taken the consequences. Others might be hurt because he'd been upset and afraid. The authorities were going to blame him for both deaths, and they were probably right.

Kayla wouldn't be dead if he hadn't arranged to meet her. The lawman wouldn't be dead if TJ hadn't run away.

The lump in his throat felt serrated and sharp-edged as he swallowed. How could she be dead? The effort of holding back tears, the pain in his chest that made it difficult to breathe, was killing him. What had happened to her?

His uncle went to press the intercom that connected the

surveillance room to the men guarding the front and rear exits, but TJ's dad beat him to it. "Hold fire."

Tom Harrison narrowed his gaze at the now completely naked man who put his hands up, twirled all the way around and headed toward their home. TJ's dad might be overprotective, but he was a deep thinker. He wasn't rash or prone to violent outbursts. Unlike some of the men who lived here nowadays, Tom didn't tolerate a man hitting a woman or kids.

"I repeat, hold fire. He's unarmed."

TJ clenched his jaw. He hadn't told his dad about Kayla yet. He couldn't bear to say the words aloud. All anyone here believed was the wildlife officer had started chasing him for no reason.

His stomach churned at the idea of telling his dad the truth. The idea of disappointing the only person left in the world who he cared about. It was too much. Especially in front of the others. If he could get his father alone…

"I think he's attempting to prove he means us no harm. Anyone recognize his face?"

TJ stood beside his dad as everyone shook their heads. TJ had never seen the naked guy before but, judging by the clothing and equipment he'd removed, he was either military or police. As the military weren't allowed to engage US citizens on US soil, then he was probably some sort of tactical cop. Not that the government always followed the rules—as his father often reminded him.

"It's a trap," Malcolm snapped. "Has to be."

Tom turned world-weary eyes on the other man. "Exactly how is it a trap? You think he has an assault weapon jammed up his ass?"

Some of the men snorted.

TJ didn't. He could see the toll this had already taken on his father, and guilt added to the confusion rushing through his veins. Tom had aged a decade since TJ's mother had died. Her death had killed something inside the man, and Malcolm had manipulated that grief in order to take over the day-to-day running of the community, cementing his standing as second-in-command, even though he hadn't been here that long.

TJ didn't like him. Didn't trust him.

Tom pressed the intercom again. "Hold fire. I repeat, hold fire. But keep an eye on him."

"He could rush the walls, get inside our defenses," Malcolm argued.

"Our defenses can manage a single man, and he'd freeze to death before he got inside." Tom shook his head. "Easiest way inside this compound is via a helicopter and a long rope. Nope. He's going after the body of their man, which is fine by me." His father's mouth turned grim. "I don't particularly want a corpse lying outside the gate, rotting. Man needs a decent burial."

TJ knew his father regretted the death of the man, same way he did. The guards on the gate had been reprimanded but, by then, it was already too late. A federal law enforcement officer was dead. Now the government were going to show up in force and attempt to destroy them all.

"We need the media onside if we hope to endure this." Tom looked around at the men standing there.

"The media? State-run TV? How are they gonna help us?" Malcolm guffawed.

The other men in the room shifted their weight uncomfortably. His dad was smart, but Malcolm was cunning. TJ hoped his father sent the other man away when this was all over, but right now that was impossible, and that was TJ's fault.

TJ glanced at Malcolm, who glared back at him.

"It'll create a public outcry if we don't let the Feds collect their dead. And we'll look like a bunch of crazies if we kill an unarmed naked guy, which will turn all our potential allies against us," Tom said patiently. "We aren't holding any hostages. If we demonstrate we can tell the difference between an act of war and an act of mercy, the world might believe us when we say we had reason to fire on the wildlife officer who was shooting at TJ. Although, I wish people hadn't been so damn trigger happy." The admonishment was directed toward Malcolm and his lackies.

TJ's mouth went dry as guilt ate him up. It was his fault too. "What do you think they might do to us?"

His father's lips tightened as he held his gaze. "I don't know, son. But we always knew this day would come. We're safe here, even if they drop a bomb on us."

They had an emergency bunker another thirty feet below ground, but the idea of being bombed was not comforting. What if they were buried alive? Left to die in the darkness?

"You never explained what you were doing out there, TJ," Malcolm asked slyly.

"I went for a walk." TJ licked his dry, cracked lips. "The guy started chasing me and then shot at me."

"And we have a right to protect ourselves on our own land," Tom stated firmly.

Malcolm was staring at TJ like he knew he was lying. TJ stared right back.

His dad pressed the intercom again. "Watch that guy doesn't go for the Fed's weapon. Turn the spotlight on him."

TJ turned his eyes back to the screen as the stranger eased out of the woods, heading straight for the body of the man who'd chased him.

Bile burned TJ's throat.

Other screens focused on the other law enforcement personnel in the area. Men and women all staring at this naked guy as he hauled the dead officer over his shoulder.

Was it a trap or a distraction?

TJ's eyes shot to the monitors near the back exit and east and west, but no one appeared to be infiltrating from that direction. Maybe the Feds hadn't found the other exit yet? Maybe TJ should leave, now? Give himself up.

If he surrendered, no one else would get hurt...

———————————

NOVAK STARTED SLOWLY walking forward, cognizant of the surveillance cameras following his progress and new ones that picked up his approach from different angles along the way. Presumably, the cameras surrounded the whole compound, which was something HRT needed to deal with before they could safely insert into the area.

Rocks and sticks cut into his feet. The breeze was so cold, he was worried his dick might fall off, or retract so far he'd be peeing like a girl for the rest of his life. He'd be lying if he'd said he wasn't nervous about the idea of getting a bullet in the chest if he'd misjudged the mentality behind the concrete wall. He was gambling these guys wouldn't shoot an obviously unarmed guy who was simply intent on retrieving the dead.

They were worried about an attack on their home and one or more of them being taken away by the Feds and incarcerated. It didn't mean Novak wouldn't come back here tomorrow with a heavily armed unit and try to do exactly that, but right now, all he wanted was to reunite FWO Jones with his loved ones and treat him with the respect he deserved.

Novak began sweeping the flashlight in a constant arc a few feet in front of him. He was following a parallel track of both the running UNSUB and boot prints he assumed belonged to the wildlife officer.

The feeling of being watched swept over him again. More cameras? Probably. That was probably what had spooked him in the forest earlier. They'd have to map out the whole area for devices.

Not *Bigfoot*.

Novak stepped out of the relative security of the trees and paused and did another complete turn to prove he wasn't hiding a weapon. Every muscle in his body tensed as he imagined barrels of loaded rifles being pointed in his direction by poorly trained militia with their meaty fingers caressing delicate hair-triggers. Usually it was his HRT colleagues with weapons pointed at him, but he trusted those guys with his life. He had to.

These men he didn't trust. They would probably kill him if he looked at them wrong. Hence the extreme lengths he'd gone to prove he was unarmed.

A dark mound appeared in front of him, revealed by the shallow beam of his flashlight to be Federal Wildlife Officer Jones. Novak ran the beam from the man's boots to the top of his bald patch. The man's hat lay upside down on the ground nearby, his 9mm handgun close to his right hand. Novak could not go near that weapon unless he expected to get his butt peppered with lead.

He picked up FWO Jones's legs and dragged him a couple of yards back toward the trees and away from the weapon. Novak's movements were awkward, as he tried to keep the flashlight in play so the people inside the fortress could see what he was up to. He needn't have worried. A huge spotlight sprang to life, as dazzling as the surface of the sun. Overkill for sure, but effective as hell for blinding anyone approaching, especially if they were wearing night vision goggles.

Yep, assuming Novak survived the next thirty seconds, he'd definitely learned a few things about the capabilities of the people inside that wall.

They were professional, organized, and had access to some high-tech equipment you wouldn't normally expect in the butt crack of nowhere.

He gathered the officer's legs against his chest and walked backward a little farther, dragging the man with him.

The sound of a groan shocked the hell out of him, but he didn't outwardly betray his surprise. FWO Jones was alive. Novak kept moving steadily away from the giant spotlight and the large reinforced steel door that was set into what looked like the front of a concrete bunker. There was an embankment, twenty feet of concrete and, above that, a tall, barbed wire fence that presumably encircled the compound.

Homey.

When Novak was a good twenty feet from Officer Jones's weapon, he gently laid the man's legs on the ground and then hefted him over his shoulder in a fireman's carry.

Again, Jones groaned, and Novak prayed he wasn't doing irreparable damage to the guy who was slowly bleeding out from a bullet wound in his right shoulder. Once the man was secure, Novak turned and strode quickly back into the woods.

Praying with every step that he didn't get a bullet in the back.

"IF THEY DON'T kill him, I might," Charlotte muttered under her breath, watching Novak's tight, naked butt disappear into the trees.

The fact he'd put himself at risk, without consultation, without discussing his hair-brained plan... She wanted to wrap her hands around his throat and strangle the damn pain in the ass Supervisory Special Agent.

Not how she usually dealt with conflict.

Agent Fontaine flashed her a worried smile.

"Don't worry. He outranks you. You won't get into trouble for him being reckless," Charlotte reassured the other woman.

Fontaine didn't say anything.

What sort of macho bullshit was it to strip off and go wandering up to the door of a compound full of gun-toting killers—*alleged* killers—and pick up the corpse of the man that a dozen sheriff's deputies had failed to retrieve earlier, without even discussing it with her first?

It wasn't that she didn't ache for the dead man and his family but adding to the collection of bodies wouldn't help anyone. And if she could talk to these people, she would hopefully be able to arrange the safe retrieval of the man's remains as soon as everyone's tempers and fears cooled.

A spotlight came on, blinding her for a second. She shielded her gaze and watched Novak, now emblazoned in perfect silhouette. He bent over and hauled the wildlife officer over his shoulder, then turned to head back through the trees, walking toward them as if he were out for a damned stroll at a naturist camp.

"We probably shouldn't look," Charlotte muttered to the other agent, wondering what the Office of Professional Responsibility would say if they heard about this.

"You have got to be kidding me." Fontaine snorted. "That man's body is a work of art."

Charlotte had tried not to notice, although it was impossible to miss the defined muscles and lean frame. Her pulse gave a little zap, and she berated herself for ogling her work colleague. Then she sighed. Some days she felt like such an old maid. She needed to live a little, but now was not the time.

Novak was hurrying now, out of the direct line of fire, but not out of sight of the cameras that watched their every move.

Fontaine had placed Novak's belongings in the stream bed, out of range of the compound. Suddenly Novak started jogging, heading straight past her toward the creek.

"He's alive," he muttered.

What the hell? Charlotte hurried after her fellow SSA, no longer distracted by the sight of ripped abs or thick thigh muscles or tight butt. Nor by his penis which was a piece of anatomy she didn't usually encounter when it came to her coworkers—nor anywhere else nowadays.

Novak placed Officer Jones gently on the ground and started tearing the clothes away from the wound in his shoulder. "Where's the nearest doctor?"

"The ME," Charlotte suggested, falling to her knees beside the injured and hypothermic officer.

"Put pressure here," Novak ordered.

Charlotte did as instructed while Novak dragged his clothes back on.

"Fontaine, call the ME and tell him we're coming to him."

Novak dressed in fast, economic motions, his teeth chattering from exposure. He slipped on his footwear as the two deputies jogged in their direction.

Everyone started making so much noise Charlotte couldn't hear what Novak was saying.

"Quiet!" she yelled. So much for her sensitivity skills.

"Jones is still alive but in rough shape." Novak was replacing his weapons into their various holsters. "At this point speed is key so I'm going to carry him to the ME. One of you call for a medivac extraction at the nearest location a helicopter can safely land. Charlotte, I need you to keep applying pressure while I transport him."

Novak lifted Jones over his shoulder, keeping the gunshot wound near the center of his own spine. Charlotte dragged off her down jacket to provide some padding between Novak's back and the entry wound. Then she pressed hard down against the seeping exit-wound using an undershirt that Novak had tossed her.

She caught hold of a strap on Novak's pants to anchor herself to him, and they moved quickly in tandem. Her feet got soaked in icy water as they splashed through the small stream. Fontaine shone a flashlight to illuminate their way. The terrain was rutted and rough, but Charlotte kept a firm hold on both the injured man and Novak. Another five minutes, and she heard the noise of people heading toward them through the woods.

"What have we got here?" the ME asked with concern.

Novak laid Jones down on a patch of bare ground, and the ME and his assistants took over, pushing them aside, shouting instructions and improvising a field IV. They might deal with the dead, but they were all trained medical professionals.

Charlotte crossed her arms over her chest and tried to stop shivering, but her wet toes were like ice cubes, and her coat was now an improvised bandage. So much for her preparedness.

Something warm enfolded her. She looked up to realize Novak had draped his black fleece around her shoulders.

It smelled like him.

"You'll need it..." she protested, dragging at it reluctantly.

Novak was already striding away. "You need it more. I can't afford for you to get sick. Let's head back to the Command Center ASAP. We still have a lot to do tonight."

CHAPTER FIVE

C HARLOTTE GLANCED UP as a helicopter flew overhead in the darkness. The pilot was careful to skirt Tom Harrison's concrete stronghold. Hopefully, no one else was going to take chances the way Novak had done. The more she thought about the way he'd acted without consulting with her, the angrier she became.

He could have been killed. Then what? All-out war and goodness knew how many lives lost?

The three of them jogged down the mountain. He was in a hurry to get back. She was trying to generate enough body heat to avoid freezing to death.

Agent Truman met them with the vehicle as, presumably, the same chopper flew back overhead again, this time hopefully carrying the wounded wildlife officer to the nearest trauma center. Someone needed to interview the man as soon as he regained consciousness—*if* he regained consciousness.

The drive back to the ranch was silent as a crypt as adrenaline levels crashed, and Charlotte mulled over what had gone down.

Truman pulled down a gravel road heading toward a large farmhouse with a bunch of outbuildings, including a gigantic barn.

Maple Tree Ranch was painted on the sign.

Rustic. Quaint.

Although there were lights in the windows, there was no indication a major tactical force had taken up residence. That was the kind of professionalism that made the FBI's Critical Incident Response Group one of the best units of its kind in the world. But she and Novak hadn't worked as a unit tonight.

At the main house, Truman drew the SUV to a stop with an audible sigh of relief. Charlotte thrust Novak's fleece into the front seat and onto his lap. No way did she want to appear in front of her colleagues wearing his jacket like some winsome teen. That was not the image she wanted to project.

And she was pissed.

She shoved open the door, her frustration at Novak growing by the second. Assistant Special Agent in Charge Steve McKenzie stood on the wooden porch, hands resting impatiently on his waist.

The Incident Commander had arrived.

He had a good rep within the Bureau and had helped prevent a major bombing at HQ, saving hundreds if not thousands of lives earlier that year. He had experience with White Nationalists going back decades. Of course, no one knew the ideology of the people from Eagle Mountain. Not all doomsday preppers were White Nationalists and not all White Nationalists were doomsday preppers.

A few men spilled out of the house. Negotiators Eban Winters and Dominic Sheridan stood on one side of McKenzie. Two HRT guys, dressed down in jeans and plaid shirts and looking like LL Bean catalogue models, stood on McKenzie's left.

Lines had been drawn.

She climbed the steps to meet her temporary new boss.

"What happened out there?" McKenzie's gaze was critical and assessing.

Both she and Novak were covered in blood and needed to get cleaned up. First, there was something she needed to discuss.

Novak spoke. "Turns out FWO Bob Jones was still alive, and we helped get him to the Medical Examiner for treatment. Hopefully, he's being medivacked to the nearest hospital." His face split into a grin—because why wouldn't he be proud of that? And he hadn't even taken all the glory.

"Can I talk to you, boss?" Charlotte tried to keep her tone neutral. Novak had saved a man's life, but without even a hint as to his intentions or rationale.

McKenzie eyed her and then Novak with narrowed eyes as if the tension between them was palpable. Even her negotiator colleagues exchanged worried glances.

They all traipsed inside to the main living room where a fire was burning in the grate.

As much as she longed to stand before the flames, she remained where she was and cleared her throat. "Actually, can we talk in private, sir? The three of us?" Charlotte indicated Novak. She did not want to say what she had to say in front of anyone else.

McKenzie frowned again then preceded them to French doors that led into a smaller side room. The room had a couple of leather love seats facing one another and was lined with bookshelves, another fire burning in the grate. Any other time, Charlotte would have *oohed* over the beautiful interior, but right now she was too angry.

McKenzie crossed his arms over his chest. "Is there a problem?"

Charlotte ignored her physical discomfort. The frozen toes and shivers that wracked her to the core. "I have an issue with SSA Novak's behavior tonight." She explained exactly what had gone down. "He didn't consult with me or follow protocol," she finished.

"What protocol? We don't have a standard operating procedure for retrieving the dead or wounded from outside paramilitary complexes on US soil." Novak moved so close she could smell the woodsy scent of his skin. Maybe he was trying to intimidate her, but then he took an abrupt step back, as if he realized he might be looming. "You sound like you're mad I saved that man's life."

She reared back. "That's not why I'm mad. *You* could have been killed. You could have put other peoples' lives in danger if we'd had to come rescue you."

"I don't think I'd have to worry about you putting yourself in harm's way for my sake." Bitterness dripped off every syllable.

"What does that mean?" Charlotte snarled. "Are you calling me a coward? You think I wouldn't come for you? Protect you?"

Novak blinked as if unsettled by her vehement reaction but doubled down on his argument. "Would you rather the man was still out there, bleeding to death?"

Charlotte pressed her lips together in frustration. "Of course not."

"It's my job to protect civilians and hostages."

"That's my job too," she bit out.

"Then maybe you should have stripped down and gone to fetch him."

Was he mocking her bravery or her strength or the fact

she was a woman? "We're supposed to work as a team. Why didn't you take thirty seconds to discuss your plan with me before you went out there?"

"Because I knew you'd try to stop me," he admitted.

Anger torched her nerves. "You assumed I'd be unreasonable."

"We don't all sit behind a desk, SSA Blood." Novak rolled his eyes. "I made a judgment call." He looked at McKenzie. Charlotte had almost forgotten he was in the room. "I figured the people inside the compound would shoot to protect themselves from an attack, but that they wouldn't shoot someone who was obviously no threat to them."

"You took a huge risk," McKenzie agreed with Charlotte.

She flashed a grateful glance his way.

"A calculated risk," Novak corrected.

"SSA Novak is a loose cannon," Charlotte stated.

"Well, if it had been up to you, *SSA Blood*, Bob Jones wouldn't have made it through the night. He would have died from exposure or bled out, and no one would have been the wiser. Whether I followed protocol or not is beside the point. I acted with forethought and as safely as I was able to under the circumstances. If we'd done this your way, we wouldn't even know he'd survived that long."

Charlotte flinched because he had a point. Though it wasn't her fault for assuming the other law enforcement personnel had accurately assessed the situation. The fact she'd been the one to push for going up to the mountain tonight also seemed to have slipped Novak's mind.

"SSA Novak, if you have a death wish, I'd like to know about it before we start working together," McKenzie stated quietly. "I already have the goddamned FBI Director and

President Joshua Hague himself calling me for hourly updates. I do not need to deal with any macho bullshit."

"I don't have a death wish, boss. But sometimes a situation requires immediate action without talking it to death."

Charlotte's eyes widened. "You didn't even give me the chance to agree or disagree with you."

"Enough," McKenzie cut in with a slice of his hand. "You two obviously can't work together—"

"I never said that," they both said in unison.

McKenzie's brows jumped.

Charlotte was as surprised as McKenzie by Novak agreeing with her. "I simply don't want SSA Novak making unilateral decisions in dangerous situations. We need to communicate properly at all times."

Novak leaned back. "Next time I decide to strip naked in the woods, you'll be the first to know."

She glared at him, but his words conjured memories of his well-toned body and a reaction in hers that she was sure he hadn't intended. God-forbid he found out. "The negotiators have to be able to trust that HRT isn't going to go behind our backs and make us look like idiots or liars. You know how that can backfire."

"You two really think you can work together like professionals? It's not only your jobs on the line, it's mine. The director has made that more than clear." McKenzie's expression was void of humor.

She glanced at Novak. "Yes."

"Yes, sir."

McKenzie nodded. "The division between you both is already costing us time, and I am not convinced."

"I'm happy to work with SSA Novak if he agrees to consult

with me in the future. I'm here because of my expertise; I'm not here to sit down and shut up," Charlotte stated.

Novak stepped forward. "I'll make sure SSA Blood is better informed of any decisions I make, sir. I'm here for the mission, not internal bickering."

They waited for McKenzie to make a decision.

"How many negotiators do we have on site?" McKenzie asked.

"Four of us at present. Another arrives from San Francisco tomorrow morning."

"Arrange for another two negotiators. I don't care how you do it. This is a Bureau priority and the director promised me everything I need."

"Yes, sir." That was a lot of manpower but meant they could work eight hour shifts rather than twelve, assuming they could get the people hiding inside the compound to talk.

Novak pointedly pulled his blood-stained shirt away from his body. "If you don't mind, sir, I want to go wash off Bob Jones's blood and then get my snipers into position before morning."

"We need to not visibly escalate the situation," Charlotte interjected quickly.

"A show of force will let them know that the government means business and that they can't piss around." Novak sounded agreeable except for the edge of irritation he tried to disguise.

"Somehow, I doubt that sending in heavily armed opera-tors is going to reassure the people inside that compound that we want a peaceful resolution to this issue," she stated calmly. She wasn't sure that her head wouldn't explode, but she needed to appear reasonable and be a team player. She knew exactly which of them would be replaced if McKenzie decided they couldn't work together, and it wasn't Novak.

Charlotte continued, "Pull the cops way back from the entrance to appear less aggressive. We've successfully dealt with sieges like this in the past few years by demonstrating patience and restraint."

"There's a time for restraint and a time for force. While I accept we need to proceed with the former for now, we need to be prepared for the latter," Novak replied.

"Agreed." Charlotte nodded. Preparation was key.

Novak nodded decisively even as his brows rose in surprise.

"I'm still not convinced about you two working together." McKenzie stared at them both long and hard. "A lot of the mistakes of the past were compounded by those in charge not communicating with one another. By not listening to one another."

"Of course." She often taught the failures of the past to new recruits. It was great to find an Incident Commander who agreed with her thoughts on the matter.

"So, if you two really think you can work together..." said McKenzie.

Charlotte smiled reassuringly.

Novak crossed his arms and dipped his chin.

"I'm going to change things up slightly."

Charlotte did not like the sound of that.

"What exactly do you mean, sir?" asked Novak.

"I'm making you partners," McKenzie asserted. "By that I mean you guys are going to spend the next seventy-two hours joined at the hip and, if you can't convince me you can work together effectively during that time, you'll both be sent back to Quantico."

Charlotte frowned. "How am I supposed to manage my negotiation team if I have to tag along to HRT meetings all day?"

"And vice versa." Novak scowled.

"That's why I want more negotiators. At least three teams of two with SSA Blood overseeing everything. You both have competent people working beneath you who can run this show blindfolded. Correct?"

Reluctantly, she and Novak both nodded.

"We all know that these types of situations, especially when there are no hostages—" McKenzie began.

"We don't know for sure there aren't hostages," Novak pointed out.

"—can take weeks and even months to resolve." McKenzie ignored the HRT team leader. "I don't want to be here for months. I want to spend Christmas with my fiancée back home, but that's irrelevant. What is relevant is making sure everyone in that compound comes out alive and whosoever killed that woman and shot both of those law enforcement officials is arrested and charged accordingly. Then we will hopefully leave these people alone to celebrate their own holiday season however they wish to do so."

McKenzie's eyes glinted. "In fact, as space is gonna be crammed, there's a kids' bedroom at the end of the hallway that has a single set of bunks in it. You guys can share that. Unless you have objections because of gender?"

She shook her head.

"Divide your time between tasks that need to be accomplished. I want you to have breakfast, lunch and dinner together and sleep in the same room at the same time. Joined at the damn hip until I know I can trust you to respect and include one another in any important decision-making processes. Objections?"

Furious protests were screaming through her mind, but if she let any escape her mouth, she'd be off the case.

"None from me. She's already seen me naked," Novak joked.

"Which won't happen again, SSA Novak," McKenzie snapped.

Novak's shoulders went ramrod straight. "Of course not. I was joking."

"SSA Blood? Any objections?"

Charlotte shook her head. She was stunned by this turn of events.

"Charlotte?" McKenzie pushed. "Do you want to switch out as Negotiation Commander with one of the others?"

Anger surged through her blood, making her hands tremble. Switch out because she didn't want to share a room with a guy she didn't know, didn't trust?

"No, sir."

McKenzie still looked dubious. "Go get cleaned up, both of you. Let me know where to meet you in thirty minutes for the first briefing."

"Yes, sir." Charlotte turned away, astonished by McKenzie's decision. Novak looked equally shell-shocked.

Great. This was just great. Now she had to try to make peace when her whole being felt like she was at war.

NOVAK ANGRILY SLUICED soap off his skin as he scrubbed

away the itch of dried blood. The fact his fellow SSA had tried to throw him under a bus and get him reprimanded was a kick in the gut. While his actions might have been unconventional, they'd been successful, and any alternative would have almost definitely resulted in someone's death. Bob *fucking* Jones for one.

He rinsed the stains out of his shirt and, after a few minutes under the hot spray, he washed his hair with shower gel.

He got out of the shower, dragging a microfiber towel all over his body then rapidly scrubbing his hair. One of his team had dumped his kit bag inside the bathroom door as requested so at least he had clean clothes to wear. He wrung out his wet t-shirt in the sink and pulled on fresh pants, t-shirt, holstered his weapons. Felt like a human being again.

He couldn't believe he was going to be bunking with Ms. Holier-Than-Thou for the next few days, but he'd endured much worse over the years. *Much* worse. He only hoped she could deal and didn't go off whining to the boss every time he looked at her sideways.

Once things were running smoothly and they stopped trying to scratch each other's eyes out, he was certain McKenzie would back off this arrangement. Novak would return to his team. She'd go back to her boys. They simply needed to demonstrate that they could communicate and get along without bloodshed.

He held a pile of dirty clothes and decided to search for a washing machine. He stepped into the empty hallway. The rest of HRT had been billeted in the barn and a couple of outbuildings, and he hated being separated. His men would be busy checking gear and setting up what they needed, fighting for the best bunk.

And here he was waiting for Charlotte Blood to get ready. He refrained from tapping his foot impatiently. He'd never met a woman who didn't take twenty minutes to wash hair or shave legs or whatever else went on in the bathroom. The only time he spent that long in the shower was when he had female company. The image of Charlotte Blood standing naked under a jet of water suddenly seared his brain.

Oh, no.

Hell, no.

He was not thinking about that incredibly irritating agent that way. Sure, she was pretty and had a hot body. Neither of those things made up for the fact she was a pious know-it-all intent on standing in the way of him getting his job done and generally making him lose his mind.

Nope.

In fact, if he was going to be sharing a room with her, there was no way he was even thinking of her as female and certainly no way he was thinking of her as attractive. He'd worked too long and too hard to get reprimanded simply because someone didn't like his methods—read "having the balls to do his damn job"—or had simply decided to screw with him.

Shit. Not *screw*. He shook his head.

Fuck him over.

Nope, not *fuck* him in any shape or form. What the hell was wrong with him? He gritted his teeth against the lack of suitable words that didn't involve sex.

Mess with him. *Annoy* him. *Sabotage* his career. *Undermine* him. *Judge* him. *Undervalue* him.

He'd been there before.

Thoughts of his ex wanted to invade his mind, and he forced them aside. She certainly hadn't thought his opinion mattered about anything, so he wasn't going to waste brainpower on past failures.

The bathroom door next to him opened. Charlotte Blood appeared wearing black leggings and an oatmeal roll-neck sweater. Her wet hair was darker now and slicked against her skull. Clear blue eyes were huge, with dark circles shadowing the delicate skin beneath. She appeared tired and vulnerable and not at all like the firecracker who'd gone after him earlier. She clutched her own pile of dirty laundry.

The anger went out of him. The fact she'd stood up to him showed guts. And she hadn't done it behind his back, which showed honesty and balls. They had to work together so he may as well get on with being polite so they could speed this along. He cleared his throat. "I'm going to throw these things into the nearest washing machine so they can be dried by morning."

"Good idea. Let me dump my wash bag on the bunk, and I'll come down and do the same."

"I'll take them." He held out his hand. "If you want."

"Okay. Thanks." She looked surprised and hesitant about the offer. Did she think he didn't know how to operate a washing machine?

"I'll meet you in the kitchen in five minutes. We'll grab some food before deciding who to brief first," she said, still clinging to her things.

He held out his hand once again. An olive branch. Charlotte passed over the pile of damp, dirty clothes. She'd attacked the bloodstains in the sink the same way he had.

McKenzie appeared at the end of the corridor, talking on

his cell. Perfect. Look at them, making nice and polite. Cooperating. He and Charlotte both smiled like prisoners up for parole.

The Incident Commander nodded curtly and went back around the corner at the end of the corridor.

"You have another coat?" he asked Charlotte. It was too cold outside to go far without one.

She shook her head. "I messaged the negotiator who is coming in tomorrow and asked her to grab one on the way to the airport."

He nodded. He'd see what he could scrounge up from the guys in the meantime because his stuff would be huge on her. He'd noticed she propped her boots against the radiator too. They'd gotten wet when they'd been rushing Officer Jones to safety. Hopefully, they'd be dry by morning, otherwise her going outside for any length of time would be a problem.

Damn. He needed to stop worrying about her. Despite her delicate blonde looks, she was a tough-as-nails agent who'd gone nose to nose with him without flinching. Plenty of guys wouldn't.

But looking out for his people was what he did—a team was only as strong as its weakest link, and you became the weakest link if you neglected things like wet boots or cleanliness in survival situations. Charlotte was part of his team now, whether he liked it or not.

She disappeared into her room—*their* room. The idea made him shudder. When was the last time he'd bunked with a woman? Years. Apparently, he was hard on some people's nerves, generally women he slept with judging by his relationship record.

He headed down the back stairs to the kitchen and mud

room. He found an industrial-sized machine and stuffed everything inside. A silky scrap of jade green fell onto the floor, and he quickly scooped up the panties and tossed them in the machine. He would not imagine what Charlotte Blood looked like wearing those, and he would not think about what she might be wearing right now.

He closed his eyes and banged his head on the top of the washer. He. Didn't. Even. Like. Her.

Since when was *like* necessary?

He growled.

"Everything okay?" Charlotte asked from behind him.

He drew in a long, calming breath. "Dandy." He found the powder, threw in a pod, and started the washing cycle. "Let's flip a coin about who to brief first."

"Actually," she raised up her hand like a first-grade teacher. "I had an idea about that."

He braced himself.

"Let's grab the negotiators from where they've set up communications and bring them into the barn. We'll do a full team briefing with HRT. That way we can all get up to speed faster."

He looked at her in surprise. "That's a good idea."

"I have my moments," she said dryly.

He grinned at her. This was going to be a cinch.

CHAPTER SIX

"**W**HAT DO YOU think they're doing, Dad? I mean we haven't seen much activity. Have they left?" TJ knew it was wishful thinking, but the way Malcolm snorted made him feel like he was ten years old again.

His father sighed, keeping one eye on the television monitors and one eye on the surveillance cams. "No, son. They're out there. Setting up. My guess is that guy who walked in here naked was probably either from a SWAT team or the FBI's Hostage Rescue Team. That means they'll be weighing the pros and cons of our defenses. The fact they haven't blacked out our cameras is telling. They want to give us a false sense of security. Probably try to talk us out of here first."

TJ's mood sank. He'd hoped the lack of movement on the cops' side meant they were going to leave them alone, especially as the wildlife officer was alive, at least according to the news media. Relief had filled TJ at that announcement. Maybe there was still a way to fix this mess.

The news channels were playing endless loops of film showing environmental protesters and logging trucks and old aerial shots. Most of their home was underground, hidden beneath the garden where they grew vegetables.

There was a lot of speculation as to what they believed in and whether or not they were a cult, which was bullshit. The media used the word cult to scare people. Sometimes people here went to a church in town but, more often, his mother had led them in prayer. Malcolm had taken that over after her death. That didn't make them a cult—it made them self-sufficient.

His father had bought and rebuilt this property to ease his mother's fears and to escape the world, but then people had started arriving at the door and asking for refuge, and his mother had rarely turned anyone away. They were her family, whether she liked it or not.

The image of a black woman in a suit flashed up on all four television screens set into another wall. She was standing outside the hospital where they'd taken the wildlife officer. Bob Jones was his name.

TJ's stomach clenched. Had he died?

"Turn that up," Tom demanded, pointing at the news.

According to the label on the screen, the woman in the suit was from the FBI's public relations office. She began the statement with news that the wildlife officer had survived surgery and was expected to make a full recovery although it was still early days.

"In a statement, FWO Jones said that, while fulfilling his official law enforcement duties, he came upon an attack on a young woman in progress and gave chase to the assailant. The suspect fled inside a fortified structure on Eagle Mountain. People inside the facility shot at FWO Jones as he tried to arrest the assailant."

Shit. TJ felt eyes on him but didn't look away from the screen.

The agent finished by saying that, when the sheriff had arrived to conduct his investigation, the people here had fired at them, injuring another deputy, which was when the FBI stepped in. The public relations woman looked into the camera. "We wish for a peaceful resolution to this situation, but we do want to question any individuals in the area who may have information regarding the young woman who was found dead on Eagle Mountain and the subsequent shooting of law enforcement personnel."

The silence felt like lead pressing against TJ's skull.

"You murdered someone?" exclaimed Malcolm.

TJ's head shot up. "Of course not."

But the FBI agent's words damned him as a liar. TJ looked around at a room full of eyes regarding him with distaste and disgust. "I found a girl," he admitted.

Tears flooded his eyes at referring to Kayla like she was some anonymous stranger. Nothing. Nobody. Unimportant. But he couldn't admit he knew her.

"I went over to check her pulse, and then this guy turned up." He pointed at the screen that was showing an official photograph of FWO Bob Jones grinning at the camera.

Anger burned. The world was calling the wildlife officer a hero and labeling TJ a cowardly murderer, and the only person who really mattered was the one who'd died.

"I ran before he could arrest me. He tried to shoot me in the back." His voice was hoarse. "You'd have all done the same. I don't know what happened to the girl. I didn't know her." He felt like Judas. His stomach cramped at the lie. But she was dead now, and he couldn't do anything to bring her back. "I found her dead. Maybe he killed her and decided to blame me." TJ pointed at the screen. His heart was pounding, and sweat broke out on his brow.

Even his father looked unconvinced.

Malcolm sneered. "That's some story, TJ."

TJ blinked. It did sound crazy.

"I guess," he admitted slowly. "I probably wouldn't believe it if I didn't know for a fact it was true. But it is. I swear it."

His father sat heavily on a chair in front of the monitors and held his head in his hands. TJ's heart contracted at the sight of him suffering because of him.

"I say we give the cops what they want and send TJ out to face the consequences of his actions like a man should." Malcolm raised his voice to the room in general, and there was a murmur of consent.

"That's enough." His father looked up. "This is my land, and TJ stays right here with me. Any of you have an issue with that, you are welcome to leave." Tom stared at Malcolm until the other man looked away. "Anyone?"

No one moved.

"Dad." TJ stepped forward. "Perhaps I should give myself up? Sort this thing out with the cops so no one else gets hurt."

"You think they're going to believe a boy like you over one of their own?"

TJ shook his head.

"Who do you think I built this place for, son?" His father's voice turned anguished. "Who do you think your mom and I wanted to protect?" His dad's brown eyes held an unfamiliar sheen that made TJ's throat ache with suppressed emotion.

"I don't want anyone else to get hurt." TJ looked around at the other men in the room, the condemnation in their faces plain to see. "And I want the chance to prove I'm innocent."

His dad shook his head. "This country is falling apart. I don't trust the justice system as far as I can spit, and I am *not* giving up my son." His dad pressed the general intercom.

"Anyone wanting to leave needs to pack up their gear and be out of here in the next two hours. No one will try to stop you. Anyone who stays...I cannot guarantee your safety. Those who are staying, I want four-hour watches on the front and back exits. Two men on each entrance. Two more in the surveillance room. No one shoots at anything unless we are under attack. Everyone else get some sleep. We're gonna need it."

The phone attached to the wall started to ring.

The men in the room looked at one another in shock. TJ hadn't even known it worked. No one ever called that number. It could only mean one thing. His father walked calmly over to the wall and unplugged the cord. The silence felt like a portent.

CHAPTER SEVEN

C HARLOTTE SHIVERED AS she strode outside, intensely aware of SSA Novak on her heels. Eban had told her the negotiators had set up in a building a few steps from the back door of the main ranch house. Considering she'd envisaged them working out the back of a gas station somewhere, this place was palatial.

Inside it looked like a small canteen with a basic kitchen area and a large open space where the negotiators had arranged four tables pushed together in front of one wall that was now covered in a series of white board material. Max Hawthorne was writing headings on the sheets.

She caught Novak staring at their large "Things To Remember" board which went everywhere with them and outlined reminders of how to proceed so they didn't go off track when things got heated on a call. It included "Active Listening Skills" and "Feeling Words."

His eyebrows started climbing his skull.

First line said, "Reduce anger and establish rapport." Another, "Use first name" and "Use non-judgmental language—LISTEN!!"

She needed to apply negotiator skills when dealing with Novak. And she needed to start calling him Payne.

"Payne," his first name felt unnatural on her lips, "and I

are shadowing one another during the setup phase to ensure CNU and HRT are both fully informed and onboard with operational decisions."

Novak shot her a look of amusement, obviously recognizing the first-name thing for what it was. A ploy to foster closeness that felt weird and uncomfortable.

Dominic coughed out a laugh which she also ignored.

"We saved you a bunk." Eban didn't pause as he tested the sat phones. Cell phones wouldn't work in the remote mountains, although FBI techs had set up a secure cell tower that would serve the immediate ranch area.

"McKenzie insisted we have three teams of two negotiators working with myself in an overseer's capacity, actively liaising with HRT, so you can give that bed to one of the other negotiators when they arrive." She swallowed to clear the knot of tension in her throat, but it was too big to dislodge. "I'll be sharing a room with Payne for now."

All three of her colleagues stopped what they were doing and straightened, staring hard at Novak.

Novak held up his hands in defense. "Wasn't my idea, guys."

"McKenzie," Dominic gritted out.

"It doesn't matter where I sleep." She wasn't a child. She was a law enforcement professional who never went anywhere unarmed, but the negotiators were protective of one another, and she appreciated their concern, even if it was unnecessary. "Right now, we're all going to sit in on an HRT team briefing and talk strategy."

Eban shoved back his chair and grabbed his jacket. "Secure phone lines are all set up. We found an old landline number for the Harrison property, but no one answered the first time we tried it."

She held the door for everyone as they started heading to the barn where HRT were stationed. She'd forgotten to grab her hat and gloves, and the wind cut through her sweater. The men provided a windbreak, but it was still bitterly cold.

"Sounds like McKenzie is worried about this one," Eban muttered close to her ear.

"He knows how quickly things can deteriorate." The Incident Commander had infiltrated the Pioneers, a White Supremacist organization, two decades earlier. When the police had finally gone in to make arrests, a shootout had broken out, despite the presence of children on the premises. People had died.

A black-clad HRT operator on the barn door let them in. Inside she was blasted by the scent of hay which made her sneeze.

"Bless you," Novak and Eban said in synchrony.

A few horses whinnied at the other end of the barn. The HRT vehicles were parked snug against a tractor. The Hostage Rescue Team's aircraft were being kept at the airfield but were ready to deploy if needed.

Another HRT operator met them at the door of an inner structure. "We're set up this way."

A large portion of the barn had been partitioned off, and there was a series of small workshops and tack rooms, but also several four-people bunk rooms and a kitchenette area. The men had created a mini conference area in the common room with foldout picnic tables and chairs, not unlike the area the negotiators had carved out, but with more weapons and less "Feeling words."

"The ranch caters to school visits and summer camps,"

Eban explained the bunks.

Most of the HRT operators regarded her and the other negotiators with open curiosity. Although they regularly worked together, they rarely joined each other's briefings.

McKenzie strode in behind them.

Novak stepped up to the table and looked at the map spread out there. "Where we at?"

"Getting a feel for the local topography." An operator pointed to areas on the map. "There's some pretty rugged terrain we might be able to utilize for overwatch sniper positions as long as the weather cooperates."

"They have surveillance cameras spread out throughout the forest on the east side. We need to locate any others and neutralize," Novak said.

"Or use them to our advantage," another operator put in. "Get in and out without being seen by the cameras and give the people inside a false sense of security."

McKenzie tipped his head. "How feasible is that?"

"Right now, we can do it," Novak answered. "But as soon as there is snow on the ground, it'll be more difficult to mask our tracks."

"We need more information." McKenzie looked up. "Set up the sniper teams with the remit to provide observation only at this juncture."

Novak took over. "Sniper teams, Birdman and Demarco, Hersh and Rockwell. Get your gear together for the first shift. Be prepared for winter conditions. I want you here." He pointed to a location on the map. "And here. The cameras have infrared so be on the lookout."

Charlotte knew HRT had three tactical units in total, Gold, Blue and Red, which rotated between operations, training, and support. Each unit was comprised of one eight-man sniper team and two seven-man assaulter squads, Echo and Charlie teams.

"Angeletti, take Griffin to map out the locations of all cameras and any other technology they might have guarding the perimeter. Let them see you—they will be expecting this— but also deliberately miss a few." Again, Novak pointed to the map. "Let's give them what they feel might be a safe corridor for escape and have a few sheriff's deputies staking out that area in case people make a run for it. After tonight, sniper teams will do twelve-on twelve-off shifts so they can switch out in darkness. Make sure you are equipped appropriately. No winter storms in the immediate forecast, but that can change any time, and we will need to reassess."

McKenzie paced. "I want observation teams to help figure out exactly what we are dealing with. I have analysts at HQ determining how many people are inside and their names and pertinent background information. I have an agent digging up blueprints for the compound and tracking down whoever delivered the goddamned concrete for the structure. Novak, break out your cool toys and see if there is some way of getting eyes and ears inside. We need to find out as much information as possible regarding the occupants. Anything to add, SSA Blood?" McKenzie asked.

Charlotte took a step forward. "Whatever we do, try not to inflame the situation."

Novak shot her a look, and she tilted up her chin.

"Right now, we want to talk to the people on Eagle Mountain because of a woman's death and the shooting of the Federal Wildlife Officer and another deputy. We don't want a war." She looked at the IC. "Any word on their conditions yet?"

McKenzie propped a hip on the table. "Deputy is stable. The cold temperatures kept the wildlife officer alive. It was damn good work getting him out of there, Novak."

There was a beat of acknowledgement for Novak's bravery.

Charlotte would never forget the way Novak had gone after the downed officer. She might be mad he'd done it without consultation, but she'd carry those images to her grave.

"With all due respect, SSA Blood," Novak spoke softly, and she knew she wasn't going to like whatever came out of his mouth. "They started this conflict. Someone in that compound probably killed that woman. They shot a federal law enforcement officer and left him to bleed out. When the sheriff tried to rescue him, another deputy was injured. Are you really suggesting we walk away, no harm no foul?"

"No. Not at all. But given the personality types probably involved, if we lay siege to that building, we risk sending it into a lockdown and creating a dangerous standoff for no reason. We risk turning this into a crisis that doesn't need to happen."

Novak pressed his lips together in disapproval, but she was saved by the boss.

"SSA Blood is correct. We need to gather information and figure out what actually sparked this conflict." McKenzie nailed her with a direct stare. "I want negotiators calling in to the compound until someone answers the damn phone. And if they won't talk on the phone, use a goddamn bullhorn."

"No one ever made friends over a bullhorn, boss," Charlotte said calmly. She saw an operator exchange a glance with Novak but didn't know how to interpret it. "We are assuming there's a landline hooked up, but we should also arrange to drop a satellite phone within the walls in case there isn't."

McKenzie nodded thoughtfully.

She pressed on while she had the floor. "I was thinking they most likely have some sat phones on the premises," she stated. "I say we work on getting those phone numbers and then, rather than trying to call them straight away, we listen in on any conversations before we take control of those lines. Get a handle on who their allies are."

"Good idea. Number one priority." McKenzie pointed a finger at a guy beside a whiteboard who picked up a marker and started writing. "We need to figure out if there are hostages being held or not. Secondly, who are these people, and who are their associates, and what is the risk to others at this point? Third, nail down any communication channels into or out of that facility. SIOC is monitoring all media and internet outlets. Fourth, figure out what the hell happened up there on that mountain."

The local agent, Devon Truman, received a call and turned away briefly. After a few seconds, he turned back and raised a hand. "Sheriff says they picked up a group of women and children exiting the compound. He wants to know what to do with them?"

"Where's the nearest church hall?" Charlotte asked quickly. This was good news.

"Probably Eagle Creek," Truman responded.

McKenzie nodded sharply. "Arrange beds and food for them there. I want them made comfortable, but I also want them photographed—quietly—and backgrounds run. I want to know who they are and what they know."

Charlotte raised her hand. "I could go talk to them."

"No, you can't," Novak muttered under his breath so only she could hear, "because I don't have time for that shit."

Charlotte pulled a face, but McKenzie was unrelenting. He turned to Truman. "Take another agent with you and question everyone there. Be *nice* and gather as much information as possible. Provide and encourage counselors, especially to the minors in the group. They probably consider us Beelzebub personified, so let's dispel that notion. Does the local sheriff's office have a community liaison officer?"

"I don't know," Truman admitted tiredly.

"Find out. If not, bring a local deputy along to try and get a feel for these people. A woman, if possible. In the morning, go talk to local shopkeepers. The information we need is out there, we need to track it down."

"Can we cross 'holding hostages' off the list?" Charlotte asked McKenzie.

McKenzie shook his head, his gaze unflinching. "I agree we can lower the risk of that being the case, but until we account for everyone, then no, we can't cross it off the list. Let's get to it, people. Back here at eight AM for the next briefing."

McKenzie sprang to his feet and headed out of the room.

Charlotte stared over at Novak, but he had already turned his back on her and was leaning over the map.

"What do you want us to do, Char?" Eban asked.

"Get hold of whoever is in control of that compound. We need to talk sense into them before this whole thing blows up and more people get hurt."

NOVAK CHECKED HIS watch. One AM. First teams were in place, but it had taken way longer than anticipated. They'd also developed their Immediate Action Plan should the situation dramatically head south.

"Why don't we ride horses up there as far as this point here?" This from Cowboy who'd grown up on a ranch in Montana—hence the nickname.

"We're not all comfortable on horseback, especially in the dark," grumbled Cowboy's partner.

"You just have to sit in the saddle and not fall off. We're not going to travel at speed, but it'll still be a lot faster than traveling on foot. Beats walking."

Cowboy was right. Riding on horseback was faster than hiking up the mountain and quieter than ATVs.

"It's a good idea," Novak conceded. "Talk to the people who own the ranch. If anyone falls off and injures themselves, I'll blame you." He pointed at Cowboy. The guy grinned.

"Now that's arranged, it's my turn to check in with the negotiators," Charlotte piped up cheerfully from behind him.

Novak stiffened. He'd forgotten she was there. "I've barely gotten started here," he said with frustration.

"And I haven't gotten started at all. It's my turn, Novak."

Novak blew out a loud breath. She was right, but he didn't have to like it. "You guys all good to go?" The men nodded. They were already geared up or resting while they had the chance.

"You need a bed, Novak?" Angeletti, his second in command and best friend on HRT, asked. "There's one last empty bunk in my room."

"I'm good."

Angeletti's brows rose in question.

"He's sharing with me," Charlotte said with a sweet smile. "Courtesy of the IC."

"Seriously?" Angeletti didn't look like he believed Charlotte, which made Novak grind his teeth. He should be here with his men, not hanging with management.

"Don't worry." Charlotte smiled. "I don't bite."

"More's the pity." Cowboy flashed her a smile that Novak knew had seduced more than his fair share of women.

"Enough," Novak said sharply. He wouldn't feed gossip or innuendo. This was work. Nothing more or less. His bark had nothing to do with the unusual flash of jealousy that went through him when prim and proper Charlotte Blood smiled back at one of his team members.

"Time to go," Charlotte insisted like a terrier who wouldn't let go of a bone.

Novak exchanged a look with Angeletti, one that said *what the fuck?* But Charlotte was right, she'd been patient, and it wasn't her fault they had to do this dumb *joined-at-the-hip* thing—although she had been the one to complain about him to McKenzie, so maybe it *was* her fault.

Dammit, he could think of a million better *joined-at-the-hip* options, and every one of them was inappropriate for a work situation.

"Call me with any updates." Novak helped himself to a radio and an earpiece because, while he might not be physically in this room, he didn't want to miss out on any action. He followed Charlotte out of the barn, moving slightly in front of her to cut out the icy blast of the wind as she still didn't have a jacket, and he'd forgotten to borrow anything for her.

He held open the door of the Negotiation Center and saw

McKenzie on a video call to a profiler from the Behavioral Analysis Unit. McKenzie glanced at them as they entered then went back to his meeting.

Novak followed Charlotte over to where Dominic and Eban manned the post.

"CNU is arranging for two additional negotiators out of Seattle and Salt Lake City to arrive by noon tomorrow," Dominic told Charlotte quietly, obviously aware the IC was in conversation a few feet away. "We've been trying the Harrisons' landline constantly, but no one has answered yet. We don't even know if it is plugged in."

Eban Winters nodded to them both then ignored them. He was wearing a headset and had a notepad in front of him. High tech recording equipment was set up ready to go as soon as required.

"Anything from Truman regarding the people who left the compound?" Charlotte asked.

Dominic shook his head. "But McKenzie might have heard something."

McKenzie was busy.

Charlotte pulled out her cell and started dialing. "Agent Truman? Can you talk?"

She sat down and started twirling her hair as she spoke to the local agent. Novak pulled up a chair, leaning back and crossing his arms over his chest, watching her. What the fuck was he doing wasting his time here?

"Can you send us the list of names? I'd like to get people tracing them ASAP." Charlotte's tone with Truman was sugary sweet. The way she spoke to everyone who wasn't him. Go figure.

She hung up. "According to the people Truman interviewed, they don't know exactly what happened yesterday morning, but the general conjecture was a young man, name of TJ Harrison, came running back to the compound with Federal Wildlife Officer Bob Jones in hot pursuit. They said the FWO shot at TJ, and someone guarding the door returned fire. No one was naming names as to who that shooter was. They said they then defended themselves when the sheriff arrived, guns blazing."

"How come the women and children left?" Novak asked.

"Tom Harrison, leader of the group and owner of the land, gave anyone who wanted to leave the chance, and eight people took it. Two women with six kids under ten." Charlotte pushed her hair behind her ear and suddenly looked exhausted. "Truman's gathering a list of names of people inside from the women, but he's not sure how accurate it's going to be or how truthful these women are. They are waiting for relatives to come pick them up. He hasn't told them that they can't leave quite yet. Not until we say so, anyway."

"Bob Jones woke up again," McKenzie shouted over his shoulder. "Told the agent by his bedside he saw TJ Harrison strangling the dead girl and, when confronted, TJ ran."

"What was Jones doing up there?" asked Charlotte.

"He received a report of a cougar stalking someone on the trail. He was checking it out."

Novak got on his radio and updated the sniper teams on a possible cougar in the area. Not that it was exactly news given the location. Cougar, bears, wolves were all possible. Although hopefully Bigfoot was holed up for winter.

The danger posed by the terrain, weather, and wildlife was equal to the danger from the armed men in the compound and getting more dangerous as winter approached. No one wanted to take any chances.

"What do we know about the dead girl?" Charlotte asked the boss.

McKenzie checked his watch. "Virtually nothing. ME isn't planning to start the postmortem until nine AM and we haven't been able to identify her yet. AFIS came back with nothing on her fingerprints. Her DNA isn't in CODIS. Scene is contained as much as is possible but contaminated as hell."

Charlotte tried to cover a yawn.

"You two should catch a couple hours' rest."

Novak opened his mouth to suggest he head back to the barn and help HRT gear up.

McKenzie caught his gaze before the words left his mouth. "Both of you. I'm here to respond to any issues. If anything changes before the briefing, I will let you know. Get some sleep. That's an order."

CHAPTER EIGHT

C HARLOTTE STOMPED UP the steps to the main ranch house. "I'm not a two-year-old. I don't need to be told when to sleep."

"He has a point," Novak argued from behind her. "After today, it's only gonna get busier."

"Oh, please." She rolled her eyes, though the former Special Forces soldier couldn't see as she walked into the house via the mud room.

She headed to the washing machine and tossed their wet gear in the dryer. Novak waited for her near the doorway. This shadowing one another nonsense was starting to get old. She liked her own space.

"Did you sleep on the plane?" He leaned against the doorjamb as she set the timer.

"No." Those aircraft were noisier than a fairground ride. She headed up the back stairs to their room, once again leading the way, hyperaware of the guy following her.

"Did you?" She lowered her voice as other people were already trying to sleep. Dammit. This probably was a good idea. McKenzie could rest tomorrow when she and Novak were awake.

"No," he said, barely above a whisper. "But I train regularly on little or no sleep."

He spoke as if he were talking to some civilian who worked nine to five.

She thought about the endless barricade and hostage situations she'd been called to. The untold hours of patience and common sense required to talk people out of impossible situations when the only escape they could envision was violence and death. By the end, she was showing them the light. Yes, they had to deal with the consequences of their actions, and things became a lot more problematic when people had been hurt. But it was her job to concentrate on extricating them from the incident and enabling them to move on with their lives.

She drew in a long deep breath and forced herself to let go of the irritation. She needed to think of her relationship with Novak as some long-term hostage situation in which they were both trapped and needed to figure out a way to work together to gain their freedom.

Inside their room, she grabbed her toothbrush while he simply climbed the ladder and fell fully clothed onto the sheets. It was chilly in the room.

"Are you going to be warm enough?" she asked. "I can find more blankets if you're cold."

"You don't need to mother me, Charlotte. I'm not one of your boys."

His tone grated on her nerves.

"I don't 'mother' people any more than you do," she said pointedly.

He grunted, apparently admitting she had a point. They both liked to look after their people.

She turned off the light and then went across the hall to the bathroom, brushing her teeth and smoothing on some moisturizer before returning to the lower bunk. She sat on the thin mattress, toed off her sneakers, and decided to pull on a sleep shirt but leave on her leggings and socks in case she needed to move fast.

She tossed her shirt and sweater on the back of the nearby chair. Pulled on the nightshirt and then took off her bra, throwing it with her other stuff. Then she lay staring up at the unfinished planks, wondering how she'd ever get to sleep when there was so much going on in her brain and so much she needed to do.

She turned over and sighed. Like half of the American population, she'd been traveling the weekend before, spending Thanksgiving with her mother and stepfather and half siblings in Miami. Back at work Monday morning. Then the negotiators at CNU had gone on an impromptu night out to celebrate the fact that Dominic had proposed to Ava at his father's mansion over the weekend, and the rookie agent had actually said yes. Charlotte couldn't be happier for the pair, although she'd have been lying if she said she hadn't experienced a small amount of envy, not so much over the engagement as finding the right person to love.

She pictured her perfect life. A handsome and attentive husband who possibly at this moment resembled Special Agent Devon Truman. A nice house in the 'burbs with a flower garden and vegetables, and possibly even a real picket fence. Instead she had a lonely apartment and occasional dog-sitting duties for Dominic.

Why did it have to be so damn hard?

She yawned. Tuesday had been spent at work but slightly hungover, and Wednesday had started with a bang as this situation unfolded.

Someone walked down the corridor outside their room, and she braced herself for a knock on the door. Instead the person went into the bathroom. She released a breath.

"You have earplugs?" The wooden frame creaked ominously above her as Novak peered over the edge.

She'd thought he was asleep. "Why? Do you snore?"

He laughed, and that sound jolted her. She didn't think she'd heard him laugh in that soft, genuine way before. He was too hard, too domineering to demonstrate much of a sense of humor. Or so she'd thought.

"They'll help block out the ambient noise. Allow you to sleep a little better."

"Do you use earplugs?" she asked.

"All the damn time."

She had some in her toiletries bag. "What if I sleep in? Miss the meeting?"

"Joined at the hip, remember? I won't leave you behind," Novak said quietly.

"Promise?"

"I already did."

She snorted. Novak was very much a "my word is my bond" sort of guy. Rough around the edges. Gruff. Uncommunicative.

Did she believe him?

For some reason she did.

She slid out of bed and found the small, plastic case, then slid the plugs into her ears and lay back down. A sense of fatigue swept over her, bones suddenly weighted and heavy. Her eyelids closed despite herself.

She checked her watch one last time, and finally allowed herself to drift off to sleep regardless of the strange man doing the same thing only a few feet away.

———————————

AS TEMPTING AS it was to sneak out early, Novak had reluctantly held onto his patience and let Charlotte get a little more rest. He'd woken an hour ago, showered and dressed. Collected their laundry from the dryer and folded it into two neat piles, pretending he wasn't handling her freaking panties. Charlotte Blood was still out for the count. From her pale skin and REM movements beneath her eyelids, she needed another half hour but, unfortunately, she wasn't going to get it. He couldn't wait any longer.

"Hey, Charlotte. Time to wake up."

Nothing.

He leaned over and touched her shoulder. "Hey, SSA Blood. Rise and Shine."

He found himself flat on his back with her elbow jammed in his windpipe as she bent his arm to an angle that would pop the joint if he tried to move it.

It took her a full second to blink awake, and another to realize where she was and who she was with, and what she was doing to him. She reared back. Dragged her hands over her face. "God. Sorry."

"What the hell?" Novak lifted himself up and caught her arm, but she jerked away. "Is that how you always wake up?"

"Don't be ridiculous." She checked her watch and swore. "Why didn't you wake me earlier?"

"You looked like you needed your rest."

She glared at him, blue eyes still clouded with sleep and anger. *Great.* So much for trying to look out for her. "Not your choice to make."

He folded his arms over his chest. "This morning it was."

She grabbed her bra off the chair and somehow managed to put it on without taking off her nightshirt. Her nightshirt had two W's on it.

"Turn around," she ordered.

He did as she asked. "You changed the subject and tried to deflect me with anger. Why did you attack me when I woke you up?"

She let out a weary sigh. "It's nothing."

He wasn't about to let it drop. "That how you treat the other negotiators when you bunk together?"

"Of course not." Her words were muffled by the shirt she was pulling over her head.

Of course not. But something about him triggered a reaction.

"Damn, I don't have time to shower. I'm going to smell like a goat by the end of the day."

He caught the scent of her deodorant as she applied it under her shirt. "You smell fine."

Shit, where the hell had that come from? But he liked her scent—like limes—and she better not figure that the fuck out. "We're working in a barn, so you'll fit right in," he added.

There went his natural charm again.

She snorted out a laugh.

He waited a beat. "Am I the only person you attack when you first wake up?" Even though she hadn't actually even known who he was? He risked a glance over his shoulder, and she was pulling on her sweater, then adjusting the shoulder holster and slipping her service weapon home. Then she pulled on a black fleece hoodie but didn't zip it up.

She finally looked at him, those blue eyes of hers clear and calm now. "In recent history? Yes. But it isn't what you think."

He raised one brow. He couldn't think of any other explanation for someone to react that way. Fear. Deep, instinctual, fear.

"Okay," she conceded. "It kind of *is* what you think in that I was once attacked in my sleep."

A bolt of fury seared his nerves.

"But I wasn't raped." She looked away as she said it, and he wasn't sure whether or not he believed her. He watched her jaw flex as her teeth clenched. "I had a stepbrother for a few years, and he tried a few times."

"How the hell did he get to attempt that more than once?" Why the fuck hadn't someone beat the shit out of him or removed his dick with a fishing hook via his throat?

She slipped on her boots and then dragged her hair back into a pony. "I didn't tell anyone the first time but managed to make enough noise to make him stop. Then I started karate lessons." Her smile was satisfied. "Second time he tried it, I broke his nose."

A relieved smile caught one side of his mouth. "Good."

"Yeah. Well, I guess my dad figured it out after that and put a lock on my door. He also arranged that Brad lived with his father during the school year and with them for the holidays. And as I spent school time with my dad and holidays with my mom, I rarely saw the jerk after that."

So, Little Miss Cupcake was the product of a broken home. Kind of made sense that she tried to fix situations as a career.

"I'm sorry for whatever I did that triggered the reaction," he said quietly. Frankly, it sucked. For her. It wasn't a lot of fun for him either.

Charlotte shook her head as she brandished her toothbrush at him. "No. I'm sorry I lashed out that way. It wasn't about you. I was unprofessional. It hasn't happened for a long time but sleeping in a room with someone I don't know very well obviously precipitated some subliminal anxiety."

Her words hit him like a grenade to the chest. "I would never attack you in your sleep or anywhere else, Charlotte."

"I know that."

Did she? He wasn't convinced. "I guess we'll find out tomorrow." He gave her a shit-eating grin because he knew if he offered pity or concern, she'd be pissed. "Try not to shoot me."

"No promises." She headed across to the bathroom, and he checked his phone for updates. Nothing. He grabbed the radio which he'd turned off last night. They knew where he was if anything happened. She came back three minutes later, and they both headed downstairs. The smell of bacon and coffee wafted up the stairwell, practically making him salivate by the time he got to the kitchen.

So much for being up early. About thirty people stood around the large space, eating bacon rolls and drinking coffee like there was a shortage. He wanted to go talk to Angeletti, but as soon as he walked into the room, he spotted McKenzie. He followed Charlotte over to where the other negotiators were digging into their breakfast. Following orders so he could get back to his damn job sooner rather than later.

Goddamned brass making shit up as they went along.

Angeletti crossed the room to talk to him.

"Any updates?" Charlotte asked Dominic.

Novak knew Dominic Sheridan was connected to some very important people in the highest places in DC. He appreciated the guy didn't use those contacts to give himself an easy ride. Most people had changed into either tactical or casual gear, but Dominic had been working since he arrived and was still in his suit. He looked exhausted. Shirt out. Tie askew.

"No one picked up the phone at the compound, although we tried the number all night," Dominic said between bites. "This roll is freaking delicious. We found a current email address for Tom Harrison, and one of our techs in Quantico downloaded those email servers before we sent him a letter asking him to pick up the phone and talk to us. Nothing yet, but that was only half an hour ago."

"Anyone else come out?" Charlotte asked.

Dominic shook his head. Max Hawthorne, the former SAS soldier, was listening attentively while chewing his own breakfast. He looked alert and rested. Novak leaned over and grabbed two plates, and Charlotte grabbed a couple of mugs of black coffee. They each swapped a plate and a mug.

"I wasn't sure how you took your coffee. I can get cream," she said politely, using almost the same tone she used with everyone else. Progress. All it took was forced proximity and cutting off his air supply.

"Black is fine."

Everyone was watching them interact like they were some sort of social science experiment.

Charlotte pulled a face at him because she noticed it too.

He grinned before hiding his expression with a huge bite of bacon roll. The salt hit his taste buds. He groaned. Almost as good as sex.

"Why can't every assignment be like this?" Charlotte echoed his thoughts, speaking with her mouth full.

He'd eat anything to fuel his body, but they'd lucked out

that this place had its own cook.

The woman in question stood in the doorway to the mud-room clearly bemused how her kitchen had been taken over by thirty-plus heavily armed Feds. They needed to be mindful there were civilians onsite.

"Briefing in five minutes," McKenzie shouted above the din before heading past the cook. He shook her hand.

Novak would kiss her feet if she made him a bacon roll for breakfast every morning.

He and Charlotte both took their dishes and stacked them in the industrial-sized dishwasher like everyone else did.

"I'm going to get some sleep. Call me if you need me." Dominic headed toward the stairs.

"Get some rest." She turned to Max. "Tell Eban to meet us in the barn before he turns in. In case he has any relevant input. You attend too. They've ignored the phone all night. It's unlikely they'll call back in the next twenty minutes. Leave an agent there who can grab us if someone miraculously does call."

The man nodded and walked away.

Novak was impressed how well they worked as a team. They'd obviously been together a long time and knew their jobs inside out. What made a warrior like Hawthorne want to use his words rather than his fighting skills? Novak knew the value of words, but he also knew the duplicity of man. Trust had to be earned, and he'd bet on his use of force over his ability to talk someone out of a crisis any day. That's one of the things his ex had cited in the divorce—inability to communicate. Pity he'd been thousands of miles away in a classified location when she'd decided that was a deal breaker.

They headed outside. It wasn't quite as dick-snapping cold

as it had been yesterday, but it was still freezing. He hoped his men were okay.

Charlotte was wearing her boots which were dry now, but would anyone remember to pick her up a new winter jacket?

"What?" she asked, clearly sensing him looking at her.

"Nothing," Novak said quickly.

"You're not a very good liar," she said, surprising him.

He scowled. "I am an excellent liar."

"*Really*?" she said.

"Really. We should play poker sometime."

"You'd play poker with a woman? And not the strip variety?"

Novak almost choked on his tongue at the images his mind came up with. "I have never played strip poker in my life."

"Really?" she said again. Her eyes sparkled, and she laughed at his discomfort, but not in a way that felt vindictive.

"Considering I usually play cards with teammates, hell no. I've no desire to see these guys naked."

She glanced around at his fellow HRT operators who were all pretending not to listen to their conversation and grinned. "Why not? You don't seem bashful. *I've* already seen you naked."

Heat crawled up his neck. God, the woman wouldn't let it drop, and he knew every member of HRT would be ribbing him for months now about strip *fucking* poker.

"You never played it? Not even in college?" she pressed.

He shrugged. "I was on the varsity rugby team. Between that and keeping up my grades, I didn't have a lot of spare time." He'd gotten a full ride to Princeton, but he'd had to work hard to stay there.

Her breath came out in a cloud of mist. "That is very true. I waitressed all through college and lived with my dad. He was single again then."

Novak nodded, no longer teasing, but remembering the pressure of her forearm against his throat. He hadn't told her how easily he could have reversed the situation. He did not want to take away her power. Most assholes wouldn't have his training or hers, and most would have begged for mercy. He cleared his throat. "What did you study?"

"Psych." She shot him a look.

They were almost at the barn door, but he couldn't resist teasing her a little.

"So, psych major with a minor in strip poker. I'll remember that next time I'm playing Texas hold 'em." He'd meant it as a joke but, again, his brain betrayed him by exploding with a full color image of SSA Charlotte Blood sitting at a poker table in nothing but the underwear he'd already seen.

He tripped over the step into the barn.

"Holy crap, Novak, are you always this clumsy?" Charlotte teased.

As soon as she turned away and continued walking to the meeting room, Angeletti shook his head and leaned close to his ear. "You are so fucked."

"I'm doing my goddamn job," said Novak.

"Sure, pal. But I'm betting a full house to your ace high that you recently realized the pretty lady negotiator is *hot* and that is *not* how you do your goddamned job."

Novak growled and shoved past the guy. Angeletti shoved him back, and Novak grinned, reminding him of the real reason he was here. No way was he falling for her. He was doing what McKenzie wanted so he could get back where he belonged. Sleeping in the barn with his men. Nothing was more important than his team except for getting the job done and finding justice for the dead woman and the men who'd been shot. He couldn't allow the deceptively soft-looking Charlotte Blood to derail him.

CHAPTER NINE

W HEN CHARLOTTE WALKED in, she saw Eban at the far side of the barn deep in serious conversation with the HRT operator everyone called Cowboy. Eban spotted her and came over.

"You two know each other?" Charlotte asked him.

"Grew up in the same town."

"You're kidding me? Small world."

He grunted.

There were shadows beneath his eyes that never used to be there. She was pretty sure they had something to do with the redhead he'd helped rescue in Indonesia, but whenever she raised the issue, he refused to discuss it.

McKenzie started talking.

She looked around for Novak, but he was standing with his arms crossed, leaning against the wall with some of the other black-clad operators. His absence felt like a small moment of loss and then she realized she was being absurd. They had to be together to make sure they both had access to all the information and to satisfy McKenzie's ridiculous instructions, not because they were besties. She'd sensed a softening in him, probably pity after her pathetic story about her asshole stepbrother. She hadn't seen the jackass in more than a decade, but some memories latched onto your DNA, and it didn't matter how long it had been. Something about Novak trying to wake her that morning had flicked the switch.

She didn't need his pity, but she was starting to realize he wasn't the knuckle-grazer she'd first assumed. He was prickly and irritating, but he also looked out for people, and she was a sucker for that. She did it too.

"We believe there are about thirty individuals inside the facility, according to the women who left last night. Ranging in age from five months to about seventy-five."

Charlotte closed her eyes. There were babies in that place. *Babies.*

"Any records backing up this information?" This from Novak who was naturally suspicious that this was disinformation designed to limit their response.

McKenzie looked at Truman who Charlotte hadn't even noticed. His hair was ruffled, and he was wearing the same shirt and suit as yesterday. Still smokin' hot. The realization was almost a relief. She flashed another glance at Novak who caught her eye and looked away.

"No medical records. Apparently, the people in the compound are not big believers in hospitals."

"Great. I'm sure the women love that when they're in labor." Novak rolled his eyes. "They say anything about this TJ character?"

Truman nodded. "They all like TJ, even the kids. He plays with them and taught some of them to read and write as well as ride."

"They have livestock?" Novak asked, coming off the wall.

Truman nodded his head. "Four horses. Also have a pig and some chickens. They had a cow, but it got sick and died, and they haven't replaced it yet."

"What did they say about the accusations against TJ?" Charlotte asked.

"Lies because TJ would never hurt anyone," Truman answered.

"What's his mental capacity?" Novak asked.

Charlotte bristled. So nice people had mental issues now?

"He's a smart kid. Was home-schooled but is known around the community for being kind and polite. He's eighteen, and the parents did actually register his birth in a hospital in Utah. More interesting is his father. Tom Harrison was an engineer for the Army for twenty years and worked for the US Army Corps of Engineers, primarily based out of Fort Belvoir. He left within a year of meeting his wife Martha who died this past spring. Martha came from a large family and, according to local sources and the two mothers who left the compound last night, it's her family members who live there. The building is well fortified and supplied, and they are well armed," said Truman.

"Quantico and HQ are compiling as much background information as possible on the names Truman got from the women," McKenzie put in. "Any word from the teams of observers we have in place?"

She liked that they called the snipers "observers." It helped calm the tone of the meeting.

"They have eyes on the outer defenses, but no one is moving around outside," Novak said.

Charlotte wondered when he'd received that update. Probably when she'd been sleeping like a log. "Did we get the ME's report yet?" Charlotte asked.

McKenzie shook his head and checked his wristwatch. "He hasn't conducted it yet."

She ground her teeth in frustration.

"We've been examining the original blueprints." An HRT operator pointed at the drawings laid out on the table.

Charlotte moved forward for a better look. The building was circular with two marked exits.

"The doors are fortified steel. We have to assume Harrison reinforced them after he bought the property and possibly made other modifications."

"Who wants to live in a bunker?" asked Truman.

"Asked no Gen-Xer ever," one older man quipped, receiving a laugh and lightening the mood.

McKenzie continued, "Someone who thinks it's gonna save his family from the coming apocalypse, which is more common than you'd think."

Charlotte knew he'd lived with a White Supremacist antigovernment group led by David Hines. She also knew McKenzie was now engaged to Hines's daughter. He had a lot more experience dealing with that type of personality than most FBI agents. But they still didn't know the exact ideology of all the people involved in this incident and wouldn't until they started talking this out, which could take months. She held back a sigh. The thought of being here that long when there were so many other cases to solve and people to help was depressing. However, the thought of people dying because she lacked staying power was worse.

"What's this?" Novak pointed at a thin line that led out of the building.

"Sewage or ventilation shaft?" The guy next to him suggested.

"We need to get eyes on it. It could be our way in." Novak's eyes sparked with interest.

"We're a long way from storming the place," Charlotte reminded him quickly.

Novak sent her an exasperated look. "I realize that, but we plan for all eventualities and train for those circumstances in the meantime. Knowledge about the layout is a basic requirement for figuring how to get inside with minimum risk to my men and allows us to train for differing scenarios."

His tone suggested she didn't care about the safety of his men, and that pissed her off.

"We get eyes or ears inside yet?" McKenzie asked as his eyes assessed her and Novak's interactions with a frown.

She forced her face to relax.

Another operator shook his head. "Most of our traditional methods won't work. The concrete is too thick to drill, even if we could get to them without being spotted. The seals around the doors are tight. I'm thinking we could try to get fiberoptics in either via a sewage line to the septic tank or via that other exit we want to investigate or via some of the slits that seem to be designed for observation and defense purposes."

"My vote is the ventilation system because I do not want to dive into a septic tank," an operator joked. Charlotte was one hundred percent in support of that sentiment but knew they'd do whatever was necessary.

"We'll take a look at other options later this morning when some of our other toys arrive from Quantico," Novak said enigmatically.

She held back her questions because this was how these guys worked. They had secret methods that they guarded even from other agents. The fact remained, if the worst-case scenario did happen and people's lives were threatened, HRT needed to get inside ASAP.

"I want assessments of how long they can conceivably survive if this becomes a drawn-out incident," McKenzie said. "What water sources do they have? Can we utilize them?"

Novak shrugged. "We might be able to add a sedative to the water but as people don't generally all drink at the same time, it is an unreliable method. Plus with small children inside I would not recommend it."

McKenzie nodded as if satisfied. Had that question been a test? Charlotte suspected it might have been. He looked at her. "No communications from anyone inside?"

She shook her head. "It's not unexpected in this kind of situation for people to stick their head in the sand and pretend nothing has changed and the federal government is not parked on their doorstep. It's why I believe that the less obvious we are, the more likely they are to emerge from the building before spring."

Faces fell at that. No one wanted to be here for months.

"Are you suggesting we pull back completely?" McKenzie asked.

"Right now, the threat to life seems low. So, yes, or we at least *appear* to pull back."

There was a murmur of disagreement from the HRT guys. Novak stayed silent, which she appreciated, but she could feel him watching her. Judging her.

But it was her turn and, despite her negotiator specialty, she wasn't here to make friends. "We pull back visibly. We investigate the death of the woman, determine if it was a homicide, and watch the compound. Wait for TJ to start venturing out again and then detain him in a location least likely to put anyone else in danger, especially the children. Hopefully, he will be alone. We can start questioning him and others and figure out who fired those shots. Then we arrest them."

McKenzie's lips firmed.

A muscle ticked in Novak's jaw.

"Or we could devote months laying siege, spend millions of taxpayers' dollars simply to prove our strength. We aren't going to blast our way inside when there are babies at risk, and they know it. We cannot afford to be seen as the bad guys here. It would destroy the public's trust in the FBI, once and for all."

"We can't afford for every militia in the country to think we are afraid to confront them if they hide behind women and children," Novak stated calmly, but Charlotte could hear the edge in his voice.

None of the options were good.

"You're both right," McKenzie announced. "This is a shitty operation at a shitty time of year. Unfortunately, we don't get to pick what we work on or when. The director is watching this closely and so are most of the world's media, which in turn means so is every domestic and foreign terrorist who has even thought about taking us on. I want this whole incident de-escalated, but I don't want every antigovernment yahoo or terrorist wannabe thinking the FBI is too scared of the consequences to act decisively. We are not."

Charlotte pressed her lips tight together, so she didn't interrupt and get herself thrown off the job. She liked that McKenzie listened to more than one opinion, she just wanted him to support hers.

"We're here for now. Let's not incite anyone further. No one talks to the media except through me or the public relations officer who is currently at the hospital but will be here later today. This whole area is a tinderbox of conflict, and we don't want to ignite that fuse."

With more personnel arriving every minute, Charlotte wasn't sure how the FBI could be seen as doing anything except escalating the situation.

"I also want lockdown on information coming out of this ranch. The owners have agreed to confidentiality."

"You trust them?" Novak crossed his arms over his chest. A sprinkling of golden hair was visible on his forearms.

"The owners are leaving the area and seem to have no great love of the locals. Plus, they're making bank, and I doubt they want to risk losing the fatted calf or getting arrested. HQ will monitor them," McKenzie said. "In future, let's keep the number of operatives visible on ranch property during daylight hours down to four or five max. We'll arrange food to be brought over to the barn from the main house during the day." He looked over at all the black-clad operators. "The media is hunting for our accommodations, and the locals will have figured it out already. I don't want images of this building on TV or the internet, and I don't want us to be vulnerable to attack." McKenzie looked grim. "The number of domestic terrorist and antigovernment groups who would like to take a potshot at us keeps growing and so does their armory. We consider them a bigger threat than anything coming out of the Middle East right now. I don't want anyone dropping their guard."

Everyone sat up with that pronouncement. They needed to remember they didn't work in a vacuum, and they were vulnerable too.

"Has there been chatter somewhere about an attack?" Novak asked.

McKenzie pulled at his bottom lip. "Only what's to be

expected. But I know how these people think, and this situation is an opportunity for them from several different angles."

Charlotte spoke up quickly while she had the chance. "If we're going with the status quo in the short term, and as Harrison and his buddies aren't yet talking to us, and we'll shortly have *seven* top negotiators here, I'd like permission to go speak to the people in the protest camp. See if they can help us discover the identity of the dead woman, or if they have interacted with the people in the compound."

Truman spoke up. "Sheriff's deputies were going to interview them this morning."

Charlotte narrowed her eyes. "I thought we were doing it?"

"Didn't have the manpower," McKenzie admitted.

"Even more reason for me to go," Charlotte pushed.

"You can't go because I can't go," Novak argued.

They both stared at McKenzie, each trying to use ESP to make him do what they wanted, which was to go their separate ways. The guy shook his head.

"Nice try. You two are stuck with each other until I say so." McKenzie stared at her thoughtfully. "Go talk to the people in the camp."

Charlotte knew not to betray any feelings of victory on her face and dared not look at Novak.

McKenzie continued. "We need an ID on the dead woman. I also want to know who reported the cougar incident that got Bob Jones up there. US Fish and Wildlife have no record of a call, and we hope to gain access to Jones's phone records with his permission. It has to be someone who lives or spent time in that area. There's a good chance it's someone from the camp."

"Maybe the young woman died of natural causes, but the kid found her and ran when confronted," Novak suggested.

McKenzie nodded. "Then, aside from shooting the two law enforcement officials"—which carried major prison time if they could figure out who to charge—"there are lesser offenses to answer for, which is something we could relay to the people in the bunker via the media. Assuming they have some sort of cable service?"

"They're hooked up to satellite TV. Not paying for the service but definitely hooked up."

"Do we want to block that?" Novak asked.

"Not yet," McKenzie said thoughtfully. "I've run some options through the BAU to see what the profilers can come up with. Let's see if we can manipulate them into thinking it's safe to come out."

It was a good idea. Charlotte expected someone from BAU to turn up any moment and start working on a strategy, but maybe they were doing it from Quantico.

The meeting broke up, and everyone got to work on the jobs they'd been assigned.

She glanced at Novak, noticing the pale blond stubble on his cheeks and the way the dawn rays slanted over his hair. He seemed to feel her gaze and shot her a glance that told her he wasn't happy with events but recognized he didn't have a choice.

"You and Novak okay?" Max asked quietly from behind.

She loved his British accent. They used it on female hostage takers every opportunity they got. "He's a lot more bark than bite."

Max grunted. "If he barks too much, let me know."

Charlotte smiled slightly. "I can handle him."

"I have no doubt." Max raised a brow. "One potential problem we might have though is McKenzie. His crew has taken over one part of the canteen, and if Harrison's group start talking to us, you'll need to kick them out."

Great.

"Something tells me these people don't want to negotiate though." His dark eyes held hers.

Charlotte agreed. "Not yet anyway. They hope we're going to go away."

It was wishful thinking. The FBI didn't forgive and forget. They might bide their time though. It was an improvement on the old, more bullish ways, but in the end, the Bureau always got its man.

CHAPTER TEN

NOVAK DROVE ONE of HRT's specially outfitted Chevy Suburbans. Thankfully, his hands were too occupied to strangle his fellow SSA. It helped that Charlotte sat beside him wearing a wooly hat with a freaking furry bobble and looking so cute it was hard to believe she was a hard-as-nails Federal Agent. He bet she used that a lot. That deceptive gentleness. That old *too-sweet-to-be-dangerous* nonsense.

She had balls of steel, challenging him in front of everyone, challenging their boss. Going out on a limb and doing some investigating of her own? Dragging his highly skilled operational ass with her? Yeah, the innocent package masked a bulldog personality, and he better remember that next time they were fighting for the upper hand during this incident.

Although, this *was* as good a time as any to go asking questions they desperately needed answers to. They were in a waiting game, and until they built a mockup of the fortress where they could practice tactical entries, he had little to do but supervise his guys and wait for information to pour back in. Angeletti was more than capable of handling what needed to be done.

Let the people inside the compound live on edge for a few days before they became bored and sloppy. Let them grow complacent. HRT operators did not get bored or sloppy. They were not complacent. That's why they trained constantly for these situations and the more information they had to prep, the better the potential for an outcome where no one was hurt—on their side anyway.

"It's along here." Charlotte pointed out as if he couldn't see the row of cop cars and brightly colored tents in the background. "Looks like the sheriff beat us to it."

Duh.

There were a hell of a lot of police cruisers around for conducting interviews. He pulled up at the end of the row, and he and Charlotte climbed out.

It was chaos. Civilians running and screaming, deputies chasing and tackling people to the ground, handcuffing them. Half the residents weren't even dressed properly, suggesting this had been a dawn raid when people had still been in their sleeping bags.

"What the actual hell is going on? This is his idea of conducting interviews?" Charlotte swore under her breath, which was a first. They spotted the sheriff and headed in his direction.

Novak saw one deputy look at his fellow SSA like she was someone worth tackling but when he caught his eye, the cop seemed to belatedly notice the FBI badge Charlotte wore around her neck and her sidearm.

The deputy backed down, but Novak reinforced the idea with a scowl. At Charlotte's insistence, he'd changed into less intimidating clothing. Jeans, t-shirt and a plaid over-shirt to "fit in." He still wore his tactical boots and carried all his weapons. But he was not happy to be walking into the middle of this madness without a ballistics vest and backup.

Charlotte held up her creds as she approached the sheriff

who was standing with his hands on his hips surveying the clearing. Three men lay on the ground in front of him, all wearing handcuffs.

"Supervisory Special Agents Blood and Novak." Charlotte introduced them both. "What's going on here, Sheriff Lasalle?"

The man straightened and narrowed his gaze at her gold shield. Then he spit out of the side of his mouth and looked up to meet Novak's gaze over Charlotte's head.

"Evicting trespassers."

There were angry protests from the men who lay on the frozen grass. "We have a legal right to peacefully protest." The sheriff gave the man a sharp nudge with his boot.

Novak grinned a little, waiting for Charlotte's response to that. The sheriff mistook his expression for approval.

"Call off your men, Lasalle. The FBI are in charge of this incident and right now, you are impeding my ability to carry out my part of the investigation."

The sheriff looked over her head and made no move to stop his men. Women were screaming.

Jesus.

Novak clenched and unclenched his fist.

Charlotte got into the sheriff's eye line by rising on her tiptoes. "Call off your deputies. Otherwise, myself and my colleague here will start arresting people, beginning with you." She flicked out her cuffs.

Charlotte might be someone who espoused peaceful resolutions, but she was no pushover. Novak felt a rush of lust. The woman was hot when she was pissed.

He pushed the feelings aside. They meant nothing. Animalistic reactions from a guy who, despite knowing better, liked confident and assertive women. And one of these days he'd get over being treated like he was worthless by two of them. Then again maybe not.

He got on his sat phone and told Angeletti to get some of the guys geared up and in the transport ASAP. He gave him his location. Closed the call.

When he refused to undermine Charlotte's position, the sheriff finally met Charlotte's gaze. "You wouldn't dare."

Her expression suggested otherwise.

"You called the FBI for assistance because you needed our help. I can't tell you how to police your county, *normally*, but we're here now and our remit covers all aspects of this incident, including questioning potential witnesses."

"If these scumbags weren't here causing trouble, none of this would have happened."

"You've already questioned everyone?" Charlotte asked with fake politeness. "Point me in the direction as to which one of them caused the woman's death yesterday? And please tell me who shot Federal Wildlife Officer Jones? And which one of *these* people shot and injured your deputy?" She didn't raise her voice, but anyone looking at her body language would know she was incensed.

The sheriff chewed his mustache.

"Call off your men, Lasalle, or I swear to god I will cuff you and transport you to the nearest federal holding facility, and I will not be happy with wasting hours of my day on a man who should know better."

Contempt washed over Lasalle's features, and Novak shifted his stance.

"She isn't bluffing," Novak said quietly.

The sheriff's upper lip curled. Then he barked an order to a uniform who stood nearby watching them with huge eyes.

"Call everyone back, Deputy. Let the Feds figure it out on their own from now on."

"Deputies are to return to their cars. Release your prisoners. The Feds are taking over."

Novak winced as that announcement was made over the car's loudspeaker. No way was he spending all day talking to freaking hippies. He scanned the surroundings and saw several heads swivel nervously toward them.

Great.

"I assume that means you won't be needing my deputies for any other things regarding this situation." The sheriff gave Charlotte an arrogant smile that suggested he held all the cards. "I'll make it clear to the State Attorney that before they even ask for my assistance again, I'll require a very personal apology from you, young lady." The sheriff looked down his nose at Charlotte. The implication was both sexual and misogynistic. It made Novak want to step in and handle the arrogant fucker. Then he remembered Charlotte was a Supervisory Special Agent in the FBI who knew how to play high stakes poker. She could hold her own.

Charlotte nodded. "The State Police can take over anything you are unable to handle, Sheriff. We would not want to put undue stress on a department that is already reeling following the injury of a deputy. We totally understand. Very few sheriff's offices have the capacity or ability required to cope with this sort of crisis—"

Local and State police often vied for power.

Lasalle blustered, "I never said we couldn't cope. I don't want the State Troopers all over my county."

"So you *can* handle it?" Charlotte asked brightly. "All the roadblocks and patrols already agreed upon, because all the

State Police require is a phone call, and they promised to send as many people as we request—"

The sheriff's mustache twitched. "We'll deal with it. You deal with these nuisances. I want them out of here." He cast a look around like he wasn't even seeing real people. Then he raised his voice to his men who'd gathered around to listen. "Let's go."

Novak radioed Angeletti and told him to turn around, crisis averted.

"Want me to ask him if they can send a few plain clothes agents to help conduct interviews?" he asked his fellow SSA.

She shook her head, watching the sheriff's office cruisers speed by one after another. "Let's ask around first. See what we find out."

The sheriff glared at them as he drove past. Novak was pretty sure he was giving them the bird out of sight.

Novak turned back to face the rag-tag army of tree-huggers.

Charlotte went over and helped a woman onto her feet. Then she moved on, to another, and another. She knelt beside a young man who was crying, wrapped her arm around his shoulders.

Novak huffed out a small frustrated breath. As much as he wanted to get back to his team, he also knew there would be no rushing this. Charlotte was doing what Special Forces often did abroad. You got more results from winning hearts and minds of local people than by running roughshod over their homes and lives.

He stuck his hand out to one of the gentlemen who was sitting on the ground in front of him.

The man eyed him suspiciously before taking it. Novak

hauled him to his feet and helped him stand. "Is this some elaborate 'good cop bad cop' routine because I'm ready to confess all."

Novak smiled. "No, sir. The FBI are trying to discover the identity of the woman who died up on the mountain yesterday. Have you seen a photograph of her yet?"

The man shook his head.

Novak pulled up an image on his cell. "You recognize her?"

The man's eyes widened, and he covered his mouth with his hand. "She stayed here in the camp. Was it murder? That's what they said on the radio."

"We're not sure yet." It was more than Novak should have said. Shit. "Who am I addressing?" He pulled out a notepad and pencil. Charlotte's hunch that these people might know something was already paying off.

"Professor Alan Kennedy." The man sighed. "I should have packed up and left yesterday but I was worried…"

When he trailed off and stared up the mountain, Novak asked impatiently, "Worried about what?"

The professor scanned Novak's face, looking for something. If he was after warm and fuzzies he was staring at the wrong goddamn federal employee.

"I was worried that someone was going to start blaming Sasquatch for that poor woman's death, but they've never shown any signs of aggression that we know of…"

Novak held his pencil poised over his paper. "You're worried someone is going to pin this on *Bigfoot*?"

The professor rolled his eyes. "I am aware of how crazy it sounds to anyone who doesn't believe these creatures exist."

Novak forced himself to write it all down. The professor

had no idea how crazy it sounded, but at least Agent Fontaine had warned him about this possibility. He'd have to thank her later. "Most of us like a little more evidence."

"Like the Patterson-Gimlin film? No one can discredit that old movie and yet no one believes it."

"That movie was taken in the sixties. It doesn't really explain how in this day and age there isn't more evidence of a large primate existing in a country with a population of 300 million people."

The professor sighed. "Unless you've studied the sightings and videos as I have, I'd say there's a lot of hubris associated with ignorant people declaring Sasquatch *doesn't* exist, don't you? I like the idea that we don't know everything about our planet and primates. Keeps life interesting."

Novak was pretty sure he'd just been insulted. "There was a credible sighting around here?"

The professor ran his fingers through his hair that was blowing in the wind. "August fourth, two hikers came upon a female Sasquatch carrying a baby. She ran before they got a good photo of her although they snapped a few shots on their phones. Researchers from the Bigfoot Researchers Organization, of which I am a member, came out and cast some footprints."

"You've been here all this time?" Sounded like the guy had a cushy job.

"No. I've been back and forth. This trip I arrived last Thursday night and met up with a group of like-minded friends." The professor seemed to take umbrage at Novak's expression. Novak got that a lot. "We often spend weekends and vacations camping out and hiking at night, scaring ourselves witless by howling in the woods. It's harmless fun."

"Were you hiking in the woods night before last?"

The professor shook his head. "We spent Friday and Saturday night out there. Most of the others left on Sunday, but I decided to hang around for a few extra days. I like this part of the world."

Sure. "See anything?"

Kennedy sighed. "Not this time."

"What can you tell me about the woman who died?" Novak needed to get the guy back on track.

The professor's expression cleared, and he looked away. "I don't know her name. She and her friend very much kept to themselves in terms of social activities."

"Friend?" Novak's ears perked up.

"They shared that tent over there. The yellow one with blue guidelines. I think the friend's name is Kate or something similar." The man scanned the milling crowd. "I don't see her."

"Does she have a surname?" Novak probed.

"I am notoriously bad at remembering names. Ask my students." The professor's lips pinched. "And now I better get out of here before my college sees me on the evening news and fires me. Or the sheriff comes back and arrests us all because we don't side with greedy corporations who fund his reelection campaigns."

Novak got the man's contact details and a business card. Then he strode toward the yellow tent, weaving through people and their belongings that had been scattered around the place like trash. People were gathering their stuff and avoiding eye contact.

Charlotte looked up. He jerked his head, and she moved to join him. When she got close enough, he leaned in closer, noting the smell of limes from her skin. Definitely not *eau de goat*.

"According to the professor over there, the dead woman shared a tent with another girl, who he thinks is called Kate but didn't sound sure."

"The yellow tent?" she asked as he pointed.

"Yup."

He went to let her take the lead, but she waved her hand forward. "After you, SSA Novak."

"You don't think I might scare a woman alone, especially under these circumstances?"

She smiled, and he was caught again by her calm confidence, not to mention her pretty face. "It's your lead, Payne. And I think you can be as scary or charming as you want to be."

Charming? Was that a compliment? He didn't even know if anyone had called him charming before.

The tent was close to the edge of the forest, and the trees rose up all around them. A crow cawed loudly from the top of a large pine. He stared at the tightly zipped entrance. Clearly the deputies hadn't got this far before he and Charlotte had arrived.

They stopped outside. "Whoever is in the tent, this is SSA Novak and Blood with the FBI. Come out. We'd like talk to you." From Charlotte's expression, he wasn't quite as charming as she'd hoped.

"Please," he added belatedly.

No one answered. He put his hand on his weapon as he leaned forward and gently eased up the zipper. There was that sound that reminded him of death again, just like the body bag. He didn't let it distract him.

Charlotte stood on the other side of the canopy and had her weapon drawn but pointed at the ground.

At least she wasn't a pacifist. Not that the FBI employed many pacifists.

He drew back the edge of the canvas. Inside were two sleeping bags. One was open and empty. Someone was tucked deep into the other, barely visible under a pile of clothes and bedding.

"Ma'am? I need you to step out of the tent for a few moments so I can speak with you."

Her head moved from side to side, and she groaned.

Was she faking it? Did she have a weapon down in that sleeping bag or hidden beneath the covers?

"Ma'am." He spoke louder but the only response was the rasping sound of her breath.

"I'm not sure she's conscious," Charlotte said tightly.

They were starting to gather a crowd.

"Leave her alone," someone shouted.

"Leave us all alone!"

Novak frowned and looked over his shoulder, then crouched down, peering inside to better assess the threat. He needed to know they weren't going to be rushed by a mob before he could deal with what looked like a sick woman.

"I think she might be ill," Charlotte addressed the agitated crowd. "Did anyone check on her recently?"

The mood changed. Shifted to reason and calm. Part of it was her gentle tone, part of it was the obvious concern ringing in her voice. People shuffled their feet and glanced around guiltily.

"I haven't seen either of them since the night before last."

"The one girl talked about visiting Arizona over Thanksgiving. Haven't seen them since."

"Didn't realize they were back…"

"I should have checked on them after the reports."

The crowd edged away to deal with their own business.

Novak exchanged a look with Charlotte, and she tucked her weapon away and indicated she also thought it was safe.

Novak crawled inside and saw that the woman was young, a teen. She didn't react to his presence but groaned as if she was in pain. He put his palm on her forehead, and her skin sizzled beneath his fingers. "She's burning up. She needs a doctor or an ER."

Charlotte leaned down. "Can you carry her?"

He shot her a look.

"We need to get her to the ranch and have a medic look at her. Arrange a helicopter to transfer her to a hospital if it's urgent."

Novak slipped his arms under her shoulders and under her knees. He lifted her easily and shuffled awkwardly out of the low canvas on his knees. He straightened as soon as he got outside the tent.

"Where's Brenna?" A woman who'd stuck around asked. She looked to be in her mid-sixties. Five-six. Long gray hair under a multi-colored scarf wrapped around her head.

"Brenna share the tent with Kate?" he asked.

"Kayla," the woman corrected and then looked away. People were starting to figure out exactly where Brenna was.

Charlotte pulled on latex gloves. She ducked into the tent and quickly searched until she found two purses. She photographed them *in situ* before removing two wallets, opening them to IDs and then placing them in evidence bags she had in her pockets.

"You get her to a doctor, ASAP. I'm going to secure the scene." She was already dialing McKenzie.

Novak shifted the sick girl higher in his arms. She was reed thin and small. He didn't want to leave Charlotte alone with a crowd of strangers who may or may not be harmless.

"Let's both go, and evidence techs can come back later." Even as he said it, he knew she wouldn't agree. If this was where the dead woman lived, they needed to process the scene. And the woman in his arms urgently needed to be seen by a physician.

He looked at Charlotte indecisively, something he never was. "I'm sending backup."

"If only we hadn't sent the sheriff away." Her tone was light and gently mocking. "Go. Get that poor girl some help. I'll be fine."

Novak was wasting time, so he headed for the Chevy. The people here seemed generally harmless, and Charlotte could look after herself. The memory of the dead woman flashed through his mind.

He got to the car and slid Kayla into the backseat. Her eyes half opened. "TJ?"

A bolt of satisfaction shot through him. Here was a solid connection to the case. She had to know what was going on. "No, honey, but you're gonna be okay. Rest up. I'll get you to a doctor."

He climbed in the driver's seat and pulled away. He drove fast but not as fast as he wanted.

One minute into the journey he was already cursing himself for leaving Charlotte behind. He pulled out his sat phone to call Angeletti but as he did so, one of their armored Suburbans shot past. Novak should have known they'd come back him up, even though he'd told them to stand down. He didn't stop or slow as the call connected.

"What's up, boss?"

"Find SSA Blood at the campsite. Canvass the people there about what they know about the dead woman and her friend, Kayla."

"Okay." It sounded like a question.

"We pulled the friend from their tent. She's delirious, but she's definitely involved somehow. I don't like the idea of a single agent being out there when we don't know what threats are present." He'd have been worried about anyone. It wasn't because Charlotte was a female agent, although he definitely worried more about female agents working in the field. He knew it was a bias, and he was trying his best to get over it.

"Roger that. We've got her back, boss."

Somehow, Charlotte had burrowed under his armor plating and become another one of his responsibilities. *Just what I need.* He knew Angeletti would make a big deal out of it at some point but right now, the priority was getting the job done.

Novak turned into the entrance of the ranch without slowing and pulled through the open barn door and slammed on the brakes. The door closed behind him.

Novak jumped out.

"What have we got?" McKenzie barked, striding toward him.

A former combat medic was already in the backseat, leaning over the sick girl.

"A man at the camp recognized the dead woman from the image we have of her. He told me she shared a tent with another girl. When we investigated further, we found this woman unresponsive. SSA Blood insisted I bring her here so she can be medically assessed. Charlotte stayed behind to guard the scene." Novak leaned closer to McKenzie so only he could hear. "The girl is delirious and called me TJ."

McKenzie's eyes widened. "Any idea what's wrong with her?" This last question was directed at the medic who pursed his lips.

"No obvious injuries. She has a fever and is severely dehydrated. Right now, I'm guessing she's fighting influenza or some other infection."

"Great. I hope to god everyone here is up-to-date with their vaccinations," McKenzie muttered.

"Always, but it might be a good idea for anyone treating her to wear a face mask until we know for sure what she has." The medic pulled an N95 mask out of his kit and put it on.

Novak grabbed a bottle of hand sanitizer from the glove box and doused his hands with it. He rarely got sick and didn't want to start now.

"What are the options, boss?"

"I need to talk to her, and I can't do that until she's better." McKenzie put his hands on his hips.

The medic jumped out of the vehicle. "My advice would be to get the nearest doctor to pay a house call. I can set her up with a saline drip and get fluids inside her. If she needs to be hospitalized, we can arrange it. If it's the flu without any complications a hospital would send her home anyway and, as she lives in a tent that is probably about to be torn apart by evidence techs, she'll be homeless. At best we might lose her in the system, at worst she could die on the streets. She's probably better off somewhere close by where we can keep an eye on her."

McKenzie frowned. "She can have my room in the ranch house. It has a private bathroom. I want to limit potential exposure of FBI personnel, but keep her somewhere we can question her. I want to know how she knows TJ. What her friend was doing on the mountain. Attend to her until I can get a doctor out here. Assume she's contagious for now."

"What if she is the one who killed her friend?" Novak asked quietly.

"We'll keep the door locked to help with quarantine and put a guard on it. I'll talk to the attorney general and get the director to sign off on a nurse."

"He might want her locked up in a holding facility," Novak said.

"I'll convince him. I don't want to spook her. If she goes into the system, she might clam up. I need to know what the hell happened on that mountain," McKenzie said.

"And why she thought TJ might be the one to rescue her," Novak murmured, watching his boss stride away.

CHAPTER ELEVEN

CHARLOTTE BIT DOWN on her impatience when all she really wanted to do was crawl into the tent and start investigating. They finally had a lead on the dead woman. Someone had to know what she was doing up on the mountain and who might be responsible for her death. Kayla definitely had information they needed to gather. She sent McKenzie images of both women's drivers' licenses. Brenna Longie and Kayla Russell. Then she forced herself to stand still and stay outside. Without backup, she needed to keep her eyes on her surroundings, so she wasn't ambushed by someone with a hidden agenda.

Most of the activists had moved away, but there were a few stragglers.

"Did you know the women who lived in this tent?" she asked a woman nearby who was dismantling her site.

The woman, wearing dirty jeans, a purple fleece, and well-worn hiking boots stood and wiped her hands on her thighs.

"My name is Charlotte Blood. Did you hear about what happened up on the mountain?"

"Yes." The woman edged a step closer, and Charlotte held out her hand to shake.

"Judith Thomas." The woman introduced herself even though she looked like she didn't want to give her name. Habit and social norms were useful in Charlotte's line of work. "There was a shootout between the cops and the yahoos who live inside that concrete monstrosity. We heard the shots. It was terrifying. Then the news last night said they found a dead woman. Was it Brenna?"

Charlotte felt a wave of sympathy at the sadness she saw in Judith's eyes. She pulled out her phone and brought up a tightly cropped image of the victim's face as she lay on the autopsy table.

After a reluctant glance, Judith bent over, bracing her hands on her knees as she took a deep breath. "Yes. That's Brenna. Oh, she was a such sweet girl."

"I am sorry for your loss," Charlotte said gently.

"How did she die? Was she shot?"

"We'll know more after the autopsy. We're still trying to figure out exactly what happened on the mountain yesterday."

Grief was a powerful emotion that took time to grapple into submission. Longer to move through. Silence was the greatest tool a negotiator had. Charlotte waited patiently as Judith wiped at the tears that had started to flow.

Seconds ticked by. Ten, twenty. Thirty.

"The girls have been here since spring," Judith said weepily. "They were both quiet and a little shy. They cared deeply enough to come out here and try to save the old growth forests, but they kept to themselves and didn't want to get involved with camp politics."

"Camp politics," Charlotte mirrored.

"Yes." Judith laughed bitterly. "Believe it or not there are people here—usually men—who believe they get to tell us how we should behave. They say we can only act effectively if a committee agrees on what action to take." She looked out across the array of tents. "Most of us came out here to protest, to raise our voices against huge conglomerates, and we end up silenced by our fellow protesters."

"There was infighting amongst the protestors?"

Judith huffed out a sour laugh. "So much. There's no doubt we needed a degree of organization. Half these people can't even decide what time to get up in the morning let alone arrange any meaningful demonstrations." Her eyes narrowed. "In fact, some of them are so detrimental to our cause they are probably being paid by the logging company to make our group dysfunctional or get us shut down. We do have the right to peaceful protest."

Charlotte made a soft sound of encouragement. Whatever her views, she wasn't here to agree or disagree with this woman. She wanted to create some rapport and milk her for information, which was a little calculating, but that was how she got things done.

"The people who decided they were in charge of organizing others are a bunch of autocratic know-it-alls who like delegating tasks to the point they do very little actual work themselves." The woman's indrawn breath was a shudder that shook her shoulders. "They remind me so much of my ex-husband, I almost left a dozen times."

"I'm sorry." Charlotte touched her arm in sympathy. "Perhaps you could give me some of their names so I can question them?"

Judith's mouth curved into a smile. "I'd be delighted."

Charlotte wrote down all the names to give to the analysts.

Some people were packing up to leave. Charlotte needed to question them all. But she wanted more particulars on camp dynamics and, more importantly, she needed to know about Brenna. "Anything you can tell me about the girls would be a help. Do you know where they came from?"

"Why?" Judith asked suspiciously.

"We were hoping to inform next of kin rather than have them hear about it on the news."

A look of shame swept over Judith's features. She covered her face with her hands. "Of course." She swallowed convulsively. "I used to be a nice person, I swear. A trusting fool. I've been fighting big business and corruption for so long now I've become secretive and distrustful of authority, a bit like those people holed up inside that compound."

"Did you ever encounter them?"

Judith shrugged. "I encountered men in the woods. They could have been hikers or even from the logging company, but I don't think so." She shivered. "It was the way they looked at me..." She stamped her sturdy boots on the hard ground. "They never smiled or exchanged greetings. They always seemed suspicious about what I was doing there, although it was none of their damn business."

A frigid gust of wind swept across the campsite, fluttering the tent canvases like sails on a boat. Charlotte glanced up at the milky gray sky and hoped it didn't snow. She also wished she had more than a fleece hoodie to keep warm.

Judith turned red-rimmed eyes up to the sky. "Brenna and Kayla are both good-natured girls. I'm pretty sure Brenna was the older sister, but they never said they were related. Only friends. They told people they were planning to visit Death Valley over Thanksgiving, but now I'm not convinced they ever left." A crinkle pinched the woman's gray brows. "I always felt as if they were hiding from something, but then that's how I feel about a lot of people here, even the professor."

She nodded toward the man Novak had been talking to earlier, who was busy efficiently packing up his tent.

"He's one of the Bigfoot enthusiasts." Judith bit her lip as if that was a confession.

"Are you a believer?" Charlotte asked.

"I never used to be. But Alan can be very persuasive."

Charlotte's brows hiked. Sounded like they had been close. "Was anyone here particularly friendly with Brenna and Kayla?"

Judith pursed her lips. "Not really. I hadn't realized it until now, but they kept very much to themselves. They were polite and always came to protests and attended meetings, but they spent a lot of time in their tent, or in the woods, nature watching. Brenna had a nice SLR camera she took everywhere with her."

Charlotte wondered if the camera was somewhere in the tent or if Brenna had it up on the mountain. Charlotte remembered the report that had dragged the wildlife officer out here.

"Any mention of a problem cougar being in the area?"

"Aside from me?" Judith snorted out a laugh then grew serious. "They're around, but we haven't had any serious run-ins with the wildlife out here. We're careful with food supplies and trash." She indicated the bear-proof garbage containers near the road.

"When did you last see Brenna or Kayla, aside from today?"

The woman thought about it. "I spotted Brenna coming back with some groceries on Tuesday morning."

It was now Thursday.

"Which is her car?" Charlotte asked.

"The blue Toyota hybrid." Judith started wringing her hands. "I should have come over and asked if they were all right. Offered them some food or a warm drink. I'm so used to everyone being self-sufficient that I've stopped asking if people need help. What sort of human being does that make me?"

Normal. Charlotte touched her arm. "I am sure you were kind. Kindness counts a lot more than anyone realizes."

The woman snuffled. "I suppose. I think I'm going to leave now. I think we'll all leave." Sadness hung heavy in the air. "The logging company finally got what it wanted. A pity it took a dead woman and two injured law enforcement officials." The woman tilted her head. "Ironic that the FBI wouldn't have come because Brenna died. The sheriff certainly wouldn't have cared. Her murder would have been added to all the other dead women in the world no one cares about."

"Other women?" Was that a general statement about the number of unsolved murders or something more specific? "Do you believe there's a serial killer operating in this area?"

"No." Judith crossed her arms tightly over her flat chest and shuddered. "Not that I know of anyway. It's a commentary on the number of missing and murdered indigenous women who no one seems to give a damn about."

"I care," Charlotte said firmly. "I've always cared. That's why I joined the FBI." She needed the woman to know she wasn't some government drone. But the FBI did not investigate murder under normal circumstances, that was left to local jurisdictions. "I do appreciate you being so candid with me. Would you be willing to give me your phone number and address so I can get in touch with you if I have follow-up questions?" They held each other's gaze for a moment.

After a long beat, the woman gave her the information but looked annoyed now. "I suppose I'll be added to the system as some sort of subversive now."

"The FBI isn't looking to take away people's constitutional rights. I am interested in figuring out exactly what happened to Brenna." Charlotte handed her a business card. "Please, call me if you remember anything. Or if you have any trouble anywhere—assuming you didn't cause it," she added with smile.

Judith slipped the card into her fanny pack as a black Suburban arrived, and four HRT operators climbed out, looking like badasses.

Judith fanned her cheeks. "Well, if I'm ever going to be arrested, I want to be arrested by them. They're hotties, though not as hunky as that man you showed up with." A dimple hit her cheek as she smiled. "Twenty years ago, I'd have given him a run for his money."

Charlotte's lower jaw dropped, but the woman walked away. Charlotte hadn't really noticed Payne Novak as sex god material. Except when he was naked. And when Fontaine had ogled the guy like he was a hot fudge sundae, and she was on a low-carb diet.

"What would you like us to do first, SSA Blood?" one HRT operator asked when he reached her side.

Charlotte blinked away the image of Novak wearing only his skin.

"ASAC McKenzie is sending an Evidence Response Team here ASAP to process this tent and the blue Toyota. In the meantime, interview the people packing up. Ask them for names and addresses and match it to vehicle license plates. Ask if they had any knowledge of Brenna and Kayla, the women in this yellow tent and ask when was the last time they saw either woman. And ask if they were on the mountain on Tuesday night or Wednesday morning."

"Anything else, SSA Blood?"

"Yes." She met the intensely serious stare of the HRT operator. "Call me Charlotte."

"Yes, ma'am."

CHAPTER TWELVE

T J COULD BARELY keep his eyes open as he sat in a plastic chair in the corner of the room.

"Go get some sleep, son." His father's hand landed heavily on his shoulder and squeezed.

TJ shook his head and sat up. "I want to stay here so I know what's going on." He absently rubbed his thumb on the grip of his pistol.

Tom put his hands on his hips and stretched out his back. "You need to rest at some point, you were up all night. Did you eat yet?"

TJ shook his head. "I'm not hungry." How could he eat when he'd lost the girl he loved and brought shame on the family name and danger to them all? He'd watched the ticker tape scroll across the bottom of the news screens all night long. His and his dad's names emblazoned on every television channel, even though the only thing Tom Harrison had ever wanted to do was to fly under the radar.

"You haven't eaten since breakfast yesterday morning. You have to keep your strength up." Tom smiled patiently.

TJ blew out a tired breath. He knew it was a waste of energy arguing with his father, and he was relieved his dad was standing staunchly by his side. "Want me to fetch you something?"

Tom nodded. "Sure. After you've eaten bring me a bowl of soup and a hunk of bread back here."

TJ nodded. He knew it was a ploy to get him into the canteen. It wouldn't make him feel any more hungry. The idea of food made him nauseous.

He slipped out of the room, aware of the silent disapproval from the other two men watching the surveillance feeds with his father. Outside the door, in the main corridor that ran around the lower level of the complex, TJ glanced right, toward his and his dad's living quarters.

Even though he was exhausted down to his marrow, he wouldn't sleep. Every time he closed his eyes, he saw Kayla's translucent skin and inky black hair as she'd lain there in the dirt. He shook away the shudder as he remembered the sensation of her cool lifeless skin beneath his fingers, and guilt roared through him. How could he have been repelled by the woman he loved? How could he have left her? How could he have run?

He didn't know. He'd made so many mistakes. He hadn't even started to process her loss yet. He was still in a state of shock and fear.

He turned left and numbly climbed a flight of concrete steps to the communal kitchen area. His father had bought their home from a guy who'd been sure the Cold War had been going to go nuclear. It hadn't. The old man had died of cancer, too paranoid to receive radiotherapy treatment. He'd been another of TJ's mom's million cousins, and TJ's dad had gotten this place for a song because it was so remote.

The corridor was wider on this level, and TJ forced himself to walk slowly down the hallway. He knew everyone who lived here and got on with most people, with the exception of his uncle who always found fault with everything he did.

This morning no one was meeting his gaze. The room went quiet as he entered. His smile faltered. One woman scooped a little girl back into her arms as the child rushed toward him.

The choking sensation in his throat threatened to expand and cut off his airway, but he ignored it and calmly grabbed a tray, placed a bowl of soup and bread roll on it, along with a glass of water and an apple. Realizing he had no desire to come back here any time soon, he added another serving of everything.

"Don't be greedy. We're on rations here in case you didn't notice," the cook told him sharply.

TJ flinched. He'd never been accused of being greedy in his life. Then he'd never been accused of murder either.

"I'm taking my father his lunch as well as fetching my own. I assume you don't object to that, considering you're standing in his kitchen?"

The woman pinched her lips and looked away. "Of course not. Tell Tom I can send a tray down anytime he needs anything."

"I'll be sure to mention it." The disapproval he felt in his wake was a frosty breath against his back. He gripped the tray tighter as he negotiated the stairs back to the surveillance room.

Two men were talking in the corridor but stopped when they spotted him. They watched him cautiously. One was his uncle, Malcolm.

TJ tapped on the door of the surveillance room with his foot. "It's me."

Once inside, tension pressed down on him again. The air

stirred with all the words spoken in his absence and settled under the weight of disapproval.

"Here, Dad." He placed the tray on the desk beside his father.

"Thanks." Tom took up the bowl and spoon. Blew on the soup before sipping it. "You not eating?" He nodded pointedly to the other bowl.

TJ took the soup from the tray but couldn't bring himself to taste it. He glanced up at the TV screens, expecting to see more of the same continuous news loop. He froze as an image of a woman appeared on screen.

"Turn that up," he ordered.

The man with the controls sent him a sullen glare that his father didn't miss. Even people who'd known TJ for years thought he'd killed a woman and purposely brought trouble to their door.

The woman on the screen looked a lot like Kayla, with the same dark hair and general build. But it wasn't Kayla.

"The woman found dead on the side of Eagle Mountain sparking an armed standoff between the federal government and an armed militia has been named as one Brenna Longie, originally from Pennsylvania. No details have been released about how she died."

The news cycle moved back to the same regurgitated information from earlier, but TJ had one thought whirling around and around in his mind.

It wasn't Kayla. It wasn't Kayla. It wasn't Kayla.

She looked so like her... Had the cops made a mistake? Was Kayla dead, but the cops had somehow misidentified her? Put the wrong picture on the television? Was it a trap?

It didn't seem likely, which meant Kayla might still be

alive.

Where was she? Why hadn't she been at their usual meeting place? Was she in danger? Had she told the Feds about the two of them? Did she still want him after everything that had happened? He needed to find out.

"Son?"

His father's voice broke through his whirling thoughts. Obviously, Tom had been trying to get his attention for some time.

TJ shook his head. The situation here hadn't changed. The FBI still wanted him for questioning.

"Son. Do you know that woman?"

"What? No. I've never seen her before yesterday when I found her and even then I didn't see her face."

"From your expression it sure looked like you knew her," Malcolm said snidely.

TJ hadn't seen his uncle enter the room.

"I swear upon my life I have never seen that poor woman before."

Malcolm's lip curled.

TJ wanted to punch him, but that would only demonstrate a lack of control and prove his guilt in some people's eyes.

"Sure she wasn't your sweetheart?"

TJ nailed Malcolm with a narrow stare. "What do you mean?"

"Maybe you snuck out for a little forbidden fruit and accidentally killed her. I know you snuck out most Wednesdays. Seen you a few times."

Forbidden fruit? Kayla wasn't a freaking apple.

"I said I don't know the dead woman." TJ raised his voice as sweat began to coat his skin. Malcolm's guess was close enough to what happened that the truth could appear damning, even though the conjecture was completely inaccurate. "Are you suggesting I'm lying?"

Malcolm shrugged, not brave enough to go directly against his father.

Emotions fought within TJ. Part of him was elated with the possibility Kayla might be alive, but what if she was in danger? Then there was the mystery of whatever had happened to that other woman. Did Brenna Longie know Kayla? Were they related? They sure looked alike, but Kayla had never mentioned a sister. She had mentioned a friend she was traveling with...

TJ didn't want to share his thoughts with anyone. He didn't want Malcolm knowing Kayla existed. Nor the authorities. What if they used her against him? Or worse, against his father?

He needed to keep Kayla safe, and the best way to do that was to keep her a secret.

A phone rang, and Malcolm pulled a satellite phone out of his jacket pocket. His dad had hooked up a relay inside the building a few years ago to boost the signal underground.

Malcolm went to answer it, but his father stopped him.

"You don't think the Feds are monitoring your calls?" His dad's expression was reserved, but TJ noticed the slight curl of contempt twisting his lips.

Malcolm looked at the phone as if it had grown stingers.

"It's possible they could use it as a listening device too. I'm not sure what their capabilities are nowadays, but I do know some politicians should be a lot more concerned than they seem to be. You need to destroy it."

Malcolm swore and then glanced around. He stuffed the

cell back in the pocket of his jacket. "It was expensive."

Tom shrugged his shoulders as if all these people didn't live on his charity. "I'm not saying take a hammer to it. Turn it off and leave it in your quarters in the freezer or under a sweater in your drawer." He sent a stern glance around the room. "Tell everyone, I want all cells left in bedrooms with the battery and sim cards removed until this is over, even the ones the kids play on. Who was calling you anyway?"

Malcolm stuttered before spitting the words out, "Probably Grandpa Ray. He's been calling on and off all morning after watching the news. Wants to know what's happening."

TJ's mom's paternal grandfather was still alive. At nearly a hundred, he'd rejected the need to live with them in the bunker. Said he was looking forward to seeing his maker, and he'd be underground soon enough. TJ was beginning to agree with the old man.

Tom glanced up at the news monitors. "I suspect Grandpa Ray's got as much idea as the rest of us."

A rush of premonition raced over TJ's skin. "Maybe we should talk to the Feds. Tell them this is all some terrible misunderstanding." He looked at the phone sitting nearby disconnected from the phone jack.

His dad came to stand in front of him. "Did you kill that woman?"

TJ straightened his spine. "No, sir."

His father ran his finger across the scratch on TJ's cheek. "Sonofabitch almost took your eye out."

TJ flinched. He'd forgotten about the wound from the ricochet.

"I'll talk to them eventually," his father said quietly. "I'm waiting for the right moment."

"When do you think that will be?" Malcolm asked, recovering from his distress about the sat phones.

"When I'm good and ready." His father raised his voice, which he rarely did, but these were not normal times. "In the meantime, we make sure our home is secure both physically and electronically, agreed?" Tom gave Malcolm a nod which the other man returned slowly.

TJ walked back to his chair and picked up his soup. It was cold now, but he realized he needed to be ready for whatever happened. He ate the meal mechanically though he wasn't hungry. And he watched the TV though he didn't want to be constantly reminded of everything that had occurred. And he thought about Kayla and where she might be and what she might be doing. Was she scared? Did she believe he'd killed this Brenna woman? The idea soured his mood. He needed to set the record straight. He just wasn't sure how.

CHAPTER THIRTEEN

N OVAK USED THE opportunity of having escaped his pretty shadow for a few minutes to catch up with the rest of the guys. The first sniper teams had set up a live feed of the compound, but no one was moving around outside. The second sniper teams were now in position, waiting until dark to switch out again. He and Romano planned to head up the mountain to see if they couldn't get a little additional, much-needed information regarding the insides of that facility.

"Let me know how it goes," McKenzie said, striding through the barn, having dropped his belongings on a spare bunk.

"Will do, boss."

The IC stopped mid-stride and Agent Fontaine, who was working closely with him, almost crashed into his back.

"Where is SSA Blood?" McKenzie asked.

Novak felt his skin prickle. "Still at the campsite."

"Don't forget to pick her up on your way out," McKenzie said pointedly.

"No, sir." Novak and Romano exchanged a glance. *Shit.*

Thirty minutes later, Novak strode over the grass to where Charlotte was orchestrating the systematic questioning of the environmentalists in their ramshackle camp. "Time to go."

"I'm busy." She frowned at him and looked away as she

ordered one of his guys to question another group of people.

"McKenzie's orders."

Her spine snapped straight. "Shoot. I'd forgotten about that."

"Tell me about it. Anyway, we've spent the morning doing your thing, and now it's my turn."

She surveyed the area with frustration. His Charlie team of assaulters were busy taking statements, and an Evidence Recovery Team was processing the yellow tent and the blue Toyota in the makeshift parking lot on the opposite side of the road. He knew it made sense for his guys to do this—they were all former field agents—to save the Bureau having to send out another bunch of people. But anything that prevented his men from training or took their focus off what they were here to do could cost someone their life. The fact he wasn't grinding his teeth or yelling at them all to get back to the Command Center showed a massive amount of restraint on his part, restraint Charlotte Blood wouldn't even realize he was exhibiting.

"McKenzie seriously made you come get me?" She climbed to her feet. "He isn't over his stupid idea yet?"

"Not even close to being over it." Novak was getting kind of used to having Charlotte at his side. Work wise. He was a lot less disappointed than she seemed to be.

"Where are we going?" she asked.

"For a hike."

She nodded without asking more questions and followed him back to the Chevy. She addressed all his guys by nickname as she passed them. She was fast at assimilating information, but then so was everyone at CIRG. He thought about opening her door for her but climbed into the driver's seat instead. It wasn't that he wasn't a gentleman. This was work, and they were equals, and others needed to see her as such.

Romano sat in the back with his boxes of tricks on the floor beside him. Out of sight.

"What's going on?" Charlotte asked, buckling up as Novak put the car in gear and pressed his foot on the gas.

"Romano wants to take some toys for a test drive, and I want to get a look at the mountain in daylight."

"Sounds reasonable. Any word on Kayla's condition?" Charlotte rubbed her hands together then picked up her gloves from where she'd left them earlier in the console. Little good they'd done her there.

"One of my guys is a former combat medic, and he put her on a drip to get her hydrated, and a local doctor is on his way to see her ASAP. General assumption is she has the flu." He tossed her a small bottle of hand sanitizer.

She sighed and removed her gloves and applied liberally.

"McKenzie wants to treat her at the ranch."

Charlotte bit her lip. "Obviously, if she's seriously ill she'll need to be hospitalized."

"Yeah. But this way we don't risk losing her."

Charlotte huddled into her fleece. Dammit, she needed something warmer than that. "It's a good solution. It's not as if she has anywhere else to go right now anyway."

He nodded. Yesterday they'd have been fighting over this decision but somehow, over the last eighteen hours, they'd fallen in sync. Maybe McKenzie had been right about forcing them to work together. Not that Novak wasn't itching to get back to HRT.

He scratched his shoulder then caught Romano's smirk in the rearview and narrowed his eyes at the man. Novak knew what the smirk meant, and he was not rising to the bait. The guys all thought it was hilarious he was being forced to partner with Charlotte and were probably placing highly inappropriate workplace bets.

He drove back toward where they'd started their hike with Agent Fontaine yesterday. Parked a hundred yards from two sheriff's cruisers.

Charlotte waved a cheery hand, and one of them even waved back. The news media had been moved back another mile down the road and aircraft banned so they couldn't report on the FBI's activities.

Novak climbed out and scanned the area. Didn't see another living soul. Didn't mean they weren't out there though.

"Wear a ballistics vest under your fleece," he instructed Charlotte, then winced as he remembered he wasn't her superior.

She shot him a look but grabbed what she needed out of the cargo area. At least she was smart enough not to fight him on the common-sense stuff.

He grunted to himself.

Did she think the same about him or not? He knew she thought he was a meat head. It really shouldn't matter what other people thought of him outside his team, but for some reason it did. He needed to get over his fragile ego.

Romano slammed the door and handed Novak one of the metal cases. Romano carried the second larger case.

"Can I take something?" Charlotte asked.

"This from the woman who has wheels on her luggage," Novak teased.

She put her hands on her hips. "I knew you had an issue with that."

She was still wearing the bobble hat, and it was hard to

take her seriously and yet, he suddenly realized, he did. Despite being soft and fluffy on the outside, she was a damn good agent.

"You can carry this if you don't mind." Romano offered her a laptop bag, and she slung it over her shoulders.

She grinned at the man, and Novak felt a swift kick in the gut. She smiled at everyone like they meant something to her. Everyone except him.

He had to stop taking everything so damn personally.

"Sheriff's deputies are supposed to have the place sealed off, but I'm not convinced someone couldn't slip in or out without notice," Novak said quietly. "The snipers haven't seen any movement, but their line of sight is limited to the west of those trees. Keep your eyes wide and let's keep the volume down. I don't want anyone paying attention to what we're doing."

They hiked silently, Novak leading the way, avoiding the cameras that his team had mapped out that morning. They'd also found a series of laser tripwires that presumably set off alerts inside Harrison's bunker. Novak wasn't going anywhere near those suckers.

They found a spot near the creek, out of visual range of the cameras he'd stripped in front of last night. No one had ever accused him of being modest. If it saved lives, he'd walk around naked all the time. He didn't care, except his skin wasn't well camouflaged and certainly wasn't bulletproof.

There were some low scrub bushes and a downed tree that provided good cover. They placed the cases on the ground, and Romano flicked open the catches on the lids.

Charlotte's eyes lit up when she got a look inside.

Romano sat cross-legged on the frozen grass as he started

warming up the miniature drones.

Charlotte knelt at his shoulder, watching as the camera went live.

Novak scanned their surroundings for danger. At least he tried to but kept getting distracted by the way Charlotte's lips curved in delight as Romano launched the first machine, something about the size and shape of a hummingbird.

Novak heard the soft whirr of mechanical wings followed by Charlotte's delighted gasp as her grinning face appeared on the small monitor. The camera could be swiveled from side to side or up and down, which Romano demonstrated.

The machines were pretty damn cool. Space-age gadgets that the public knew little about. The guys in the FBI's tech department were working with the military on a bunch of Top-Secret shit. The machines had tiny solar panels all over their surface to help supplement battery power which was the major limiting factor to size reduction. Power could prove an issue when flying long distances or if below ground for too long—hence getting as close as they could to their target rather than flying the drones in from the ranch. The drone transmitted data using technology a physicist in DC had been developing that was virtually undetectable. As long as someone didn't actually see the drone or hear it, they'd never know it was there.

Romano flew the machine straight up in the air until it was clear of the trees. Novak took a knee on the other side of Charlotte and got a whiff of her scent which, despite the lack of a morning shower, still made him want to breathe deeper. Romano flew the drone west, fighting a gusty breeze.

"Oh my god, that is so cool," Charlotte whispered. The hard-assed HRT operator grinned at her like a little kid.

"Keep your eyes on the monitor," Novak growled. The last thing they needed was to crash million-dollar tech because Romano was distracted by a woman.

Romano winced and went back to flying using the joystick.

"All those years of playing video games finally came in handy for someone," Charlotte commented wryly.

"Sure did." Romano took an overarching view from above, one they'd already assessed from larger drones flown at high altitude. Then he flew it slowly down, hovering about twenty feet above the concrete structure. There were holes in the concrete, probably ventilation and drainage related, but they could be defensive like the arrow slits of old medieval castles. Nothing large enough that they could use to get inside, unless they stuffed the cracks with plastic explosive, which was a possibility. Romano zoomed in on the front entrance. The reinforced door looked like it was made out of armored steel. It would probably be easier to destroy the walls. The small door within the frame though... if they could blow those hinges, they might be able to get inside fast.

The problem with Harrison having been an engineer for the Corps was he knew how the military thought. He could boobytrap all the entrances and exits. Novak wanted to get a look at the insides of these structures to check that out before anyone attempted to gain entry via those portals. And these drones were his best chance.

"Go around the whole thing and then head to the rear."

Romano flew a little higher, traveling slowly enough that the onboard cameras could clearly capture every inch of the outer fortifications. The feed was being relayed straight back to the Incident Command center via military satellite.

The drone circled once and then focused in on the rear door that was a lot less intimidating than the front but equally fortified. It was a double-garage-sized portal made of solid steel. Novak suspected it would be braced on the inside.

He frowned. The concrete construction, combined with the razor-wire topped fence, meant it was a heavily fortified position. No doubt HRT could get inside if they launched a full-scale assault, but it would take time, possibly hours, and who knew how many people inside would be injured in the process. Surprise and speed and overwhelming force were part of the Special Operations playbook to achieve rapid dominance, but he wasn't yet sure how to achieve that.

He needed to figure it out.

Romano flew over the middle of the compound, which had been half filled with soil to grow vegetables. The other side was basically a parking lot and animal holding pen.

Movement caught his eye.

A young boy, about eight years old, darted from the hen house carrying a bucket of eggs. The kid looked up, and Romano held the drone steady. The machines were quiet but not silent. The kid looked terrified, searching for signs of the coming apocalypse. Poor little bastard.

He started running again.

"Follow him. Let's see how he gets back inside."

Romano swooped down after the kid. The boy dashed to the west wall and down a side corridor not readily visible from above. After about fifteen feet, the kid slid through another large metal door that was being guarded by a man with an assault rifle. The door slammed shut before Romano got close.

Novak swore under his breath. It was probably just as well. The drone was bound to be noticed if it had flown inside at that moment.

"Park this somewhere unobtrusive so it can watch that entrance without being seen. Then let's go see if we can find the opening to that ventilation shaft with the other one."

Romano did as instructed. They'd pre-programmed the GPS coordinates, and Romano simply had to avoid any obstacles and surveillance along the way, so he flew above the tops of the trees.

"We're supposedly right over the shaft now," Romano announced twenty seconds later.

"I don't see anything," whispered Charlotte.

"Fly lower. Aim the camera at the ground," Novak instructed. Sure enough there was a small indistinct path through the foliage which had excitement sparking through him. "Follow it."

Romano went to almost ground level and then hovered and followed the path. He came to something that looked like a drainage culvert.

"Bingo," said Novak. "See how far we can get our friend here inside."

Romano's expression was a mask of concentration. Although the drone had sensors that should prevent it getting too close to the sides, the slightest miscalculation by the operator could mean crashing the expensive machine straight into a wall.

Novak switched on the infrared camera so Romano could see better.

The agent dipped the tiny drone inside the metal tube, and the hum of vibration grew louder on the monitor. Novak turned the volume down and hoped there was no one inside the tunnel. After about ten feet, the metal tube opened out into a concrete passage three-foot wide by five-foot tall.

"Looks like a secret exit to me," said Novak.

"Damn straight," Romano replied.

"A bit of a tight squeeze for HRT to maneuver," Charlotte noted.

"We've worked in worse."

At the end of the tunnel, twenty yards in, they came to a steel door. Presumably locked. They had no idea if it opened inside the actual bunker or inside the perimeter of the fence, which would leave them no better off than they were now.

"What do you want me to do?" Romano asked.

Novak thought about it. "Land the drone in the tunnel, and we'll watch the feed from the IC. If and when that door opens, we will have eyes on it. It might be our best opportunity to sneak inside."

"Sounds like a plan." Romano landed softly and then walked the machine to a position against one wall, pointing the camera toward the closed doorway and switching the machine to dormant mode with legs and wings retracted. As soon as the machine sensed any vibration, it would automatically wake in stealth mode.

It was a cool piece of kit.

The hairs on Novak's nape stood up. He glanced around, placing a hand on Charlotte's shoulder to stop her from standing or making a sound.

Romano instantly sensed the change in the atmosphere too. The guy had been a Navy SEAL and knew when to trust his instincts.

"Pack up. Take SSA Blood and the equipment back to the SUV. I'm going to take a quick look around."

CHAPTER FOURTEEN

A BULLET TOOK out a piece of bark a foot over their heads, and they all scrambled behind the fallen tree for cover.

Charlotte unclipped her weapon. "What's the plan?"

Novak looked irritated. "We can't sit here. They might change position and get a bead on us. We cannot afford to lose that kit or for the people holed up inside that bunker to suspect what we were doing out here. I'm gonna get eyes on whoever took that shot and coordinate the appropriate response. You two head back to the vehicle until backup arrives." Novak didn't wait for an answer but took off through the trees.

Charlotte was torn. The technology was important, but Novak needed backup. As the other Hostage Rescue Team member in the group, she knew Romano was better trained at these sorts of scenarios than she was, but she didn't like admitting it. "You assist Novak. I'll take the cases back to the vehicle and alert the sheriff's deputies. Hand over the keys."

"Novak told me to stay with you." Romano's expression looked determined, but she knew he'd want to be part of the action.

"That was before a shot was fired. I don't need a body-guard. That's a damn order, Agent Romano," she snapped. She slung the laptop bag over her shoulder and took the cases out of his hands. She knew how important it was for them to be kept safe. He stuffed the car keys into her fleece pocket and zipped it up.

"Be careful. There may be others out there. We'll meet you at the Suburban." Romano took off at a run in the direction Novak had taken.

Charlotte nodded and pulled out the sat phone, but when she tried to turn it on, the screen declared it was out of juice. Eban had charged them all last night so she must have taken a dud.

"Dammit." She gritted her teeth as she picked up the two unwieldy steel boxes and chose speed over stealth. She kept low and stayed within the banks of the creek as she jogged down the hill. Presumably, the shooter would be making their escape from Novak and Romano if they had any sense.

Her heart thumped a little harder than usual as adrenaline flowed. Nothing like getting shot at to wake you up. A bird took off in fright from a tree overhanging the stream. She swung around, fear drumming her chest. Unseen eyes seemed to follow her progress, and she hoped it was only her overactive imagination coming out to play, or maybe the knowledge there were surveillance cameras in the woods to the west. She adjusted her grip on the cases, but the muscles in her hands and wrists were sore and needed a rest. She paused beside a big conifer, trying to hear over the rush of blood through her ears.

Who'd taken a shot at them? Were there more shooters out there? She checked the sat phone again, turning it off and on. Nothing.

It seemed quiet enough, but Charlotte couldn't shake the sensation of being watched. She reached down for the cases again, wishing she had another hand with which to hold her weapon. She started trotting down the side of the creek bed again, concentrating on not slipping or twisting an ankle on the occasional patches of icy mud.

A man stepped out from behind a tree twenty feet in front of her, and she slammed to a stop. He pointed a rifle straight at her chest, finger curled around the trigger.

"You need to put the gun down, sir," she instructed firmly.

"Now why'd I want to do that, little lady?" He spoke with a drawl, but Charlotte couldn't pinpoint the accent beyond the US.

She forced her racing thoughts to slow. Panic was a waste of energy. Ask open-ended questions. Make him feel like he was being heard. Paraphrase his comments. Work in a few emotional labels.

Did he know she was an FBI agent? Her fleece covered her ID, ballistics vest, and the weapon on her hip. Nor was she dressed in business attire which was normally a dead giveaway.

She didn't know. "You live around here?"

Was he from the compound? He didn't look like an environmentalist. He didn't answer her question.

"Know anything about that gunshot I heard a few minutes ago?"

He didn't say anything, but something flickered in his eyes.

She was doing a terrible job of getting him to talk. She decided to mislabel an emotion to draw out an emotion. "I realize you're scared of me—"

His face scrunched in disbelief. "Scared of you? I'm not scared of you." He took a step forward and lowered the gun a few inches.

"Then I don't understand why you're pointing a gun at an innocent woman, sir?"

The gun lowered another few inches, but it was still pointed straight at her. If it went off it would take a miracle to miss her at this distance. His eyes ranged from her bobble hat down to her boots as if he couldn't quite figure her out.

His gaze focused on the two cases she held. "Put the cases on the ground and the laptop with it."

"The cases?" she mirrored, stalling for time.

She didn't know if the guy was from Eagle Mountain or an outsider. Either way, he should not be here. Someone had messed up.

"Those things in your hands. You stupid or something?"

She raised her arms a little. "Are you intending to rob me, sir? Am I being mugged?"

If he had any inkling of a moral code, the words should have made him pause.

The man's expression tightened.

"Why do you want these?" She took a couple of steps closer. Novak and Romano had gone haring off in the other direction because that was where the shot had come from. Had it been a deliberate act to split them up or had this guy outmaneuvered the two HRT operatives?

"Drop them on the ground and step away."

"Why are you doing this?" she asked.

"None of your business."

"I beg to differ under the circumstances." Her tone was non-judgmental.

He brought the gun up and took a step toward her. Spoke between gritted teeth. "Put. The. Cases. Down. And. Step. Away!"

The words hung loudly in the air.

She hoped Novak and Romano heard the guy yelling at her. She licked her lips nervously and took another step closer to the wrong end of that gun barrel.

"Fine. Fine. But you have to be careful with them else you'll break them." She laid both cases gently on the ground as if the contents were eggshell-fragile, before taking a few steps back. He moved forward and glanced down.

This was going to be interesting. How did he expect to keep pointing that rifle at her *and* pick up the cases? The only answer to that conundrum was if he shot her.

Yikes.

His expression hardened, and his finger started to tighten.

"Of course, you'll need the combination to open them to get rid of the tracking beacons if you hope to get away with this."

He looked confused for a second. "You're bluffing."

"Dude, if you have any idea what you're trying to steal, then you know there will be added layers of security." In reality, she had no idea if there were trackers inside the boxes but the important thing was, he was about to lower the rifle.

Or maybe not. "Get over here and unlock these things. First, toss the Glock." He indicated the woods.

Damn. She couldn't afford for someone to steal the boxes even if the actual drones were gone. Confidential operating instructions and specifications were inside, not to mention the military-grade encrypted laptop. She couldn't afford for this guy to even know the boxes housed a drone. Maybe he hadn't seen Romano flying the machines. Maybe he was simply taking the opportunity to rob her.

She slowly removed her weapon with her fingertips and

tossed it away. She approached him, looking for weakness. He was a heavy-set man about six feet tall. Gray-blue eyes and a ginger beard.

She wasn't stronger than he was, but she didn't have to be. She was probably faster. And, unless he was a martial arts master, better trained.

"What do you want this stuff for, anyway?" She leaned over the case and made it look like she was about to open the thing. Not that she could, because it turned out there was a biometric lock on it. Excellent.

She didn't wait for a reply. She sensed more than saw him take a breath. Her fingers closed around the handle of the laptop bag, and she whirled, shoving the gun barrel to the side with one hand while at the same time connecting the bag solidly to his temple. The rifle went off, but she didn't let go of the hot barrel. She dropped the bag and straight-armed her free palm into his nose, causing a gush of blood to pour from his broken snout. He cried out as his head went back, but Charlotte didn't relent, wouldn't relent until he was disarmed and no longer a threat. She brought her knee hard into his crotch and head-butted him when he jerked forward. He finally let go of the rifle but tried to grab her around the waist. She smashed the side of her fist into his ear, and he toppled to his knees, groping for his weapon. She kicked, connecting her shin to his jaw and, finally, he went down.

Charlotte snatched the rifle away from his fingertips and then unzipped her jacket to access her cuffs. She was turning him over and clamping both wrists together when she heard the sound of footsteps running in her direction.

She snapped the cuffs tight and raised the rifle as Novak burst through the bushes and stopped short.

A slow grin spread over his features, and Charlotte was shocked at how attractive he suddenly looked.

"What?" she asked, walking over to pick up her Glock.

"We caught the idiot who took the potshot. Then he started laughing, saying we'd 'walked right into their trap.' I came as fast as I could to make sure you're okay."

The man on the ground groaned.

"Of course, I'm okay," Charlotte said with a hint of smugness. She'd be lying if she said she wasn't happy to show that she could take care of herself. Negotiation was something she'd actively pursued, not something she did because she wasn't capable of taking bad guys down any other way. She scanned the surroundings.

Novak matched her stance. "Backup is on the way."

"Good. I tried to call the IC, but my sat phone wasn't working." A wave of tiredness washed over her. Probably the adrenaline ebbing in her blood. "You better bring him along, and the rifle. I'll carry the cases."

"Yes, ma'am," Novak said respectfully and, for once, Charlotte didn't doubt his sincerity. This was the sort of thing he valued. Violent action and overpowering strength. She was disappointed she hadn't been able to talk her way out of the situation. It wasn't like there had been time to establish a behavioral stairway but still…

Romano arrived with another prisoner in tow, this one barely out of his teens.

Charlotte blew out a frustrated sigh. Why did people make such dumb choices? Why did they sabotage their lives this way?

"Read him his rights, would you?" she asked.

Novak did as she asked, for once not questioning her

reasons. They began picking their way back down the mountain to their vehicle, waiting as the deputies ran along the road to meet them. Charlotte didn't want to talk. She stowed the cases in the back of the Chevy along with the other equipment.

She took photos of both men in custody and would bet all her meager savings they were part of some antigovernment group and already in the system.

"Ask the deputies to transport both prisoners to the county jail but keep them separate and isolated," she told Novak under her breath. "I don't want them talking to anyone. No lawyer. No media. Not even the sheriff."

"Want me to interview them?" Novak asked although he didn't look happy with the idea.

She shook her head. She appreciated Novak was letting her lead on this. She had a lot more experience than him in this area of investigations. "You need to get your team back together, and I need to get back to base." She wanted to check in with her people. See if there were any developments, although they would have called her. Then she remembered the sat phone she carried was defective so maybe not.

She thought about their options. "Send Romano to make sure these guys are handled properly by the deputies. We'll call McKenzie, and he can dispatch agents from the ranch to interview them ASAP. I want to know if they're part of Harrison's group or from elsewhere. I want to know exactly what they were planning."

One side of his lips curled up, and she was hit by the fact that his rugged features were actually sickeningly well put together. How had she really not noticed before today?

"Sounds like a plan."

She knew they'd have to fill out FD 302s for this, which was a pain. But these men might have valuable intel they might be willing to barter in exchange for lesser charges. Right now, they were looking at serious prison time.

She looked up at the mountain. "Think there are more of them out there?"

Novak stared along the dirt path. "Maybe. And we need to deal with the possibility before we do anything else."

"Agreed. Can I borrow your phone?"

He frowned as he handed her his sat phone, and then he turned back to Romano to give him instructions. And Charlotte forced herself to stop staring at Novak like she'd never seen him before.

The sooner they got through the next two days the better.

NOVAK DROVE THE now familiar road back to the ranch. He was still trying to process the train-wreck his emotions had been when he'd heard that gunshot and realized Charlotte was alone and in danger. The relief that had engulfed him when he'd found her not only safe, but in charge of that motherfucker had been like a shotgun blast to the chest. He'd wanted to run over and give her a hug, but she had more than proved she didn't need his help or approval. As far as she was concerned, she was simply doing her job. It was his problem that he had a visceral reaction to seeing her in danger.

He checked his watch as Charlotte spoke to McKenzie. Still a couple of hours until the sniper teams changed over. He'd spoken to them via secure comms, and the assholes who'd shot at him, Romano, and SSA Blood had not come out of the main exits. Novak doubted they'd come out of the secret tunnel either as they'd had eyes on it for some time prior to the gunshot.

Either there were access points to the compound that the FBI didn't know about, or these two jokers had infiltrated the perimeter the deputies had set up. The latter seemed much more likely.

"Ask him if we can request a drone with thermal imaging capabilities to be parked over the area so we can see if there are any more of these clowns out there." He held Charlotte's clear blue eyes as she nodded and then did as he asked. She covered the microphone. "He's going to put in a request to headquarters."

Novak breathed out through his nose, trying to lessen the tension in his body. He didn't like the breach in security, and he could hear McKenzie making the same complaints into Charlotte's ear.

"Put him on speaker."

Charlotte raised her brows but did as Novak asked.

Oh boy, McKenzie was as pissed as a scorpion in a skillet.

Novak finally found a gap in the man's tirade against local law enforcement to interrupt. "As much as I agree with your feelings, sir." He never wanted to relive the fear he'd felt for Charlotte when that second gunshot had sounded. "We need concrete action in the meantime."

He watched Charlotte tense up and knew she was going to hate what he was about to suggest. "Why don't we call up the Enhanced SWAT teams out of Atlanta and LA to take over guarding the perimeter?"

Charlotte's eyes narrowed.

"I realize that it might look like an escalation to the people inside the compound, but I need to know someone has my men's backs if we're to operate safely. If we have a bunch of disparate nationalists lining up to try to infiltrate the area and 'help' Harrison's group, then the situation is gonna go south fast. Someone will get shot. Someone will die. I do not want it to be one of my men."

Silence reverberated around the cab.

"They're my men too," McKenzie said softly. "I'll make the calls."

Novak released a long pent up breath as McKenzie hung up.

Charlotte hunched deeper into her hoodie.

He didn't like the defeated look in her eyes, but this was the right thing to do. "Sorry." Jesus, since when did he apologize for doing what was tactically appropriate?

She slowly shook her head then sat up straighter. "No. You're right. We need to make sure we have a secure perimeter, and the sheriff's deputies are obviously incapable." She caught his surprised expression. "What? You think I want agents in more danger than they are already? I want everyone to go home safe, but especially my colleagues who put their lives on the line every single day."

He swallowed tightly thinking how close she'd come to being shot today. "I know you wanted to have less of a police presence."

"Yes." The muscle in her cheek flexed as she clenched her jaw. "But even if we have more personnel, it doesn't mean the people inside the bunker have to know about it."

That sounded like a strategy he could get behind.

"What do you suggest?" The ranch house was coming into view in the distance.

"Let's go talk to McKenzie. We'll have to dig a bit deeper into our toolbox to get these people to talk to us."

"How do you propose to do that?"

A smile curved her mouth, and he found his eyes drawn to her lips. He dragged his gaze away. *Stop it. She's not interested in someone like you.*

"I have a few ideas. Let's go have a chat with the boss."

CHAPTER FIFTEEN

"THIS SITUATION ISN'T going to work," Charlotte said to their boss after surveying her kingdom, which had been gradually taken over by McKenzie's people. Novak was relieved McKenzie was here rather than in the barn with HRT. Bad enough the boss was bunking with them now. "We need room dividers in here that allow us to do our jobs without distraction or interruption from whatever is happening in the Command Center."

McKenzie looked unimpressed. "So far all you guys have done is sit on the end of a phone that no one picks up."

Charlotte's brow crinkled. "And do you think that's easy, boss? Do you think it's not incredibly tiring simply waiting for the other person to pick up the phone, knowing it could happen at any moment and also knowing you need to be totally on your game if and when they do pick up? Especially when your boss is conducting sensitive meetings a few feet away?"

"You're starting to make me feel unwanted, SSA Blood."

"It's nothing personal, boss. But ideally I'd like you to set up elsewhere."

"There isn't anywhere else." McKenzie's eyes were reddened with fatigue but also filled with humor. Novak appreciated the guy didn't object to people pushing back as long as they also followed orders.

"What about the den we were in last night?" Charlotte suggested.

"I moved out of the barn, and I'm sleeping in there now. Sorry." McKenzie rubbed his eyes. "I couldn't stop thinking in the barn with people still actively working the case all around me."

Novak mentally fist pumped.

"Try earplugs. They work wonders." Charlotte shot Novak a glance, and his lips twitched. "You want us to be able to work effectively, and you want to be well rested, correct?"

McKenzie nodded. "That's right."

Charlotte grinned. "Use the might of the federal government to beg, borrow or steal, five or six room dividers to give us the privacy we need and don't knock it down the list because it seems unimportant. It is important if you want us to be effective at doing our jobs."

"On it." One of McKenzie's team was already on the phone.

McKenzie smiled then sobered. "Despite my inefficiency with office design, I did do a few things you might approve of. I sent SSA Makimi to interview the men who shot at you today. She's one of the best interrogators we have in the Bureau. Also, SWAT teams are being dispatched from LA and Atlanta. Not sure how we can keep the increased numbers of agents in the region under wraps from the media."

"I have an idea." Charlotte crossed her arms over her chest. She was on a mission, and Novak was too smart to get in her way. "I'm assuming we have identified all the phone numbers being used on Eagle Mountain at this point?"

McKenzie nodded. "Yup. They turned them all off a few

hours ago anyway. I think they realized the potential security issues. We have several hundred contacts outside the facility to follow up on. It'll be interesting to see if the cell numbers from the two idiots who attacked you turn up on that list."

"Let's cut all communications to the bunker now except the news channels."

"Go on." McKenzie leaned back in his chair with his hands behind his head.

"They've been playing loops of the same thing over and over for hours on the news. Let's take control. Keep playing the loops and maybe add some of our own material at regular intervals. Either we get the networks to help us or we do it ourselves. I know we have the expertise in the media department. BAU can advise us on what content to add to influence what scenario or outcome we hope to achieve."

"I like it." McKenzie nodded then yawned. "Sorry. I need some sleep. I still don't know how we get the people in the compound to talk to us, but we *need* to start a dialogue."

"I was wondering if we might be able to track down Harrison's former commanding officer in the Army? Record a message from the guy that we can vet. Play it on our fake news show. Persuade Harrison to pick up the phone and start talking to us."

"That is a good idea." Novak approved. "If I was holed up with my back against the wall my old 5th SFG CO would be the person I'd have most time for."

McKenzie yawned again. "Fine. Arrange it," he said to his team. "Have agents talk to the Department of Defense. Find his CO, interview everyone we can track down from Harrison's old unit. Let's figure out why this guy ended up hiding away in the middle of Washington State for the last sixteen years. I'm going to find some earplugs as per SSA Blood's suggestion and crash for a few hours. You two are in charge," he pointed to Novak and Charlotte, "but I want to be woken immediately if something changes or when SWAT arrives. They'll be staying at an old motel back on the highway. Tell them to keep a low profile. The less people who know about this the more likely we are to pick up subversives hoping to join the cause. And let's put eyes on any groups of people who come out in support."

Timothy McVey had turned up in support of the Branch Davidians. He'd taught the Bureau lessons about watching the margins of a conflict. With David Hines's supporters flaring up to attack the Feds earlier in the year, it was worth the additional leg work.

"Any news on Kayla's condition?" Charlotte asked quickly as McKenzie shrugged into his jacket. They followed him to the door.

"Probable urinary tract infection."

Novak experienced a rush of relief. Influenza could wreak havoc with their personnel even with the flu shot.

"Doctor set her up with intravenous antibiotics. We have a nurse coming in to check on her every few hours and a guard on the door. It's the best I could do."

"I'd like to visit her."

"Don't tell her about Brenna yet," McKenzie warned.

"I won't," Charlotte's expression twisted. "Did the Medical Examiner send the autopsy report yet?"

"Preliminary finding was she died from blunt force trauma to the head, but we don't know whether or not it was accidental. Like I said. Preliminary."

"Time of Death?" asked Charlotte.

"Between five and ten AM Wednesday morning. Medical Examiner says the low ambient temperature made it more difficult to pinpoint."

It was a wide window. "Don't forget to write up your reports on the incidents that occurred today." McKenzie looked at both of them for a second to make sure there were no more questions before he nodded and headed out the door.

A wave of sadness settled on Charlotte's features. "I wonder if Kayla has anyone else in her life."

"Pretty sure she knows this TJ kid." Novak didn't like the way Charlotte's grief made him want to envelop her in a big hug. He was getting soft.

Charlotte crossed her arms over her chest, looking miserable. "You don't have to come with me. McKenzie won't know if you go to the barn while I go up the back steps."

Novak grunted. "Something tells me he'd know. I'm not willing to risk getting sent home when things are getting interesting." It had nothing to do with the fact he enjoyed spending time with Charlotte. "Hey, we survived the first twenty-four hours. Only forty-eight hours of prison time left. How hard can it be?"

"I think I'm growing on you, SSA Novak."

Charlotte headed outside, and he followed her, closing the door after them, unwilling to admit she might be right.

———————

CHARLOTTE STEPPED SOFTLY on the back stairs, aware that even though it was only six PM, people might be sleeping or concentrating on work, and she didn't want to disturb them. Novak followed her, moving silently. He'd grown quiet. His expression going from teasing in the Command Center to closed down as if something was bothering him.

She went into their room and spied a thick winter jacket one of the negotiators had picked up for her laid out on the bed. Charlotte needed to remember to pay her back for the coat. "I finally get to feel warm again."

"You should have told me you were cold. I'd have found you something." Novak's quiet murmur sounded grouchy rather than considerate. He went over to his bag and started digging around, effectively closing himself off from her.

Charlotte hid her disappointment. His emotional responses were all over the place. She didn't know what she'd done to upset him, and then she kicked herself for assuming his moods were her fault.

She'd spent years studying the psychology of relationships, which was probably why she refused to settle for anything less than perfection in her own love life. She'd seen her parents fall in love with several partners and each time, they'd grown apart and stopped communicating. While she might crave closeness with another human being, she wasn't going to risk the pain of heartbreak. When she was convinced it might last forever, then she'd let herself fall in love.

But that had nothing to do with Payne Novak. He was hardly *love of her life* material. And she was not taking responsibility for his shitty mood.

Her stomach growled, and he looked up from where he knelt on the floorboards with a slow grin. "Hungry?"

His words stroked over her senses and raised a shiver in its wake. Even though he was simply being considerate to the other people on the floor by keeping the volume down, his voice sounded sexy and intimate. And she was a fool for thinking that way.

Apparently, she'd lost all sense of judgment when it was her job to understand the tone and nuance of conversation. And she realized Novak wasn't being moody, he was being quiet and reflective after a long, fraught day. Taking a moment.

Maybe she was the one who needed to lighten up and not overanalyze a man she didn't know very well and was struggling to understand.

"I'm starving. I skipped lunch. Not to worry, I'll get something after I speak to Kayla."

He frowned at his watch. After six and dark as pitch outside. She knew he was worried about his men.

"Or I can scrounge up a power bar and head straight to the barn if you'd rather," she offered.

"No." He scratched his head, looking a little confused. "You go see Kayla. I'll grab some dinner for both of us and wait for you in the kitchen. If McKenzie turns up, I'll say I'm grabbing some food for Kayla. Pretty sure the sight of me might scare the shit out of the kid anyway."

"You helped save her life today."

"I carried her to the car." He made a dismissive noise.

She smiled. He didn't like praise. Even after his heroics yesterday, he'd deflected the attention.

"You got her to safety."

Novak shrugged.

She went to touch his arm but thought better of it. Instead she joked, "Look at us, communicating like adults."

A flash of heat burst in his eyes and then was gone.

She blinked.

Was he *attracted* to her? Or had she imagined it? She'd

probably misread him, again. Novak was the opposite of an open book.

"Don't get excited. I'm sure we're going to butt heads again before this is over."

But his words reminded her of the fact she'd already butt-ed heads with someone today which might explain the headache that pinched her eyes. She rubbed her forehead and reached down into her toiletries bag to grab a Tylenol.

"You okay?" he asked.

"Yeah. By-product of my badass hand-to-hand combat is making its way into my brain."

He peered closer at her, and she was suddenly hyperaware of his height, the breadth of his shoulders.

"I'm sorry my actions put you in danger."

She laughed. It came out a little squeaky. "I'm sorry we have so many FD 302s to fill out."

"I'm serious, Charlotte. I made the wrong choice. We should have found cover and waited for backup."

"And let those guys find another angle and pick one of us off? Hell, no." She tilted up her chin. "I don't need you treat me like some weak female when I am an experienced FBI agent whose job it is to go after the bad guys."

"I don't think you're weak. Did he punch you?" Novak moved close enough to stare into her eyes as if he were searching for signs of a concussion.

Her cheeks heated. "No. I gave him a Glasgow kiss."

Novak's expression stayed blank for a full second. "Are you fucking kidding me?"

"I tricked him into getting close enough to grab his rifle and, after that, I let him have it. I'm going to have to send my trainer in Quantico a crate of beer."

Unsettled by Novak's intense stare, she grabbed a bottle of water out of her bag. She swallowed the tablets and drank deep to wash them down.

"You spar with a trainer at the academy?"

She drank more water and then capped the lid. Wiped her lips with the back of her hand. Novak tracked her movements and, for some reason, she suddenly felt self-conscious. "A couple times a week when I'm at CNU. One of the New Agent in Training instructors puts me through my paces. Hey, maybe I could work out with HRT while we're here?"

Novak swung around, and she couldn't see his face anymore. His shoulders looked stiff. "Maybe."

"Don't sound so enthusiastic." She shook her head. Hot and cold. She never knew which Payne Novak she was going to get.

"I'm hoping we're finished here before we need to set up a training gym."

"Aw, you're no fun." She punched his arm in jest and found her hand gently captured in his. He was giving her a funny look again, like he was struggling to figure her out when really, she was an open book.

"I'm not here to have fun." His expression was grim, and his voice cracked. His hand trembled slightly before he released her.

She frowned. "Here in Washington State, or here on this earth?"

"Both." He huffed out a small breath, maybe realizing how much about himself he was revealing. She wanted to smooth a finger over his brow and ease the tension in his jaw. He looked incredibly vulnerable in the moment.

"Anything you don't like food-wise?" He pulled away and

changed the subject.

"I eat pretty much anything and everything, except shell-fish, which will send me into a death coma."

"Good to know. You carry an EpiPen?"

"Yeah." She kicked her bag. "I have two in there. So next time we argue, you know how to get rid of me."

"Christ. I'm not that big an asshole." Pain lanced his expression. "I respect your opinion even when it's wrong. And I want to find a resolution to this situation that doesn't involve my men being put in danger or the bad guys getting away with shit."

She choked out a laugh, not sure if she should be insulted or flattered. "I was joking. I didn't seriously think you'd want to get rid of me. Maybe tie me up and lock me in a closet until this is all over, but not full-on anaphylactic shock."

He stilled for a moment, wincing as he realized he'd over-reacted. Then he held up his hands in surrender. "I guess I'm used to working with HRT guys, and I'm overthinking everything."

She grinned. "Leave the thinking to the negotiators."

She found herself actively searching for signs she'd amused him—that he *liked* her. Because that's what she did. Made everyone like her. It was a weakness she hated about herself.

"You talk to Kayla. I'll go warm up some clam chowder," he deadpanned.

She lobbed a pillow at him which he caught and placed back on the bed.

"Don't be long." Novak grew serious. "I want to see what the sniper teams have to say before they get some sleep."

The seriousness of the situation once again washed

through her mind. She didn't have time to mess around or have fun. She straightened her shoulders and lifted her chin. She needed to get back to work.

She wasn't looking forward to lying to this girl about her friend, but she had to remember Kayla was technically a suspect.

"Don't start any trouble without me." Charlotte picked up the winter jacket and ripped off the tags, trying not to wince at the price which was high for a government salary.

"Charlotte, you almost arrested the local sheriff and then fought an armed assailant who was twice your size into submission. I'm not the one who got into trouble today."

Charlotte rolled her eyes behind his back.

"I saw that." He gave her a sardonic smile over his shoulder before he turned away again.

She watched him head down the stairs, but he didn't look back. She was actually starting to like the guy, so maybe McKenzie's draconian tactics were working. She didn't need to like Novak to work with him, but it sure did help.

She walked down the hallway and turned the corner. An agent sat in an uncomfortable-looking kitchen chair outside Kayla's door.

"I'm going to check on her."

The agent nodded, and she opened the door to a beautiful room with a queen-size bed. She left the door open and walked towards the tiny figure lying so still beneath the covers.

Kayla was sleeping peacefully with her skin deadly pale except for the slight flush of fever across her cheeks.

Charlotte wondered where she'd come from. The team must have a lot more information about her by now, and Brenna's autopsy report might be in. She needed to catch up on all the details and then help implement her idea to interview Tom Harrison's CO, but she couldn't drag herself away from the bedside.

A drip was attached to Kayla's arm. Someone had changed her clothes, and she was now wearing a plain white t-shirt with the ranch logo on it. She had long, thick, blue-black hair and beautiful features, but she looked so damned alone and vulnerable. Charlotte's heart ached for the girl.

Did she have a family out there somewhere waiting for her? Or was her only family lying on a slab in the morgue and her only home on its way to the lab for analysis? Or had this girl with her hauntingly beautiful face somehow been involved in her friend's death?

Even though Charlotte wanted to talk, she knew Kayla needed to recover her strength before she could be interviewed properly.

Charlotte turned and walked away.

CHAPTER SIXTEEN

T J STUFFED A spare set of clothes into his rucksack, followed by his Bible and his mini survival kit, water bottle, purification tablets, straw, space blanket, sleeping bag, first aid kit, and foldable shovel. He drew on his winter hiking boots and laced them tight. Slipped into his camouflage, waterproof, winter jacket. TJ stuffed his gun in the holster on his waistband, picked up the big winter mitts that went over his gloves and stuffed them in his pack.

He could walk to Canada in this gear and disappear forever into the wilderness. If he wanted.

He didn't.

He needed to find Kayla and see why she hadn't been there to meet him yesterday morning. Was she safe? Had she been hurt? Was she sick? Who was the other girl? Or had the news outlets made a mistake, and Kayla was actually dead? The need to know the truth ripped at his mind with sharp talons.

He needed to find out.

After that, he'd tell her the truth about what happened and do whatever she wanted him to do. Go on the run, give himself up, whatever she wanted. Whatever she needed.

He headed out of his room, through the living room, small kitchen, and past the huge master bathroom where his mother had liked to soak in the massive tub that his dad had blasted a hole in the wall to bring inside. Past his parents' bedroom and the laundry room. Maybe once he was gone, and his safety was no longer an issue, his father would pick up the phone and talk to the Feds. Stop this going any further. But there was no way his father would give him up. TJ knew that with every fiber of his being.

He knocked on the door to his father's study, hoping Tom didn't answer. After a few seconds TJ tried the handle, relieved when the door opened.

"Dad?" he called out.

No answer.

Good.

TJ headed over to the corner of the beautifully furnished room. Most of the compound was dour concrete, or utilitarian furniture. But wherever his mom had had a hand, there were brightly painted walls, thick, vibrant rugs, comfy seating and solid wooden furniture, much of which his father had assembled in place as it was the only way it could fit inside the room without widening all the doors.

Behind a chair, beneath a rug, was a floor safe only he and his parents knew about. They had other larger caches dispersed around the building, one buried beneath the potato patch, another near the septic tank, one buried under the garage area that would require a jackhammer to retrieve, and yet another large one buried outside the concrete walls.

No one knew about the gold. They might suspect, they might even have their own caches buried around the place, but he and his dad had buried their treasures before anyone had started arriving on their doorstep, looking for refuge and free board.

TJ opened the safe and pulled out four thick rolls of hundred-dollar bills that he stuffed into the side pocket of his pack. He took a handful of gold coins and slid them individually into a gap he'd picked in the stitching of his jacket. He arranged the coins so they were evenly spaced and less likely to tear the lining.

He closed the safe and hoped his dad forgave him for stealing, even though he'd always told him to use the money if he ever needed it. TJ knew Tom had meant if he was no longer around.

He'd never defied his father before. Aside from sneaking out on Wednesday mornings, he'd been the perfect son.

Now it was time to stand on his own two feet, time to find the woman he loved and decide what the next move would be for their future. If Kayla was alive, he wanted the chance of a life with her. Dying in a standoff was not part of that plan. Hiding in the desolate shell of a home for the next decade held no appeal either. Not anymore. He wanted to see the world.

TJ headed out of his dad's study and their apartment. He glanced up the stairs, into the part of the compound where other families lived. He used to feel guilty for having so much more space than the others, but it was something his father had insisted on when TJ's mom had welcomed more and more "family" into their home. They could stay, but everyone pulled their weight, and the Harrisons' living spaces were off limits. It was the only time TJ had seen his dad deny his mom anything. TJ was glad for that now.

He headed north along their private corridor and approached the back of the structure. It was dark here. Shadows streaked the bleak 1960's mud-colored walls.

Guards had been positioned at the front and rear exit, but TJ wasn't going out the main door. There was another way, a way no one knew about except him and his dad. The one he'd used for months to sneak in and out of the place without anyone seeing. A storage room led to a tunnel that came out in a culvert beyond the tree line.

No lights shone nearby, but he knew his way blindfolded. He paused for a few moments, thinking he heard something scuff in the darkness, but decided it was his imagination. He put his hand on the doorknob and started to turn the handle. A powerful flashlight flicked on out of nowhere and dazzled his eyes.

"Where do you think you're going?" Malcolm's voice sliced through the darkness.

What the hell? The guy was hanging out in the shadows, waiting to catch TJ unaware? TJ held up his hands to shield his eyes. "Mind your own goddamn business."

Someone grabbed his pack off his shoulders, and someone else caught hold of both his arms to restrain him.

What the actual hell?

Malcolm started going through his stuff.

"What are you doing?" TJ struggled with the man confining him, but the guy was huge and didn't budge.

Malcolm pulled out a roll of bills. "Where d'you get the cash? You don't have this sort of money."

How did he know what TJ had? Had Malcolm gone through his belongings?

"Give that to me. You have no right to go through my things." TJ tried to twist out of the grip of the man imprisoning him, but another one joined the first. They weren't kidding around.

TJ saw Malcolm's fist heading toward his face a moment before it connected. Blood spurted from TJ's nose as pain flashed bright white through his brain. He bit back a cry of agony.

"I've wanted to do that for a long time." Malcolm started laughing as he shook out his fist. "Hurt like a bitch but was worth it."

"What's going on here?" Tom Harrison's voice echoed down the corridor. Brisk footsteps followed. Someone turned on the dim wall lights, and TJ blinked as Malcolm shone the flashlight into his face.

"Your precious son was making a run for it," Malcolm taunted.

Shame crawled over TJ's flesh as his father stared at him.

"TJ wouldn't do that," Tom stated slowly.

"His knapsack says different," Malcolm amended.

TJ hated the disillusionment he saw in his father's eyes. Someone handed him the roll of cash, and Tom took it and flicked through it, knowing exactly where it had come from. Knowing TJ had stolen from him.

"I was going to go talk to the Feds. Tell them what happened. Make them understand this was my doing and to leave you alone," TJ said desperately. No way was he mentioning Kayla.

"He's running away. He murdered his girlfriend, and he's running from justice, leaving the rest of us to take the fall."

"That is not true," TJ snarled. "I never saw her before in my life."

His dad met his gaze but, for once, TJ saw doubt there. The fact his dad didn't one hundred percent believe him was a kick in the gut.

"Is she the one you've been sneaking out to meet?" Malcolm continued to pry open secrets that didn't concern him.

"Have you been sneaking out to meet a girl?" his dad asked him.

TJ held his father's gaze. "No, sir."

The disappointment in his father's eyes almost defeated him, but he couldn't tell anyone about Kayla. He couldn't risk getting her involved in this mess until he knew what had happened on that mountain. What if she'd had something to do with the other woman's death? What if they'd struggled, and the other woman fell or hit her head and died? What if it had all been a terrible accident?

Right now, he was the only other person in the world who knew Kayla should have been on the mountain waiting for him. How would he find her if she'd left the campsite? Endless questions raced through his brain, and he needed answers.

"What do you want to do with him?" One of the men holding his arms asked.

Silence followed the question. Every man held their breath waiting to see what Tom Harrison would do with his normally pliable son.

Malcolm spoke loudly, as if anyone doubted his point of view. "Send him out the front door and let the cops deal with him accordingly. Once they have him, they won't be interested in the rest of us. He's who killed her. He's the one they were chasing. End this thing before anyone else gets hurt because of this monster."

TJ sucked in a shocked breath. Malcolm was painting him as a deranged killer. "I never hurt that woman. I never touched her." TJ tried to take a step forward but, once again, two men held him back. "Dad!"

"Place him in his quarters." Tom stuffed the roll of cash into his pants back pocket.

Malcolm rolled his eyes. "Not exactly the punishment I was thinking of."

Tom shoved Malcolm against the wall and got in the man's face. "TJ isn't the only one who goes sneaking in and out of the compound every now and then, now is he?"

Malcolm's lips narrowed, and he looked away. "That's my business."

"Well, this is *my* property. *My* land. *My* son and *my* rules. You don't like it you can gather your stuff and get the hell out." Tom wasn't shouting, but no one thought he was bluffing.

Malcolm's mouth twisted, and he fell away from Tom's grasp, his jaw clamped shut in anger.

What secret was Malcolm hiding? Why hadn't his father mentioned it before?

Tom looked at the men holding TJ but didn't tell them to release him. "Put him in his room. Lock him inside." He handed one of them the key he usually kept in his pocket. There was a spare in the drawer in the security room, which usually doubled as a general office.

"*Dad,*" TJ implored.

Tom took a step towards him, shaking his fist. "Do not speak to me."

"I didn't do it! I don't know her—"

"I don't *care*! You stole from me. You looked me in the eye and lied to my face." Tears shone in his father's eyes. "You tried to leave without talking to me first." His voice broke. "You are all I've got, TJ, and I cannot lose you now. Lock him in his room until I say otherwise. It's for your own safety."

TJ opened his mouth to defend himself, but his father was already striding away.

Malcolm's eyes glistened in the dim light, and TJ knew he'd played right into the man's hands. A horrible feeling spread through TJ.

Was Malcolm planning something? Had TJ somehow aided his cause?

As he was shoved along back the way he'd come, TJ wondered what the hell was going to happen next.

Once in his room, they tossed his backpack at him, and he caught it, standing uselessly in the middle of the familiar space. The other men left, and he heard the soft click of the lock.

Had they locked the other doors that led into the apartment? Presumably.

He needed to get to Kayla. He had to make sure she was safe.

TJ wanted to yell and scream. How had he lost control of this situation? How had Malcolm figured out what he'd planned to do? How long had he known about the secret tunnel?

Endless questions looped around his brain, but TJ was no closer to figuring out the answers than he'd been when he'd found the dead body in the woods.

CHAPTER SEVENTEEN

NOVAK PEELED OPEN his eyes, instantly wide awake. He and Charlotte had called it a night at about two AM. The agent questioning the two men they'd caught on the mountainside still hadn't returned, and McKenzie hadn't been able to give them an update. Novak might have stayed in the Tactical Center longer, except Charlotte's eyes had been drooping, and there was a general lull in activity. Usually being on someone else's schedule would have pissed him off, but she'd had a hell of a day and hadn't made a single peep of complaint.

The negotiators hadn't been able to contact anyone inside the facility. The FBI was in the process of tracking down Tom Harrison's former military buddies and any close friends who weren't cooped up with him on Eagle Mountain. Media and tech people were busy preparing to isolate and switch the video feeds without being noticed. On top of that they were still waiting on tests the ME was running and the reports on the trace evidence from the crime scene, the tent, and the SUV.

The reconstruction of the fortress being built on a nearby military base was halfway finished. Charlotte had not been happy when she'd heard about that development, even though she knew it was standard operating procedure.

He checked his cell for any urgent updates, but there were none. It was six thirty AM.

The drone had sensed some movement on the other side of the door last night, but no one had come through it. Novak was convinced that this tunnel was the key to getting inside and planned to explore options later.

He heard Charlotte turning over. Last night, he'd promised to wake her in time to shower before the eight AM team meeting, but he was reluctant because she obviously needed more than four and a half hours of slumber.

He sat up and crawled down the ladder as quietly as he could. He was wearing his boxers and needed a shower. He glanced at Charlotte's sleeping form, hesitant to wake her because she looked so freaking peaceful. But he'd promised, and he always kept his promises. Plus, he wanted to earn her trust. He leaned down and very gently touched her shoulder.

Rather than finding himself flat on his back, her lids fluttered opened, and she yawned, throwing the covers back.

Was that disappointment he was feeling that she wasn't stretched out over him with her arm across his throat? Or some sort of primitive pride that her subconscious no longer considered him a threat? He told himself to be relieved not to have an elbow in his gullet, but paradoxically he missed the physical contact.

Yeah, he was that desperate.

"What time is it?" She sat up, leaning back on her elbows. He was so close to her the warm scent of her skin flooded his senses.

"Oh six thirty." His voice was low and gravelly with sleep and something else. Something he was working hard to quell.

He realized he was a bit too close than was reasonable for a colleague and jerked away, only to whack the back of his head on the top of the bunk. He ducked out, stood, swearing under his breath.

"Are you all right?" Worry colored her tone. She swung her legs out of bed and ran her fingers through his hair and over the back of his skull.

"I'm fine." He leaned into her touch, absorbing the comfort.

"You know, you might be the clumsiest operator I've ever met." She seemed oblivious to the way her arm wrapped around his, or her warm breast pressed against his back.

But he wasn't and, suddenly, wearing only boxers was a big mistake. *Massive* mistake. Sweet Jesus he needed to get out of here before she realized how fucking turned on he was.

She stepped away, and he thought he was saved until there was a knock on the door. Rather than waiting for them to respond, the door started to open. Novak swung away and reached for the black pants on top of his kit bag. He saw Charlotte's eyes widen to saucers as she spotted his tented shorts. Then her gaze shot to the door as her cheeks turned scarlet.

McKenzie flicked on the light, and his voice cut through the quiet of the morning. "SWAT teams are almost here. Novak, I want you to tell them where to position themselves. ETA ten minutes. I want them deployed before dawn breaks."

Charlotte cleared her throat, and Novak swore she shot another look at his erection which was rapidly fading, thanks to the presence of his freaking boss.

"What about me?" Charlotte's voice was so high-pitched it was more of a squeak.

"You two are glued at the hip," McKenzie said sharply.

"Remember?"

Novak and Charlotte stood in frozen silence after McKenzie closed the door with a firm click.

Glued-at-the-*damned*-hip was turning into a unique form of torture for Novak and probably terrified his female colleague. He stuffed his legs into his pants. "Sorry. I, hmm." *Fuck.* He dragged on his socks and shirt, not knowing what the hell else to say.

"It's okay. I'm so sorry. I know it's a morning thing. I apologize for invading your personal space a few moments ago. It must have made you very uncomfortable. Now, thanks to McKenzie, I still don't have chance for a shower, but I appreciate you waking me."

He was fully attired by the time her mouth ran out of steam. He grabbed his cell and was on his way out, hand on the doorknob, when he paused and looked back at her. She stood there uncertainly in a baggy nightshirt that came almost to her knees but draped loosely over her shoulders, revealing the smooth hollows above her collarbones. Her arms drew up and crossed nervously over her chest.

She was looking at him like she was worried she'd done something wrong, and he hated that.

He cleared his throat. "For the record, it wasn't a morning thing, and it wasn't your fault. I apologize. It won't happen again. I'll let you get dressed and wait for you in the kitchen."

CHAPTER EIGHTEEN

C HARLOTTE HAD NEVER been so confused in her life. The fact she was in a barn teeming with prime male specimens who were much more her type made her preoccupation with Payne Novak even more puzzling.

Did Novak mean that he'd been thinking of someone else this morning, and that's why he'd been aroused? Or that his body's responses were his own responsibility? Or was he so packed full of testosterone that the simple proximity of any female near a bed made the blood pump south?

Was it less about her and more to do with primitive male hormones?

Had she imagined that flash of heat in his gaze yesterday?

She wanted to know, but then why push the issue if she didn't intend to do anything about it? He'd apologized, even though she was the one who'd touched him, she realized with a recurrent bolt of humiliation.

She was a very tactile person, but that was no excuse. If he'd done that to her? She'd have been indignant and made uncomfortable, right? She wanted to close her eyes with humiliation. She especially shouldn't have touched him when she was in her nightshirt and he was in his boxers, and they'd been alone in a room with two dense but totally functional mattresses a short step away. He could easily have gotten the wrong message.

It was the wrong message, right?

She watched Novak's features tighten, brows clench, eyes narrow, lips pinch as he leaned over a map to figure out exactly how to distribute SWAT teams to form a secure perimeter. The sheriff's deputies and state troopers would be moved back another half mile.

Novak really was much better looking than she'd first appreciated. Apparently, it took working in close proximity and the viewpoints of two other women to even admit that to herself.

She worked with good-looking men all the time. Dominic, Quentin, Max and Eban were all men who women fluttered over like nitwits—except their partners who were way too sensible to exhibit that nonsense. She'd witnessed it a hundred times and had women tell her how *lucky* she was to work with such hunks of men. It made her gag a little because they were her friends, more like brothers than potential lovers. She had never wanted to get sexually involved with any of them.

Maybe she really was an old maid.

But Novak had the kind of appeal her coworkers didn't, rugged and less refined, but honest. Brutally honest. Her fellow negotiators were all tall, dark and handsome. Payne Novak was a Viking marauder in black Kevlar.

Definitely not her type. Definitely not the man she imagined mowing the lawn every Saturday in July. She watched his hands as he pointed to different positions on the map.

Nice hands.

Capable hands.

For the record, it wasn't a morning thing, and it wasn't your fault. I apologize. It won't happen again.

Great.

Right?

Although it could have been fun.

She shut that thought down immediately. She forced herself to concentrate on the briefing, even though this part of the incident had nothing to do with her, and she was basically killing time. McKenzie had not relented. She'd heard he was a bit of a hardass, and now she knew it firsthand.

SWAT were also doing twelve-on twelve-off shifts so they could rotate in and out of position during darkness. They were equipped with proper winter gear, but Charlotte didn't like the idea of so many people being exposed to the elements in this remote location. If only they could get Harrison talking. Get him and his buddies out of there before the brass in control of this incident lost patience and ordered a tactical solution.

She didn't want to be here all winter. *No one* wanted to be here all winter. But, more importantly, she did not want anyone else to die.

The SWAT guys and girls all started moving at once, half back to the motel to rest up for the day, and the other half out into the woods.

"Watch out for the cougar," she added. Then she frowned. They still hadn't figured out who had told Bob Jones about the problem cat.

"And Bigfoot," Novak added with a grin.

McKenzie strode in as SWAT strode out. He'd taken a call at the start of the briefing just as she'd asked him what Agent Makimi had managed to glean from the two men who'd attacked them on the mountain yesterday. Charlotte had the impression it had been President Hague on the line, not exactly someone he could blow off.

McKenzie nodded and spoke to a few of the SWAT guys as they filed past. "Watch your backs out there. Don't take any unnecessary risks."

Charlotte appreciated that the Incident Commander's priority was his people's safety. So was Novak's, but he had so much confidence in HRT's abilities that she worried he forgot they were human.

"Blood, Novak, get over here." McKenzie stood in front of one of the news channels set up on a massive computer monitor while one of the HRT guys turned up the volume. McKenzie looked at his wristwatch. "First one is due to switch…" He held his fingers up. Five. Four. Three. Two. One…

There was the barest flicker on one of the screens.

McKenzie looked back over his shoulder. "Think they'd notice that?"

Charlotte realized Novak was standing beside her when he said, "I wouldn't have thought so."

"They're waiting on the commercial break before they do the next one."

It took ten minutes until all six of the networks that the FBI knew the men in the compound watched were being controlled remotely by the media people in HQ. Every other news channel had been blocked.

The FBI couldn't do this indefinitely, but they could control the narrative in the short term.

"Okay, General Veldman, Tom Harrison's former CO is up in the next segment. The interview won't go out at the same time for each channel because that wouldn't look realistic. NBC is first. Or rather, our version of NBC." McKenzie propped himself on the work bench. He seemed surprisingly at ease in the rustic setting despite the sawdust clinging to his expensive suit pants. Charlotte had heard rumors he'd started life as a cowboy.

"Have a seat." Novak indicated a chair to Charlotte beside HRT's central tables.

She looked up, but he didn't meet her gaze. She felt her cheeks burn in a wave of embarrassment. "Thanks."

Did anyone notice? Jeez, the two of them couldn't be more awkward if they'd had blinding sex all night long rather than the barest hint of *it's-not-your-fault* attraction.

She dropped to the chair Novak suggested and then felt a widening chasm stretch between them as he went over to stand with his men.

She swallowed the sudden tightness in her throat. She must be coming down with something to be so goddamn sensitive. She hadn't gotten this far in the FBI by being a wimp.

The segment they were waiting for came up on the screen. General Veldman, a retired two-star general in the United States Army, stood outside his modest California home wearing khakis and a buttoned-up polo shirt, talking to an FBI agent who was masquerading as a reporter.

"Did General Veldman have any objections about doing this?" Charlotte asked McKenzie.

"None I was made aware of," McKenzie said without taking his eyes off the screen.

The reporter made a brief introduction, spelling out the respected status of the retired military man.

"What do you want to say to Tom Harrison, the man at the center of the armed standoff in Washington State? I believe he was under your command for five years so you must have known him well?"

The general straightened his back and looked directly into the camera. "Tom, I don't know what's going on in your life right now, but I do remember how desperately you wanted to start a family and live a peaceful life."

"So Tom Harrison is not someone you'd expect to be involved in an incident of this nature?"

The general shook his head. "This is not something that the Tom Harrison I knew would do. He liked to help people, not hurt them."

"Do you have any idea why Mr. Harrison isn't talking to the FBI agents who want to question him regarding the death of a young woman on the mountain near his home?"

CNU and the Behavioral Analysis Unit had crafted the script around the idea of prompting Tom to pick up the phone. Charlotte hoped they weren't overplaying their hand.

"The man I knew was honest and fair. He respected the rule of command and followed orders. Tom Harrison was a damn fine soldier, who always had his fellow soldiers' welfare as top priority during training and deployment."

"Sounds like you think Tom Harrison is an honorable man who doesn't present a danger to the public. What would you like to say to Mr. Harrison at this time?"

The general pressed his lips together. "Talk to the authorities, Tom. Help them figure out what happened up there on the mountain. Nobody else needs to be hurt. Tell the truth, and everyone can go home safely in time for the holidays. If someone made a mistake then they need to pay for that mistake, nobody else. You know law enforcement are only doing their job the way we did ours. Put your weapons down and come out and talk to the authorities so no one else gets hurt. I'll make sure you are treated fairly, even if I have to come out there myself. It's time to tell the world your version of this story."

The camera shifted to the fake reporter who held up his mic and looked like he was having a damn good time. "This is Steve Perkins, signing off from California."

The reporter would have a complete background developed in the event someone checked him out. Not that the compound had internet anymore, but the FBI liked to be thorough.

Silence rang around the barn as the HRT guy turned the volume back down as the news loops continued to run with General Veldman's interview staggered on each channel.

"How long do you think we need to wait for a reaction?" Novak addressed Charlotte.

Charlotte opened her mouth to answer when Romano shouted, "Activity on the drone."

Everyone crowded around Romano's laptop. Novak saved a space for Charlotte, and she couldn't believe how she was suddenly hyperaware of his closeness as she inched near to his side in order to see what was happening. What had changed?

Her attention focused on the monitor and her job.

The door cracked open, and the man who she recognized as Tom Harrison strode past, carrying a handgun and an armload of something.

"Shit, we should have had operators in the tunnel," Novak muttered.

McKenzie shook his head.

"What's he doing?" asked Charlotte.

"We'll replay the video in a moment. Get the drone through the door, Romano," Novak spoke quickly.

Romano walked the device forward. Everyone held their breath as it approached a lip but, thankfully, the drone was robust enough to climb over it, and Romano pushed the joystick hard.

The drone seemed to be in a broom closet. Romano headed toward the light, hugging the side of the wall.

"Turn it around and see if we can figure out what Harrison is doing. Alert the SWAT teams in the vicinity he might be coming out and he's armed," Novak yelled.

"Alert SWAT but get that drone all the way inside the building. It's more important than short term intel," McKenzie overrode Novak's orders.

Charlotte noticed Novak clench his jaw, but he didn't fight it. They probably only had a brief window to get inside.

Romano remotely moved the drone through the broom closet into an outer corridor and did a quick three-sixty.

"Head into the dark space. Keep her snug to the wall and watch for Harrison coming back out," Novak commanded.

They all held their collective breath as Romano moved the drone and then turned it to watch the entrance of the broom closet. After a few of the longest minutes of Charlotte's life, Tom Harrison came through the doorway, shut the door, and locked it behind him. Then he leaned against the wall, cradling something in his hand. Another two men came running down the corridor, appearing out of breath, shouting for him to stop. Harrison looked up for a long, slow second and then deliberately pressed down on a detonator. The floor shook, dust filling the air.

When the atmosphere cleared sixty seconds later, no one was left in the corridor.

"What happened?" asked Charlotte, even though she

knew.

"He demolished the passageway." Novak's jaw flexed.

"He has explosives." Charlotte's heart felt like a jackrabbit in her chest. She'd known it was a possibility but rather than encouraging Tom Harrison to talk to them, the interview with Veldman had made Harrison up the stakes.

Her cell buzzed with a text.

She checked the screen. "Someone just picked up the phone." She looked at Novak and then bolted from the barn, the HRT team leader and Incident Commander tight on her heels. They scrambled into the Command Center and hit a wall of silence.

She dashed past the new room dividers and threw herself into a chair beside Dominic who was busy writing notes as Eban spoke encouragingly into the phone.

"I understand you're concerned. We all want a peaceful end to this incident. My name is Eban Winters. Tell us what we can do to resolve this situation." He used his most soothing voice, which reminded Charlotte of a cat purring in the way it instantly relaxed her.

There was a sharp crack of laughter on the speaker from the other end of the line. "That's easy. Go. Away."

"Is this Tom Harrison? The owner of the property? Can I confirm that's who I'm talking to? Mr. Harrison?"

"Yeah, this is Tom Harrison." His voice was tired. There was a good chance he hadn't slept the last two nights, on constant alert for an incoming attack.

"You sound tired, Tom."

"I am tired, Eban. I'm tired of you people trying to attack my home. I want you all to go away."

"I can understand that, Tom. I can see how you'd interpret

say?"

"They claim they don't want anyone hurt. Wanted to talk to you to get your side of the story."

"I could do that—"

"I already told you, I don't want you talking to them. They'll end up twisting things around."

TJ didn't understand. "We can't live underground forever…"

"We could have." Tom gave a bitter smile. "If it was only the two of us."

TJ shuddered. He didn't want to live underground forever.

Tom's expression darkened. "I will love your mother until my last breath, but her soft heart means I can't protect you here anymore." Tom huffed out an exasperated gasp. "And ever since her brother arrived, people have been grouching and bitching about getting their fair share. Fair share of what? My home? My food? My money?" Tom's eyes narrowed to slits.

"But if we don't talk to the Feds what other options *do* we have? There's no other way out of here."

Tom's eyes grew sharp then. Assessing. "I've only ever had your best interests at heart, son. You know that, right?"

TJ nodded. His father loved him. He knew that.

"Do you trust me? I mean really trust me?"

"Yes, of course. But I don't want to die."

"I'm not going to let that happen." Tom put a comforting hand on his shoulder. "Do as I say. Stay inside our quarters. Gather me a pack together the same as you had. Put all the money and documents out of the safe inside it too. As much gold as we can carry between us. We can come back for whatever is buried in the woods in a few years when this all blows over. Store the packs out of sight in case Malcolm comes crawling around here." He pulled the roll of cash out of his back pocket and handed it to TJ. "I'll come get you when it's time."

TJ shook his head. "I don't understand."

Tom clasped his upper arm and held his gaze. "You don't have to. Be ready to leave. It might not be today or tomorrow, but the day will come, and we need to be ready to move fast. Okay, son?"

TJ nodded. But it wasn't okay. None of this was okay.

———————

"WHO'S THIS GUY?" McKenzie pointed to the video still of one of the two men running down the corridor toward Tom Harrison seconds before he blew the tunnel.

They were going through the nitty gritty of all the new information they'd uncovered. Charlotte sipped on fresh coffee the ranch owners had provided and wished she could crawl into a hole.

"We're trying to match photographs with names. Believe it or not, they're not big on Instagram selfies." Truman winced. "Sorry, boss, that didn't come out how I intended it to. I haven't slept in a while."

McKenzie spared the young agent a hard glance. "What *do* you have?"

"A bunch of names many of which seem to be nicknames like Bud and Chuck. They tend to use cash when they go into town. No credit cards or checks although we know some of them collect welfare."

"Most of the phones we traced inside the compound were burners," McKenzie added. "The numbers they called provided us with a lot of additional information that agents are following at various field offices around the country."

"Any connection to the guys who attacked us yesterday?" Charlotte asked.

Agent Makimi looked up from typing on her laptop. "Not that we've been able to ascertain. The man who attacked you wasn't talking, but the younger one peed his pants when I told him he was looking at three counts of twenty-five-years-to-life for attempted murder and conspiracy to murder Federal Agents."

Yesterday seemed like a million mistakes ago.

"What did he tell you?" asked Novak, sending Charlotte a concerned look.

"Someone on one of the White Supremacy chatrooms suggested they all head to Washington State en masse and get a head start on the revolution the tin pots want."

"Those 'tin pots' almost brought down HQ in the spring," McKenzie reminded them all with a glower.

"I was there. I remember." Makimi pulled a face. "These two drove over from Oregon. Hiked in from a logging road to the west. Claimed to not even see any deputies up there."

Charlotte scowled. "I take it all the chatroom users are being tracked?"

The woman nodded and tucked her ink-black hair behind her ear. "We're mapping their communication network. We plan to make coordinated arrests where appropriate and bring others in to interview if we don't have enough evidence of actual crimes being committed. Remind them no one is above the law."

"Some of them may already be on their way here," Novak said.

"That's why we have SWAT and State Police assisting.

There's always a danger." McKenzie grimaced. "The longer the standoff goes on, the greater the potential for harm."

Charlotte frowned. She was disappointed the two men weren't connected to Harrison in some way. They could have used them to instigate a phone call. The fact she'd been attacked because of some rightwing bozos wanting to burn the Constitution pissed her off. At least she'd helped put them in their place without anyone getting hurt.

"Do we know how the women who left Eagle Mountain yesterday came to live there in the first place?" she asked Truman.

"One says her husband is a cousin of Tom Harrison's late wife, Martha. The second woman is her sister-in-law. Her husband died in a car wreck a few years back."

"So they're all loosely related?" Charlotte was trying to get past the utter failure her plan to interview Harrison's old CO and air it on the news had been. It was still being shown to the compound because removing it would tip the FBI's hand completely, but it was being interspersed with other additional innocuous items as they arose on the cable news networks. Right now, McKenzie wasn't taking any more risks with predicting the behavior of the man running the show. Tom Harrison had revealed himself to be completely volatile like a stick of old dynamite.

"Yup. All related to the late wife, so far as I can tell." Truman nodded.

"Can we fill out the family trees? We know she had relatives down in Utah, correct?" Charlotte asked.

"That's a good idea," said Novak. "See if we can find a relative who can talk some sense to them."

She shot him a look. Was he trying to make her feel better because of the disaster she'd created earlier? She was grateful no one had died, but the situation had escalated fast. She'd overheard McKenzie briefing the director again, which couldn't have been fun. She knew he was under a tremendous amount of pressure.

She glanced at Novak and caught his gaze. He looked away. They hadn't even had the chance to discuss what had happened in the bedroom that morning, which was probably for the best. She wasn't sure her people skills had equipped her for that conversation, especially when she didn't know if he was actually attracted to her or not.

And she also didn't know why she was seeing him differently now. He wasn't her type. Her type was standing a few feet away trying not to yawn with tiredness. Charlotte gave Truman a sympathetic smile.

McKenzie hadn't said anything about Harrison blowing the tunnel, but she felt the weight of his censure every time his gaze landed on her.

"Run the images of the men we saw on the video through face-recognition software ASAP." McKenzie instructed the tech guy.

"Already running them, boss. But the quality isn't great so it might take a while."

"What about the vehicles inside the gates?" Charlotte suggested.

"Shit. I forgot about getting the license plate information. I suspect we can grab it off the footage from the drone flight yesterday." Novak stood, and Romano opened up another laptop to start scouring the footage.

"Get on it." McKenzie sounded annoyed.

They'd decided to leave the drone in place in the darkened corridor until the early hours of the morning when the least number of people would be around. Even underground, people followed the diurnal rhythm of the sun.

Charlotte opted to confront the elephant in the room. "I'm sorry my idea about interviewing Harrison's CO backfired. It was a bad call. I take full responsibility."

McKenzie frowned.

"It wasn't your fault, SSA Blood." Novak shifted his stare from her to their boss. "We all agreed it was the best course of action. Even BAU approved."

Charlotte shook her head. "We didn't have enough background information from after he left the Army. Eighteen years is a big gap."

"Don't blame yourself." Novak gave her a wry smile. "Anyway, you said it would make him pick up the phone, and it sure as hell did that."

McKenzie crossed his arms over his chest. "Aw, look at you two getting along so well. Next thing we know you'll be getting married."

Charlotte glared at the Incident Commander, but Novak took it a step further, sounding furious. "You don't get to make that joke, boss. You forced us into each other's pockets for this op, and we made it work. You were right to do it. Now our relationship is based on mutual respect, which was what you wanted. Don't turn around and twist it to make us look bad for following your orders."

Charlotte's eyes bugged.

Silence rang around the barn, and no one dared move, let alone speak.

McKenzie raised both hands. "You're right. I'm being a dick because I'm pissed the plan didn't have the desired results. It wasn't SSA Blood's fault Harrison went so far off the deep end." He rubbed his brow. "His reaction doesn't make sense."

"We pressed a button we didn't know existed." A black swan. An unknown unknown. The problem was, they still didn't know what it was. "We need to figure out what we're missing, and I bet it's buried somewhere in the past eighteen years."

McKenzie swore and then closed his eyes. "You're right. We're going to re-interview everyone who ever worked with or met Tom Harrison or his wife or son. That's every storekeeper in town. All the churchgoers where he occasionally worshipped. It's his relatives, his wife's relatives, it's the environmentalists who might have interacted, his Army buddies—see if he kept in touch with any of them. If these people aren't local, let's get leads out to FBI field offices around the country. If people have been questioned once, question them again, this time about what makes Tom Harrison and any of the people inside that building tick. I'm going to call the lab and light a fire under their asses, so we have some solid pieces of evidence to work with."

"Did we get the Medical Examiner's report yet?" Charlotte asked.

"Yeah, but they're still waiting on toxicology results. They're running DNA through CODIS and missing persons and any other databases they can access."

"Did the ME say if Brenna had been assaulted?" Charlotte asked.

"There were scratches on her torso that suggest she might have been involved in some sort of struggle but no obvious sign of sexual violence."

That wasn't a hard no, but as an FBI agent, Charlotte had learned to take the best she could from a case. There were things she'd seen on the job that still gave her flashbacks. It was why she'd moved off the streets into negotiation, although she still came up against violent altercations. If she wanted to avoid them altogether, she'd have to live in a sensory deprivation unit.

"Should one of us go interview Bob Jones?" she asked. The FWO was one of the three people known to be on the mountain that morning. He was a key witness.

McKenzie opened his mouth to say something and then stopped. He stared at her for a long moment. "My first instinct was to say no, you don't have time," he laughed harshly, "but I have the sneaky suspicion time is something we're gonna have lots of, because that man is not going to be picking up the phone anytime soon. Yes. Both of you go talk to Bob Jones."

Novak gritted his teeth and clenched his fist in silent annoyance.

"I hear he's doing so well they moved him to a general ward," McKenzie added.

Sunlight picked up dust motes in the air. It still hadn't snowed, but every day felt as if it were on the brink. "The rest of us are going to stay here and dig into Tom Harrison's life. We're missing something, and I intend to figure out what."

"Hey, Novak," Charlotte muttered under her breath as everyone returned to their tasks. "We pass the airstrip on the way to the hospital." She watched his entire body uncurl and unclench as the information registered. That's where the FBI was building the reconstruction of the compound.

He shot her a glance. "You don't say." Then he smiled at her, slow and hot, even though she was sure that, only yesterday, it would have been a perfectly ordinary smile. "Let's go then."

CHAPTER TWENTY

I T WAS AN estimated seventy-minute drive to Colville. Novak did it in forty.

It helped to have blue lights flashing the whole way. Which, in turn, meant he avoided having a conversation he didn't want to have.

Charlotte huffed her disapproval at his driving and maintained a death grip on the handle above the door the whole way. Up until now, they hadn't been alone even for a second since he'd left the bedroom in darkness that morning, and he hadn't thought about the potential embarrassment until he'd climbed behind the wheel. Hence the lights and sirens.

Concentrating on driving also made it impossible to dwell on the way his body had betrayed him that morning. Not that it was a problem. It would not happen again. Despite what she might think, he *was* an elite warrior and controlling his mental and physical reactions was part of that gig. He trained daily with live ammo, so he didn't flinch at the sound of a gunshot. He simply didn't have a huge amount of experience working with a woman he found attractive or having to mask that reaction while in a bedroom wearing nothing but boxers. Maybe he needed to put in the time, acclimate to her presence, and his reaction would go away—although he didn't want it to go away indefinitely. God forbid.

The fact they only had one night left together was both a curse and a blessing. But he could endure it as long as she could.

He pulled into a space rather than parking on the curb because Charlotte gave him "the look."

He jumped out of the vehicle and waited for her to join him. "What ward is Jones in?"

"Let's go find out." She strode away.

She'd changed into a trim black pant suit for this interview. He still wore his jeans but had teamed them with a dress shirt and a sport's jacket to conceal his shoulder holster. Turning up in tactical gear set people's nerves on edge...or so Charlotte had informed him.

She was probably right. Not the best way to blend.

He dragged his eyes away from a very fine rear view and pinned them to the back of Charlotte's head. Time to think about anything except the fact he was lusting after a woman he could barely tolerate two days ago.

McKenzie's plan had worked a little too well for Novak's liking.

Frantically, he searched for a distraction from his wanton thoughts. The smell of gun oil. The feel of the rope burning between his gloved palms as he threw himself out of a helicopter. The rub of new boots on long runs. Angeletti taunting his ass. His snipers...

They'd settled into a rhythm, and he felt a whole lot better about their safety with an unmanned drone for air support and SWAT teams backing them up. Wasn't foolproof and certainly didn't show de-escalation in their response, but the press was being kept out of area and, so far, none of their new efforts had made it into the public's awareness. And he was quite happy to identify as many of these domestic terrorists as possible as long as they didn't present a direct threat to his men.

Charlotte turned and waited for him under the breezeway as he crossed the parking lot. She huddled deep into her suit jacket.

"You should have worn your winter coat." *Jesus.* He sounded like her father.

"I brought it with me. It's in the back of the Suburban."

"Want me to fetch it?" He stopped walking.

"I'm fine. We're nearly at the door." She smiled at him, her nose a little red due to the sharp wind coming off the Cascades. He clamped down on the desire to wrap a warming arm around her shoulders. At this rate, she'd be filing a harassment complaint before they reached the forty-eight-hour mark.

Inside the hospital, two people sat in the waiting room that was peacefully quiet and free of TV screens. It had a large fireplace at one end. The distinctly patterned chairs were a little busy for his taste, but the whole scene had a restful vibe he hadn't observed in many hospitals. He looked up at the signs to indicate the wards, but Charlotte was already cross-examining a nurse behind the admissions desk. The counter was positioned in front of an impressive display of wormy maple that clad an entire wall.

An aging security guard who looked bored to tears sat off to one side. Novak flashed the guy his badge and gave him a nod. The man straightened and scanned the waiting area as if reminded he had an important role here although maybe not right now.

Charlotte breezed past him. "Come on. Stop intimidating people."

He frowned and then caught up. "I don't intimidate people."

She snorted.

"I don't intimidate *you*."

She looked at him thoughtfully as a smile curled one side of her lips. A dimple flirted with her cheek. "You're right, you don't. But then I'm also an FBI Supervisory Special Agent and not that easy to intimidate."

He fought a snigger. Charlotte couldn't intimidate a kitten, although she had kicked that guy's ass yesterday. He would have loved to have seen that.

"How come you joined the FBI, anyway?" he asked.

They reached the elevator, and Charlotte pressed the button for the third floor. No one else was in the car.

"I wanted to help people." She shrugged.

"Why not become a shrink or a doctor if you were interested in psychology?"

"I considered it," she admitted, tying her hair back into a ponytail with relaxed, economical movements. "But I craved action too. I mean, having a clinic and patients is a noble endeavor, but I wanted to work on the sharp end. See if I could stop offenders before they committed crimes, or before they made them worse. That's how I ended up at CNU. What about you?"

The elevator arrived.

"I'll tell you later."

"I look forward to hearing it." Charlotte sent him a smile that made him distinctly uncomfortable. No way were they having *that* conversation this side of ever.

They arrived at the nurse's desk and before Charlotte could speak, he leaned over and gave the nurse his best smile.

"Here to see Federal Wildlife Officer Bob Jones?"

The woman's eyes glinted. "Are you a relative?"

He flashed his badge and deepened his smile. "We wanted to check on how he's doing."

"I'll go see. It'll be nice for him to have some visitors."

She meant for them to stay near the desk, but he and Charlotte ambled slowly in the direction she headed off in. He spotted the guard on the door—to keep the press away from the poor guy—and immediately knew where Bob Jones was.

The deputy stirred as they got closer. He came to his feet and checked their IDs thoroughly. Novak realized that the guard was positioned between the injured sheriff's deputy and the injured wildlife officer.

"How's the other guy doing?" He pointed at the sick man surrounded by a thousand Get Well cards and balloons.

"Lost his spleen and broke his wrist in two places. He's gonna make it though. He's a great guy."

Novak grimaced. It would be a long journey back to recovery.

The nurse came out of Bob Jones's room and gave them a small smile. "You can see him now. He's awake."

"Yes, ma'am."

Novak waved Charlotte ahead of him. There were cards here too, but not as many as next door. Jones wasn't married and had no kids, apparently.

He was sitting up in bed wearing an unbuttoned pajama top over a thick white bandage. He looked a hell of a lot better than the last time Novak had seen him.

"Officer Jones?" Charlotte asked.

The man in the bed looked her up and down. Novak didn't know if he was checking her out or naturally suspicious.

"I'm Supervisory Special Agent Charlotte Blood from the FBI and this here is SSA Payne Novak. We are both so glad to see you making such a fast recovery."

The man grunted and raised his voice to reach outside the room. "No thanks to the local sheriff's department. Left me to bleed out like a stuck pig."

Charlotte blinked.

The deputy out in the hallway didn't turn around but raised his voice to answer back. "Would have gotten away with it too, if it weren't for those pesky FBI agents."

Bob Jones barked out a laugh then gripped his chest as if in pain.

"No way was I stripping off naked to go get ya," the deputy added.

"Thank God," Jones replied.

"Actually, it was—" Charlotte began.

"Great you were moved out of the ICU so quickly. The surgeon must be happy with your progress." Novak spoke over Charlotte and winced a little at her annoyed expression, but he didn't want her to tell Bob Jones that he was the one who'd rescued him. He hadn't done it for glory.

"Yeah." Jones looked between the pair of them. "Bullet went straight through and missed all major blood vessels. Doc says a half centimeter left or right, and I'd never have survived."

"Well, I am very glad you are making such a full recovery." Charlotte beamed enthusiastically.

"I'm not saying it doesn't hurt." Bob Jones grumbled as he rubbed his chest. "Hurts like a *you know what*. But I'm damn grateful to the man who carried me out of there. Saved my life."

Charlotte opened her mouth, and Novak cut her off again. Hopefully, she'd get the message before he pissed her off for good.

"I'm sure whoever it was was simply doing his job and will be gratified to know you are recovering."

"Officer Jones." Charlotte gave Novak a broad smile, finally receiving the message. "We're wondering if you can tell us what happened on Wednesday morning?"

"I already gave a statement to an investigator."

"I understand." Charlotte sat close the bed, not touching Jones but somehow offering comfort with her presence. "I know it's difficult, but you might remember something else that might prove helpful."

Novak went over to stare out the window.

Jones scratched his head. "What do you want to know?"

"Talk me through what you remember."

"I got information about a cougar stalking someone up on Eagle Mountain."

"What time was that?" Charlotte asked, making a note in her book.

"I don't remember exactly. Maybe eight AM?"

"Was the call to your cell or your radio?"

He frowned at her. "Neither. Someone flagged me down when I arrived in the parking lot. A hiker who'd just come off the trail. Knocked on my window." He grimaced as he shifted position. "Told me a cougar had followed him for a few hundred yards and looked like it was ready to attack. Hiker scared it off by making a lot of noise and brandishing a walking stick. Didn't want to make an official report and refused to give his name. I decided to go look for any evidence he was telling the truth as opposed to jerking my chain. It was a potential problem with the camp being nearby."

Charlotte's voice rose. "Do you remember anything about this man at all? Any part of the license plate?"

Jones rubbed his eyebrow. "Car was a silver sedan with California plates. Younger fellow. Maybe twenty-five. Medium height, light build, brown hair."

Mr. Average.

Great.

Charlotte curbed her obvious excitement. "What happened then? Did you see him leave?"

Bob shook his head. "I don't remember. I went to check it out. Hiked up the path to the top of the ridge. I came to a clearing where I saw a young man acting furtively in the trees."

"Furtively?"

"Creeping about and bending over."

"And…" Charlotte encouraged.

"When I got a better look, I see him with his hand on the neck of a woman who was lying on the ground." Jones scratched his head. "I hollered at him to move away. He looked up and pulled a gun on me. Then he ran. I gave chase then, when I get to within sight of the walls, someone shot me."

"Did you fire your weapon then?" Novak asked.

Jones looked at him, eyes narrowed. "I did, but I didn't hit anything. I was already falling to the ground at that point." Jones let out a gusty sigh. "I must have passed out and then woke up again when that idiot Lasalle showed up with his damn posse for a shootout that was straight out of the Wild West. They was shooting everything that moved. I froze, which I guess is pretty cowardly."

"No one thinks you are a coward, Officer Jones. People are

relieved you survived," Charlotte assured him.

Bob Jones swallowed tightly. "I appreciate that. I think I passed out again after that. It got so cold, felt like I was in a meat locker. I thought I was dead until the FBI agent started dragging me out of there."

"It was an incredibly brave act by the agent involved," Charlotte said, turning to meet Novak's gaze.

He looked away and refrained from rolling his eyes. He hadn't been brave, he'd been doing something that was ingrained in his ideology. No man left behind. And she hadn't been so impressed at the time, otherwise, they wouldn't be stuck shadowing one another.

"I don't remember much else except waking up in the ICU after surgery."

"Did you recognize the young man in the woods?"

Bob Jones nodded. "Sure. I didn't know him personally, but I've seen him around. TJ Harrison."

Novak pulled up a picture of TJ on his cell from the DMV. "This him?"

"Yup," Bob Jones agreed. Shifting uncomfortably.

"You ever see the girl before?"

"Before that morning nope. I didn't recognize her."

"Did you touch the body?" Charlotte asked.

"I might have checked for a pulse real quick. It all happened so fast. I didn't want him to get away."

"You know anyone in the compound?"

Bob Jones tried to sit up, and Novak watched Charlotte help him adjust the pillows.

"In passing. Like I said, I've seen them around. Probably even shared a joke with some of them at the bar from time to time, but I wouldn't say I *know* anyone there."

"Tom Harrison says you shot at his son while he was running away," Novak said.

"Bullshit."

"It's easy to get confused in combat situations," Charlotte assured him. "But are you absolutely sure they fired first?"

Charlotte was correct. Joe Public expected picture perfect recollections of these events, not understanding how the brain worked during extreme situations.

"I wouldn't shoot someone in the back, even if he did murder an innocent woman." Jones's face was pasty white, and sweat began to gleam on his brow. He yawned widely. "Sorry. I can't believe how tired I feel."

"You've been a great help. We appreciate you taking the time to talk to us. Please continue to rest and recover." Charlotte patted the man's hand and stood to leave, placing her card on the bedside table. "Feel free to reach out if you remember anything else, Officer Jones. Even the smallest detail."

They said their goodbyes. When they were standing in the doorway, Jones said loudly, "I want to come to your headquarters and shake the hand of the man who saved my life."

"No problem." Novak nodded and hauled Charlotte away before she could give him away. He let go of her arm halfway down the corridor.

"Why didn't you admit it was you who carried him out of the woods and save the guy a trip?"

Because it was embarrassing? "Let him recover in peace."

"He'll find out eventually."

"Hopefully, I'll be long gone by then."

Charlotte looked up at him. Her eyes almost violet in the bright sunlit corridor. Her lips pressed together. "Hopefully, we both will be."

CHAPTER TWENTY-ONE

CHARLOTTE WAVED UP at the FBI techs who were fabricating the reconstruction of Harrison's fortress in a massive unused hangar at the secret military base northeast of Colville where they'd landed less than two full days ago. The structure was monstrous and looked like an Iron Age fort or something from a Mad Max set.

"Is it really that big beneath the surface?"

"According to the blueprints." Novak was walking quickly around the base. The whole thing was being constructed mainly of scaffolding and wood for the purposes of speed. "We have to assume Harrison modified it in some ways but not the basic layout. Outer walls are three feet thick, reinforced concrete."

"Well, that might be an issue," she said dryly.

Novak chuckled, and she felt that little shot of delight that she'd made him laugh again. He was so much more fun than she'd given him credit for in the beginning. It was almost as if he kept the lighter parts of his personality a secret. In the past, she'd only seen the domineering, tactical commander, but it wasn't like they spent time together outside of work, and they were usually on opposing sides of any argument.

They reached the model of what had been the secret tunnel, and guilt ate her up once more.

Novak pointed to it and raised his voice so the FBI techs could hear him. "Forget about this part. He demolished it with explosives."

One guy looked up. "What about using earth moving equipment to expose the entrance?"

"Perhaps. But the guy said he'd blow the lot if he sees or hears us approach, which pretty much rules out bulldozers."

"Well, fuck," the tech said. "What's the plan?"

Novak slid a glance at her as if uncertain of her reaction. "We're trying to figure out if he has explosives already in place or not."

Because if explosives weren't already in place, it might be preferable to launch a preemptive strike. Before Tom Harrison rigged the whole place to blow and killed everyone inside.

She shook her head. "I can't believe they'll sit by and let him wire the place."

Novak shrugged. "Maybe they don't know about the threat. Maybe he's bluffing. Or maybe they've all drunk the Kool Aid. End of days and all that. Kill themselves before the government does it for them and get ahead in the queue for the second coming of Christ."

Charlotte pressed her lips together. The idea of children being involved made her stomach churn even worse than normal. They'd hopefully obtain more information if they could move the drone closer to the action and pick up some valuable intel.

"Where'd he get the explosives?"

"Good question." Novak rolled his shoulders. She'd pulled on her down jacket, but he hadn't bothered and didn't appear cold. The guy must have antifreeze in his veins. "But a man like that, I bet he has plenty of connections for ordinance."

She and Novak moved through one section where the boards weren't properly installed yet. The upper story soared above them.

"According to the women who left the bunker, the main canteen area is over there." Novak pointed to the other side of the structure. He strode down the wooden corridors and pointed to empty doorways. "These rooms belong to the Harrison family. They have an entire third of the lower level to themselves, and no one else is supposed to go near their space. I bet that seeds a little resentment when there are almost forty people sharing the other living quarters."

"Especially when people get sick or babies start crying at night."

Novak grunted. "Why'd they all start arriving there anyway? Some sort of prophesy I don't know about?"

"I think it's more a case of economic hardship from what Agent Truman has been able to piece together." Charlotte didn't miss the narrowing of Novak's gaze when she mentioned the devilishly good-looking agent. *Interesting.* "First folks arrived on Harrison's doorstep during the housing crash. Apparently, they'd lost their homes and Harrison's late wife didn't have the heart to turn them away. I suspect that when Harrison started accepting people into his bunker, others decided to take advantage of the isolation and protection it offered."

"Looks like the act of charity might backfire."

They walked the entire circumference, then Novak hauled himself up onto the upper level without bothering with the ladder.

Charlotte allowed herself a moment of admiration for the sheer perfection of a man at the peak of physical condition.

She might be fit, but there was no way she could lift herself up using her fingertips. She spotted the closest ladder and climbed up to find Novak waiting for her at the top. He was grinning, a twinkle in his blue-green eyes making him look like a naughty schoolboy and almost irresistible.

Almost.

Her mouth went dry. Somehow, over the last two days, she had managed to become seriously attracted to this man. Whereas before she'd thought him gruff and uncommunicative, now she realized he was quiet and thoughtful but tended to wear a scowl as his default expression. And whereas she'd once considered him rugged, now she realized he was jacked.

She went to step away from the reaction she was having to him, but he grabbed her and pulled her against his chest.

"Careful," he warned.

She looked down and realized she'd almost stepped through a gap in the wood. She sucked in a quick breath, trying to ignore the palpitations of her heart at both the danger and the feel of his arms wrapped around her.

He shuffled them backwards until they were safely away from the edge. Her fingers clenched on his hips, gripping his jeans. She swallowed her fright as her heart continued to hammer. "Thank you."

She turned around in his arms and found herself staring up into eyes the color of the ocean, surrounded by spiky blond lashes. The world slowed.

Suddenly he pulled away.

"Christ. Sorry. I wasn't trying to manhandle you I just—"

Charlotte placed a hand on his chest, and he immediately stilled. "Novak. I understand why you grabbed me. Thank you for saving me from a nasty fall."

Novak nodded slowly.

She could feel his heart matching the frantic beat of hers beneath her palm. "Why do I make you so nervous all of a sudden?"

His expression grew incredulous. "I don't know what you're talking about."

Denial.

"Hmm." She stared at him a moment longer, but the sound of footsteps approaching on the lower level had her moving away from him, careful to watch her step this time. She continued to walk through the structure because she knew he'd want to explore every inch, and this might be his best opportunity.

She wanted more information. "I thought we were starting to like and admire one another, but I can see now you are actually only tolerating my company."

"What? That's bullshit. I like and admire you just fine."

Charlotte felt a twinge of guilt for deliberately mislabeling his emotions, but he was a straight up guy who wouldn't tolerate lies or inaccuracies.

"I don't scare you?"

"Scare me?" He looked as if she'd told him she planned to pluck his soul from his body with a toothpick. "Why would you scare me?"

She decided to soothe his agitation with a simple, "I'm glad."

So why was he nervous? Did he worry she was going to throw herself at him and cause a scene if he rejected her? Anger stirred. Well, she hadn't been the one sporting the screaming erection that morning. No, that had been all him.

That had been all him...

They walked around the rest of the structure with Novak pointing out a couple of possible inaccuracies to the techs as she turned over her and Novak's interactions during the last few days. She was pretty sure he was attracted to her but obviously didn't want to act on it. Or maybe he was worried about her reaction. After all, they were working together in a high intensity case, and if she objected to his advances—should he make any—then the rest of this incident would prove mortifying.

Same if he rejected her…

Not that she planned on acting on any of this craziness that had started to buzz between the two of them. It was probably a simple by-product of forced proximity.

He helped her down the ladder, and the fact he seemed worried about her even though she was perfectly capable of managing something as simple as a ladder stirred warm feelings inside her. But what if she'd misread everything, and he was working super hard at being polite and keeping everything professional between them?

What if he'd realized she was starting to lust after him…?

Mortifying.

He walked to another part of the hangar where two men were welding a smaller door inset into a massive steel structure that represented the entrance to the compound.

"You're not seriously contemplating going in the front door, are you?" she exclaimed.

Novak shrugged. "They certainly wouldn't expect it."

"Because it would take too long."

"Not if we got someone on the inside."

"Or persuaded one of the people already there to do it for us," she added. That could be the negotiator's job.

"That would be the perfect win-win scenario for me, followed by everyone filing out with their hands in the air and weapons left behind."

They headed back to the Suburban.

"There are babies in there, Novak," she said quietly.

He kept his eyes on the ground. "I know."

Silence strummed between them. The breeze had a cutting edge, and the dense gray of the clouds suggested Mother Nature was finally about to switch gears and deliver on her promises. A storm was forecast for tomorrow.

They climbed into their seats and buckled up. Charlotte was sure it was going to be another hair-raising trip back to the Command Center.

Novak slid on his sunglasses, turned the key, but the vehicle sat idling.

She looked at him to see what was up.

He grinned. "So, you *like* and *admire* me, huh?"

She smacked his arm, and he let out a belly laugh. Then he put the Chevy in drive and peeled across the tarmac.

Her other hand clenched around the edge of the seat. "Do you always drive like you're in a bank heist or are you trying to impress me?"

"Is it working?"

"No!"

Novak eased up on the gas. He flicked off the flashing lights and turned onto the main highway. "You're no fun."

She shook her head.

"Any other mention of the man Bob Jones reported seeing in the parking lot?" he asked, getting back to the case where they were both more comfortable.

Charlotte checked her cell. "No. McKenzie is having

someone go over all the interview statements again. I wish we'd known about that potential lead yesterday morning before we went to the campsite."

"We can re-interview and canvass the area for information, but I don't see him as a potential killer. I mean, he went out of his way to identify himself to law enforcement and then sent the officer up the same path to where his victim lay," said Novak.

"Killers have been known to do worse. I meant to check if there had been any other murdered women in the area or if Brenna showed any similarities nationally," she said.

"You think this death has links to a serial killer?"

"I know it isn't likely, but we can't assume anything, especially when our chief suspect is holed up in an impenetrable fortress."

"Nothing is impenetrable with enough time and enough explosive," Novak said quietly.

Charlotte shivered. "Seems weird that he threatened to blow the lot. Harrison obviously loves his son. If he bombs the place surely that'll kill him too?"

But they both knew of many instances where men decided they'd rather murder their children than lose control of their fate.

"Hey, what happened to Bob Jones's vehicle?" Charlotte didn't remember hearing anything about it.

"I expect someone from the US Fish & Wildlife Service drove it back to their office."

"Let's drop by and see if we can swab any contact DNA from it. Jones said the guy tapped his window."

"UNSUB might have been wearing gloves," Novak pointed out.

"And he might not have." Charlotte understood Novak wanted to check on his men, but there were no new developments. They would have heard if there had been. "We go past the office."

"Of course, we do."

"I have an evidence kit in my bag."

"Of course, you do."

His dry response made her laugh. She watched his hands clench around the steering wheel and felt an unexpected wave of lust.

"May as well make the most of our escape. I doubt it'll happen again any time soon," she said, concentrating on anything except the attraction she was feeling.

"You'll be able to go back to working with the negotiators tomorrow evening."

She couldn't read his reaction to that, although she knew he was eager to get back to his team.

"Yeah." She cleared her throat. "You won't have to put up with my spur of the moment suggestions any longer." She focused her sense of despondency on their lack of progress in the case and not on the fact that she couldn't figure out where she stood with him on a personal level. "Since negotiators haven't been able to effectively communicate with these people, the others haven't exactly needed my skills. Maybe we will be reduced to shouting via the bullhorn tomorrow like McKenzie originally suggested."

Novak shot her a long look, but his eyes were hidden behind his sunglasses. "Well, if anyone can make friends over a bullhorn, it'll be you, SSA Blood."

"Aw. Did you give me a compliment?"

"Don't get used to it." But the way his lip twitched suggested otherwise, and she hated the fact that it filled her with joy.

———————

THEY MADE IT to the US Fish and Wildlife Service office minutes before it was set to shut down for the weekend. Charlotte went to grab them both coffee and a sandwich. They'd somehow missed lunch again, and Novak was ready to gnaw off his own arm.

He headed in the front door and received a gimlet stare from the receptionist who clearly was on her way out. "FBI Supervisory Special Agent Payne Novak." He held up his creds. "Can I talk to whoever is in charge?"

The woman placed her jacket back on the chair and headed over to where two men were standing discussing something in the open-plan space behind her.

"This fella here's from the FBI. He wants to talk to the boss."

A tall, lanky man with thinning hair and a ready smile came over and lifted up the counter. "Come on through. What can we do for you?"

Novak showed his creds again. "I'm part of the team working on the Eagle Mountain incident. My colleague and I are hoping to get access to Bob Jones's vehicle."

The man braced his hands on his hips. "It's out in the parking lot. We drove it back Thursday morning. I can't tell you how grateful we are to you guys for getting him out of there. I hope they give the guy who rescued him a medal. Makes me sick to realize Bob was lying there suffering all that time."

"FBI is real grateful Bob was found alive too." Novak nodded firmly, grateful Charlotte wasn't around to try to out him.

Novak followed the guy to his office where he grabbed a bunch of keys off a hook near the door.

"Can I ask what it's regarding?" the FWO asked.

Novak grimaced. It was a long shot. "We visited Jones in the hospital. He gave us a possible lead on a potential suspect or witness who we want to identify and interview."

The man moved to the window and widened the white venetian blinds to peer outside. "This 'we' happen to be you and a pretty blonde?"

Novak moved around the desk to see Charlotte scoping out the vehicles in the lot. "Yep. She's with me."

And he liked that. He thought he'd be desperate to shake the other SSA by now, but in reality, the fact their seventy-two hours were up tomorrow evening filled him with a hollowness he hadn't expected and didn't like.

"It's the third truck along. How long is it gonna take?" The man glanced up at the large clock on the wall. "I'd hoped to go visit Bob myself before heading home for dinner with the family."

"Not long. We don't even need to look inside. Just want to swab the outside." Novak handed the keys back. "You don't need to hang around. We can take it from here."

"Appreciate that." The FWO grabbed his jacket. "I'll let you out the back as Doreen has probably already locked the front door." He lowered his voice. "And around here we don't like to upset Doreen."

Novak followed the man through the office and out the back door into the rear parking lot. Charlotte stood talking to the other wildlife officer Novak had seen when he'd first come inside. He didn't miss the way the guy was pulling in his stomach and puffing out his chest.

"That's Duane. He's a bit of a lady's man. Unlike Bob who tends to keep to himself and hasn't dated since his wife left him a couple years ago."

When Charlotte handed the eager-looking officer her card, Novak wasn't sure if it was for professional reasons or personal. Did she date? Did she have a boyfriend? Before he hadn't cared. Now he wanted to know everything about her and that irritated him.

CHAPTER TWENTY-TWO

NOVAK SAID GOOD night to the FWO chief and headed over to where Charlotte had peeled herself away from her admirer. Novak supplied a narrow-eyed stare when the guy looked as if he was about to approach Charlotte again.

"You're doing it again," Charlotte muttered.

"What?"

"Intimidating people."

"Sorry." He smiled, but it was cold and razor thin. "Did I interrupt something?"

He headed to the third truck along as Charlotte sucked in an angry breath. It was a white Ford with the Fish and Wildlife shield on both front doors.

"What is wrong with you?" She caught up to him real fast.

"Wrong with me?" He lowered his glasses as he checked out the driver-side window. Then he turned on the flashlight on his cell and angled it over the glass. "Nothing is wrong with me. I'm doing my job."

"So am I."

"Looked more like you were busy collecting the phone numbers of potential admirers." *Shit.* He hadn't meant to say it out loud.

She hissed out a breath. "Dammit, Payne Novak, I swear to god if we weren't in a public place, I would smack you around the head."

"*Tut, tut.* Violence isn't always the answer, Charlotte." He pointed to the window while she silently raged. "There's a smudge or two here that might be from human contact."

He tried to ignore the elusive scent of her. Whatever it was that drew him in and made him want to lean even closer and inhale.

She shoved him out of the way, and he was reminded he'd pissed her off again, big time.

But this was good. This was better than falling deeper and harder for the woman. He'd lied earlier when he'd told her she didn't scare him. She scared the ever-loving crap out of him, but not how she probably meant. He wasn't good with women. Not after being married to a woman who'd vowed to love him and then left him within a year, as if their wedding vows had been nothing more than a children's dress up party.

Also, the idea of starting something with a colleague that could explode all over his life was not a good idea. He needed to back away from the grenade, not jump on it.

Charlotte peered closer without touching the vehicle. "I don't see any distinguishable prints, not even a partial."

Novak grunted.

"It could belong to anyone and will only prove useful if we find the same DNA on Brenna's body, and the DNA is uploaded into some database. Even then, it's not proof, simply information."

"I understand the process," he said tersely. Jesus. She treated him like a such a moron sometimes. Just because he hadn't enjoyed being a field agent didn't mean he hadn't been good at it.

Charlotte's lips tightened as she took photographs with

her cell, then pulled two small vials from her pockets and stroked the tip of the sterile swab over the surface of a grease smudge before sealing it in a sterile container which she labeled with a Sharpie that she also had in her bag. Then she repeated the process with another smear. She capped that sample and put them both into her pocket.

She wagged the pen at him and moved closer. "You know, it's exhausting trying to keep up with your moods."

"My *moods*?"

"Hot one minute. Cold the next."

"Then don't bother trying." His voice was low and terse. He sounded mean. Good. He removed his sunglasses and gave her his flattest stare.

Charlotte rolled her eyes. "For some reason I keep giving you the benefit of the doubt, that you're not actually an ass. That you actually do like and respect me like you said back at the base."

Novak opened his mouth to respond, but she never gave him a chance to speak.

"But you're grumpy every time I talk to some guy—" She cut herself off and stared at him with eyes that kept growing bigger.

He folded his arms over his chest. "What?"

She held his stare, and he wished he had the strength to sever the connection.

"You're jealous," she said.

"Ha." He walked around her waving a hand in defeat as he strode back to the Suburban. "That's ridiculous."

"Ridiculous?"

"Nonsensical. I'm not jealous. You're delusional."

He got in the cab, and she opened the passenger door.

"Not delusional. Spot on. Oh my god. I've seen more than a few signs. Like when I talk to or about Truman, you scowl."

"That's my resting bitch face." He grabbed the coffee she'd purchased and left in the cup holder and took a slug.

"We've already established you're attracted to me."

The coffee spurted out. *Oh god.* She was talking about his hard-on that morning. He almost choked and grabbed a tissue to clean up the mess.

"You're an attractive woman. I'm not blind." He wasn't gonna blush because of an autonomic biological reaction. Fuck.

She strapped herself in and reached for her own cup as he went to pick up his sandwich. Their hands brushed. Both froze.

She didn't move her hand away, and he couldn't remove his. The connection felt both ephemeral and fragile and like something he wasn't equipped to deal with, was not trained for. He wanted to turn his fingers over and interlink them with hers. All the anger and embarrassment drained out of him. But the frustration built. Frustration that he wasn't the sort of guy a woman like Charlotte Blood would want.

"I'm not good with women, Charlotte."

"You make us sound like a subspecies," she said quietly.

"No. If anything, that's how you think of me. Like some Neanderthal with more muscles than brain cells."

She remained silent, which was a confirmation.

"It hurt, actually." God, next he was gonna be admitting he didn't like being judged by his looks alone and start freaking bawling. Like a fucking baby.

"I'm sorry. I was wrong," she said softly.

Emotions welled up inside him. Gratitude for her saying

that, envy that she could forgive so easily. Guilt that she was more honest than he would ever be because she was right. He was jealous as fuck. He was a selfish, jealous asshole, and he would die before he admitted any of it.

He forced himself not to stroke the silky skin on the back of her hand.

He wasn't good with women. He had his reasons. Not just an ex-wife who hadn't given a shit about him.

He forced himself to finish reaching for his sandwich and to move away from her warmth. He took another swig of coffee hoping to dislodge the rock stuck halfway down his gullet. Finally, he spoke. "You asked me earlier why I joined the FBI."

He thought at first she wasn't going to say anything. That maybe she knew it would be terrible and didn't want to know.

"Why?" she asked. Because, of course, she did. Charlotte did not run away from the tough questions.

"I need to fight the bad guys. I need to protect people who aren't strong enough to protect themselves."

The silence in the cab gained a life of its own until it vibrated like a tine on a tuning fork.

She finally broke the tension. "Who in your life wasn't strong enough to defend themselves?"

Her voice was soft. She was really good at listening, which was a shame, because he was really fucking awful at talking. Did he tell her the truth or hide behind a lie? But if there was one person he didn't want to lie to, right now, it was her.

"Me. I'm the one who wasn't strong enough to protect themselves. Not until I started to grow and push back. Not until I became more of a *Neanderthal.*" He growled the last word.

He didn't want to open a vein and bleed all over her so he put the car in drive and pulled out of the parking lot. Bumping back onto the main road. He stuffed his mouth full with another bite of the baguette that he was too emotionally constipated to say thank you for. Somehow he knew it wouldn't matter to Charlotte. That she'd understand. And he hated that. He chewed, the bread like sawdust in his mouth. Then he took another bite.

His trauma had been a long time ago, but the psychological harm was still a factor in how he lived his life. He *hated* that. Hated that his bitch of a mother still had a destructive impact, all these years later.

But he didn't want to talk about his childhood and was grateful Charlotte didn't seem to want to either. The hum of the pavement beneath the tires was the only sound he heard all the way back to the ranch.

———————————

TJ PACKED HIS father's rucksack and distributed gold and money evenly between them to help disperse the weight and in case one of the packs was lost. He added the passports, birth certificates, his parents' wedding certificate, his mother's death certificate.

He ran the tip of his index finger over the passport photograph of his mom. The family had driven to Alaska once because his dad had wanted to visit his parents. They'd died the next year, and TJ didn't really remember them.

Considering their current notoriety, TJ doubted passports would be much use, but he did as his father asked and packed them carefully in a plastic envelope.

He was glad his mom wasn't still suffering but wished they could go back in time, wished that they'd taken her to the hospital despite her objections. That he could have one more day with her walking through the forest, maybe introduce her to Kayla—assuming Kayla was still alive.

He clenched his jaw. He didn't even have a photograph of Kayla, although she'd taken some of him with her phone.

He'd find her. His father had connections.

They'd get out of here together and figure it out. No one else needed to get hurt.

Once he'd finished packing, he began pacing the apartment.

Being idle drove him crazy, so he pulled out all the flashlights and spare batteries, assembled all the matches and candles in their quarters and put them on the kitchen table, ready for action.

It was water that would provide the biggest obstacle. Their home was fed via a natural spring, but if the authorities diverted it or somehow contaminated it, they'd struggle. He knew the others had filled a massive plastic tank they had in case of nuclear war, but it wouldn't last forever. At some point people would surrender or die.

TJ filled several large vessels from the tap. Set full buckets near the toilets. After ten minutes, pans and jugs filled every surface in the kitchen, full of pure, life-saving water.

Then he surveyed and stacked the dry goods and went through the freezers. Although they ate lunch with everyone else in the cafeteria, they usually cooked dinner for themselves here in their quarters. TJ threw a deer stew in the oven and then lay on the couch, already tired of waiting.

He did not want anyone suffering on his account. But the authorities were also after the people who'd shot at them, so even if he gave himself up, it wouldn't be the end of this nightmare. Thankfully, no one had died in the exchange of gunfire so the punishment shouldn't be too harsh if they gave themselves up. They might even be acquitted.

And, assuming the world didn't come to an end, the men would be back with their families in a couple years.

Whoever killed Brenna Longie though, they'd serve a lot longer and would deserve every second. Surely the cops would require proof rather than the say-so of one guy who'd simply seen him checking a prone woman's pulse and jumped to a million conclusions? Maybe if there were other suspects the Feds wouldn't be so focused on him?

He sat up suddenly.

Why had Malcolm been skulking in the dark corridor? There was no way he could have predicted TJ was about to leave, which meant he'd heard him approaching and hid in the dark. But why had he been there in the first place?

Malcolm knew about the secret tunnel. Obviously. His father had suggested Malcolm had been sneaking outside too. Where had he been going? What had he been doing?

Had *he* killed Brenna? Had he thought Brenna was Kayla and killed her because Malcolm knew Kayla was TJ's girl-friend?

He needed to find out. One way would be to watch the surveillance tapes, but it would be impossible to do that without alerting Malcolm or one of his cronies. The other option would be to search Malcolm's room…

TJ checked the time and climbed off the couch. Most of the people who lived here ate dinner around five, and Malcolm rarely skipped a meal. TJ's fingers curled around the spare keys to the apartment that had also been in the safe. Time to see what the hell was going on.

CHAPTER TWENTY-THREE

C HARLOTTE NEEDED TIME alone to think, but she wasn't likely to get it any time soon judging from the fact as they pulled up to the ranch, McKenzie stood waiting for them on the porch looking like a bad omen. It made her feel raw and put upon that the only solitude she'd had recently was when she went to the bathroom, and she didn't even get a lot of that right now.

She wanted to mull over what Novak had said to her. All of it. That he found her attractive but dismissed it as irrelevant. It was *not* irrelevant. Not even a little bit.

That he'd needed protection from someone in his life when he'd been smaller and more vulnerable. How small? How vulnerable? Why had he needed protection? From whom? What had happened? Why had no one stepped in?

Had she been insensitive, treated him poorly? Maybe she had in the beginning, but he'd earned it.

Hadn't he?

Or had she completely misread those smirks he used to send her? Seen condescension where instead there had been only disguised male interest?

McKenzie looked impatient as they hit the bottom step.

"Kayla's fever broke. She just woke up."

Charlotte snapped her attention away from her personal

issues and back onto her job where it needed to stay. People were counting on her. Most of them didn't even know it.

"Has she spoken to anyone?"

McKenzie shook his head. "Nurse was helping her bathe and then getting her to eat some soup. I want you to talk to her."

"Did we find out anything about the family yet?"

McKenzie tilted his head. "I'll brief you after you talk to her, but we don't know much."

"Going in blind," she said. "Got it."

"What about me?" Novak asked.

Charlotte knew he was itching to get rid of her and get back to his men. He'd opened himself up, and he'd retreat from that level of vulnerability. Even "evolved" guys did not like to reveal their weak spots, and she wasn't sure she'd classify Novak as evolved.

And she *still* wasn't being fair.

"Both of you. Together. When I said seventy-two hours, I meant it." McKenzie led the way inside the ranch house. "Did Bob Jones have anything new to add?"

They trailed into the kitchen after him. A massive vat of chili bubbled on the stove, the aroma filling the steamy air.

"The cougar sighting was reported by the man who approached him in the parking lot below the hiking trail."

"So you said on the phone. Did he get a name or any useful details?"

She shook her head. "No. But we took DNA swabs off the side window of his work vehicle." She pulled the samples out of her pocket and handed them over. "He told us the guy tapped on the window and then drove off in a silver sedan. Might be worthless, but you never know."

"Good work."

She rolled her shoulders. "Do we tell Kayla about Brenna?"

McKenzie pressed his lips together, clearly deciding. "Question her first. Tell her Brenna is dead after you think she's told you everything she knows and check her reaction."

Great. A tactical death notice. The thought made the chicken sandwich she'd eaten earlier churn in her stomach.

She nodded and trailed over to the stairs, aware of Novak in her shadow, but not wanting to talk to him when she needed to concentrate on how to approach Kayla. He stayed silent, and she was grateful he was giving her space. He caught her arm when they reached the hallway outside their room.

"I can wait outside the door if you'd prefer."

"McKenzie said both of us." Charlotte stared into his chest.

"Fuck McKenzie," he muttered vehemently.

Charlotte laughed. "Do you really want to test his resolve when we only have twenty-seven hours to go?"

"I don't think Kayla is gonna feel comfortable with me in the room."

"Just don't scowl at her." Charlotte raised her eyes to meet his doubtful gaze. She smiled up at him then, wishing she hadn't started to like him quite so much. It had been easier, before, when all she'd seen was the operator, not the man. "And maybe sit close to the door. And don't react to anything she says."

"Got it."

Charlotte carried on walking and nodded to the agent guarding the door. "Take a break and grab some food. One of us will find you when we're done."

She tapped on the door and a nurse opened up. The woman was young, short, and built like a tank. "Kayla managed to eat some soup and walk to the bathroom and back. I think she's feeling a lot better, but she's going to tire easily. I'll come back in the morning for a final check, but now it's a case of staying hydrated, eating well and getting lots of rest and taking her pills."

The nurse grabbed her coat. "I need to get home. Bye, Kayla. See you tomorrow."

Charlotte blinked at the assertive energy the nurse took with her—impressive in a den of FBI agents.

Kayla's eyes darted nervously between Charlotte and Novak. As Charlotte approached the bed, Kayla sat up and drew her knees toward her chest, dragging the covers over her as if she were cold, even though the room was warm.

"Hi, Kayla. My name is Charlotte Blood, and this here is Payne Novak. We're with the FBI."

"I don't understand." Kayla's voice was scratchy and thin. "Why am I here? Where's Brenna?" Her fingers gripped the bedcovers tightly.

"You were sick. We brought you back here to recover."

Kayla's eyes went a little wild. "I don't understand why the *FBI* would do that?"

Charlotte drew a hardback chair to the side of the bed. She heard the creak of wood as Novak settled into a similar seat near the door. "Mainly because you were *very* sick, and we *really* wanted to talk to you."

Kayla swallowed. She looked unsure but was listening.

"Can you tell us the last thing you remember before you got ill? Did you go away for Thanksgiving?"

"We'd planned to for a few days. Maybe visit Monument Valley or somewhere. Then I got sick so we didn't go anywhere."

"Uh huh."

Kayla relaxed a little and leaned back against the pillows next to the headboard. "Brenna wanted to pack up and head farther south before the snow came, but I wasn't ready to leave yet. But I didn't mind going for a few days."

Kayla reached for her water, and Charlotte passed it to her.

"Where's Brenna? Is she okay?"

Negotiators generally only lied when the next step was a tactical solution. "I have some questions I need to ask you. Do you feel comfortable talking to me?"

"Why? What about?" Kayla shrugged her shoulders and laughed nervously. "Sure. Unless you're planning to arrest me."

"I'm not planning to arrest you." Didn't mean it wouldn't happen if Charlotte found evidence of a crime, but she didn't think Kayla was a serious suspect in this case. No one could fake that kind of fever. "Are you two related? I mean you have different last names, but you look so alike."

Kayla's bottom lip wobbled. "People always think we're sisters. I guess that's kind of what drew us together at school."

"This was back in Pennsylvania, right? How come the two of you ended up in a tent on a mountain in Washington State?"

"We both love animals and nature. We realized that the only real way to fight for conservation was on the ground. We heard about the protesters here and decided to join them."

Charlotte tilted her head to one side and flashed her brows in a universal facial expression that built rapport. "Not many people have the determination to live their principles that way."

"Complacency isn't enough anymore. If we don't protect the planet, millions of people are going to die or be displaced. Billions of animals have already died. Wars will be fought over water. Rather than figuring out alternative fuels or investing in desalination facilities or finding ways to scrub carbon dioxide from the atmosphere, corporations are chasing profit. It's business as usual for the rich, while the world burns."

"It takes a special person to stand up to the machine."

Kayla eyed her sideways. "Well, if the FBI has a database of environmentalists then that makes you part of the machine."

"We only keep databases on criminals. Being an activist is not illegal as long as people follow the law."

Kayla let out a long sigh. "Which is okay in principle, except when the corporations don't follow the rules, they get some measly fine or a slap on the hand. It's like there're different rules depending on who you are, or who your daddy is."

"The FBI is a big supporter of the law being applied equally to everyone. No one should be above the law." Charlotte sighed too. "I know that's not always how it appears." The justice system was a complicated beast and subject to political corruption and manipulation. "How do you support yourself?"

Kayla rubbed at her forehead as if she were tired. Charlotte hated this part of her job. But while she might not consider Kayla a serious suspect, it was possible that she had been involved with murdering her best friend, or conspired with someone else, to do the deed. No one could be eliminated until they figured out the truth.

"I had some money put aside, and Brenna sells her photographs on the web. That's why she wanted to move on. New places, new images. Also, she hates the cold."

That was the second time someone had mentioned Brenna liked taking photographs. Where was the camera? Charlotte made a mental note to ask if it was one of the items recovered from the tent or car. She hadn't seen it, but it didn't mean that it wasn't there.

"She's a good photographer?"

Kayla nodded fervently.

"So what about you? What do you like to do when you're not actively protesting and trying to save the world?"

Kayla gave her a quizzical smile. "Why do you want to know?"

She looked so small and alone in the big bed and seemed to have no idea about what she'd lost. Charlotte wanted to reach out and give the girl a hug.

"I remember when I was eighteen," she said instead. "I spent a lot of time either working or meeting friends or going to the movies with boyfriends, but there's not a lot of those things in this remote part of Washington State."

Something flashed in Kayla's eyes. "I like to draw. I write and read a lot of books. I have a boyfriend." She looked away, and her fingers played with a loose cotton thread she'd found on the duvet cover.

"TJ?"

Kayla's head whipped around. "How do you know about him?"

"You said his name to SSA Novak when he carried you out of your tent and brought you here for treatment."

Kayla's eyes shifted to Novak over Charlotte's shoulder. "I didn't remember how I got here. Thanks for helping me."

Charlotte glanced at Novak. He nodded to Kayla and gave Charlotte a small closed-lip smile. No more resting grumpy face.

Charlotte waited patiently, employing silence as a tool.

"TJ is my boyfriend, but it's complicated."

Charlotte laughed. "Isn't it always." She felt Novak's eyes burning holes in her back.

Kayla reached for her water again, and Charlotte helped her.

"How did you two meet?"

"There are a breeding pair of Northern Spotted Owls up in the forest near where he lives. Brenna took a bunch of photographs to sell, but I liked to sit and sketch them, which took longer. One day I saw another person watching them too."

"You weren't scared? Alone in the woods with a strange man nearby?"

Kayla gave her a look. "Of course, I was nervous. But he didn't approach me that first day. Nor the second. He gave me a nod of acknowledgement but kept his distance. Eventually I was curious enough to walk over to where he sat and strike up a conversation."

Kayla's fingers continued to play in a restless motion with the bedspread. "He offered to show me some of his favorite spots in the mountains, and we started going for hikes. Then he said he couldn't get away every day so we made a date to meet up once a week."

"Once a week?" Charlotte mirrored.

"Every Wednesday morning. He's gonna wonder where I was this week."

So that explained why TJ was out there on the mountain.

Kayla glanced anxiously over to the window. "Did it snow yet?" She sounded a little desperate. "TJ said he didn't think I'd be able to hike up the mountain once the snows came. That it would be too deep and too dangerous." Her lips downturned. "He doesn't have a cell phone. He has an email address but…"

But it wasn't quite enough to satisfy the craving of an amorous teenage heart in the golden age of technology. The FBI already knew his email address. The tech people had hacked the server at the compound.

"It hasn't snowed yet. Threatens to every day but hasn't delivered yet. What does Brenna think of TJ?" Charlotte asked.

Kayla lay back against the pillows, tiredness pinching the corners of her eyes.

"Brenna hasn't met him properly, but she thinks I'm stupid to waste my time hanging around here for a guy. It's not like that though. He's not like that."

Charlotte frowned. "Like what?"

"He's not a user." Kayla inhaled sharply. "Brenna, well she has terrible taste in guys and thinks all men suck. But I keep saying to her that not everyone is like Simon."

"Simon?"

"Her most recent ex-boyfriend." Kayla hunched her shoulders. "He's an abusive asshole. And then there's this one guy in camp who's sniffing after her. She thinks I haven't noticed the way he flirts with her."

"What's his name?"

"Alan Kennedy. Some professor." Kayla's expression became a little petulant.

Funny. Charlotte had read Novak's 302 and, from what he'd written, the professor had acted like he'd barely known the two women.

"Don't tell her I was talking about her. God, why is the FBI interested in Brenna's crappy love life?"

"We all make mistakes when it comes to our love life." Again she felt Novak's interest in her words.

I'm not good with women, Charlotte.

She tried to imagine Novak in a relationship. She couldn't fit him into all the places in her life, like grocery shopping or long romantic walks while holding hands. But she could visualize him in terms of non-stop sexual escapades. Her cheeks heated. Obviously, she suffered from an overactive imagination, which was apparently the side product of a starvation diet.

Again, she pushed the thoughts away. "Did you ever visit TJ's home?"

Kayla frowned, clearly uneasy now. "I saw it from a distance. Crazy looking bunker in the middle of nowhere. I never went inside. TJ said his father wouldn't approve of him seeing me. Why do you ask?" Kayla's lips wobbled again.

The fact she was emotionally vulnerable made Charlotte feel like crap, but she pressed on. She had a job to do. "What are you and TJ planning to do once the snow falls?"

Kayla looked miserable. "He talked about coming with us once or twice."

Charlotte forced a smile. "How'd Brenna feel about that?"

Kayla frowned.

Charlotte inwardly winced. She'd used past tense, but maybe Kayla wouldn't pick up on the difference or she'd interpret it more innocently.

"I doubt he'll do it."

"If he did?"

Kayla shrugged. "I didn't bring it up with her yet. She won't like it. She likes it being the two of us when we travel." She stared down at her covered knees. "She was raped once.

241

No one else believed her except me. It was at a party she shouldn't have even been at and someone slipped something into her drink." Kayla wiped a tear that escaped. "Bunch of guys took turns with her and posted it online. Brenna was devastated. Girls called her a slut. Boys called her a whore. She dropped out of school and then started a cycle of relationships with shitty guys like Simon. Leaving Pennsylvania was the best thing we ever did, but I don't think she likes the idea of me being with anyone, you know?"

"She's protective of you." Charlotte nodded as a sense of grief swept over her. Brenna Longie had suffered some hard knocks in her life. Setbacks and situations that would have driven many to self-medicate on drink and drugs as well as make other poor choices. The fact she'd never caught a break... it was heart-wrenching.

Had Brenna fought with TJ about Kayla? Had Kayla's boyfriend killed her best friend?

"Where's Brenna? Is she still at the campsite?" Kayla moved as if to climb out of bed. "I'm feeling a lot better now. Maybe someone could give me a ride back?"

She was talking fast as if her brain had finally recognized something seriously bad must have happened. Like she said, the FBI wasn't interested in people's love lives, not if they were adults above the age of consent.

Charlotte took Kayla's hand. "The campsite has been dismantled, and most people have left. I'm afraid I have something terrible to tell you."

There was no easy way to say this. No gentle easing into the subject matter. "Brenna died."

Kayla pulled back her hand as if she'd been bitten. Her eyes filled. "I don't understand. How could she die? Did she get sick too?"

Her eyes shot between Charlotte and Novak. He stood.

Charlotte shook her head. "No. She was found dead on Eagle Mountain not far from where TJ lives."

Kayla's mouth curved in grief. "She can't be dead. What did she die of?"

It would have been so much easier to tell Kayla that Brenna had suffered a heart attack or been attacked by a cougar.

"The Medical Examiner believes Brenna suffered some sort of blunt force trauma to the skull."

Charlotte watched Kayla's expression crumple. A noise started emitting from her throat. A deep keening sound that immersed Charlotte straight into the other girl's wretched grief.

"I am so sorry, Kayla. I am so very sorry." She forced her emotion to the side as she tried to comfort the other woman, but Kayla turned away from her.

"Leave me alone. Leave me alone!"

Charlotte nodded. She understood. This was not the time to prod at the open wound or ask if Kayla thought TJ was capable of killing her friend.

"I'm so very sorry for your loss. If you want to talk to me or Novak," she caught the way his eyes widened in alarm, "tell the agent at the door. We'll come straight away."

Kayla turned away from them, curled on her side into a ball. Sobs shook her small frame.

Charlotte walked out of the room and closed her eyes.

"I'll go track down the guard. Tell him we're done here," Novak said quietly.

Charlotte nodded, bracing a hand against the wall as he walked away. She straightened when she heard people return.

"Well, that sucked," Novak muttered as she led the way back to McKenzie.

Charlotte's eyes suddenly flooded with tears, and she needed a moment to find her usual professionalism. As they passed their room, she took the opportunity to reach for the door handle and duck inside. "I need to grab a charging cable for my phone. I'll be right down."

She quickly shut the door and stood by the window looking out into the darkness. Sadness welled up. She heard the door open and close and forced herself to say as normally as possible, "You don't need to wait. I'll be right down." She needed five minutes to get herself together. Five minutes alone so she could move on and do her job or whatever version of it McKenzie had settled on.

A moment later, strong arms wrapped around her waist and tugged her against a strong male chest. A chin rested on her shoulder.

His comforting her was like a hug for her soul. She wished he wasn't here to witness her distress, but at least he wasn't giving her hell. She squeezed his wrists in acknowledgment of the quiet solace he was offering. It helped.

"I keep thinking about that poor girl who died. All the terrible things that she'd overcome to get here. All the horror. Only to die on the mountain."

Novak's arms tightened further.

Emotions that had been building up for some time wanted to come unstoppered, but she couldn't afford to break down. Usually she was better able to distance herself, but fatigue and the pressure were getting to her, the emotional toll of other people's grief wearing away her mental barriers.

Novak spun her slowly around until he was cradling her

against his chest. "She deserved better."

Charlotte nodded. Life could be cruel and turn on a dime. She knew that better than most.

She looked up at the dark shadows that coated Novak's face. There was enough light under the crack beneath the door that she could make out his concerned expression.

"You gonna be okay?" he asked gruffly. And even though he held her in his arms, he hadn't crossed that line. He was giving her comfort and she knew if she pulled away, he would let her go.

She didn't want him to let her go.

Life was too damn precarious not to take a risk now and then.

She ran her palm against his sandpapery cheek. "I thought you said you weren't good with women, Novak."

And then she kissed him. Giving him time to run, then nibbling his lips, drawing out his response. Telling him she was interested in him if he was interested in her. That, whatever this thing was between them, it wasn't one-sided.

NOVAK KNEW THAT comforting Charlotte was probably not a good idea, but he had never imagined the danger would be from her kissing him. It was so unexpected but so welcome, he wanted to dive in so deep and fast she'd end up naked and against a wall with him inside her in twenty seconds flat.

Instead, he closed his eyes and savored the touch of her lips against his. Held back for a few seconds to enjoy the sensation of being kissed. The soft drag of her lips catching his in tender supplication.

There wasn't a lot of tenderness in Novak's life.

Dedication, hard work, sweat, grit, blood and pain. No gentleness.

Sensing she might be about to pull away, he finally allowed himself to kiss her back. He started in kind. Small sips of connection. A sensory exploration of the softness of her lips. Her hand slipped up into his hair, and he took that as permission for more.

He angled his mouth across hers, and she opened willingly, tangling her tongue with his, absorbing him. He wished he could capture the feeling in a bottle and keep it with him forever. That silky volcanic heat. The sharp edge of teeth, the sweep of her tongue into his mouth.

His pulse crackled along his veins. His hand found its way to her breast, molding the cotton of her shirt over the perfect handful of flesh. He reveled in the hard press of her nipple against his palm.

Blood headed south, and his dick was so hard he was in danger of passing out. She brushed against him and holy shit, that felt better than the past five years of his sex life.

He broke away, panting.

He was in big trouble here.

"Damn." She shifted, pushing away from him.

And here it came. The regret. The "what the hell were you doing" and "that was a mistake."

"We better go report to McKenzie before he comes crashing in here looking for us and finds me all over you."

"I was all over you too." His voice was rough. It did that a lot around Charlotte. Like his base instincts upped the testosterone in his veins and thickened his vocal cords.

She straightened her shirt. "I noticed."

What did that mean?

She walked to the door, and he stood like a fool wondering if she was going to pretend like this never happened. Or maybe it didn't mean that much to her. Hell, maybe she made out with all the guys she worked with. The thought tore through his mind with a burst of rage.

Perhaps she was right about the jealousy thing…

She stood near the door and opened it a crack, enough he could see her face. She kept her voice low. "It's probably better if we don't mention this to anyone."

He stiffened. "Who exactly do you think I'm going to tell?"

She blinked, clearly surprised by his pissy attitude. "Right. I simply meant—"

"Forget it. I know what you meant." He turned away, ashamed at his surliness when she was always Miss Sunshine. But did she really think he was going to go running to the guys bragging he'd kissed the hot negotiator he'd been forced to partner up with?

That wasn't who he was.

But she didn't know that…

She didn't know that he'd started to have *feelings* for her. Feelings he knew she wouldn't reciprocate because, at their core, they were both so fundamentally different. Feelings that would make working together damned uncomfortable for both of them if she found out about them. He would not make her uncomfortable, but he could maybe explain that he respected her. That he liked her.

"Charlotte…"

But the sound of the door catching told him it was already too late.

CHAPTER TWENTY-FOUR

TJ STRODE ALONG the corridor and nodded as if nothing was wrong to one of the women who was heading down the stairs to deliver a tray of food to the surveillance room.

"Hi, Tara. How you doing?"

She smiled back at him, perhaps unaware he'd been confined to his room earlier.

He kept walking purposefully.

Malcolm had finagled one of the best rooms, not counting the Harrisons' suite. The old man who'd stayed there before had died peacefully in his sleep not long after Malcolm arrived. Malcolm had claimed the space by virtue of being TJ's mom's brother, although she'd never been particularly fond of the guy.

TJ didn't hesitate. He inserted the master key into the lock, turned it and ducked inside and closed the door softly behind him. It was dark, so rather than put on the overhead light, he pulled a flashlight from his pocket and swept the beam around the room.

The bed was empty so Malcolm was probably eating dinner.

TJ started with the bedside table. There was a Bible. A glass of water with scum around the rim. In the cupboard he found a pile of well-worn porn magazines. *Ew.* TJ slammed the door closed and tried to stop his stomach from turning over by pressing down hard on his abdomen.

He scanned the room. Headed to the modest gun cabinet. Inside was the usual array of rifles, shotguns, four pistols, boxes and boxes of various sized ammunition. His dad had set up a way for people to make their own lead shot, but Malcolm obviously preferred manufactured varieties. TJ checked the top shelf, but there was nothing.

Shoot, TJ didn't even know what he was looking for.

He headed over to the small kitchenette that contained a microwave, small refrigerator, and sink. TJ looked in the fridge. Lots of beer but little else. In the freezer were some small plastic wrapped packages of white powder. TJ picked one up and twirled it in his fingers. Then he put it down fast, slamming the icebox closed. TJ didn't know much about the outside world, but he knew those packages contained narcotics. If his dad discovered Malcolm had those drugs in his home, he would toss him out the front door, siege or no siege.

TJ went through the few cupboards quickly, running his hand underneath the drawers and countertops the way he'd seen in spy movies.

Nothing except a splinter in the middle of his index finger.

His uncle had a table pushed against one wall serving as a desk. A laptop sat there, and TJ opened the lid, surprised when the screen flicked to life but disappointed it was password protected. TJ flipped the lid back down. He checked out the bathroom, including the cistern, but there wasn't anything hidden there. He went back into the bedroom and scanned the area, but there was nothing he could see that would point to Malcolm being a killer. The sound of footsteps in the corridor alerted TJ to someone's approach, and he desperately searched for somewhere to hide his six-foot-plus frame. He moved the bedcovers and saw there was enough space for him to squeeze beneath the bed. He'd scarcely shuffled under when the door opened, and the light flared on. Malcolm's voice echoed off the bare concrete walls.

"Put a guard on the kitchen area if people can't be trusted not to ration themselves. Make sure the little brats only take half portions."

Whoever Malcolm was talking to mumbled a response, and Malcolm slammed the door shut on him. TJ did a quick check on his body parts to make sure his feet weren't sticking out the end. They weren't. Dust made his nose tingle, and he concentrated on not sneezing.

Malcolm was bitching to himself but not loud enough for TJ to make out what he was saying. TJ traced the man's position using sound as the bed covers hung over the side of the bed, shielding him from view.

He heard the fridge door slam and a tapping noise followed by two hard snorts and a long sniff.

The drugs.

TJ had had no idea Malcolm was an addict. Where'd he get his supply? No wonder he was desperate to end this siege with the authorities. What happened once the asshole ran out? What happened if he was detained?

Malcolm threw himself down on the bed, and TJ had to turn his face to the side to stop his nose getting broken. He blinked. An expensive camera lay under the bed.

Malcolm did not strike him as an artistic type. Not even a little bit.

The man above him shifted, and TJ said a silent prayer

that the guy didn't pull out a magazine and jack off. It was one thing to know he did it, another entirely to be an unwitting witness.

A knock sounded at the door.

"Can't a man get a few hours' sleep around here?" Malcolm yelled.

"Sorry, boss."

Boss?

"One of the generators isn't working properly. I tried to fix it…"

Malcolm hauled himself off the bed. "Don't put your filthy maws on it!"

One thing his uncle was good at was repairing anything mechanical. "I'm coming."

The man broke wind and then crossed to the bathroom, and TJ heard him taking a piss. The door opened, the overhead light flicked off, and the door closed. TJ breathed out a sigh of relief. He counted to ten then wriggled out from beneath the bed. At the last moment, he grabbed hold of the camera strap and dragged it toward him. As he did so, something glinted in the beam of his flashlight.

What was that? He groped around in the filthy carpet, and his fingers closed around a gold coin. TJ turned it over a few times. It looked the gold coins he and his dad had bought from the US mint.

After a few moments, TJ tossed it back under the bed. He wasn't a thief.

The weight of the camera over his shoulder mocked him, but TJ only wanted to take a look, then he'd bring it back. Malcolm would never even know it was missing.

———————

NOVAK WAITED FOR Charlotte in the hallway outside the bathroom, needing to clear the air before they got back to work. People's lives depended on them not fucking this up. Their careers depended on it too.

McKenzie found him. "Glad you're taking 'glued at the hip' to heart."

Novak rolled his eyes. McKenzie had no idea how desperate Novak was to be *right there* with Charlotte.

"Don't you think it's a little extreme?" he asked.

"When I arrived, you two were ready to get in the ring and go ten rounds. My solution made you work past your differences quickly. I wouldn't have done it if I hadn't wanted you both on the team, but I was serious about sending you home. I need a team that's cohesive, not divisive."

Novak grunted. McKenzie's decision had consequences none of them had anticipated.

He heard the toilet flush and it startled him.

"We should move." Novak started herding McKenzie down the stairs even though his boss was also a big guy. He didn't care if it annoyed him or not. He didn't want to blindside Charlotte. "I don't want to look like a stalker."

McKenzie nodded. "Good point. Let's grab some food and debrief at the Command Center afterwards."

Novak was itching to get back to his men, but he knew there were no real updates. They were still in a holding pattern. Sniper teams and SWAT had rotated again, and those not on duty were getting some rest.

Novak was worried about the weather. A winter storm was forecast for tomorrow. While they trained in winter conditions, he would not risk HRT lives if a blizzard blew in. They had the technology to watch the compound, although even that could be disrupted by the adverse weather conditions. He wasn't happy about it, but at some point, they might have to withdraw and wait out the storm.

He was scooping chili into a bowl when Charlotte appeared in the doorway. He prepared another serving while McKenzie hunted for clean cutlery.

They kept conversation to a low hum as the cook bustled around, tidying away things and prepping for breakfast. Novak scowled at the pot of oatmeal she had bubbling on the stove. He definitely preferred the bacon option.

Charlotte had applied some makeup and lipstick, and no one would know she'd kissed the fuck out of him a few minutes ago.

No one except him.

When they were done, they cleared the dirty dishes into the next load of the industrial-sized dishwasher and headed outside into the frigid night. Thankfully, Charlotte had remembered to grab her jacket this time.

"You aren't cold?" she asked him as they both ducked their faces out of the wind.

Was she kidding? His heart rate was still revved up with nowhere to go. He was grateful he wasn't sporting wood.

"I'm fine."

They went inside the Command Center. Charlotte hurried over to the negotiators he didn't know. They looked bored shitless. The one woman was cleaning her gun.

When it was obvious nothing had changed, they stepped toward the other side of the screen. Charlotte kept throwing him uncertain glances, and he remembered her telling him earlier that she didn't like him blowing hot and cold all the time. At the time he hadn't understood, but now he realized he'd snapped at her in the bedroom seconds after comforting and kissing the hell out of her. He was an asshole. He stopped her before they went around the corner to speak to McKenzie.

"Charlotte, I'm sorry. I shouldn't have—" He opened his mouth to explain further, but McKenzie yelled, "Novak, Blood, get in here!"

Rather than clearing the air, if anything, his apology appeared to make her angry.

They didn't have time to sort this out. They hurried around the corner into the space McKenzie had commandeered. Agent Truman smiled at Charlotte and Novak breathed in deeply through his nose. He was not jealous of the fucker.

Nope. No.

Liar.

"You'll want to hear this. We received an ID on one of the men we isolated in the video."

Another agent had two images open on a laptop. One was a wanted poster. Beside it was a still from the drone footage they'd taken that morning.

The wanted poster was for a man called Mark Roberts.

"Truman asked the women who left the bunker to identify this man for him, and they named him as Malcolm Resnick." McKenzie pulled up an old DMV picture of a much younger man with no mustache and a lot more hair.

"Which identity is the real one?" Charlotte asked, leaning forward.

"Malcolm Robert Resnick is the name of Tom Harrison's late wife's brother. Half the people there are named Resnick.

Mark Roberts was a false identity he apparently used for many years when he was involved with Nationalist and White Supremacist groups out east."

"What did he do?" Charlotte pointed to the wanted poster.

McKenzie's expression pinched. "Killed a reporter who infiltrated their organization. By the time the cops found the body 'Mark Roberts' had disappeared."

"So he has good reason not to want to come out." Charlotte frowned. "I still don't understand Tom Harrison's reasons though. The fact he won't even let TJ talk to us. Any updates on his life over the last eighteen years?"

McKenzie leaned back in his chair. "All he's done is settle into his burrow with his wife and child. Locals say he was never any trouble, always polite but aloof and unassuming. Moved here when TJ was two or thereabouts."

"Did they go to church?" Novak asked.

"Some of them do," McKenzie acceded. "Harrison and his wife went occasionally but generally kept to themselves. They never really interacted with the town socially. TJ never went to school or had sleepovers with friends. Interestingly enough, Malcolm Resnick has been leading some prayer groups at the compound."

"Is he a godly man?" asked Charlotte.

She sounded doubtful, but murder and religion weren't mutually exclusive in some parts the US. The twenty-first century was a lot more "Old Testament" than "turn the other cheek" even if a lot of people were too blind to recognize the difference.

"Or is he staging a coup?" Novak asked. "When did Resnick arrive here?"

"The journalist went missing in February. They didn't find

the body until late March. The women said Malcolm Resnick arrived sometime around then but weren't a hundred percent sure of the date."

"When did Tom's wife die?" Charlotte asked.

"You think he killed her?" Novak asked sharply.

Charlotte shrugged. "I don't know. But it feels like this has been a big year for the Harrisons, one way or another."

McKenzie scratched his neck. "It's an interesting thought. Let's see if we can find out if and where she's buried. We can exhume her body."

"That might anger Tom Harrison and his son."

McKenzie looked unimpressed. "He lost his right to too much consideration when he threatened to blow the place up with everyone in it. What did you get out of Kayla?"

"She and TJ met in the late spring. They've been seeing one another every Wednesday morning for most of the summer and fall." Charlotte looked at him. "My guess is that, when Kayla became sick, Brenna went to meet him. I don't know if that was to tell him to stay away from Kayla or simply to tell him his girlfriend was too sick to meet him."

Charlotte repeated the information Kayla had given them about Brenna's background, and McKenzie's team started tapping into other databases.

"Did we find their families yet?"

McKenzie looked over his shoulder at them. "Brenna has a mom in Pittsburgh. Alcoholic and an addict. Father unknown. Kayla comes from a middle-class background and has some money. Her parents died in a car wreck about eighteen months ago. There's an elderly grandfather, but he's got dementia and is in a nursing facility."

"She told me she had some money put aside."

McKenzie nodded. "She has a trust fund created with the compensation she received, but she doesn't get full control until she's twenty-one."

"So she's roughing it for a couple of years?" Novak asked.

McKenzie rolled his shoulders. "I guess. She can afford a lot more than a tent, but I have to give her props for standing up for what she believes in. The lawyer handling her estate wants permission to come here and take her back home. I'm sure he'll be drawing up papers."

"Kayla's an adult," Charlotte said crossly. "She has the right to choose how she lives her life."

"Think Brenna didn't want to lose her golden ticket so told TJ to get lost?" Novak asked.

"Cynic." Charlotte crossed her arms, looking as if she'd forgotten what he tasted like.

Whatever was in his eyes made her remember though. Color rose in her cheeks, and she turned away.

He frowned. He needed to figure out how to hide the feelings he had for her. It wasn't like this was usually hard for him. But she'd *kissed* him. She'd kissed him like she meant it. Not overwrought with emotion. She'd kissed him with intent. With heat. With lust.

And although he might not have admitted it to himself before, hadn't allowed himself to, he'd been attracted to her since the first time he'd seen her last summer on the way to a prison siege in New York State.

But he was taking everything way too seriously. He needed to go with the flow. People kissed one another. It happened. It had just never happened to him on the job before.

"Novak has a point," McKenzie stated. "Brenna could have told TJ to back off and that Kayla didn't want him anymore, and he might have lashed out."

"Or maybe Brenna went up to pass on a message to TJ but met someone else instead. Maybe she bumped into Malcolm Resnick, and he worried she might recognize him and killed her," Charlotte suggested. "Or maybe it was the man who reported being stalked by the cougar to FWO Jones."

Novak suppressed a smile.

"What?" Charlotte eyed him narrowly.

"You don't want to think badly of Brenna because she had a tough life," Novak told her honestly. "But people with tough lives often end up as hard-ass people."

Ask him how he knew.

"None of it explains why Tom Harrison won't even talk to us," Charlotte grumbled. "I want to go over the transcript of what he said to us earlier again."

McKenzie nodded. "Do we tell them we know about Malcolm being a wanted man?"

Charlotte shook her head. "Malcolm Resnick probably thinks he's flying under the radar. Tom either doesn't know and telling him won't change anything unless we prove Malcolm had something to do with Brenna's death. Or Tom does know and wants to protect his brother-in-law."

"Also, if Malcolm discovers that we know he's in there, that might prompt them to look for surveillance bugs," Novak added.

"License plates didn't come back in his name?" Charlotte asked.

McKenzie shook his head.

"It could also prompt a change in leadership if Tom decides to surrender. Malcolm knows he's facing the possibility of the needle if we arrest and convict him," said Charlotte.

McKenzie jerked his chin in acknowledgment or approval. "Kayla say anything else?"

"Don't forget the camera and the professor," Novak prompted Charlotte, who looked like she was about to shake her head.

"Oh yeah. According to Kayla, Brenna was a decent photographer and sold her pictures online. Check to see if she has a website, would you?" Charlotte directed her question at one of McKenzie's team. "Also, check if there was an SLR camera found in her tent or car. If there wasn't, it might be worth getting a search team to scour the hillside."

"The evidence guys did a pretty comprehensive search on Wednesday afternoon." Truman rested a hip on the desk.

Even Novak could see the other agent was handsome enough to set hearts a-fluttering. He gritted his teeth.

"Enough that they'd have found a camera if it had been there." Truman finished.

"We should expand the search area," said Charlotte.

"You thinking she might have photographs of her killer?" Novak asked.

"It's possible."

"Perhaps the killer took it?" Novak suggested.

"Bob Jones didn't mention anything about a camera." Charlotte's cheeks bunched as she drew her lips tight. It was her thinking expression. Cute as fuck.

"Maybe he didn't notice it? Someone should ask if he saw anyone that morning carrying a camera. Want us to do it?" Novak asked McKenzie who quickly shook his head.

Novak quelled the shaft of disappointment that went through him. It was almost eight PM and this time tomorrow night he and Charlotte would no longer be required to work so closely together. He'd be back with his men where he belonged. Charlotte would be in here with the other negotiators. He didn't understand why this didn't fill him with insane amounts of satisfaction.

"According to Kayla, Brenna was gang raped in high school and had a series of abusive relationships culminating in a guy called Simon who Kayla thought might be violent. I'll try to get a surname from her in the morning."

"Ex could have followed her here and killed her. It's extreme, but if this guy held a grudge and figured out where the women were…it's definitely possible," said Novak.

"And the professor?" McKenzie prompted.

Charlotte looked at him.

Novak unfolded his arms. "Alan Kennedy. He's the one who initially told me which tent Brenna stayed in. When I spoke to him, he gave me the impression he barely knew the women, but Kayla said she'd seen him and Brenna flirting."

McKenzie pulled a face. "I know a lot of guys who flirt with women they barely know. It's kind of the point. I also understand why he might not have admitted it after seeing a photograph of the woman in question lying on a slab." He stood. "Have an agent visit him again. Push him hard on exactly how well he knew the girls and his alibi for Wednesday morning." Then he jerked his chin. "We need to get a look at the inside of that building tonight."

"Agreed." Novak checked his wristwatch. "After midnight, when most of the inhabitants have gone to sleep."

McKenzie looked frustrated. Novak knew how he felt on about a hundred different levels.

"Okay. We'll reconvene in the barn at midnight," McKenzie agreed.

CHAPTER TWENTY-FIVE

EVEN THOUGH NOVAK looked like he was about to crawl the walls with frustration, Charlotte had called the CNU team together for a quick debrief and to inform them they needed to be in the barn at midnight.

Eban came in the door. He gave her a tired grin, having recently woken up. Lines of strain bracketed his mouth and eyes. He sat next to her and dragged his hand through hair that was getting shaggy. The others were discussing possible ways to use the media channels they'd created to reach out to the people inside the compound.

"What did I miss?" he asked.

"We suspect Brenna went to tell TJ Kayla was sick as the two had a standing Wednesday morning date. There's a wanted killer inside the bunker name of Malcolm Resnick, oh, and FWO Jones met a guy who reported being stalked by a cougar just before Jones headed up the trail."

She took a sip of water from the bottle she carried. "I want us to come up with a narrative that will work well over the bullhorn as well as construct a general email to all the inhabitants of the facility reassuring them we mean no harm."

"Why not print leaflets?" Eban joked.

"That is actually a good idea. I'll ask McKenzie to send a requisition request into Quantico."

Eban groaned. "Jesus."

"We can get a drone to deliver them. A great big one. It'll serve two purposes. They know we have drones but let them think of them as these huge things, not the sort that can crawl inside the place and act as a listening device." She told them all about the bug that HRT had inserted and how they were going to try and take a little tour of the facilities as soon as the inhabitants went to sleep.

"Cool." Dominic sprawled in the next chair over with his hands cradled behind his head.

"The leaflets will tell everyone inside that we don't mean to harm them."

"They might not believe us," Eban said.

"And they might. Maybe someone will open the door or people will simply leave. We could put a phone number on there to reach the women in the church hall. They can ask how they're being treated and reassure those inside we don't eat babies."

"At least not yet," Novak said with a sly grin creasing one side of his mouth as he leaned against the wall, looking like the hottest piece of man flesh Charlotte had ever laid eyes on. And it wasn't even the primary reason she was attracted to him. She actually was more drawn to the fact that he listened to her now and supported her. Dammit.

It had been so easy to be attracted to Agent Truman. So damn easy. He fit into every fantasy of Happily Ever After she'd ever had. Novak? Not so much.

But how had a phenomenal kiss and moment of intimacy gone so off track?

She'd messed it up by saying she wanted to keep the kiss a secret. But it wasn't because she was ashamed of him. It was because no matter McKenzie's seventy-two-hour edict about them teaming up—as soon as they revealed a personal relationship, Bureau policy demanded they be separated. She didn't want that. She wanted to see this incident through. She wanted these people safely out of that fortress before anyone else got hurt.

That included HRT.

She also wanted to explore the unusual feelings she had regarding Supervisory Special Agent Payne Novak while they had this chance. But couldn't do that if they went public. She knew this chemistry wasn't a common occurrence. She'd been forced to spend time with the opposite sex before. She, Dominic, and Eban often shared quarters, but that had always felt like bunking with a BFF. She'd certainly never wanted to kiss the face off one of her CNU colleagues.

Novak however... she was all for kissing his face off.

His gaze turned quizzical. She'd been staring too long.

She turned back to the table and found both Dominic and Eban looking from her to Novak with matching expressions of surprised irritation. Shoot.

Charlotte divided the tasks up between the negotiators and told them to run whatever text they came up with past the Behavioral Analysis Unit and their boss.

Novak came up behind her. "My turn?"

It was a question rather than a statement which proved how far they'd both come. She pushed back her chair and grabbed her coat off the hook by the door. Felt Dominic's and Eban's brooding gazes follow them out the door.

They were met by a ferocious wind that attempted to slice off the top layer of her skin.

They put their heads down, and she noticed Novak tried

to shield her as much as possible even though he was the one without a proper jacket. He did that a lot, she realized.

She caught the top of his sleeve, dragged him down to her level. Shouted rather than whispered in his ear as the howling gale tore the words off into the night.

"The reason I suggested we shouldn't tell anyone about that kiss was because I wanted to do it again sometime. Not because I'm ashamed of you or it." She scanned his face for some sign of understanding. "I wanted you to know that."

She held onto him determinedly. He looked confused, probably wondering what the hell she thought she was doing.

His gaze moved over her head, and she twisted to see McKenzie striding toward them. She didn't let go of Novak's arm.

He met her eyes and, finally, a smile tugged at the side of his mouth. He nodded. "Understood. I think that's a good idea."

McKenzie reached them, and she let go.

"What's a good idea?"

"To get a taped video statement from Kayla to send to TJ's email address," Charlotte yelled.

"It is a good idea, but let's see if you can save any more of them until we're out of this weather. Damn, I hope the snipers and SWAT guys are protected." McKenzie walked on, chafing his hands.

They strode quickly to the barn, and she was hyperaware of what Novak had said to her. He thought it was a good idea that they kiss again sometime. A quiver of lust rushed through her. Then she made herself focus. She needed to do a better job of hiding her feelings in front of these highly trained, intelligent agents. She'd given it away to Eban and Dominic, but they knew her inside out and sideways. She couldn't afford for anyone else to figure it out.

They headed through the corridor inside the barn. Novak caught her fingers from behind and gave them a quick squeeze. Over in less than a second but printed indelibly on her being like the most ardent of kisses.

It spoke of understanding and hinted at a promise.

CHAPTER TWENTY-SIX

FOUR HOURS LATER, after reviewing, editing, and forwarding to Quantico their proposed script for emails, leaflets, and for Kayla's video message, Charlotte rubbed tired eyes and sipped the coffee some angel had brought her. Novak and Romano had connected the laptop feed to a giant screen. They merely needed popcorn and soda to complete movie night.

Dominic came and plonked himself next to her. She was careful not to look at Novak, but the way Dominic's lip twitched, she knew he had already guessed she was infatuated with the guy.

He leaned close and murmured in her ear, "So…you and Novak, huh?"

She scowled at him. "Shush. It's not like that."

It was totally like that.

Agent Fontaine went up to Novak and fluttered her long dark lashes, and Charlotte had to physically force her body not to react. When Fontaine touched Novak's arm he glanced at Charlotte, looking almost nervous, she felt both a burst of relief and irritation at herself.

"Ha," Dominic muttered. "At least it's mutual."

"Shut. Up." She gave him a kick under the table to reinforce her pronouncement.

McKenzie strode in, and everyone found a seat or places

along the wall. Charlotte barely managed to keep from grinding her teeth when Fontaine hoisted herself up next to Novak on the work bench.

He moved a fraction of an inch away from the gorgeous agent, and Charlotte released a breath.

She looked at Dominic. "Don't say a word."

"What's up?" Eban dragged up a chair behind her and Dominic and leaned his head through the gap.

"Just studying human behavior," Dominic said laconically.

"If you say anything, Dominic Sheridan, I'm going to find pictures of every woman you ever dated and send them to Ava."

"Don't even joke about that." Dominic shuddered. "Greek women have a temper."

"You love it," Charlotte teased.

He grinned. "I do love it." His gaze shot between her and Eban. "I want my friends to find the same sort of relationship I have. Minus the crazy future mother-in-law."

"Who's your best man?" Eban asked. "Because I am available."

"It better not be your asshole brother," Charlotte muttered. Dominic's brother was a drunk and a creep. The first she could forgive but not the latter.

"He's not invited." Dominic yawned. Charlotte felt guilty because he and Eban were on the early shift. But everyone was here except one agent manning the phone in case it finally rang. Charlotte had given up hope these people would talk to them until the status quo was broken.

Novak pushed off the bench and went and stood beside Romano. Fontaine looked disappointed.

Romano warmed up the miniature drone and then took it

up to the ceiling of the concrete corridor where they'd concealed it.

"Power level is sixty percent," Romano noted.

Lack of sunlight meant it hadn't been able to recharge, which could be an issue long term.

"Head to the front door," Novak instructed. They'd pre-programmed some of the routes but needed to go slowly in case Harrison had modified the structure or there were people in the corridors. "We assume there will be guards at the gate and can't afford for anyone to even suspect we have this device inside, so I want you to land it out of sight and walk it forward to get a visual."

Romano nodded. Even though all eyes were on him, he looked laid back and confident.

Charlotte couldn't resist the draw any longer and walked up to the front, beside Novak, so she could see the drone's progress overlaid on a 3-D rendering of the compound that had been digitized.

Romano flew slowly. Past a series of doors and then to an opening in the corridor.

"Head up the stairs and then right."

The entire audience held its breath. Harrison had threatened to blow the building if he found out they were attempting anything. Charlotte suspected infiltrating his home with a multimillion-dollar drone would count.

A bead of sweat formed on Romano's temple.

He flew the tiny machine around another corner in the labyrinth and then landed it softly on the hard, concrete floor. He didn't waste any time and scuttled forward. It took a lot longer to get anywhere on the ground, but all eyes were glued to the screen as the drone raced through the darkness.

Charlotte scanned the barren walls for signs of explosives. Nothing visible.

Voices came over the mic, and everyone quieted to see if they could pick up what these people were saying. Romano slowed but kept moving cautiously forward.

The space was dimly lit with two sconces that glowed a dull amber. Two shadowy figures were on duty either side of the door. The long narrow slits in the concrete allowed the men to scan the clearing in front of the fortress. These slits were strategically placed around the building.

"If we could get to the walls without being detected, we could stuff a few of those slits with C4 and blow a hole in the wall," Novak said.

"But probably not without Tom Harrison pressing the button and killing them all," said Charlotte.

"Only if he already placed the charges."

"What do BAU say about the likelihood of that?" Charlotte asked.

"I spoke to Lincoln Frazer, and he couldn't see anything in Tom's profile to suggest he'd carry out his threat of mass murder, but he also said they wouldn't have predicted his response to seeing his commanding officer on national TV either. The guy is unpredictable. That's a problem," McKenzie answered.

"We haven't seen any evidence the place is set to blow," Novak said.

Charlotte tried to unclench her jaw, but the tension was growing and impossible to ignore.

Novak peered closer at the monitor, taking interest in the hinge mechanisms and locks. The inset door was a heavy-looking thing with a wheel on it that looked like something you found on the inside of a submarine.

The drone couldn't pick up the muttered conversation between the two guards so Romano backed it away as soon as Novak had gotten images of everything he wanted.

"Head back down to the lower level," Novak said suddenly. "I want to check out the points immediately below the cafeteria for explosives."

"We won't have much juice left if you want to stake out the cafeteria area for any length of time," Romano told him.

"If Harrison is serious about killing everyone, then all he needs to do is call a meeting in the cafeteria and bring down the roof," Novak stated. "That's where I'd pack explosives."

"But he said he was only going to blow the place up if *we* made a move. Why would everyone congregate in the cafeteria at that point if they thought they were under attack?" argued Charlotte.

This was Novak's decision, and she could see him weighing her statement as carefully as he weighed Romano's.

"Ideally, we want to listen in on Tom Harrison's conversation." McKenzie pressed his lips together.

"We don't know where he's spending most of his time," Novak sounded frustrated.

"I know finding explosives means we don't want to risk an assault, but not finding them might simply mean we're looking in the wrong place. It's not a green light," Charlotte pointed out.

Novak's eyes flicked to her. The operator assessing the negotiator's statement, not the man assessing the woman. Charlotte felt a thrill of pride.

"SSA Blood is right. We don't have time to search the whole structure for bombs." Novak expelled a breath. "We don't want to use up all the juice, so let's pick up intel instead and work on getting the other drone in through one of those slits in the wall now we know there aren't any internal barriers."

That was a good idea except those positions were all guarded.

"A bullhorn might disguise the sound of the second drone flying inside the facility," Charlotte suggested.

McKenzie grinned at her. "I knew you'd see it my way eventually."

"Sure, boss." She laughed.

Romano flew the first device near the roof of the corridor, and everyone held their collective breath as he reached the cafeteria. No one was around, thankfully. Romano scanned the area. It was dark. The community was apparently conserving power, which was smart if they were planning a long siege.

Romano headed up into the rafters, which was the only homely feature in the entire place. Carefully, he set the drone down and then walked the device to a joist that was hopefully out of sight from the ground.

And now they waited.

———————

THE MEETING BROKE up, and everyone went back to their individual assignments or to catch some sleep after working an eighteen-hour shift.

Novak and Charlotte headed back to the room they shared without speaking. Although it was late, he wasn't tired. She'd told him earlier that she wanted to kiss him again. Did that mean tonight? Or back in Quantico?

Did it mean kiss or something else? Something *more*?

But Charlotte needed her rest. She already had dark shadows under her eyes. He forced the thoughts of kisses out of his head. Sleep. Now.

They both used the bathrooms, and he cleaned his teeth. He heard the shower go on in the room next door and did his best not to imagine Charlotte naked. But it wasn't easy, especially as he'd felt her pressed against him a few times now and could more accurately picture her naked.

She needed her sleep.

He might be horny, but she was exhausted.

He made himself go back to their room and climb into the top bunk. Closing his eyes to at least try to pretend he was dozing. He heard the door creak open then close. His heart beat faster when he heard her flip the lock. But maybe she didn't want McKenzie barging in on her when she might be getting dressed. It had certainly been an unwelcome shock that morning.

This was their last night together. The bleak realization kept booming through his brain like fireworks.

"Novak?" she whispered.

He grunted. He wanted her to call him Payne.

"You awake?"

"Sure am."

She stood on her bunk and leaned over the edge of the guard rail. He rolled on his side and faced her. The drapes were open, and there was enough ambient light that he could clearly see her wide eyes and the way her teeth pulled at her lower lip.

Their mouths were only inches apart.

"How would you feel about another kiss?" she whispered.

His heart pounded so hard he could feel it against his ribs. She was propositioning *him,* and it was the sexiest thing he'd ever experienced. Was he dreaming? He frowned.

"Unless you don't want to." Her expression became uncertain. And he was done playing games.

"Do you want to come up here or shall I come down there?" he asked.

She shivered, and her eyes widened. "I think our combined weight might break the bunk."

Blood heated in his veins. *Combined weight.* "Jesus, Charlotte. You say that, and all I can think of is having you naked beneath me and pounding into you."

She blinked, but she didn't appear put off by his words. In fact, she looked eager. "Okay."

He laughed and leaned a little closer. Kissed her mouth. "What do you mean, okay?"

"Okay, yes. I'm saying proceed with the pounding. Yes, please."

Holy fuck. She was green lighting the fantasy of doing a lot more than kissing. He jumped over the side of the bunk, landing quietly on his feet, and caught her to him. She wore her over-sized t-shirt. Nothing else. The material was thin and stretchy, and he used it to draw her even closer.

"Are you serious?" He needed to know he wasn't crossing a line.

She swallowed audibly. "Only if you want to. I'm not trying to force myself on you."

Relief seared his brain at the same time as amusement. "Feel free, honey. Any damn time."

Her hands skimmed up his chest and over his shoulders. "How about right now?"

She rose up on tiptoe and nipped at his lower lip.

His fingers curled even tighter into the material and then slipped under the thin cotton and whipped it up over her head. Rather than seeming shy about her body, she stood there naked in front of him, letting him look his fill. Her fingers traced the edge of his boxers, then up his oblique muscles and across to his navel. Women liked his body. He knew that. Usually he found it a little disconcerting, but Charlotte wasn't salivating over the muscles he worked hard for so he could do his job. Instead, she touched him as if she was matching the texture of his skin to her imagination, and he liked that idea—that she might have fantasized about this. Her hands skimmed over the sprinkling of hairs on his chest and touched the brown nub of one of his nipples.

He was busy trying not to marvel over her body. The soft breasts and trim waist and toned legs. She might be a negotiator, but she was also a Federal Agent so she kept in shape. He ran his hands down her sides and cupped her bottom, pulling her against him, trapping his erection between them. It was a glorious form of torture.

She rubbed herself against him, and he almost blacked out.

He tilted her chin up, wanting to kiss her almost as much as he wanted to have sex with her. Her mouth opened beneath his, and she tasted like sensible mint toothpaste, but he knew there was a lot more to her than that. His one hand roved, finding the rigid tip of her left breast and tweaking it hard enough for her to close her eyes and drop her head back on a moan.

"Like that, huh?" he asked.

"Love that."

They spoke in whispers. Aware that if they were caught

they'd be left sexually frustrated and immediately sent back to Quantico with letters of censure in their files. He didn't know which would be worse.

Her fingers wrapped around the length of him, and she made a little pleased humming sound that for some reason made his cheeks burn.

He cupped her ass, rubbing her clit against his hard length, and feeling her push against him.

"Wanna be fucked against the wall, Charlotte?" he whispered. His hand slipped along her seam, his fingers easing inside and finding her hot and ready. "Or on the bed?"

"Both," she whispered back, taking a gentle bite of his ear lobe.

His knees almost dissolved.

He grabbed a condom out of his wash bag. He carried them as much for his team as for himself. As much for survival reasons as for sex. He'd never been so glad that he was prepared for anything.

He hadn't been tempted by a woman in what felt like forever. It wasn't that he didn't like sex. He loved sex, but anonymous hookups left him feeling dissatisfied and were no better than a hand job.

As much as he wasn't good with women, as much as he didn't want another relationship that left him feeling empty, he wanted more than casual sex. He wanted fire. He wanted to burn. But he didn't want to be consumed.

This didn't have to be anything other than a little raw passion between two unattached adults. Two very horny unattached adults.

She took the condom out of his hand, and he ditched his boxers. She carefully slid the silky latex over his oversensitized flesh. He shivered, removing her hand when she went to stroke him and turning them both so she was the one with her back against the wall.

Uncertainty flitted through her expression.

He let go of her hand and stroked the hair off her brow. "What is it?"

"I haven't done this for a while."

"The wall?"

Her mouth quirked. "Any of it, but especially the wall."

He went to take a step back, but she grabbed his hand. "It's not that I want to stop. I really don't. I'm worried I've forgotten what to do and won't measure up."

He cradled her head between both his hands and kissed her slowly. He pulled back, cocked his head. "How hard can it be?"

The fact he was throbbing against her like a piece of molten steel had her laughing as he'd hoped.

"Very. I hope."

She ran her fingers over him, and he closed his eyes, concentrating on not losing it. On not embarrassing himself and disappointing her. Jesus.

"Let me know if you need any pointers, but I'm pretty sure we can figure it out together." He took her hand and placed it on his shoulder, then did the same with her other hand. Then he hoisted her up so her legs were wrapped around his waist, her moist center pressed against his hard length, making him shake with need. "I've got you. All you need to do is hang on. Think you can do that?"

She nodded, eyes huge and a little bit serious. She was honestly worried she was going to be something less than perfect, and yet she was already more perfect than any other woman he'd been with in years.

He adjusted himself until he was poised against her entrance. He stared at her expression as he slid slowly inside. Her eyes widened, and her mouth opened. And then she closed her eyes as a whole-body shiver overtook her, clamping down on the snug fit of him inside her.

He gritted his teeth as the waves of her orgasm subsided.

When she opened her eyes, she gave him an endearing grin. "Told you it had been a while."

"Well, I think you're getting the hang of it." He used one arm under her butt to help hold her up. With his other hand he cupped her chin and tilted her head, kissing her mouth deeply, wanting to absorb her taste. Then he started thrusting slowly, careful not to make a giveaway rhythmic noise that everyone else in the building would identify as someone, somewhere, getting some.

The effect of slow, sensual thrusts dragged out the erotic sensation, and the need to climax built inside him in small incremental steps up a very long spiral staircase.

He wanted to give her endless pleasure. Wanted to make this good for her. His competitive spirit was finding an outlet he hadn't thought of before. He didn't simply want to have great sex with Charlotte Blood. He wanted to be the best lover she'd ever had.

He felt her breath hitch and the tension build in her body as he drove her slowly and relentlessly towards another orgasm.

She started to make a sound, and he kissed her harder, holding her breath captive in his lungs, swallowing her groan, feeling her shatter around him a second time.

It broke him. He drove harder, but the noise was too loud,

so he pulled them away from the wall, planted his feet wide apart and held her in place, as he pounded into her deeper and harder. Thrilled when she moaned quietly in passion once more. Despite all his lauded self-control, he couldn't stop himself from making a similar groan of pleasure. Her hand clamped over his mouth as he pistoned in and out of her slick flesh. Finally, the orgasm hit him like the crest of a wave flattening him against the bottom of the ocean as sensations pummeled his entire body. He came with the force of an explosion, the rush of heat, the blinding light wiping his brain clear of everything except that moment of pure unadulterated ecstasy.

When his heart rate slowed enough so he could risk opening his eyes, he looked down at Charlotte who was cuddled contentedly against his shoulder.

He eased her off him and onto the bed. She didn't want to let go and that made something inside his chest tighten.

"Give me a second." He got rid of the condom, carefully sealing it in an airtight plastic bag. But the musky scent of sex would give them away if anyone came inside the room. "How do you feel about me opening this window for a few minutes?"

She held out a hand. "As long as you keep me warm."

He stared at her. When was the last time he'd fallen asleep with a woman in his arms? He knew exactly when—and it had been years ago.

But for her... It took a lot of trust to sleep beside someone. A lot of trust.

"We've come a long way since you were pressing your elbow into my jugular," he commented.

She smiled contentedly. Hell, he liked this Charlotte Blood. Liked her a lot.

He pulled on his boxers and opened the window wide.

An icy blast brushed his skin.

"Holy smokes," Charlotte complained.

He crawled in beside her, and she plastered herself against him, snuggling into him, pulling the covers over them both.

He lay on his back and assimilated all the sensations of her body touching his. The brush of her satiny hair against his stubbled chin. The tangle of her smooth limbs with his hairy ones. The lime scent that teased his nostrils. The soft cushion of her breasts against his chest. The feel of her heart beating reassuringly against his.

The air became frigid, but he didn't want to disturb this tableau of contentment in the barren sea of his life.

Charlotte fell asleep, and the utter peace on her face was something he could stare at for hours, days even... The thought terrified him. She'd wanted sex, but he had the disastrous feeling he'd given much more of himself than his body. And if he wasn't careful, she'd waltz away with his heart, and he'd be once again left with nothing.

TJ PACED THE room. His father hadn't come back to their suite yet, and he was starting to worry about him. TJ had eaten the stew alone, and the scent hung heavy in the stale air of the apartment. He was reluctant to use the range hood though he couldn't imagine how the Feds would be able to use it against him.

Paranoia was taking over.

He glanced at the SLR camera he'd taken from beneath Malcolm's bed, frustrated because the SD card was missing.

Why hadn't he checked for it before he'd left the room?

He eased open the door, but it was quiet as death outside, and he was pretty sure Malcolm would be sleeping. He couldn't risk another foray into his uncle's quarters. Best to wait until breakfast or lunchtime, even though the delay was killing him.

He spied his computer and decided to check his email, cognizant of the fact the Feds might have taken control of his account. Still, he could look at his messages. See if there was anything from Kayla, even though he knew the Feds might attempt to trick him. He wasn't dumb. Well, aside from running from that Federal Wildlife Officer and starting a mini war, he wasn't dumb.

That was definitely the stupidest thing he'd ever done.

Before he turned the computer on, he covered the camera with a sticky note. When the messages downloaded, he saw there were several from the FBI and nothing else. The lack of spam meant for sure the Feds had control of his email account. He read the messages, and they were all variants on the same theme. Talk to them. Tell them what happened. He started typing out an explanation but heard footsteps in the hall. He quickly shut down and closed the lid. He kicked the camera under his desk.

"How you doing, son?"

"Dad." TJ climbed to his feet. "Is it time to go?"

His father shook his head tiredly. "Not yet. I need to sleep, and there are a few things I need to finish."

TJ itched to do something. To get out of here. "Want me to go hang out in the surveillance room? Take a turn watching the camera feeds?"

Tom stared at him for a long time. "I don't think that's a

good idea."

"You can't protect me all the time, Dad." He stretched to his full height, six inches taller than his father. His mom had been short too. They'd always joked TJ was a throwback to his paternal great-grandfather who'd been 6'4 and built like a grizzly bear. "I'm a man now."

Tom smiled slowly, a look of pride coming over his features. "You are, and I respect that. But there are things you don't know."

"What things?" asked TJ.

"I'll tell you soon enough but not tonight." Tom yawned. "Look, son, I can't tell you what to do, but if you go out there and Malcolm or his goons catch you, I have a feeling they'll toss you out the front door."

TJ grimaced. "Maybe that would be for the best."

Tom's mouth pulled to one side. "I didn't say you'd be alive when they did it."

TJ's eyes widened until the skin hurt. "You think he wants me dead?"

"I think he wants us both dead, but most people here still remember that I'm the one who gave them a place to stay."

TJ was stunned by that declaration. "What are we gonna do?"

"Tonight, we're going to lock the door and get some sleep. There's a storm coming, son. We need to be ready. You packed our bags?"

"Yes, sir." He nodded toward the two packs he'd placed in the bottom of his tidy cupboard. His father didn't tolerate mess. "How are we going to get away without them seeing us?"

His father yawned widely. "I got it all figured out. It's what your mother would have wanted."

"I miss her," TJ admitted.

His father looked at the carpet. "So do I, son. So do I." He looked up. "Think she'd have liked your girl?"

Hot tears stung TJ's eyes. "Yes. I do."

His father nodded sadly and walked away.

TJ watched him go, knowing he should have told his father he believed Kayla was still alive, but also knowing his father was exhausted and would demand a thorough explanation.

He'd tell him tomorrow when they had more time. They'd figure out how to find her together. He wasn't sure what sort of chance of a future any of them would have, but he could at least try. His dad would have an idea how to pull it off. His dad always had a plan.

CHAPTER TWENTY-SEVEN

CHARLOTTE WAS SO content and cozy. She rubbed herself against the warm flesh pressed against her side and woke up enough to remember exactly how they'd ended up this way.

The large white digital display of the alarm clock said five AM.

Novak seemed to be asleep, and she drew back to see his features. It was still dark out, but her eyes had adjusted enough to make out his expression. His broad forehead was smooth and free of lines. The tension that usually surrounded his eyes had disappeared, and his lips were slightly parted.

He must have closed the window at some point because it wasn't an arctic gale anymore. She hadn't stirred. She'd slept for four hours solid and, though her body might disagree later, right now, she was hoping to make the most of whatever time they had left together.

She brushed her hand over his thigh and found him hot and heavy. She leaned up and murmured against his ear, "Now I know you're awake."

"How?" he whispered back.

"Because nobody could sleep with this."

"You'd be surprised." He sounded like he was in pain. It was definitely something she could help with.

"Do you have another condom?" she asked.

He reached over the side of the bed and groped around for a moment.

"Thankfully, I do." One side of his mouth curled up.

She went to take it out of his grasp, but he jerked it away, and she ended up sprawled across his chest.

"Impatient."

"Worried McKenzie will be at the door and ruin the mood," she muttered. "And I'm definitely going to need a shower this morning."

Novak's ocean eyes crinkled at her. "Unless it's an emergency, McKenzie can wait. I've got a few immediate action plans that take precedence."

A quiver shot through Charlotte. What would it be like to spend the entire day in bed with this man rather than these last few stolen hours?

Dangerous thoughts. He was probably quite happy with a fling but would run a mile if she mentioned the "R" word.

"What plans would they be?" she whispered.

"You'll see." He turned on his side and leaned on one elbow, the covers falling off him to reveal packed muscle and strong limbs. She ran her hand over the smooth skin of his pecs. "This is all a little intimidating," she admitted quietly.

"You don't like it?"

"I didn't say I didn't like it, but it makes me realize my idea of fitness is pretty basic."

"If I'd wanted to have sex with someone who could bench-press a truck, I'd have hooked up with one of the guys."

"I have no doubt," she said with a smile.

She went to kiss him, but he inched away from her.

"Where are you going?" she said, a little exasperated, not to mention cold.

And then he kissed her breasts, her ribs, navel, the sensitive skin where her leg met her torso, the inside of her knee, and she understood exactly where he was heading.

"You said you wanted it all, Charlotte." His hands wrapped around her legs and pulled them wide apart, and she felt overwhelmed by lust. His tongue licked along the seam of her vagina, and her muscles turned to warm wax.

She breathed out a moan. "If McKenzie knocks on the door, I'm going to shoot him."

"I'll help bury the body." His tongue was relentless, like the rest of him. He worked her clit before moving back to her entrance and licking inside. His breath against her sensitive flesh made her quiver. Then he scraped his unshaven chin over her vulva, had her almost shooting off the bed.

"Oh my god. I've finally figured out why women like beards so much."

He laughed and then ignored her. Concentrated instead on making her lose her mind with the dexterity of his tongue and the gentle scrape of stubble. When one of his hands reached up to tweak her nipple, she dug her heels in the mattress and bowed her back as release sheared through her. After the orgasm ended, she lay panting, wanting more.

She heard the tear of a wrapper and bent her knees, needing to feel his weight pressed upon her.

She reached down and guided him to her because she didn't want to wait any longer. Was in no mood to be teased. He slowly forced himself inside and held himself up with his arms as he started thrusting in and out, each stroke dragging across her clit.

His eyes never left her face, searching it for clues as to what worked for her and what didn't.

Spoiler alert. It *all* worked for her. The perfect complement of fullness and friction.

She gripped his ass and pulled him even closer, fighting him every time he tried to retreat. It turned into a beautiful synchrony of frenzy, and an orgasm ripped through her. She opened her mouth to scream, and Novak planted his hand over her mouth as he pounded harder. The lack of springs in the mattress meant they were almost silent, and she wasn't sure she'd have cared even if they hadn't been.

Stars dazzled her, and her muscles spasmed in a cascade of pleasure that shimmered inside.

Finally, his face tightened and expression contorted. He started to groan, and she placed a palm over his lips while wrapping her legs tight around his hips and clenching around him.

A few ragged breaths later, he collapsed on top of her. Heavy as lead. Warm as the sun. Their heartbeats slowing in union.

She wrapped her arms around him, not wanting to let go even as the first distant tread of footsteps warned them the world was waking up and that they had to rejoin the rest of the human race.

He thrust his hips into her one last time and then gently extricated himself. He disposed of the condom, then pulled on his boxers again. She lay in bed watching him, wondering what he was thinking. But he wasn't revealing any emotion.

"Novak," she said softly.

He looked up, wary. She still didn't know why he was closed off or who had hurt him, but Charlotte's weapons were empathy and honesty. "That was amazing. I hope we get to do it again. Soon."

He grinned, and his body seemed to relax by a thousand degrees. "You were incredible. You haven't forgotten a thing, but I'm willing to be your workout buddy if you want to practice."

She shook her head, laughing, and fell back against the pillow.

"I'm going to open the window because the room stinks of sex again. If you want a shower before McKenzie comes looking for us you better get up now." He leaned down and kissed her, and Charlotte felt it like a possessive stamp on her heart.

"If I could sneak into the shower with you, I'd do it in a moment, but not at the risk of both our careers. So get out of here while you still have the chance." She eyed the tented shorts.

He shook his head and moved away. "This is not a problem I usually have, but you naked appears to short circuit my control."

Charlotte laughed and pushed the covers off, deliberately tempting him even though she didn't plan on missing out on this morning's shower. Not after last night.

She grabbed her nightie off the floor and heard Novak swallow loudly as she dragged it over her head. She picked up her wash bag and towel. Sashayed to the door and looked over her shoulder. "Bet I'm ready first."

"Accepting that bet would be taking advantage."

"If you're so confident, what's the problem?" she asked.

Novak opened the window while shaking his head. The icy blast had her teeth instantly chattering. "It would be like stealing candy from a baby and wouldn't be fair."

Charlotte let her gaze scan his body before rising to meet

his eyes. "I never said anything about candy, Novak. Nor money. I was thinking more along the lines of granting sexual favors." She beamed at him, knowing she was going to shock the hell out of him and glad. Maybe he'd realize there was more to her than he thought. "And, frankly, win or lose, I'd be more than happy."

She went out into the corridor and grabbed the bathroom that was free, grinning as Novak was forced to wait his turn.

CHAPTER TWENTY-EIGHT

ONCE IN THE Command Center, she tried to ignore Novak, but it was impossible when she was hyperaware of the guy's every move. Every time she looked at him, she felt like she had hearts in her eyes. She also didn't want to confuse the guy by ignoring him, but they both had important jobs to do.

If only she could wipe the satisfied smirk off her face. She glanced over at Novak and noticed he suffered from a similar affliction.

Then she caught Eban's gaze. He was glowering at her.

"Can I talk to you in private?" he asked.

"Sure." Was he finally going to tell her what was going on with him? She thought he'd head to a quiet corner in the large space but, instead, he went out the front door into the subzero temperatures. Great. She grabbed her coat. Novak walked over to join her.

She shook her head. "I need a private moment with Eban. McKenzie isn't here. I'll be back in five minutes."

His eyebrows flashed, and he jerked his head toward McKenzie's team. "I think his people report back on everything, including us."

"This won't take long." She touched his arm and saw Dominic's gaze flicker over them. She removed her hand even though she regularly touched her fellow negotiators this way. *Dammit.*

Outside, she ducked her chin into the high neck of her coat and stuffed her hands deep into the pockets. She glanced around. Eban was nowhere in sight, but then she spotted him at the corner of the building and followed him until they were out of sight around the back.

"What's up?"

Eban's dark eyes were narrowed. "You slept with him."

"I was ordered to, remember?" She tried to brazen her way out of being blindsided by the accusation.

"Don't bullshit me."

Charlotte's eyes went wide. She opened her mouth to deny it, but there was no way she could lie to one of her best friends.

"How could you be such an idiot, Char?" Eban kept his voice low, but it struck a blow.

Charlotte gritted her teeth on a moment of hurt and anger. "It's none of your business. And I don't remember you giving Dominic hell when he hooked up with Ava in New York State."

"They weren't working together."

"Technically, they were." Hot fury rose up inside her at his double standards. "Plus, Ava was a rookie."

"Ava is more than capable of looking after herself," Eban bit back.

Charlotte's jaw dropped. She advanced a step. "And I'm not?"

"That's not what I meant."

"It's what you said, and as a negotiator you understand the importance of words." Did he really think she was some weak, ineffectual female? Was that how he viewed her? As someone who couldn't read men and had no right to take a lover of her own?

"Listen, Charlotte. Guys like Payne Novak are after one thing and one thing only."

"One thing?" Charlotte echoed.

"Come on. Don't be so naive. I know you're looking for a relationship, but Novak isn't that kind of guy."

"What kind of guy is he?"

Eban rolled his eyes and looked off toward the woods. "I spoke to my buddy about him. He does one-night stands and is not the type to send flowers the next day. He's never even known Novak to go on a date, ever."

Ice formed on Charlotte's insides. "Maybe he hasn't found what he's looking for before now?"

"Grow up, Charlotte. You don't think the entire Hostage Rescue Team aren't taking bets on whether or not he bangs you during this incident?" Eban's cynicism was like acid dripping on her heart.

Hurt pierced her. "Do you know that for a fact?"

"I heard one of the guys speculating. I told him to can it." He put a hand on her shoulder and leaned close, pity in his gaze.

"That is not Novak's fault. That's what people do." Charlotte jerked away from Eban. "How dare you think you get to comment on my love life when you won't discuss your own." He reared back. "And don't think I don't know what's made you into such a miserable grouch these last few months."

"Hey. I'm not talking about me. I'm trying to protect you." His nostrils flared, and he went to turn away.

She grabbed his arm. "That's not how this works. You don't get to interfere in my love life and not expect a little tit for tat."

"I don't have a love life," he said bitterly.

She moved closer again because she did not want anyone overhearing this conversation. "Apparently, you want to make sure I'm as miserable and alone as you are."

Eban's eyes widened. "He's taking advantage of you. I don't want to see you hurt."

"What about him being hurt by me? Why is that not an equal possibility?"

Eban's expression told her everything she needed to know about what he thought about the chance of that. He obviously didn't find her worthy of a man's genuine affection.

"Maybe I wanted sex."

Eban flinched.

"Women do, you know. Actually want to have sex now and then without a wedding band or an FBI interrogation."

"I'm trying to look out for you."

"Well, whippee. For the record, I seduced him. Twice. And, yes, if I'm honest, I'd like to actually spend more time with him, get to know him outside work. Hang with someone who isn't in CNU for a change." Rage heated her veins. "But if he isn't interested in anything except sex, then I'll take that too. Because I deserve to be loved, Eban. In every sense of the word."

"You do deserve to be loved. You deserve to be happy."

But Eban obviously didn't think Novak could value or love her except in bed. It showed exactly what he thought of her.

"What about Darby O'Roarke?" She pushed because she was incensed.

"What about her?"

"Doesn't she deserve to be happy?"

292

He crossed his arms over his chest on the defensive. "Of course, she does. What's that got to do with you or me?"

It had everything to do with why he was so miserable and determined to take them all down with him. "Doesn't she want you?"

Eban glared at her. "That is irrelevant. She was traumatized."

Charlotte wanted to snarl but reminded herself she was usually good at talking to people. That was her job. It was his too. "True. But she's a smart female and maybe you should start listening to what she's saying rather than shoving your world view down her throat."

"She was brutalized. She was almost destroyed." His eyes glittered.

Charlotte hardened her heart. She wasn't the pushover everyone assumed.

"Then offer her love. Offer her devotion. Treat her like she's the only important thing in your life. Make her life worth living."

He shook his head. "You're such a goddamn idealist."

She got in his face and yelled, "I'm the most practical person you will ever meet!"

"Bullshit. You're already in love with him!" Eban swung away from her before he could see how well that barb struck home. "Is he worth your career?"

"It won't come to that."

"What if it does?"

She looked down at the broken blades of grass beneath their feet. "Then that will be my choice to make."

Novak chose that moment to walk around the side of the building.

Eban clearly wasn't done making her life miserable. As Novak got closer, he said, "You need to leave her the hell alone."

Charlotte's mouth dropped wide open.

Novak kept coming. He looked from Eban to her. "Are you okay?"

"She doesn't need you negatively impacting her career."

"Negatively impacting…?" she exclaimed.

"What are you? Her fucking brother?" Novak stopped next to Charlotte.

Eban lunged for Novak, accidentally knocking into Charlotte. She caught herself on the side of the outbuilding, but she wasn't a fragile flower. She was a goddamn Federal Agent. Eban landed a blow on Novak, and the next thing, he and Novak were both on the ground, grappling. Novak outweighed Eban by thirty pounds and trained daily. She could tell he was trying to hold back, but Eban was no slouch, and he wasn't pulling his punches.

Charlotte tried to drag Novak off the other negotiator, because this was insane, but Eban used Novak's distraction to get him into the exact same hold she'd gotten Novak into the first morning he'd woken her. And she watched Novak easily flip Eban onto his back using his legs, to end up pinning him to the ground. She realized how easily he could have reversed their positions that first day. But he hadn't. Because he'd wanted her to keep her power.

Novak let Eban go and rolled to his feet. Then he reached out and held his hand out to pull Eban up.

Eban stared at her and seemed to realize he'd completely fucked up. He waited a beat before he took Novak's hand and let the other man pull him to his feet.

"You better treat her right."

"We slept together, Eban. Doesn't mean we're going to get married." Charlotte shook her head at her friend. "Go fix your own love life before you try to interfere with mine."

She walked away, even as Eban opened his mouth to argue with her more. She ignored him. She had work to do. They all had work to do, and she should never have allowed herself to be distracted.

Novak caught up with her. "Are you all right?"

She blew out an exasperated breath. "I wasn't the one brawling."

He blinked as if she'd hurt his feelings.

She stopped walking and faced him. "Sorry. Yes, I'm fine. He shouldn't have attacked you that way." She raked her fingers through her hair and wondered how she'd got into this mess. "Eban is worried about me getting hurt."

Novak drew back, and she rolled her eyes in exasperation. "I'm not expecting any sort of commitment from you, Novak. I'm simply telling you the facts. Despite what Eban might believe, I have actually slept with guys before, and I didn't want or expect a ring from any of them." The fact anything worth mentioning had been years ago was irrelevant. "What I don't want is for our"—she searched for the right word—"intimacy, to interfere with our jobs."

His expression closed down, and she had to wonder if she'd somehow managed to say the wrong thing again. So much for being a top negotiator. Right now, she couldn't negotiate her way out of a wide-open prairie field. Although it was hard to employ active listening techniques when the person you were talking with didn't *say* anything back to you.

McKenzie chose that moment to open the back door of the

ranch house and jog down the steps.

Novak looked from their boss to her and back. "You're right. We probably need to cool it."

"What?" she choked out.

All the joy she'd experienced last night evaporated. She swallowed. Maybe Eban had been correct in trying to warn her that having sex wouldn't equate to anything but a passing distraction for the HRT leader. She had literally thrown herself at this guy last night.

She froze with the knowledge that maybe she'd simply been there, convenient and willing. Her stomach rebelled, and she had to swallow back the bile that crawled up her throat.

Apparently, she'd been lying to herself. She wasn't equipped for some purely physical fun, no matter how much she wanted that to be the case.

She wanted more.

Then McKenzie was giving orders and not seeing anything amiss even as her heart ping-ponged against her ribs. She nodded woodenly, going through the motions as tiredness swept over her in an inexorable wave.

"You two okay?" McKenzie frowned.

She nodded quickly. "Discussing today's joint itinerary." Which was basically the end of what they'd started last night.

Well, it had been fun while it lasted. But considering her emotions were going through the shredder, she wasn't sure it had been worth it.

McKenzie took her words at face value.

"You two have proven you can work together. You're released from having to spend every moment shadowing one another. Weather supposed to change this afternoon. Novak, the mockup building is finished. Get your men practicing to infiltrate the compound. Blood, go talk to Kayla and see if you can get her to tape that message to persuade TJ to give himself up."

McKenzie checked his watch. "Meet back at the Command Center at noon." He stared at them both expectantly, having no clue as to the quagmire of lust and confused hurt his orders from three days ago had wrought.

"Yes, boss." Charlotte nodded miserably.

The two men walked away. Novak looked over his shoulder, but his expression was unreadable.

Dammit.

She blew out a long breath and headed into the ranch house, because she wasn't ready to face Eban or Dominic, who knew her well enough to read the signs of misery. She felt battered, but she had to get her act together. Lives depended on it.

Did McKenzie's change of orders mean HRT were planning to storm the compound before the blizzard hit? Or use it to disguise their activities?

She didn't know. Didn't want to know as it might taint what she said to Kayla or the people inside the building, should they actually communicate with the negotiators. The feeling of hurt and heartbreak in the background of her mind reminded her that even though she had found someone she connected with on multiple levels, and even though she was surrounded by dozens of people, she was still just as alone as she'd always been.

CHAPTER TWENTY-NINE

NOVAK HAD FUCKED up. He knew it.

Maybe he should have walked away from Eban, but when the guy knocked into Charlotte, anger got the better of him and he reacted before he regained control of his temper. By the time he had a hold of his emotions they were on the ground, battling for dominance.

He might not start a fight, but he wouldn't run away from one.

But maybe he should have.

Eban had obviously figured out what they'd done last night and didn't think Novak was good enough for his friend.

The guy wasn't wrong, but it didn't mean the insult didn't sting.

That's why he'd suggested to Charlotte that they cool it. It wasn't what he wanted, but it would probably be better for her in the long term. He really wasn't good with women.

Who was he kidding? He was protecting himself from when she figured it out too. Rejection sucked.

And then McKenzie had arrived.

He shook his head at himself. What a fucking coward. Have sex, brawl with her friend because the prick said Novak would hurt Charlotte, and then fucking hurt her because he was too chickenshit to tell her how he really felt. Like the world was brighter and the air smelled fresher and every cell in his body was fucking *happy* for once in his miserable life when he was with her.

Fuck. He couldn't even text her because he didn't know her personal number, and no way could he say what he wanted to say on their government issue cells.

Fucking fuck.

He walked inside the barn, not hearing a single word McKenzie said on the walk over, except something to do with the bullhorn.

"Sitrep," Novak shouted as he strode to the tables where they'd set up their maps and computers. All he could see was the hurt and betrayal etched across Charlotte's features.

"First drone is in a good position to receive quality intel we're relaying straight to Quantico for analysis. A team of image and sound engineers are dissecting as much information out of the noise as possible." Angeletti frowned in concentration. "No sign of Tom Harrison or his son yet."

"Assemble Charlie team. They'll spend the morning practicing assaulting the bunker and figuring out the best DA plan." Deliberate Action—the best-case scenario where HRT controlled the assault rather than being controlled by the need to get inside and rescue hostages when things had spiraled out of control.

"No live fire. The construction material isn't bulletproof, but it'll give the guys the opportunity to get a feel for the space. I want them to know it blindfolded. Echo team swaps in this afternoon." One team needed to remain here in case the situation went south, and they had to respond immediately.

"Yes, sir." Angeletti flicked a glance at McKenzie before he left to hustle Charlie team into action.

Novak stood staring down at the map not seeing a thing, instead remembering the stricken expression on Charlotte's face when he'd told her they should cool it.

Like he'd kicked a puppy.

He felt the boot in his gut. She'd never let him near her again. Why should she? No one needed that type of rejection, especially not a smart, beautiful woman like Charlotte Blood. *Christ.* He ran his hand over his face.

"Negotiators are going to start using the bullhorn, and leaflets are going to be delivered by drone at ten AM," said McKenzie from behind him.

"That was quick." Usually it would take a week to even get permission to spend the money, let alone print the leaflets.

"I made an executive decision."

"Oh, the Bureau loves those." Novak snorted.

McKenzie grinned. "Tell me about it." Then he sobered. "You think SSA Blood is up to the job of being Negotiation Commander on this incident?"

Novak's spine snapped straight. "Yes, sir."

McKenzie shook his head wryly. "Think she'll say the same 'bout you when I ask her?"

Numbness spread over Novak's body. "I have no idea, boss. I only know you'd be a fool to underestimate her ideas or approach. She's a smart agent. And you're no fool."

"Thank you, SSA Novak," McKenzie said seriously, then he grinned. "I happen to agree with you about SSA Blood."

Novak looked away as his mouth went dry. While he might have resented the heavy-handed approach McKenzie had taken, it had worked and now, rather than being desperate to hang out with his men and get the job done, he was mooning around the barn like a love-sick teen.

Time to snap the fuck out of it before someone got killed.

———————————

WHEN TJ WOKE, there was a note on his bedside table. "Be ready."

His father had obviously already left.

He checked the time and groaned. It was the start of breakfast so he changed into some clean clothes and slipped out of their rooms, carefully locking the door behind him as he didn't trust Malcolm not to come in and steal their stuff if provided the opportunity.

He had the man's camera slung over his shoulder and hidden behind his back, striding confidently along the corridor as if heading for breakfast. He wore sneakers and kept his tread light. Thankfully, there was no one at the stairs or outside the surveillance room so he kept going, walking quickly until he came to Malcolm's door.

His mouth went dry as he stopped and listened with his hand on the knob. If Malcolm was in here, TJ was screwed.

After a few silent seconds, TJ inserted the key and tapped quietly on the door. "Uncle Malcolm?"

There was no reply. TJ went inside, but the light was on so he didn't bother with his flashlight. The bed was unmade.

The sound of the shower running made TJ's heart constrict. *Crap.* Malcolm was still in here. Sweat formed on TJ's palms. This was probably his only chance, and he needed to act fast unless he wanted to get caught. He went over to the laptop and spotted the card. He ejected it into his palm, swung the camera under the bed, kicking at the strap. Then headed straight out the door, closing it quietly behind him as his heart nearly punched its way through his chest.

Damn.

He slipped the SD card into his pocket and walked back down the hall to his room. He kept his head down, footsteps soft, and prayed every step of the way no one was gonna catch him.

CHARLOTTE KNOCKED ON Kayla's door and poked her head inside. "May I come in?"

Kayla nodded.

"How are you feeling today?"

Kayla shrugged. "Better, I guess." She looked miserable.

"You ate?" A breakfast tray sat on the dressing table. The plate still half filled with food.

"The nurse insisted."

"You need to build your strength." Charlotte tried to smile reassuringly. It was natural for Kayla to continue to be upset about her friend's death. It was natural to feel survivor's guilt. "Can I ask you a few more questions?"

Kayla nodded a little uncertainly. "Can I ask you some?"

Charlotte hesitated. "I'll tell you what I'm able."

"Where's Brenna?"

"With the Medical Examiner. He'll release the body soon."

Kayla swallowed. "I want to bury her properly. I have money." Her tone was defiant.

Charlotte nodded. "I'll make sure the office knows."

"I don't want people to think she's unloved." Kayla wiped at her eyes. The news was still fresh, and the young woman looked like she'd been crying for most of the night. Unlike

Charlotte, who'd been having sex with a man she could easily have fallen in love with had she had the slightest inclination he might feel the same way.

We probably need to cool it.

Obviously not.

"I'll get you the contact details today. Brenna will be well taken care of, I promise."

Kayla nodded. "Okay. What do you want to know?"

"Do you have a surname and address for Brenna's ex, this Simon guy?"

Kayla's brow pleated in confusion then cleared. "You think he killed her?"

"We aren't sure yet how she died. We want to eliminate him from our enquiries."

"You think he'd drive all this way?" Kayla's expression showed she was thinking hard.

"What do you think?"

"He was pissed when she left him. Threatened to kill her. Threatened to kill me too." Her lip wobbled. "But I can't see him bothering to travel all this way. He's a bully and a pig, but a lazy pig." She gave Charlotte his surname and the street he lived on. Charlotte texted it to McKenzie and forced thoughts of Novak out of her mind. She'd have to get used to working without him around and ignore her mortification until this was over.

"Was the last time you saw TJ a week ago last Wednesday?"

Kayla nodded then frowned. "Did he find Brenna?"

"Yes."

Her dark eyes lifted. "What did he say?"

"That's the problem," Charlotte admitted. "TJ didn't say

anything. He ran when confronted by a Federal Wildlife Officer who gave chase. When the officer got within sight of the walls, the people inside opened fire, wounding him. He's in the hospital lucky to be alive."

Kayla still looked confused. "Why would TJ run?"

"Because he was scared?"

"Why would he be scared?"

Charlotte let the silence work for her.

Kayla kicked off the covers. "No. I can tell what you're thinking, but there is no way TJ would hurt Brenna."

"What if Brenna told TJ you didn't want to see him anymore?"

"Then he'd have either gone home or come down to the camp to talk to me. He wouldn't hurt anyone."

"Maybe he didn't mean to? Maybe he lashed out in anger, and Brenna's death was a terrible accident?"

Kayla stood and started pacing. She looked frail in the borrowed nightshirt. "TJ isn't violent. He's a gentle person. You think I'd be attracted to someone who couldn't control his temper? No. Nope. No way. I've seen that cycle too many times to fall for that crap."

Her passionate defense was convincing.

Charlotte sighed heavily. "We need TJ to talk to us, but his father won't cooperate. I was hoping you'd be willing to record a message to TJ that we can send via email or play over a loudspeaker. I'm hoping you can persuade him to come out and talk to us."

"Are they like, holed up inside their bunker and surrounded by the FBI?" Kayla suddenly seemed to understand the gravity of the situation.

Charlotte nodded. "I'm doing everything in my power to

get them to communicate with us, but they won't pick up the telephone. We want to end this thing without violence, but they aren't helping achieve that goal."

Kayla's mouth tightened. "Please don't let anyone harm TJ. He wouldn't hurt anyone. Ever. I won't be able to live if I lose him too."

Charlotte reached out and squeezed her arm. "A message from you might persuade him to talk to us."

Kayla swallowed noisily. "I'll do it. I'll do anything to help get him out of this alive." She picked at her shirt. "But not wearing this. Do you have any of my other clothes?"

Charlotte almost smiled. Kayla must be feeling better if she was worried about her appearance. "I'll see where your things are." It was possible the lab had finished with them and could release them, but not likely. "We're about the same size so I'll fetch you something of mine to wear in the meantime. One thing. Would you be willing to work with a basic script from us? One that encourages TJ to give himself up for questioning so we can figure out exactly what happened to Brenna?"

"I'm not lying to him," Kayla said tersely.

"I'm not asking you to lie. I don't want you saying something to him that he might misinterpret and possibly put his life or those of the others inside the compound in danger."

Kayla looked upset and confused, but Charlotte couldn't tell her about the threat TJ's father had made. It was possible the other people in the bunker hadn't heard Tom utter that threat to the Feds. She wanted to avoid cornering Tom or creating panic and that meant treading very carefully indeed.

Kayla nodded. "Okay."

Charlotte headed to the door. "I'll fetch you something to wear and a brush for your hair. We'll tape downstairs so you don't have an entire crew of Feds in your bedroom." It was important to have a safe space to retreat to.

Charlotte headed down the corridor and opened the door to the room she shared with Novak. She stood paralyzed for a few moments as the memories from last night flooded her mind. But she didn't have time to dwell on the fact it hadn't been enough for him while it had been almost too much for her.

Instead, she grabbed another pair of black leggings, a t-shirt, and a gray FBI sweatshirt from her small case. The room smelled of their night together so she opened the window a notch. She'd close it after they finished filming. She dropped the clothes off and left Kayla to change in privacy, heading downstairs to where a tech was setting up the recording equipment in front of the roaring fire.

Kayla came down five minutes later, looking young and scared and delicate after her illness. But there was a determined set to her jaw that Charlotte recognized.

"Sit over here by the fire." Charlotte encouraged.

Kayla sat on the couch, and her sock-covered feet didn't quite touch the floor. The sweatshirt looked bulky, but at least it would keep her warm.

"Read off the teleprompter. If you want to run through it first, that's fine. And if you want to say something a little more naturally, then go with it."

Kayla stared at her, looking young and uncertain and overwhelmed. Who wouldn't be?

It took almost an hour to get a take they could use despite the fact she'd gone off script a little at the end talking about how much she wanted to see him again at their special tree. Kayla was now sitting shaking while drinking hot cocoa.

"Send it to McKenzie and BAU and get them to review it ASAP. If we don't hear back in thirty minutes, we're using it anyway," Charlotte murmured to the tech working with her on this.

Charlotte went back over to Kayla. "You look tired. How about I take you back to your room."

"You'll let me know how it goes? If TJ sends a message back for me, right?" Kayla shuffled along in a pair of house slippers the ranch owner had found for her.

Charlotte nodded. "As soon as I get the chance. Yes."

Kayla turned outside the door to her room. "Please don't hurt him. Don't hurt TJ."

Charlotte swallowed. "We are doing our very best to get everyone safely out of this, Kayla. You have my word. This agent will get you anything you need in the meantime." Charlotte indicated the guard.

"No problem. I'm here to help." The man smiled cheerily.

Kayla nodded and tried to disguise a yawn. They'd definitely exhausted her more than they should have.

"Get some rest." Feeling guilty, Charlotte turned around and left. She needed to head up the mountain and see if her team had made any progress knocking down the wall of silence the people in the compound had erected. She needed to stay busy to keep her mind off the wreckage Supervisory Special Agent Payne Novak had made of her heart.

CHAPTER THIRTY

FORTY MINUTES LATER, Charlotte watched intently as Eban, speaking from the cover of the woods, used the bullhorn to work through a monologue that they often used in these sort of barricade situations.

How can I help you?

What do you need?

Everyone wants a peaceful resolution.

No one wants anyone to get hurt.

We know you don't want to go to prison.

We understand your fears.

Help us resolve this peacefully.

The words echoed eerily through the air, swirling through the trees and bouncing off the bare rock of the mountainside—hardly conducive to surrender.

HRT had knocked out the camera feeds and ground sensors as they didn't want the people inside the bunker to have any information regarding the FBI's intentions, or help them potentially pick off targets with a sniper rifle. Charlotte was back in the same creek bed she'd visited several times already—a safe zone for the FBI to assemble personnel.

She tried to pull her wooly hat farther down over her ears but damn, it was cold. A storm was gathering. The tension grew thicker around them, putting everyone on edge, pulling tighter and tighter until Charlotte thought her nerves might snap.

Novak paged her on the radio. "Leaflets are inbound."

"Roger that." She sounded so lame, but it wasn't like she could scream at him, "I don't want to cool it!" At least not without humiliating herself in front of everyone and possibly losing her career.

Yippee-kai-yay, mother trucker.

She heard the quiet buzz of the large drone approaching from the east and looked up at the overcast sky. The tops of the trees swayed violently in the wind, and the forecast said it was going to get much, much worse.

The drone zipped overhead, and she twisted to watch its progress as Eban kept up his monologue.

Even though there were no defensive slits on the inner walls—probably so defenders didn't kill one another in the crossfire—the plan was to do a rapid delivery to avoid anyone inside the bunker getting a line of fire on the drone. The drone would dip inside the barbed-wire fence, release its cargo, and head straight out again.

"Leaflets deployed." Novak's deep voice crackled in her ear again, and she hated how the memories of their intimacy conflicted with his clipped military precision. He seemed remote and not simply because he was still back at the base.

She keyed in the radio channel that connected her to the negotiation team. "Tell them about the leaflets, Eban. Before they freak out."

She hated being distracted about a personal issue during an incident—which was why the FBI didn't allow agents in a relationship to work together in the same unit. But she and Novak technically weren't in the same unit, and they were equals in terms of rank and authority. They hadn't broken the rules, but their affair, if you could call it that, would be frowned upon by people with too much time on their hands at HQ.

Not that *anyone* would ever know about it.

And what did it matter? Novak had proven he wasn't interested in her for more than a one-night stand. She wasn't the sort of woman who needed to have the message repeated. Communication was her expertise. Cool it? She was happy to shove the entire disastrous episode in the deep freeze. She wasn't stupid or desperate. Nor would she ever admit exactly how close he'd come to changing her idea about the sort of man she wanted to fall for.

The drone flew overhead again as Eban explained over the bullhorn that the FBI wasn't trying to attack them or scare them. It was simply delivering some information by drone as the people inside had allowed them no other option. Then he was back to the calm reassurances that were both comforting and lulling.

Novak had told her he wasn't good with women, and she'd thought he was using that as an excuse to avoid relationships. But she'd been wrong—he really wasn't good with women. He was grumpy and difficult. He was also attentive and kind.

She hated him. She really hated him.

A fierce blast of wind had her staring up at the sky with concern. The first flake of snow catapulted out of the air, followed by another and another. Winter had arrived, and she was pissed.

———————————

TJ STARTED VIEWING the photographs on his laptop. Hundreds of images. Thousands. Of the mountains. Of the owls that had hatched in the late spring. Beautiful images that showed his world in all its magnificence. At dawn. At sunset. In bright sunshine and drenched in rain.

At first, he didn't understand.

Then he came across one of Kayla sitting in her sleeping bag looking as if she'd just woken up inside a sunny yellow tent. His mouth went dry.

He printed the image out, needing that physical connection to the girl he loved, the girl he thought he'd lost. He touched the screen, wishing he knew where she was and whether or not she was okay.

Why did Malcolm have this camera? Had he stolen it?

Of course he'd stolen it. But from whom?

TJ kept going through the images with mounting trepidation. The answers came toward the end of the pictures as he'd known they would. The ones taken on Wednesday morning. The ones taken by the girl who'd died. The girl who looked so like Kayla. Kayla's friend.

He went through each single photograph until he finally figured out what had happened, and exactly why Brenna Longie had been murdered.

A calm rage settled over him. Now he understood. Now he understood everything.

His email dinged and, although he expected another plea from the Feds to end this thing peacefully, instead the sender was Kayla, and there was a video attachment.

His heart was on fire when he clicked play.

NOVAK TOSSED THE radio on the counter and then winced when Romano shot him a startled look.

"Sorry."

"No problem, boss."

Romano had warmed up the second drone, and they were using it to monitor the inner door and the leaflet delivery. The small, white postcard-sized pieces of paper fluttered around every inch of the enclosure like a giant ticker-tape celebration at the end of the Super Bowl.

"You gotta be missing hanging out with a beautiful woman rather than me and a bunch of hay bales." Romano shot him a grin.

"Shut the fuck up." Novak's teeth were clamped so hard together it was like breaking his jaw every time he needed to speak.

Romano sobered, and Novak didn't miss the face he pulled as he went back to his monitor.

Novak sighed. What he should have done was made a joke about the hassle of working with women in general or Charlotte in particular, but there was no way he was doing that. Not even to disguise the fact he was absolutely miserable. These were smart guys. It wouldn't take them long to do the math.

"Movement on the door," he said instead.

The people in the compound sent out the young boy again. He ran like a rabbit, zigzagging this way and that, collecting handfuls of leaflets before heading back to the door. Clearly terrified.

"Fucking cowards," Novak snarled.

Romano shot him another wary look. "Everything okay, boss?"

Novak scratched his eyebrow. Dammit. "Sorry for being an asshole. I'm getting a little sick of these guys running the show. I know the negotiators are right. We need to exhaust all peaceful avenues unless something changes on the inside. But I think the people in that bunker are a bunch of paranoid fools." And Novak had hurt someone he cared about, whether he wanted to care about her or not. No wonder his ex had decided he wasn't worth the effort.

The first drone was picking up movement inside the cafeteria.

"I'll let you kick my ass when we get back to Quantico but right now, fly the second drone to the observation slit while these guys are distracted."

They'd picked the location out earlier based on the fact it would get the greatest noise distortion from Eban *fucking* Winters talking through the bullhorn. Fucker. The slit they'd chosen wasn't in the direct line of sight to where the negotiators had set up through the thick stand of trees and where the guards were most likely to be keeping a close watch.

And perhaps Eban Winters wasn't the only fucker here.

Novak had seen Charlotte's injured expression when he'd said they should cool it. And, as she'd been the one to make all the moves so far, why should she be the one to tell him, that no, they shouldn't fucking cool it. That, in fact, they should keep the burner turned all the way up on this thing that was going on between them because he hadn't had sex like they'd had last night since he was in his late teens. And he hadn't felt this emotionally wrecked since his wife dumped him.

They'd clicked.

As bizarre as it seemed, her easy-going calm was the perfect complement to his default grim. And whereas a few days ago he'd thought her low-key diplomacy was a cop out, now he knew she was as determined as he was to help make the world a safer place. Unfortunately, the other thing they had in common was a will of iron.

There was no way in hell she'd make the next move. Not now.

To have any kind of chance, he needed to fix what had gone wrong between them. Except then what? Was he really ready for a serious relationship again? Part of him craved it, but was it worth the all-consuming holistic pain? Hell, no. His ex had destroyed the fantasy of coupledom for him. He should content himself with being grateful for the scorching bedroom antics last night. Instead he was down-to-the-bone miserable.

He wanted more.

And was too scared to go after what he wanted.

The irony wasn't lost on him. The negotiator was the one with the bigger balls in their personal skirmish.

He turned his attention to the monitors.

Romano was struggling to fly the drone through a two-inch gap in the blustery wind. The guy was completely focused on his task, and Novak realized something serious was kicking off in the cafeteria.

Novak backed away from the table so he didn't distract Romano and called McKenzie.

"You need to get over here. Now."

"Drone's inside." Despite the coolness of the barn, sweat dripped down the side of Romano's face.

"Good job." Novak braced his hands on the table and stared at the screen. "Start searching the lower levels for explosives while most of them are occupied in the canteen. Let me know immediately if you find anything."

"What have you got?" McKenzie strode up to him.

"Some sort of meeting. Doesn't look friendly."

"Turn it up. Let's hear what they have to say."

"I think we should get Charlie team back here and Echo team up on the hillside." Novak did not like the look of this mob. He especially did not like the idea of Charlotte being up on that hillside even with SWAT for backup.

"Scramble Echo team into position but let's listen to what's going on before we call back Charlie," McKenzie overrode him.

But Novak knew what things looked like when something was about to go south. It looked like an angry mob in an underground bunker. It looked exactly like this.

CHAPTER THIRTY-ONE

T J STRODE TOWARD the communal kitchen with a growing sense of fury. He could hear raised voices and shouting, including his father's voice.

When he walked in the room, everyone went silent. The only noise was the constant sound of the bullhorn the cops had started using about thirty minutes ago. It was already grating on his nerves.

"And here's the little prince. The bastard that started it all." Malcolm stood on a table and jeered at him.

Anger seared TJ. He twisted away as one of Malcolm's friends went to grab him and next thing he knew, his dad was by his side with his hands raised.

Thankfully, people still respected Tom Harrison enough to listen to what he had to say, so they quieted down.

"My late wife and I gave you shelter when no one else would help you." He cocked his head and stared at people individually. Most of them had the grace to look ashamed. He put his hand on TJ's shoulder. "We shared our food and our home with you. Built you beds to sleep on. Provided heat for your rooms. A safe place for your children to grow up. And you repay me with this? Wanting to kick my son out to the very authorities most of you are running from?"

His voice didn't get louder, but the condemnation was

clear.

"Isn't safe if we're living with no murderer."

"TJ is no murderer." His dad tried to talk sense into them. It didn't work.

Malcolm waved a white piece of card at them. "The Feds are gonna storm the gates if we don't give them what they want."

"How about we start with whoever shot the wildlife officer and deputy?" Tom countered.

"How about we start with whoever killed Brenna Longie." TJ's voice rang out through the space.

"That's what I've been saying all along you little cur," Malcolm sneered.

TJ stared at Malcolm until the other man faltered. "I know what you did. I know you've been stealing our gold. I know you killed Brenna Longie. I know it, and I've got proof!" TJ yelled as all hell broke loose.

His dad grabbed his arm. "Time to go, TJ."

TJ wanted to confront Malcolm further, but it was clear no one believed a word he said.

"Now!" His dad dragged him out of the room, and they started jogging down the steps.

Malcolm yelled after them, "You can run, but there's nowhere to hide. I'm coming for you."

His dad was full-on sprinting now and had his key out and in the lock. TJ dove inside and helped hold it closed while his dad flipped the deadlock.

Someone started banging on the metal portal.

"What about the spare keys in the office?" TJ asked suddenly.

"I swapped it out a couple weeks ago when I realized Malcolm was sneaking in here and trying to break open the safe." Tom applied the other bolts and nodded with satisfaction. "Go grab the packs and lock every door securely on the way back. It won't hold them forever, but it'll hold them for long enough."

TJ wasn't sure how they were going to escape, but there wasn't time for questions.

"Did you know he'd been stealing our gold?" TJ asked as he hefted the two heavy packs and locked the door between the living room and the kitchen.

"I knew he wanted to but hadn't realized he'd found any of it." Tom strode into the bathroom and grabbed a crowbar out of the linen cupboard. He inserted it into a narrow gap between marble slabs that formed the floor. "Grab the other side of this."

TJ did so and together they slid the heavy marble slab to one side. Directly below ran a two-foot-wide drainage pipe.

"I added this when I installed the tub for your mother and figured it wouldn't hurt to have an emergency escape no one else knew about." Tom slipped into his winter jacket.

TJ swallowed. "Where does it come out?"

"Top of the hill. I covered the top with grass seed years ago so it might take some lifting, but it's our best chance of getting out of here alive."

"You really think they want to kill me? Malcolm is the one who must have killed Brenna."

Tom glanced at him but didn't say anything.

"Kayla's alive, Dad."

"Kayla?"

"The girl I'm seeing."

His dad smiled almost sadly and patted his arm. "I'm glad, son. Now let's get the hell out of here."

TJ grabbed his dad's arm. "Won't the FBI pick us up as soon as we exit the tunnel?"

"Snow's started now. We're in for a hell of a blizzard." Tom shook his head. "Climb on down, son. I need to slide the slab back into place so they don't know where we went."

The banging on the door was getting louder as if they were using a battering ram.

TJ tossed the crowbar into the tunnel and shimmied head-first down the tight space, dragging his pack behind him until there was room for his father to climb in after him. He heard the heavy scrape of stone across stone. As soon as the slab settled into place, darkness pressed down upon him. The drain smelled like musty earth, icy dirt. It smelled like a frigid grave.

He put on his headlamp and started crawling one inch at a time through the pipe heading uphill.

"Drain goes under the other exit, but we might need to dig our way through if the explosives damaged it," Tom said behind him. The words echoed eerily.

Great. Panic expanded through TJ's lungs and his body. How had his world morphed into this nightmare in the space of a few short days? He forced the terror and the alarm out of his mind. Concentrated instead on moving his large frame through the narrow pipe toward the exit.

It was fine. Everything was fine.

Even when he got to a pile of dirt, he didn't allow the fear to intrude. He pushed the panic to one side. Concentrated on the next breath. His father passed him his collapsible shovel, and he started digging his way through loose soil that had fallen through a crack in the side of the pipe.

Everything is fine. Everything was going to be fine. His dad always had a plan.

———————

KAYLA LISTENED AT the door for a long moment. The whole house was so quiet that every creak and groan of the wooden beams resonated through the peaceful space and echoed off the walls.

None of which helped her.

She glanced around and noticed the TV. She turned it on and then climbed into bed, pulling the covers up to her chin.

The agent who'd been assigned guard duty popped his head in after a few minutes.

"Feeling okay?" he asked.

He seemed nice and reminded her of her old geography teacher from back in Pittsburg.

She nodded. "I was bored. Do you mind if I watch something? Am I disturbing you?"

"Not at all."

"I think I'll take a bath in a little while."

He nodded. "Sounds like a plan. I'll be outside if you need anything."

She swallowed. "Thanks. I appreciate it."

She found a particularly clappy-clappy talk show but didn't put the volume so high that it would disturb anyone. It helped disguise her movements. She went into the bathroom and started running the faucets, adding bubble bath that sat on the shelf.

Then she went back to the window and opened it up, applying a little force that produced a noise that made her freeze. The agent didn't seem to have heard. She shivered at the frigid blast, but she couldn't let the discomfort deter her. A cause worth fighting for was a cause worth suffering for.

The pitch of the roof was steep, and snow swirled around as the wind gusted. She really didn't want to do this.

She moved a chair beneath the window, grabbed the knickknacks off the sill, and put them on the bookcase so she didn't break anything or make a noise. Then she ran back and turned off the taps, pulling the bathroom door shut behind her. Back in the bedroom, she moved as quietly as possible. Climbing onto the sill using the chair and then crawling out onto the roof.

Oh God. Her stomach lurched as if she was on a roller-coaster. Immediately, the wind snatched at her hair, effectively blinding her. She shuffled along carefully, the shingles scraping her palms and knees.

The icy-cold took her breath. She twisted back and closed the window behind her, grateful it was old fashioned enough not to have a mechanical winding mechanism. Instead it shut snugly due to the amount of paint on the woodwork.

She made her way gingerly along the steep rooftop, trying not to make any noise in case people were sleeping inside and realized there was someone on the roof.

She froze when she saw the big man who'd accompanied Charlotte yesterday, the one who'd carried her out of the tent and brought her back here. She was completely visible should he look up, though she wore black and gray like the roof tiles and stayed perfectly still beside a chimney stack. She held her hair down, leaning back until she was pressed flat against the roof near the brickwork of the stack.

Novak—she remembered his name—opened the barn door, and another man came out leading two horses. The snow was thick now and getting thicker by the second. She stayed perfectly still as Novak closed the barn door and then climbed onto one of the horses. The two men rode away, and she *knew* this was her chance. She crawled across the roof and came across an open window. Kayla's teeth chattered as she lifted the latch and opened the window wide, praying there was no one in the room. She climbed inside, holding on to the frame so the wind didn't catch it. She eased the window closed behind her and slid slowly to the floor.

Her heart pounded.

Her hands were already numb, as was her face.

Quickly, she rifled through the case that sat on the floor. She pulled off the thick sweatshirt and pulled on another long-sleeved t-shirt and a thin black sweater that felt as soft as cashmere. Then she pulled the sweatshirt back on again. She spotted sneakers in the corner of the room. They were a size too big so she pulled on another pair of thick socks and tried again. Not perfect but not bad.

Her hands hesitated over the windbreaker and ball cap. Both had "FBI" emblazoned on them in thick yellow letters and wearing them was probably illegal unless it was Halloween. The problem was, there was no way she'd survive long without something to cut out the wind.

She tied her hair into a thick pony at the nape of her neck, pulled on the cap, and grabbed the jacket. She had no idea if TJ had a way to get out of the place where he lived or not. He'd always alluded to sneaking out, but she didn't know exactly what that meant. She'd added the bit about meeting her at their tree in the hopes he could do that. He'd understand as soon as he saw her message and, if he could, he'd be there.

She needed to know what had gone down. They'd figure out what to do after that. When he'd told her what had happened on the mountain with Brenna, she'd bring him back here and get him to talk to Charlotte, and pray she wasn't making a massive error in judgment.

But TJ wasn't a killer. He wasn't.

Kayla listened at the door for a slow count of ten. Then she headed out, acting confident and focused as if she belonged here and had a very important job to do. She walked softly down the corridor, down the stairs, and outside into the storm.

CHARLOTTE GLANCED UP at the burgeoning sky. The thing that kept bothering her was Brenna's missing camera. A woman might lose a hat or gloves, but a photographer would never mislay her camera.

Charlotte had checked the evidence logs, and a camera had not been found in the tent or the car. She glanced up at the sky again and knew this would be her last chance to search for it before spring. Bob Jones hadn't recalled seeing a camera before he'd been shot either.

What if the camera had photographs of Brenna's killer on it? How would that be for evidence?

Eban was still on the bullhorn with Max supporting him. Dominic was manning the phone back at the Command Center with the other negotiators. She felt surplus to requirements. Everyone knew exactly what they were doing. Until something changed, they didn't need her. Even then, the negotiators here were the best of the best. McKenzie's edict that she "oversaw" them left her basically jobless until these people started communicating with them.

At least when she and Novak had been shadowing each

other, they'd helped move the case forward. Out here on the mountain, she couldn't even do that.

Truman paced nearby. He was acting as her assistant today and looked equally frustrated.

She stood. "Let's go quickly scout the crime scene perimeter where we found Brenna Longie's body and look for her camera."

Truman frowned and stared up at the sky. "I'm not sure that's a good idea." He shot her a look. "Plus, SSA Novak might rip me apart if anything happens to you."

So he'd noticed something had changed between them. Something seismic.

"This is none of SSA Novak's business." The bitterness that dripped from her tone had Truman frowning. Charlotte looked away. She wasn't ready to acknowledge that Novak had caused her pain. Not publicly. Inside was another matter. Inside was a festering mass of insecurity and hurt that would take time to purge.

She started walking, and Truman quickly caught up. "I want to walk a grid pattern another twenty-five feet outside the tape in case Brenna dropped her camera and ran when she was attacked."

They could see clearly through the trees, but a thin layer of snow was already accumulating on the ground. She made a call to SWAT to warn them they were going to be in that area for a few minutes, not wanting to be arrested or shot.

When they reached the crime scene tape, she mentally marked her starting point, and she and Truman began walking in opposite directions in a systematic pattern, eyes glued to the ground.

Truman's sat phone rang. She looked up as he answered.

He jogged around to meet her. "McKenzie is on his way

and wants us there to meet him."

Charlotte glanced around in frustration. They'd already covered about a fifth of the territory she wanted to search. "You go. I'll be twenty minutes behind you."

"I can't leave you here alone."

"Don't be ridiculous. I know the way back. I want to finish up here first." She wanted to find that camera. "It won't take long."

Truman still looked unsure. "What if there's a whiteout?"

"What are you gonna do? Hold my hand?" She teased the guy, aware that a few days ago those words from her mouth would have been flirting, but both of them somehow knew today that they were not. She had the horrible feeling he knew why and wondered how many others had guessed her and Novak's not so secret attraction.

"Call me immediately if anything changes." Twenty minutes was pretty much all Mother Nature would give her anyway.

Truman pressed his lips together into a thin line and then nodded before walking away.

Charlotte put her head down and began her search again. The wind howled around her, and she shivered despite her cold weather gear. If this storm turned into the full-on blizzard it was predicted to become, then everyone would need to retreat until the snow stopped and they could reassess the situation from base.

The sense of anticipation was growing, as if this storm was foreshadowing something big. But Charlotte wasn't superstitious, and she wasn't about to give into panic. She was sure the camera contained clues about Brenna's last moments. Figuring out how the girl had died was worth a few minutes of temporary discomfort.

CHAPTER THIRTY-TWO

SOIL DUSTED HIS hair, coated his nostrils and mouth, and crept inside the neck of his jacket. TJ coughed as he clawed his way through another mound of dry earth. He felt like a worm wriggling blindly through the soil. Every breath made him choke.

"We're getting there, son."

It didn't feel like it. They'd already dug through ten feet of soil and debris. TJ was convinced they were going to be trapped down here and buried alive.

Every time terror threatened to take hold, he concentrated on one more clawed handful of dirt, one more hard-fought inch of forward progress. He'd almost lost it a dozen times already, but there was nowhere to go. Even if he lost his mind and started screaming into the void, he was still stuck in an underground pipe. Plus, he could hear his dad shuffling along behind him. The idea of looking like a coward on top of bringing every level of hell to their world because he'd made a lousy decision a few days ago was unbearable. TJ concentrated on scraping through the dirt inch by inch, even as the concrete pipe seemed to become smaller and smaller, until it squeezed his shoulders.

Was it his imagination? Sweat broke out on his brow.

"Almost there, son."

Relief made his teeth chatter. Or maybe that was the cold.

TJ reached a manhole cover set in concrete above his head—the outside world once again within reach, along with the inherent danger it contained. But he'd rather face anything that lay outside than spend one more minute in this underground hell.

He twisted and sat up, tried to unscrew the opening mechanism on the hatch. It was nice to be upright again, but at first the cover didn't budge, and alarm began to swell again, sweat slicking on his brow. Perspiration was the last thing he needed if they were heading into a blizzard. He wiped his face on his sleeve.

He needed to get out of here. To get to the tree. He needed to see if Kayla was there. He was pretty sure that's what she'd tried to tell him in the video. To meet him at the tree.

He repositioned himself to get better torque. He put every ounce of his strength into forcing the mechanism to move, and finally the satisfying grind of rusted metal on rusted metal screeched out as the wheel started to turn.

Once the lock was undone, the heavy cover still didn't budge.

"It's the grass roots, TJ. Keep trying. It'll open," his dad encouraged him.

"As long as there isn't an FBI agent sitting on top."

They both laughed, the humor relieving the excruciating tension. He looked down at his father lying in the tunnel beneath him.

"How did you know you were going to need this one day?" he asked curiously.

His father looked away, a pained expression crossing his features. "You know me, son, I like to have a backup plan."

TJ nodded. TJ's whole life had involved plans and backup plans and contingency plans. He'd always assumed it was an Army thing.

TJ once again put his shoulder into shifting the heavy metal cover. It lifted an inch, and dry clumps of soil rained down on them. His father cursed and backed down the tunnel a little to avoid getting dirt in his eyes. TJ tried again, feeling the grass roots begin to separate and pull apart.

When it finally gave, the cover went crashing over but landed with a cushioned thump.

He climbed out into a barrage of horizontal snow. His father passed him both packs before following him out.

TJ rubbed the dirt out of his hair and pulled a black knit cap from the webbing of his pack and dragged it over his head. Damn, it was cold. His father replaced the cover on the manhole and then slid his own pack over his shoulders, bouncing up and down to adjust the straps.

"This way," Tom ordered, checking his watch.

When TJ didn't immediately follow, Tom turned around.

TJ's mouth went dry. "I need to check to see if Kayla is at our meeting place."

Tom's mouth dropped. "No. No. The Feds will be all over that area."

TJ looked around and saw how far they'd traveled underground. Maybe quarter of a mile. His dad must have built this years ago because TJ didn't recall it at all.

"Dad, she sent a video. I think she sent me a secret message. To find her at the tree where we first met."

Tom's eyes were wide. "It's a trap."

"No." TJ shook his head.

"TJ, use your head. You can contact her after we get

away."

"How? Anyway, how are we going to get away, Dad? I mean we might escape in the short term, but long term? They'll know we're missing. Malcolm will see to that, even if the others don't say anything."

"They won't say anything."

"And you call me naïve," TJ said.

His dad flinched.

"I need to see Kayla. If she wants to come with us, great. If she doesn't, I'll turn myself in."

"No. No, son, no." Tom's mouth opened and closed as he gulped air. "All the sacrifices we made. Everything I did to protect you. You're going to throw it all away for some girl who might not even be true to you?"

TJ's anger flashed. "She's true to me. I know I made a mistake. You don't have to come with me. In fact, you should go." Tears burned, but TJ blinked rapidly as if it was the snow getting in his eyes. "I'll meet you at the deer hide later tonight if she isn't there."

Tom grabbed his arm. "I can't let you throw your life away!"

"I'm not a little kid anymore, Dad." He pulled away, which he could see his father hated. "I need to make my own decisions. I need to see if Kayla is by the tree." He shielded his face with his arm. "I need to make sure she's safe. The way you would look out for Mom."

Tom swallowed and took in a slow ragged breath. "I'll come with you. If this Kayla girl is there and didn't bring the Feds with her, we'll take her with us."

"If she wants to come."

Tom's lips pinched, then he started giving out more orders. "Quickly. Let's move through the trees. Careful, they'll have people out here."

TJ agreed. He knew the way. But the snow was so thick now visibility was down to ten feet. They'd literally have to bump into someone to be discovered. TJ knew it was foolish to head into a possible trap, but he also knew nothing and no one else really mattered. Only Kayla.

————————————

As THE SITUATION inside the compound rapidly deteriorated, HRT put their Immediate Action plan into play.

Novak rode a tall bay mare up the mountain with McKenzie at his side. Riding was faster than driving and then walking up from the road. They should be able to catch up with Echo team who'd left thirty minutes prior to get into position, preparing to instigate an assault that involved ballistic shields and enough C4 to bring down the main gate. Charlie team was planning to stage fifteen minutes away, waiting for the order to go. They would fast-rope down inside the concrete walls and blast the door where they'd spotted the kid entering and exiting a few times. Snipers teams were still in place, but the visibility was so reduced Novak planned to move them closer as soon as the others were in position. Snipers couldn't shoot what they couldn't see.

Romano had stayed in the barn, manning the drones with a few FBI techs and several local agents, including the gorgeous Agent Fontaine, assisting him. Novak knew without a doubt the guy would rather the female agent stay behind than his surly ass.

McKenzie was wearing jeans and a sweatshirt with his FBI

windbreaker thrown over the top and rode like he'd been born in the saddle.

Snow kept getting in Novak's eyes, and the weather looked set to become a full-on blizzard. They slowed the horses to a walk as they began a steep climb. "You seem pretty comfortable on horseback." He raised his voice to be heard over the wind.

"I grew up working on ranches in places like this. Winter is as godawful as I remember it," McKenzie said, shielding his eyes with his arm.

Novak grunted.

"I meant to tell you earlier." McKenzie gathered his reins and urged his horse to move closer. "DNA results came back on Brenna Longie. No semen but unidentified skin cells from three different people were isolated off her body. Get this, one was flagged in the Missing Persons database."

"What?" Novak frowned as he batted a tree branch out of his face.

"The lab is running the test again to confirm. The missing person DNA was processed in a different way, so someone is also rerunning that sample as we speak. Said they'd have definitive answers in a couple of hours."

They only needed a few skin cells to run Touch DNA tests, but it was also notoriously easy to get cross contamination, affecting results.

The incline eased off, so they urged the horses into a canter again, rapidly eating up the ground. They cut across the mountain south of Harrison land, hitting the now familiar stream bed before once again starting to climb.

They reached the place where the negotiators were set up and dismounted. Novak glanced around but didn't see

Charlotte. Disappointment flooded him. Was she purposefully avoiding him?

Eban Winters lowered the bullhorn, abandoned his position in the trees, and headed in their direction. "What's happening?"

He and Novak eyed each other warily, but they both had a job to do, and that came before any personal grudges.

Novak wanted to ask about Charlotte, maybe tell Eban he wanted another chance with her, but he doubted it would change Eban's opinion of him, especially now. And it was Charlotte's opinion that mattered.

"Looks like the people inside staged a coup. They were chasing Tom Harrison and TJ. Maybe it means they'll all surrender now?" McKenzie sounded hopeful.

Eban grimaced. "A change in leadership generally means the situation inside is becoming more volatile, and new leadership usually takes a harder line."

Novak swore. "Where's SSA Blood?" he asked, unable to stop himself.

Eban stared at him for a fraction of a second longer than was comfortable before saying, "She went to scout around the crime scene to look for the dead girl's camera before the snow buried it. She took Truman with her."

An evil glint lit Eban's gaze. One that said he knew Novak was jealous as fuck of the pretty-boy agent. But when Truman came tramping through the trees toward them, they both frowned.

"Why aren't you with SSA Blood?" Novak demanded.

Truman answered, "Fontaine told me that McKenzie wanted me here. SSA Blood insisted on finishing searching the crime scene perimeter for Brenna Longie's camera. She won't be long."

Anger had Novak's teeth fusing together. The snow was getting thicker now. He clawed back worry at the idea of Charlotte being alone out there on the mountain.

"I want her back here now," McKenzie said. "Situation has escalated."

Novak could have kissed him.

Truman called Charlotte on the radio. After the second attempt failed, the hairs on the back of Novak's neck sprang upright.

He checked his watch. "I know where the crime scene is. I'll return before anything kicks off here."

"And if you're not?" McKenzie asked with an edge.

Novak rubbed the soft nose of the mare he'd ridden. "Angeletti ran through this scenario a thousand times without me because of your orders. HRT know exactly what they need to do, and I'll be back in time to watch them execute."

Romano came over the radio. "We found C4 in the bottom level of the bunker, directly below the cafeteria area like you predicted, Novak."

Shit. Novak clenched his fists. He wanted to go after Charlotte, but explosives meant people's lives were in imminent danger.

"Appears to be on a timer."

"How long?" Novak demanded.

"Twenty-three minutes twenty-five seconds and counting."

Fuck.

Dominic Sheridan squawked to life on Eban's radio. "Someone new just picked up the phone."

They were standing in a small huddle now, McKenzie,

Eban, Novak and Truman, using the horses to help block out the noise of the wind.

"Ask if Tom Harrison is within hearing, Dom," Eban said loudly.

Dominic replied after a few moments. "Harrison isn't there. The guy on the radio said all the people who've been running the show have disappeared, and the rest of them want to get the hell out ASAP."

"Tell them to put down their weapons and come outside as there is the threat of a bomb inside the building," said McKenzie.

"Wait," Novak said sharply. "We can't be sure the doors aren't rigged to blow. Tell them to congregate in the center of the compound, unarmed with their arms up in surrender. We'll need to make sure the rear gate isn't rigged with explosives before they open it. Tell them to make sure everyone is wearing winter jackets, especially the kids, because they will need to walk off this mountain, and this storm is going to be a bitch."

"What's the ETA on the bomb tech?" Dominic asked over the radio.

Angeletti was the designated tech.

"Fifteen minutes away," Novak said and then swore. As much as he wanted to find Charlotte, he was the best explosives tech on site and couldn't simply walk away during a crisis, no matter how much he worried about her.

She was a professional.

"I'll do it." He expelled a long breath then gave Echo team instructions to split up and wait for people to exit the facility.

"Where the hell has Harrison disappeared to?" McKenzie asked, taking hold of Novak's mount.

Had the guy somehow slipped away? Or was he hiding in some deep bunker, while creating a doomsday scenario for all the other people who lived in the compound?

"Let's hope he stays out of the goddamn way until these people are clear of danger." Novak took off running toward the fortified walls. It was a risk, but at least he wasn't naked this time. He shivered anyway.

Where the hell was Charlotte? Was she purposefully avoiding him?

No, she'd never be that chicken.

Had she found something? Was she in trouble?

Dammit. He needed to wise up and clue in else his lack of concentration might mean he'd never see her again. He'd never get to say he was sorry. That he was an asshole who was so terrified of being dumped again that he'd retreated from getting emotionally involved with anyone who wasn't one of his teammates. People who were dependable and accepted him for what he was. People he could be close to without getting eviscerated.

But he certainly didn't want from them what he wanted from Charlotte, which was a deeper connection. He wanted to find a genuine, lasting relationship with a woman he could share his life with.

Even though the likelihood of her wanting him was minuscule.

He arrived at the rear gate without any bullet holes in him, which was a plus. Unless it was too cold to feel gunshot wounds, in which case it was still a plus.

He scanned the edges of the rusted metal. No obvious wires anywhere. He got on his radio. "Inform them a Federal Agent is climbing the walls to come inside. Tell them to keep the hell back, and no one will get hurt."

"Negative. It's too risky." McKenzie's voice came over the radio.

Novak was already scaling the outside of the bunker using his fingertips and the stiff soles of his boots wedged into the thin observation windows. He found finger holds in the cracks that marred the surface of the concrete and used the small lip at the apex of the narrow slits to lunge for the top. Shaking with effort, he hauled himself onto the wall and lay there catching his breath. Thankfully, the wire surrounding the compound wasn't electrified, and he snipped it so he could walk through.

He saw a terrified-looking man watching him and decided to hold his hands up showing they were empty. He had to yell over the howling wind. "I won't hurt you." Charlotte would be proud of him. "Get everyone into the courtyard. Someone planted explosives in the lower level of this structure, and your people are in danger."

"How do I know you're telling the truth?" the stranger yelled back.

"Wait twenty minutes, and you'll find out the hard way."

The man turned tail and ran back to his fellows.

Novak ignored him and the others who came out. People were tearing up his radio, but all he could hear was Charlotte's voice in his head.

There are babies in there, Novak.

And he'd do his damnedest to get them out alive. Twenty minutes wasn't a lot of time to do it in, but there was no rushing this particular task.

He saw the wires that confirmed his worst fear a few moments later and followed them down to a hay bale. Behind the bale, he saw a large block of explosives attached to a mechanical trigger. It appeared as if the trigger would activate when the gate opened. He walked across to the other side of the door and found a matching device. No matter which door opened, a bomb would go off.

He was about to take a step closer to the gate when he spotted a tripwire set about ten inches off the floor.

Sonofabitch.

He hunkered down. The bomb-maker, presumably Harrison, had created this as a deadly welcome for Novak's men. Fury began to grow, but Novak pushed it aside. He needed to examine the devices and disarm them. Quickly. Before Harrison detonated the ones beneath him which would also trigger these suckers.

He released the crick in his neck and blocked out everything else.

———————

CHARLOTTE HAD SEARCHED almost three quarters of her target area when she saw a flash of movement. It looked like Fontaine was heading up the hillside off to her right. The snow was blowing so hard it was difficult to see. Flakes of snow stung her eyes.

Dammit.

Charlotte carried on her search because another five minutes, and the snow would be too thick to see anything on the ground and wouldn't melt until April if they were lucky. Her encrypted radio squawked, but the weather was interfering with reception. She hoped they called SWAT and other personnel back down the mountain within the next half an hour.

She finished surveying the area and propped her hands on her hips, huffing with disappointment. Maybe TJ had taken the camera and FWO Jones had simply missed seeing it during the chase. Or maybe TJ had tossed it in the bushes somewhere. Maybe the hiker Bob Jones had spoken to in the parking lot had lifted the SLR from Brenna's lifeless body after he'd killed her.

She looked around and wondered where Fontaine had gone. Then she spotted her near an old, storm-damaged tree. Was she looking for something? Conditions were getting worse. Much worse. Charlotte decided it was time to head back to the mustering point.

She'd collect Fontaine along the way. It was definitely time to make sure no one got lost up here.

Her radio crackled again and, this time, when Charlotte put it up to her ear, she could vaguely make out the words. Things were hotting up. Definitely time to return to the frontlines.

She was about to take another step when a man slipped out from behind a tree with a pistol pointed at her head.

It was Tom Harrison.

"Drop it." He meant the radio.

Silently she swore. How had he gotten out of the bunker? Had anyone spotted him?

Had he seen Fontaine? Had Fontaine noticed Charlotte was in trouble? Charlotte let the radio fall into the snow.

Come on, come closer.

"Now the Glock. Only, real slow, thumb and index finger. If you do it wrong, I will shoot you."

Charlotte knew he wasn't bluffing. The thought of giving

up her weapon made her feel physically ill, but she didn't think she was going to have much choice if she hoped to survive the next few minutes.

A gunshot would bring other agents running, but they might not find her until it was too late. Her ballistics vest only worked if he didn't shoot her in the head.

"No one wants to hurt you, Tom." She very slowly removed her glove and reached down to *very* unhurriedly undo the Velcro of the holster she wore at her waist. She used her thumb and index finger to remove her weapon and tossed it about ten feet away from Tom Harrison.

"Back up until I tell you to stop."

Charlotte did so. The guy was intelligent. The expression on his face was wry as he walked forward to pick up both the radio and the gun. "Move an inch, and I will kill you. I don't owe you anything, understand?"

She nodded.

"Dad, stop."

"Don't hurt her!"

Charlotte recognized the voice of the woman who she'd thought was Agent Fontaine. It was Kayla Russell, and she was wearing Charlotte's clothes. TJ Harrison held her hand.

"You sent him a message in the video." Charlotte tried to disguise her bitterness at the betrayal, but she was so angry it leaked out. How could she have so badly misjudged the girl?

"I only asked TJ to meet me by the tree. I wanted to ask him about Brenna. I want him to turn himself in, because I know he didn't have anything to do with her death."

Tom pointed his weapon at the girl.

TJ immediately shoved Kayla behind his back.

"What the hell, Dad. No."

What was going on?

"She brought the FBI with her." Tom swung the weapon back to Charlotte, and she kicked herself for not tackling him, although he would probably have shot her.

"I didn't know she was here, I swear," Kayla sobbed. She was holding so tight to TJ's hand but crouching behind her boyfriend in terror. "Don't hurt her. She helped me!"

The girl was begging and crying so hard that Charlotte believed she was genuine. She was still pissed, but she didn't think Kayla had been in cahoots with these men. Only stupidly in love.

Charlotte heard people trying to raise her on the radio. Man, they were gonna be pissed she wasn't answering and, hopefully, they'd send a search party. But visibility was closing down. SWAT and HRT snipers didn't stand a pup's chance in hell of spotting them in this storm.

"He's not gonna hurt you, Kayla, or the lady FBI agent, right, Dad?" TJ asserted confidently.

Tom and Charlotte both shot him a look of disbelief.

"I didn't kill Brenna," TJ said quickly to Charlotte. "I know I shouldn't have run, but I was scared." TJ closed his eyes. "This is all my fault."

"Give yourself up, TJ. The FBI will believe you," Kayla urged.

"He's not gonna do that," Tom stated firmly with his eyes narrowing on the girl.

"Yes, I am, if that's what Kayla wants," TJ responded.

His dad huffed. "Don't be a damned fool, TJ. They'll lock you up and throw away the key."

"Not if he did nothing wrong," Charlotte emphasized.

Tom shot her a look like they were the only two adults in

the room, and Charlotte realized Tom Harrison had his own agenda that would override the opinions of his son, Kayla, and the Federal authorities.

"Let's talk to them, Dad. End this thing before anyone gets hurt."

Charlotte could see it didn't matter to Tom Harrison if anyone else got hurt. Nothing mattered except protecting his son and escaping capture. But how did he plan to do that long term?

"TJ?" Kayla said nervously.

Welcome to the family, Kayla.

"She can come with us." Tom jerked his head to the north. "But if you can't keep her under control, we leave her behind."

Charlotte set her teeth in anger.

TJ finally seemed to man up. "I'm not leaving her behind."

"How about I shoot the FBI agent instead?"

"Dad!" TJ was outraged, but Charlotte knew Tom was serious. She also knew he'd get rid of her as soon as he had the opportunity. One way or another. Otherwise she'd point the authorities straight to them.

Tom shouted over the blustery wind. "Move it, TJ. We need to get out of here before the FBI track us down. We can figure out everything else later."

Charlotte heard Truman calling for her on the radio again.

"Here." Tom tossed the radio to his son. "Listen to that in case they send out a search party for this one." The kid caught it and stuffed it in an outer pocket. Then he started moving north, his arm wrapped protectively around Kayla's shoulders.

Tom waved his gun at Charlotte. "Give them a few feet head start."

"So you don't hit them when you put a bullet in me."

"No reason to put a bullet in you if you do as you're told."

Sure, Jan. She purposefully dragged her feet through the snow, leaving a trail someone would hopefully be able to follow. She pictured Novak on the first night they'd arrived finding traces of TJ's passage over frozen ground.

Find me.

"You don't have to do this, Tom. You haven't done anything wrong yet." Except assaulting a Federal Agent and a few dozen other felonies.

"Look, lady, don't treat me like an idiot, and I'll return the favor."

"Charlotte. My name is Charlotte." Making herself human to him, not merely a Special Agent.

He glanced away. "Get moving, Charlotte. Or die. Your choice."

CHAPTER THIRTY-THREE

S WEAT POURED OFF Novak's brow, and he wiped his sleeve over his face. He'd dismantled the tripwire and then worked his way along each wire, looking for booby traps.

Echo team were searching the inhabitants for weapons before sending them across to a ladder system they'd rigged which seemed like the safest exit out of the compound in the shortest possible time. The clock was ticking. Signal blockers had been set up to prevent the bombs being remotely detonated, on purpose or accidentally, but they didn't have time to dismantle all the possible timers that had already been armed.

Novak spotted Cowboy cradling a baby as he climbed quickly over the wall.

Snipers had been ordered down from their overwatch positions as they'd been effectively blinded by the storm. And even though the FBI had some of the best pilots in the world, the wind was gusting too much to risk the helicopter. Charlie team had been dropped at the ranch and were now driving out to help escort these people to a processing center for interview.

He lay on his back on the ground and observed the device from that angle. Three wires went into the black box at the back. Red, black, green. He tried to see inside, but the thick plastic was opaque. He took photographs with his cell.

"Time to move it, boss."

He looked up at Cowboy who was now standing over him.

"We're as sure as we can be that everyone is out. Two minutes before the explosives underground are due to blow. We need to evacuate."

Damn. He was right. Novak swore and rolled away from the devices. There was no point in risking disarming them if the whole place was gonna blow anyway. Why did Harrison want to kill everyone here? If he hated them that much, why hadn't he thrown them out months ago?

"Right behind you." Novak told him.

They dashed over the ladder. The inhabitants had all been herded down a nearby trail. Cowboy went to follow, but Novak grabbed his arm. "This way."

They sprinted through the snow toward where Novak had left McKenzie and the negotiators. The creek bed would provide good cover as they had no idea how much C4 Harrison had packed into the place or how much ammunition was stored within the walls.

They threw themselves down the bank and skidded to a dramatic halt. Novak scanned the row of people who were taking cover.

"Good job back there," McKenzie told him.

Novak nodded. Where the hell was Charlotte?

"The unanimous opinion, according to the people coming out of there, was that everyone was accounted for except Tom Harrison, his son TJ, and Malcolm Resnick. They said the Harrisons had locked themselves in their rooms."

Novak frowned. He saw Eban looking at him with a worried expression on his face that told him Charlotte hadn't yet returned.

"Where's SSA Blood?" he asked.

"I don't know, but if she doesn't have a good excuse, I'm going to give her an official reprimand." McKenzie was pissed. The horses whinnied from where they were tied to a nearby tree.

"Nothing from SWAT?"

"SWAT and the locals withdrew. Conditions are getting too dangerous."

He and Eban stared harder at one another.

"I'm going to look for her," Novak gritted out.

"No, you're not," McKenzie said.

"I'm not asking permission, boss. I think she's in trouble, and I'm going to look for her."

McKenzie raised his hand for silence as Romano counted down the seconds on the radio.

"Five, four, three."

Novak hunched his shoulders and crouched low to the ground, resenting the delay.

Everyone ducked and covered their heads.

"Two, one."

The explosion was enormous and made the earth shake. The horses he and McKenzie had ridden up here reared in fright. A plume of smoke and dust blew forty feet up in the air, flames visible above the trees. Secondary eruptions rocked the ground beneath him. Holy shit. If Novak's men had walked into that, they'd all be dead.

Tom *fucking* Harrison had been serious about killing everyone within a hundred feet of that place.

A feeling of unease crawled over his shoulders, and he climbed to his feet before the debris had finished falling.

McKenzie rolled his eyes, obviously recognizing Novak's

intention. "SSA Blood had better have a damn good excuse."

Novak ran over to the horses, grabbed the reins and the horn of the saddle, and mounted up. Eban Winters was right with him.

No way would Charlotte not be here when things were going down, not when she cared about everyone as much as he did. He urged the horse into a full gallop, crouching low over the horse's neck and deftly avoiding overhanging branches.

They pulled up at the crime scene, horses blowing hard, yellow tape fluttering in the wind. They scanned the area and then quickly circled it, searching the snow for Charlotte. Had she had an accident? Twisted an ankle?

No sign of her.

Eban went to call out her name, but Novak stopped him with a firm grip on his sleeve.

"Look." He pointed at a series of footprints and a fast disappearing trail of broken snow cutting through the woods heading north. "Go fetch help."

Eban shook him off. "I'm coming with you."

Novak shook his head. "We might need reinforcements, and we can't risk using the radio."

Eban frowned and then caught on. He swore. "You think someone took her?"

Novak nodded. "She wouldn't have simply wandered off. Whoever has her possibly has access to our communications."

Eban grabbed him by the straps of his ballistics vest and shook him. "Do not lose her, Novak. Else I will fuck with your life for the next fifty years."

Novak nodded, unable to speak. He couldn't lose her. He'd only just found her.

THEY WERE OUT of the wind in a gully, and TJ took a moment to savor the relative calm. Kayla was struggling to make progress through the snow and kept stumbling against him.

He looked down at her pale features. He'd given her his mitts, but her teeth were chattering. "Are you okay?"

"She was very sick," the FBI agent shouted behind him. Her name was Charlotte. She'd apparently helped Kayla. "That's why she didn't meet you on Wednesday morning. Brenna came up the mountain to tell you she was ill. Kayla needs to get out of this storm."

Her skin was almost as white as the snow with the exception of dark shadows beneath each eye. She nodded, then stumbled again, and he realized she was exhausted. They needed to get out of the storm, but the deer hide was at least another mile through rugged terrain. TJ bent down and lifted her as his father groaned with exasperation.

TJ held Kayla's thin frame tight against him as he looked back at the FBI agent. "I didn't kill Brenna. I know who did though. I found photographs on Brenna's camera."

"Wait," the FBI lady said sharply. "You had Brenna's camera?"

"Found it under my Uncle Malcolm's bed."

"Malcolm Resnick?"

TJ watched the lady Fed's expression. She was pretty and didn't look like he'd expected a Federal Agent to look. She was nervous. She didn't understand his father wouldn't hurt her. He might tie her up and leave her at the deer hide, but he wouldn't shoot her. TJ would make sure she'd be warm enough.

"I understand you must be close to your brother-in-law, Mr. Harrison, but I'm surprised you'd shelter and protect a wanted killer," the FBI agent commented.

"Dad didn't know," TJ assured her.

"I'm not talking about Brenna."

TJ frowned.

"You knew about the reporter Malcolm killed, right?" Charlotte directed her question at his dad.

The words didn't make any sense. "What's she talking about?"

His dad was breathing hard, clouds of frozen air bellowing from his mouth. "I didn't want to let him stay, but my wife wouldn't forsake her own brother. I could hardly turn him away."

"Even if he killed Brenna?" Charlotte pushed.

TJ frowned.

Kayla gripped his coat. "Who killed Brenna?"

"My uncle," TJ said bitterly. "He was stealing gold from us. Brenna took photos of him. I think he killed her for that, tried to blame me instead."

Tom cocked his head. "I knew he was on the run, but he swore he didn't do it. When the girl was found dead, I suspected him, but he'd already established a hold over everyone. There was nothing I could do until we had a chance to escape."

"Was your wife ill before Malcolm Resnick arrived?" the Federal Agent asked softly.

Tom's nostrils flared as he absorbed her words.

The world shook beneath their feet. TJ staggered, trying to hold onto Kayla and stay on his feet. Flames and smoke billowed above the trees.

Tom glanced wearily toward the compound. "I don't think

we need to worry about Malcolm anymore."

Ice sliced through TJ. He let Kayla slide to her feet. "What did you do?"

"I did what I had to do. To keep you safe. To protect you."

TJ backed up a step. "You blew up our home?" Tears burned his eyes. "What about everyone in it? What about the children?"

"They weren't exactly willing to help you, now were they?"

The Federal Agent went sheet white. "This is your escape plan. Destroy the bunker and everyone inside and it'll be months, if ever, before anyone even realizes you weren't there."

"Keep moving," Tom said coldly.

TJ was in a state of shock, but he kept walking. He couldn't believe his father had blown up their home with people inside. People they'd lived with for years. He forced one limb in front of the other, arm wrapped tight around Kayla, helping her as she visibly struggled. He no longer knew the man who'd raised him, whom he'd loved all his life. He'd never imagined his father would harm anyone, let alone women and children.

His mother had brought some of those children into the world.

His stomach churned.

His limbs started shaking, and he staggered to one knee.

His father rushed forward. "Are you, okay, son?"

The Federal Agent lunged for Tom, but some instinct must have warned him, and he whirled toward her, and the gun went off. She crumpled into the snow.

TJ gaped in horror.

Tom raised the weapon to shoot her again, but TJ rushed his father.

CHAPTER THIRTY-FOUR

NOVAK RODE AS fast as he dared while scanning his surroundings. The tracks were getting blown away or covered in fresh snow, and he needed to use every sense and skill he'd ever developed to follow them under these conditions. He needed to find Charlotte.

He couldn't believe he'd left her feeling unsure about how much he cared. Hell, "cared" was total bullshit. He "cared" for Charlotte more than the woman he'd married.

The thought of losing her ate at him. Corroded his mind. He wasn't this cursed. No one was this cursed. He'd find her. He'd save her. He would rip the head off any fucker who hurt her again, including himself.

After that?

Who knew. But he was willing to at least fight for the chance to be with her.

The sound of a gunshot had him pivoting the horse east while his heart twisted nastily inside his chest. He spotted the trail ahead but cut higher up the mountain, cresting a small ridge behind a dense stand of conifers. He scanned the scene below, and his entire being laser focused on the most important mission of his life.

There.

A small group of people were visible through the branches.

Tom Harrison. TJ Harrison. A bolt of surprise went through him when he spotted Kayla, but he didn't waste time trying to figure it out.

Where was Charlotte?

He kept low, urging the horse forward, but using the trees to keep out of the line of sight.

Then he spotted Charlotte curled up on the ground with a patch of scarlet staining the snow beneath her.

His mind was screaming in denial, but his body kept going through muscle memory alone. Pressing forward. Making tactical decisions even as fear for her threatened to consume him.

TJ was trying to stop his father putting another bullet in Charlotte. They were struggling for control of the gun. As soon as TJ lost that fight, Charlotte would get a bullet in the head.

Kayla was screaming.

The gun went off, and TJ sagged at the knees.

The tableau in front of Novak hung in suspended animation even as he galloped toward them.

Tom Harrison dropped the weapon and held onto his son, both hands visible and empty, otherwise Novak would have put a bullet in his head.

He pulled the horse to a stop one-handed and leapt off. He tackled Tom and made him release TJ, clamping the man's one wrist and then the other behind his back and securing him with handcuffs. Novak scooped up Tom's pistol and stuffed it in one of his pockets.

"Help him!" Tom screamed in anguish.

Charlotte rolled onto her back, panting. "Glad you could make it to the party, Payne." She smiled, braver than anyone he knew. "I knew you'd come."

Her faith humbled him, made emotions and gratitude swell inside, mixing with something else. Something larger and scarier.

"Are you shot?" Novak parted Charlotte's jacket and felt fifteen thousand different bolts of relief when he touched the ballistic vest.

She grinned and grimaced at the same time and waved her glove at him, and he realized that was where the blood was coming from. "Clipped my fingers. Hurts like a bitch, but I'm okay now I've got my breath back."

The fact she was hurt but not dead loosened his normal reluctance to put himself out there. His normal cowardice. He took a leap because she wasn't dead, but she could easily have been. He leaned down and quickly kissed her mouth. "I'm not ready to cool a damn thing between you and me, SSA Blood."

And still it didn't feel like he was telling her everything, but they had to get out of this blizzard before they all died from exposure.

"Tend to my son!" Tom rolled in the snow.

Charlotte scooted over to where TJ lay in the snow, clutching his abdomen. "Kayla, I need you to come over here and help me." Charlotte tugged the straps of TJ's backpack off his shoulders and tried to open the fasteners one-handed. Kayla helped even though she was shaking.

Tom was trying to wriggle closer to TJ. "Help him! Help my son!"

Novak looked from the older man to the younger while he radioed for a medivac and updated the others. The weather was such he didn't think it would be possible to get the helicopter all the way out here. As he looked at the two men, he saw no family resemblance at all, not in size, shape, coloring, or features. Suddenly, it all clicked into place. The secure compound, the refusal to talk to the Feds, the desperate escape plan regardless of the cost in terms of human lives.

"Sonofabitch," Novak said, going to his knees while still keeping the older man in sight.

He checked for an exit wound, making TJ shriek in pain. "Sorry kid." Yup. There was blood on the snow behind him. "Pass me something to press against this," he asked Charlotte.

"There's a first aid kit in the side of my pack. I wasn't expecting to get shot though. What the hell, Dad?" TJ's voice was tight, mouth stretched in pain.

"I'm sorry, son. I'm so sorry. It was an accident. You shouldn't have grabbed it!"

Charlotte tossed Novak a red pouch and a survival blanket. She was doing everything one handed which made him think her hand was worse than she was letting on. But the kid might die without rapid emergency measures.

Novak pressed some random piece of clothing against the kid's front while he turned him to tend his back.

"There's a couple of packets of QuikClot in there," TJ told him, wheezing.

Novak grunted. Despite the freezing temps, he lifted up all TJ's layers and cleaned up the welling bullet wound he found there. He ripped open a pack of the hemostatic agent giving it a few seconds to work its magic. It might keep the kid alive until he could be transferred to a trauma center, depending on what else the bullet had hit on the way through. Novak pressed clean gauze against the wound, taping it, then rolled TJ onto his back, ignoring the groans of pain. He needed to stop the bleeding so he repeated the process on the entry wound while

Tom Harrison wept.

"I'm so sorry, son."

"He's not your son," Novak snapped.

Tom's jaw fell. TJ rolled his head in confusion.

The trees swayed violently.

"Can you walk?" Novak asked Charlotte.

"Yup." She was being forcibly upbeat, which was classic Charlotte. He gently grabbed her wrist and tugged off the glove, making sure she couldn't see the wound. *Shit.* He hid his concern and poured another pack of clotting agent onto her mangled fingers and wrapped her hand in gauze. Then he zipped her jacket closed and pulled his big mitt over her injured hand to protect her from frostbite. He kissed her again. "I was worried when I realized you weren't with the others."

Worried didn't begin to cover the emotions that had zapped his being when he'd discovered she was missing.

"My son is bleeding out while you waste time!"

"Whose fault is that?" Novak growled. "And like I said, give it up, he's not your son."

"Yes, I am." TJ sounded bitter.

Novak looked at Kayla. "I need you to stay beside SSA Blood and keep putting one foot in front of the other until we find help. Can you do that?"

The girl looked like a gentle breeze would knock her flat, but she nodded. The horse he'd ridden up here had run away. Novak hoped the animal knew its way home.

He rummaged through TJ's backpack and found a small tent. He extricated it from the case and spread the orange material on the ground next to the injured young man. Then he rolled the kid onto the canvas.

"That's a good idea. Undo my hands, and I can help pull

him. He's all I've got left," Tom said desperately.

Novak stared him down. "He's not yours, Tom. You know he's not yours, and I know he's not yours."

"What do you mean?" Charlotte asked.

"Touch DNA came back from Brenna's body, and one of the hits was to a missing person case. Start walking." He directed the last order at Tom. "That's why Tom here and his wife moved far away from civilization and locked themselves up in a concrete bunker. Not because they thought the world was ending, but because they were hiding from the authorities. It's why Tom wouldn't talk to us. He was terrified we'd figure it out, if and when we checked TJ's DNA."

"Dad?" TJ held tight to his wound. "What's he talking about?"

"Nothing, son. He's a liar. All Feds are liars, and they'll say anything to try to turn us against one another." Tom's lips pulled back in anger.

Charlotte looked contemplative as she dragged TJ's pack onto her good shoulder. Because it was evidence, and she insisted on doing her job.

It was in that moment he had his blinding epiphany. He *loved* this woman. And he'd probably never recover when she decided it was over between them.

Do the job. Get her to safety. Suffer later.

He forced this new and unwanted reality out of his mind. He wished nothing more than to kick Tom Harrison's ass all the way back down the mountain, but he needed to get these people to safety as this blizzard was beginning to shut down visibility. If he didn't get them out of here soon, they might all die.

CHARLOTTE KNEW HER hand was badly injured but ignored it. The cold helped. Having Novak save the day and declare he was interested in exploring this thing between them helped. She was thrilled, but part of her was churning with confusion. She'd wanted him to say more. To declare undying love for her. Even though he wasn't the kind of man she'd planned to marry. She tried to picture that ideal future again, but the man in her life kept morphing into Novak wearing one of his challenging grins.

How could she have fallen for a man who was so wrong for her?

Snow stung her eyes and brought her back to trying to survive and get the hell out of this storm.

She used her good hand to assist Kayla. Tom Harrison was using his bound hands to hoist one side of the tarp that cradled TJ up the side of the hill. Novak did most of the work. Tom was trying to help.

She watched Novak move, admiring everything about his strong physique and the competent way he moved. He was smart too. Really smart. She was stupid to have underestimated and undervalued him. He might not talk much, but the neurons were firing just fine in that brain of his. He'd figured out Tom Harrison's motivation and suddenly, everything the man had done made sense. TJ being a stolen baby was the Black Swan they'd been looking for. That was the one piece of information they hadn't known they hadn't known.

In the relative calm between a thick stand of conifers, she pressed Tom Harrison for answers. He'd been willing to shoot her in cold blood to protect his secret, to keep TJ with him no matter the cost. "Why did you steal a baby, Tom? What happened to your real son?"

"I don't know what you are talking about. You're all liars!" Tom started sobbing.

Charlotte ignored his protestations. "It explains everything. Especially why TJ doesn't look anything like you or your wife."

"Shut up. Shut up."

"Certainly why you freaked out when your CO told you to come out and talk to us. As soon as TJ was in the system you knew we'd figure it out. Did your wife kill the other child, Tom?"

He gasped. "No. He died." He seemed to realize his admission was the end of the road. Although maybe that had been earlier, when he'd shot her.

"Our son died, and my wife was inconsolable. She couldn't have any more babies. I thought she was going to die from grief, and I'd lose her too." Tom glanced at TJ, but the kid wasn't listening. The young man had passed out, and Charlotte was worried he wasn't going to make it.

Novak put his back into dragging TJ's inert form up another short incline before they started going downhill again, trying to retrace their original steps through the almost whiteout conditions.

"So you took someone else's baby," Charlotte shouted.

Kayla was failing fast. Charlotte grasped her arm. "You've got this, Kayla. Think of Brenna. Think of TJ. You can do this."

"Is he going to be okay?" Kayla asked, squaring her thin shoulders.

"Yes. Don't give up on him."

And suddenly there were figures running toward them.

Six HRT guys, plus McKenzie and Eban.

She had never been so happy in her life to see the cavalry. A knot of relief wedged in her throat. They were going to be okay. Everything was going to be okay.

A few moments later, she found herself swept up in strong arms. Maybe she'd fainted. She wasn't sure. She recognized the scent of the man who held her, the feel of his hard chest. She was in the warmth and safety of Payne Novak's arms, and it made her feel euphoric.

"Thank you for coming after me," she murmured.

He kissed her forehead, ignoring the presence of the other agents and Eban's stern glare.

"I'd probably be dead by now if you hadn't arrived when you did."

"Don't say that," he said harshly.

"Glad to see you still kicking, SSA Blood." McKenzie's gaze took in the way Novak cradled her protectively against him as four of the HRT operators picked up TJ and started running down the mountain with him in the makeshift stretcher.

Another operator lifted Kayla, and the other read Tom his Miranda rights as they all hurried toward safety.

"How bad is it?" Charlotte raised her hand, covered by Novak's oversized glove. The pain was bad, and she knew the bitter cold was numbing the true extent of the damage.

"It's going to be fine. A couple stitches, and you'll be good as new." But he wouldn't meet her gaze.

"I better be able to shoot after this, because I am not leaving CNU." She trained with her left hand, but it had always been weak. "I'm a freaking negotiator. Negotiators aren't supposed to get shot."

"Maybe next time you'll stay where you're supposed to," Novak admonished.

"That'll never happen." She smiled because he needed it.

"Maybe I'll report you to the Office of Professional Responsibility for not following procedure."

"As long as I get to be joined at the hip with you every now and then, I'd be happy with that."

"Really?" Even now he sounded so uncertain, as if he didn't know how much she'd enjoyed his company, how permanently he'd bound himself to that crazy part inside her that had gone and fallen in love with him even though she hadn't given it permission.

But she still wasn't ready to give him the words. "Really."

She must have fallen asleep because when she woke up, she was flying, and Novak was holding her good hand.

Medics were working on TJ. She hoped he was going to be okay.

Novak kissed her uninjured fingers. "I've got you, Charlotte."

"But will you keep me?" she joked, feeling a little punchy. But maybe she wasn't joking, because her eyes locked on his as she waited for his answer.

His fingers tightened on hers. "I am not letting you go, honey. I am not freaking letting you go."

"Good." She held those blue-green eyes of his, suddenly overcome with tiredness. "Because I think I might love you, Payne Novak, and that really wasn't part of my life plan." She drifted off, hearing him shouting at her in the distance, but unable to fight her way out of the darkness. Unable to answer his pleas.

CHAPTER THIRTY-FIVE

H E'D TOLD CHARLOTTE he wanted to pursue their relationship, and Charlotte had upped the stakes and flat out told him she loved him, even though he didn't fit in with what she'd imagined her future would look like.

And then she'd passed out, and he'd been screaming at her to stay with him. Even then the "L" word hadn't passed his lips. What was wrong with him? Emotions swirled inside him. What was he so scared of? Nothing compared to the regret he was feeling for not telling her before she passed out. Maybe when he'd found her bleeding in the snow would have been a good time to mention he was pretty sure he had heavy-duty feelings for her. What if she died? And he'd been too cowardly to confess that a few short days of being with her had destroyed all his defenses, brought down all his walls.

But she wouldn't die.

She was in surgery to save the use of two of her fingers and maybe reattach the distal phalanx of the ring finger on her right hand. The frigid temperature and speed of getting her to the hospital meant the doctors had a good chance of success. But what if there was an issue they didn't know about? What if she'd been shot somewhere else and the doctors hadn't noticed?

McKenzie strode into the waiting room, cell phone

pressed to his ear. He held up his hand to prevent Novak from speaking. "No, Mr. President. SSA Blood is still in surgery but expected to fully recover."

She'd better goddamn recover.

"We have one suspect in surgery. Serious condition after being shot by the man who raised him," McKenzie said.

Would TJ be classed as a suspect or a victim when the truth came out? It probably depended on what, if anything, he'd done to Brenna Longie.

"One suspect's whereabouts are unknown, but we believe he was in the basement of the compound at the time of the explosion and is likely dead or deep in a bunker. It'll take time to ascertain his fate. We need to wait until this storm passes."

Malcolm Resnick might have made his way out the same way Tom Harrison had escaped, but Tom swore the man didn't know about the tunnel. The likelihood was he'd hidden himself away, hoping that the FBI wouldn't be able to find him, not knowing Tom had rigged the place with enough explosive to reduce it to ashes.

Everyone else had gotten off the mountain alive, and they were being interviewed separately to try to figure out what the hell had happened.

"The owner of the facility, who we believe to be the ring-leader, is in custody. Yes, sir, it appears he and his late wife kidnapped a two-year-old name of Dale Singer sixteen years ago to replace their baby son who died."

TJ's biological parents had been informed their abducted child had been located alive but not the details. Not yet. Who the hell knew what was going to happen with that situation. TJ might not want to acknowledge them. He might not survive his wounds. Anyway, none of that mattered. All that mattered was getting Charlotte fit again, and then he could teach her to fire a gun as well with her left hand as with her right. All it took was practice and commitment. And he was fully committed. One hundred percent fully committed to helping her. To being with her. If he could only work up the balls to tell her about these feelings he was so terrified of.

"The HRT team leader who went inside the compound to check the gates for explosives?" McKenzie said as Novak winced. "He's right here, Mr. President."

McKenzie thrust the phone into Novak's hand. "You're up."

Shit. Novak put the cell to his ear and cleared his throat. "Mr. President."

He immediately recognized Joshua Hague's voice.

"Thank you for your heroic actions today, son. Your bravery turned around what could have been a grave tragedy."

"I was only doing my job, sir. Same as all the other Federal Agents and law enforcement officers out there today. I am no 'hero'. I'm part of a team of professionals."

Great. He was correcting POTUS.

Thankfully, the man laughed. "Modest too."

Novak felt his stomach pitch. He wasn't modest, he simply didn't deserve to be singled out.

"Thank you, sir," Novak added lamely before quickly handing the cell back to McKenzie like it was a live grenade.

McKenzie took it, his eyes critically assessing. Novak suspected he was about to get a tongue lashing.

Finally, the guy hung up. "Any news?" He nodded in the direction of the doors that led through to the surgical suites.

Novak shook his head. He shouldn't even be here. He should be with his men and debriefing the op. Filling in forms and packing up equipment in case they were needed somewhere else fast.

McKenzie sat on a seat across from him. "I guess my plan to get you guys on the same wavelength worked a little too well, huh?"

Novak clenched his fists, not knowing what to do with his hands. "Looks like. But don't blame SSA Blood for any of this. It's all my fault."

McKenzie rolled his eyes. "Trust me, if it's right, then you're each as responsible as the other."

Novak remained silent. He wasn't going to risk Charlotte's career.

"The other negotiators wanted to be here, but I gave them a direct order to start packing up and getting the paperwork finished. I'm sure they'll be rolling up before long."

Novak didn't want to deal with any of them. Not the negotiators, not his team, not McKenzie.

"I know what you're going through. I went through the exact same thing with Tess. I almost lost the woman I loved." The chair creaked. "Have you told her yet?"

Novak pressed his lips together. Shook his head.

"If you think it's real, then don't put it off too long."

Novak nodded again.

McKenzie laughed and then stood. Novak braced himself to disobey a direct order to get back to the ranch for the debrief. Instead, McKenzie tossed him a set of keys. "We have guards assigned to TJ and Kayla. The latter is being interrogated by Agent Makimi right now."

"For what it's worth, I don't think Kayla was involved in anything criminal. And TJ was struggling with Tom to stop him from pulling the trigger on Charlotte a second time."

Novak's stomach turned over. "She'd be dead if it wasn't for that young man. That's why he was shot."

"I need you back at base, Novak. There's a lot to do. But I'll give you enough time to see Charlotte and make sure she's gonna come through this okay." McKenzie nodded. "You know you can't avoid the paperwork forever, right?"

One side of Novak's mouth twitched. "Unfortunately, I do know that."

McKenzie squeezed Novak's shoulder before he headed out the door, and Novak sat staring at a mark on the floor. Finally, the surgeon came out to talk to him, thankfully wearing a smug smile that told him the surgery had gone well.

He blew out a massive breath of relief. "Can I see her?"

She smiled knowingly. "You can see her for a few moments, but she'll probably be asleep for the next few hours."

He followed the doctor through to the recovery ward, and there was Charlotte looking small and pale in the bed. Her hand was bandaged and restrained in a sling across her chest. That was gonna hurt when she woke up. The wound had been ugly, flesh torn, muscles mangled. But only one bone had been shattered by the bullet and, according to the surgeon, she'd pinned it and tried to put it back together the way it should be. Now they had to wait to see how well it healed.

He held Charlotte's good hand and kissed her forehead. Considering she was a negotiator, she managed to get into a hell of a lot of trouble in a short amount of time. It made a change for him to be the one left worrying.

He leaned down and kissed her quickly again, on the lips this time, but she was completely out of it. No response. Her skin felt warm and soft.

"I'll be back as soon as I can," he told her. He hated leaving her, but the nurses promised to call him as soon as she woke up. Then he'd be back. Then he'd tell her how he felt.

————————————

THE FIRST TIME Charlotte woke up after surgery, she'd tried not to be disappointed that it was Eban sitting in a chair beside her bed rather than Novak.

She went to move her right hand and found it confined by bandages and a tight sling. *Shoot.* That hurt.

"Careful." Eban came out of his chair and smiled down at her. "You're going to be okay, but the surgeon had to do a number on two of your fingers."

"What happened at the compound? Was anyone hurt?"

He told her what had gone down. "That boyfriend of yours was pretty badass." He explained how they'd discovered the explosives on a timer, and then Novak had discovered the boobytraps on the compound gates and tried to diffuse them while the people evacuated over the wall.

The fact that Eban had called Novak her boyfriend made her smile. It was an apology of sorts. A sign of approval for the man she'd fallen for, not that she needed it.

Where was he though? Probably caught up with McKenzie.

He'd told her he wasn't going to let her go. Her cheeks burned a little as she remembered how she'd told him she loved him. *Damn.* But she did.

The issue was whether or not Payne Novak could ever love her back.

She'd talk him into it. She'd literally plan out a campaign until she could convince him that she was the best thing that had ever happened to him. Hopefully, he wouldn't take too much convincing. She yawned. That was tomorrow's job. She tried not to worry about her damaged fingers. Only time would tell if she'd lose the use of them, and likely her job too.

"Everyone got out alive?" she asked, already drifting off again and unable to worry about anything right now except getting better.

"The only person unaccounted for is Malcolm Resnick, last seen near the Harrison's private quarters."

The nurses came in and shooed Eban out. He told her he had to get back to the ranch, and that he'd return tomorrow.

The nurses wanted to pump her full of morphine for the pain before they let her sleep, but she wouldn't let them. They gave her super strength Tylenol instead.

Four hours later, she felt as if her hand was on fire, and pain lanced through her wrist and all the way up her arm.

Charlotte had no idea what time it was, but it was still dark outside. Hard to believe that this time last night, she'd been having wild monkey sex with Novak.

She didn't have a phone or any clothes. And where the hell was her weapon? She hoped Novak had taken care of it for her.

Had TJ survived?

Immediately, she threw the covers off herself and swung her legs out of bed. The tiles were cold as she made her way to the door of the private room she was in. She poked her head out, aware that her rear end was flapping in the wind.

She used her good hand to hold the back of her gown together as she shuffled down the corridor. She recognized the floor she was on. The same one Bob Jones was on, but the guard wasn't at his post. Maybe with the siege over, the press had lost their appetite for the story.

She went down to the nurses' station, but there was no one around. She reached for the phone to call Novak, but footsteps approached, and she withdrew her hand guiltily.

"I was looking for my phone," she explained. But the nurse shooed her back to bed.

Charlotte was in too much pain to sleep and too stubborn to take opioids.

Maybe Bob Jones was awake too? Had anyone thought to tell him that they'd arrested TJ and that TJ had accused Malcolm Resnick of Brenna's murder?

She decided to stick her head into his room, in case he was awake and wanted to talk.

She checked for the nurse, but she'd gone again. So she walked to Bob Jones's door and paused outside. Should she knock? But what if he was asleep? Instead, she carefully eased it open an inch.

The sight of a naked man stretched out on the floor had her rushing forward.

"Wouldn't do that if I was you."

Charlotte froze and turned slowly around. Bob Jones was out of bed and wearing the deputy's uniform. He was also pointing the deputy's gun at her face.

And then she realized she'd made a rookie error. They all had. They'd treated Bob Jones as a witness when he should have been treated as a suspect.

"There never was a cougar sighting. You and Resnick were in it together," she said dully.

His eyes glinted nastily in the dim light. "We have an arrangement. Now, we're going for a little walk."

"I'm hardly dressed for a walk." Her teeth started to chatter.

His smile made her skin crawl. "I disagree." He jerked the end of the gun but was too far away for her to lunge for it. "Make a noise, and I may as well shoot you anyway."

Dammit. She'd had enough of people waving guns and shooting at her in the last twelve hours. "You'll kill me the same way you killed Brenna. It was you who killed her, correct?"

He shook his head. "Not me. Malcolm. I'd have kept her alive for a while."

Charlotte shivered at the implication in his tone. Was that what he thought he was going to do with her? "You blamed TJ. Started this whole thing." She frowned at him, trying to work her way closer to him and his gun.

He knew what she was trying to do though. "Get any closer, and I'll put another bullet in you."

"The thing I don't understand is why you were there in the first place." It clicked into place with a blinding flash. "TJ said his uncle was stealing gold from him and his father."

"Give the girl a gold star."

"Tie me up and leave me here."

"I don't think so." He smirked. "Come on. Time to go, girlie."

She looked down at the paper-thin gown and her bare feet. "If I go outside like this I'll freeze to death."

His expression was uncaring. "I guess your choice is freezing to death or a bullet. Move it."

CHAPTER THIRTY-SIX

NOVAK WAS STRETCHED across the front seat of the Chevy, fully clothed with his boots on the dash. He'd driven back to the hospital despite the blizzard. Despite McKenzie giving him an exasperated glare. Despite the mountain of paperwork he'd left behind.

The team had understood.

According to the nurse he'd spoken to, Charlotte was sleeping, so he'd thought he'd catch forty winks and then sneak in when the nursing shift changed.

Trouble was he was too cold to sleep.

He was about to turn on the engine when a car pulled up and sat idling at a side door. A second later, he watched a deputy open a fire exit. The deputy then pushed a woman in a hospital gown out into the snow. At first, he thought his eyes were deceiving him, but then he realized it was Charlotte, and the deputy had his gun trained on her.

What the fuck?

He called McKenzie, who answered too quickly for the man to have been asleep.

"We have a situation." He couldn't believe how calm he sounded when he wanted to rage and scream at the assailant to let her go. "I'm in the hospital parking lot and I see a car with a driver, plus a deputy, who looks a lot like our injured wildlife officer, holding a gun on a woman in a hospital gown wearing a sling."

"SSA Blood?"

"Yes." Novak gritted his teeth. "Not sure who the individual driving is, but you need to send agents ASAP and cops for backup. I'm going after them. In fact, I'm not letting them leave this parking lot."

Novak put the cell on speaker and tossed it in a cup holder. Then he turned the ignition key. He didn't switch on the lights as he waited for the small truck to start driving along the road that would have them passing directly behind him.

Rage coursed through his veins. Every pore in his body oozed deadly intent. He pulled an HK416 carbine from under the passenger seat and waited. He was worried about hurting Charlotte, but he didn't have much choice.

He watched them trundle sedately away from the hospital. Calmly planning to get away with murder.

They were about twenty feet away when he revved the engine and flew backwards at top speed, bumping over a small grass berm and straight into the driver's side door.

The impact spun the small truck off the road. Novak slammed on the brakes and jumped out, putting bullets into the front and back tires so the truck was going nowhere.

The driver jumped out and started running away. Malcolm Resnick.

Cockroaches always survived the apocalypse, but Resnick wouldn't get far. Novak could already hear agents spilling from the hospital in pursuit. One of them came in his direction, but Novak didn't take his eyes off Federal Wildlife Officer Bob Jones who was in the back seat of the truck with a gun pressed to Charlotte's temple. She shivered violently from the cold or from fear. All Novak knew was she was suffering, and that made him mad.

Her eyes were defiant and wide, pain creasing the corners.

A massive lump wedged in Novak's throat. He still hadn't told her how he felt. "Let her go, Jones."

"Let me go, or I'll kill the bitch."

"It's over." Novak forced the emotion out of his voice. He did this every day. Every single day. He didn't usually have someone he loved playing the part of hostage though.

"I'm going to slide out this door and walk around the truck. Then I'm going to get in your vehicle and drive away," Jones countered. "I'll leave her unharmed. I want your truck. Nothing else."

Novak nodded, his face an impassive mask.

Bob Jones eased out of the back seat, keeping Charlotte pressed tight against him.

She wasn't even wearing slippers.

Rage grew, but Novak pushed it to another part of his brain and sighted his weapon. Jones kept ducking, trying to conceal himself behind Charlotte. Making a shield of an injured woman.

"Do you want to know who saved you four nights ago, Bob?" Charlotte asked. Her voice vibrated with cold. "It was Novak here. He risked his own life to save yours."

Jones spat in the snow. "Mighty kind of you."

"I presume you decided to make TJ your scapegoat that day, but it backfired when someone in the compound actually shot you."

Jones forced out a sour laugh. "They had better aim than I anticipated. I wasn't planning on getting any closer, but someone got a bead on me. It was my own fault."

"You sure it was Malcolm who killed Brenna?" Charlotte's breath came in a sharp gasp.

"Yeah. We caught her spying on us."

"Doing what?" asked Novak.

"Malcolm has a drug habit he needs to feed. I help him out with deliveries. Then he found a bunch of gold at Tom Harrison's place and needed help getting it out. The plan was to split it fifty-fifty."

Novak doubted it had been lost.

"Malcolm caught the girl and shoved her. She tripped and hit her head against a tree." Jones dug the gun harder into Charlotte's skull. "It was an accident. I went and put the bag of gold in the truck to keep it safe and came back to move the body deeper in the woods. TJ was already there."

The gold must have still been in the back of the truck the day he and Charlotte had gone to the US Fish and Wildlife Service office.

"You must have been worried someone was going to look in your vehicle and find it." Charlotte was trying to distract Jones.

She knew as well as Novak did that Jones would try to shoot them. It was the only way he'd actually escape.

"Stay where you are and don't do a damn thing," Novak murmured to the agent who'd arrived to back him up.

He watched Bob's finger on the trigger and did not waver in his concentration as Charlotte spoke. She was trying to get Jones to drop his guard. Novak's gaze stayed on the man who wanted to rip the best part of Novak's future away from him. He'd had a mother who'd tried to do that with abuse and torment. He'd had an ex-wife who'd tried to do that with broken promises and casual disregard. He wasn't letting another human being get in the way of his happiness.

Bob went around the back of Novak's Suburban, and Novak moved parallel on the opposite side. The man had to loosen his grip on Charlotte to open the Chevy's passenger door. The moment he did so, Charlotte jerked to her left, and Novak took the shot through the glass.

Jones crumpled to the ground dead.

Novak slung the carbine over his back and ran around, brushing the shattered safety glass off Charlotte and catching her to him. He whisked her into his arms as the other agent confirmed Bob Jones was never going to be a problem again.

Novak sprinted back to the warmth of the hospital as Charlotte's teeth chattered like machine-gun fire. He rushed in the main door and whirled to where a roaring fire was burning in the fireplace.

He placed her in front of the hearth, pulled off his jacket, and wrapped it around her quaking body.

Then he sat down and pulled off his boots and socks and lifted her frozen feet so he could put the socks on her. Then he gathered her against him, careful of her injured hand, and rocked her in his arms.

"I love you, Charlotte. You constantly scare the shit out of me, but I can't stand the idea of not being with you."

She laughed, but it was perilously close to a sob. "I love you too. I have no idea why." She smiled when he winced. "Except the fact you keep saving my life, and you're smart, and you listen to me even if you don't always agree with me."

A group of nurses rushed down the hall. He wouldn't let her go, but he let them lead the way back toward her room so they could get her properly warmed up and check her stitches.

"And you are really good at sex, Novak," she said, despite

the snorts of the other people in the room.

"Call me Payne."

"I always do." She touched the side of his face, and he almost collapsed with relief. "On the inside, I always do."

The nurses and doctors rushed around, but he refused to leave. They found the young deputy knocked out next door, and they started work on him, but he was already coming around.

When they had her settled, and she'd finally accepted a shot of something for the pain, he held her good hand.

"What's the first thing you want to do when we get back to Quantico?" he asked her.

"I want to go grocery shopping with you."

He frowned. "Seriously? Grocery shopping is your idea of a fun first date? I might need to reassess this situation."

Her head rolled against the pillow. "I've always had this vision of going grocery shopping with the man of my dreams. Him being patient and kind as I choose the ingredients for a romantic dinner."

"Is there sex involved in this fantasy?"

Her lips curved. "Depends how well we get along doing the grocery shopping." Her fingers curled around his before she admitted. "My parents have both been divorced twice, and I never once saw them go grocery shopping with their exes without bickering."

"So it's a test."

She laughed. "It's a test."

"You know I'm competitive, right?" he teased, kissing her fingers.

"I'd noticed. I'm competitive too."

"I'd noticed that. We're going to be the best grocery shoppers in existence." He leaned up and kissed her lips. It scared him that she still felt cold. "Move over." He was barefoot so he crawled into bed beside her, cuddling her good side against him and holding her the way he wanted to for the next eight decades. She rested her head against his chest and, after a few minutes, she stopped shivering.

Thirty minutes later, McKenzie popped his head in the door, but Novak didn't move, and McKenzie didn't comment on the arrangement. Charlotte was finally sleeping, and Novak would defy the president himself if the alternative was disturbing her.

"Resnick is in custody," McKenzie said simply before heading out again.

Good. Saved Novak hunting the guy down.

Somehow, after only a few days, this woman had become the single most important thing in his life, and he intended to be her protector from now on. He intended to love her. And go grocery shopping with a smile on his face even if it killed him.

EPILOGUE

TJ STARED THROUGH the side window as the earth turned a brighter shade of orange, and the vegetation switched from majestic trees to cacti and rolling scrub.

Kayla slipped her hand into his. "How are you holding up? Need to stop and take a rest?"

He turned to look at her. She was so beautiful but still so fragile looking. She'd picked him up at the rear door of the hospital when he'd finally been discharged that morning.

The FBI had dropped all charges, which should have made him feel good but actually, he was still numb.

"I should be the one looking out for you, not the other way around," he told her. Shame welled up inside him. It was an emotion he was used to. The therapist who'd come to see him in the hospital almost every day had told him he needed to forgive himself and give himself time to deal with the loss and betrayal.

Kayla had experienced loss and betrayal too.

"I'm so sorry about Brenna." He'd told her before, but he didn't want her thinking he'd forgotten that she was hurting too. He wasn't sorry it had been Brenna rather than Kayla on the mountain that day. Even that private acknowledgement made more guilt burn through him.

"I miss her." Kayla's mouth squeezed tight as she watched

the road. "I was glad I was able to give her a proper service."

TJ nodded, though he hadn't attended. He'd still been under guard back then. Weeks of interviews had been required before he'd been allowed to see Kayla.

His father had tried to reach out to him from jail, but TJ had refused to talk to him. Despite everything Tom Harrison had done, TJ still loved the man. He still loved his mother. They were the only parents he could remember, and they'd loved him fiercely. Too fiercely. Tom had been willing to kill dozens of people, including children, in order to keep their secret.

TJ would never be able to forgive his father for that. Nor for the fact he'd shot the lady Federal Agent and would have shot Kayla if she'd have held them back.

TJ could never forgive him for that.

Tom and Martha's shocking secret meant TJ had another set of parents out there. People who'd suffered incredible loss all because his mom and dad had wanted a child and had taken theirs.

TJ was supposed to meet with them. Even the thought felt like a betrayal of Tom and Martha. And that wasn't fair on him or his biological parents. They were the ones who'd been wronged. They were the ones who'd endured the loss of a child for sixteen years never knowing if he was alive or dead.

Who did that?

Monsters.

Monsters did that, and TJ loved them both.

"Where we going?" he asked though he didn't care. As long as they left behind the mess of his old life.

"Brenna always wanted to visit Death Valley. I figured I'd sprinkle her ashes there so she got her wish. Is that okay?"

He only wanted to leave behind the destruction and lies and media circus his life had become in the weeks following his father's desperate escape bid. "As long as I'm with you."

She flashed him a brilliant smile. "Let me know if you want to stop anywhere along the way. I figured we'd find a motel room for the night."

"You don't want to camp?"

She shook her head. "Don't have a tent. The Feds haven't given it back yet. Anyway, one of us was shot, and I don't want him to have a relapse."

He flinched again. Not from the pain, that had been crazy, but from the anguish in his father's eyes when he'd realized what he'd done.

"I'll pay you back." He needed to get a job but wasn't sure what the heck he was going to do with his life.

"I don't need your money, TJ."

He laughed, and it pulled at the scar tissue of his abdomen. "Just as well. I don't have any."

"I thought your father ceded you all the land and gold the Feds dug up?"

"I'm not taking it. I don't want anything of his."

"He raised you. He did everything he did because he loved you. Who else is he going to give it to?"

TJ shrugged. "He'll get out one day. He can live there."

Kayla shot him a worried look. "TJ, he's never gonna get out. Stealing a baby? Blowing up the compound with the intent to kill? Shooting Charlotte? He's never getting out."

TJ bobbed his shoulder.

"Take the land. Create a nature preserve or something. You love that mountain. Protect it."

He thought of the secretive creatures who lived in that

forest. The idea of them being left unprotected destroyed him. He looked at her and asked the most important question. "Would you go back? Live in the area?"

She nodded. "I was thinking of buying that ranch where the Feds stayed. It's for sale."

TJ's eyes widened. He could work on a ranch. He knew how to ride, and he knew how to do hard physical labor.

Kayla's fingers clenched and unclenched around the wheel. "But I don't want to be there without you. I love you, TJ. That hasn't changed. You're a good person. You didn't do anything wrong."

TJ couldn't swallow. He reached out and squeezed her fingers again. "I love you too."

She smiled and lit up his world. "And when you're ready to see your biological parents, I'll come with you. I'll hold your hand, and we'll get through it together."

TJ's spirit lightened for what felt like the first time since he'd found Brenna's body on Eagle Mountain. "I spoke to them on the phone. It was weird. I know they wanted to visit in the hospital, but I wasn't ready."

"It's okay. We'll go when you're ready."

"Thank you." He swallowed tightly. Even his name was wrong. TJ. Tom Junior. He'd never be Dale Singer. Dale Singer was dead. TJ wasn't sure how they'd feel about that. Until they talked, really talked, he'd never know.

He stared at this beautiful, amazing woman who had changed his life completely and made it worth living. "Thanks for being the girl I fell in love with."

She laughed and threw him a teasing smile. "We're in this together. With luck, we've got years ahead of us, but I'm not taking anything for granted. I'm going to love you probably a lot harder than you're prepared for."

He shook his head. "I'm ready for anything. I've spent too much time doing what other people think I should. The only person I care about now is you." And maybe he'd care about his biological parents one day soon too. Maybe they could build some sort of relationship. Slowly.

Some of the weight lifted. He didn't need to figure out everything today. Like the therapist said, he could take time to figure it all out. Time to heal with this woman who'd become a part of his heart.

―――――――――――

IT WAS CHRISTMAS Eve, and Novak was cleaning his weapons in his equipment cage in HRT's compound at Quantico.

As long as there was no major incident to respond to, he had most of the Christmas holidays off. Trouble was Charlotte had flown to California yesterday to visit her father, and he was left tooling around like some lovelorn sap.

The fact he was a lovelorn sap was beside the point. They'd spent pretty much every spare moment together since Washington State. Even grocery shopping had been fun, because he'd discovered he had a sweet tooth where Charlotte was concerned, especially when licked straight from her body. Finding new toppings had become his favorite pastime.

He sighed miserably. He missed her.

She'd invited him to accompany her to meet her father, but with Kurt Montana still overseas, Novak felt as if he couldn't reasonably fly across the country.

Duty.

For the first time in his life he found himself resenting the fact his job was getting in the way of his personal life. Before it had been all he'd really had. Now it sucked. It really sucked.

Angeletti had invited him to his family's Christmas lunch tomorrow, so that was something to look forward to. He'd need to kick his morose ass into festive gear to get through it without depressing the hell out of everyone.

When every weapon was gleaming, he washed up his hands in the sink and decided to go home to his pathetic, empty apartment and make something a little more inventive than toast to celebrate the season.

When he pulled up outside his apartment, he sat in his truck looking up at his window. The sky looked exactly how he felt. Gloomy. Sullen. He pulled out his cell. Called Charlotte. "I'm getting the next flight out there."

"Wait. No—"

"Blue team is officially on standby. If an incident requires Gold team as well I'll figure out a way to get back here."

"No—"

"Charlotte, I'm doing this. I need to pack and call the airline. I love you. See you soon." He hung up before he changed his mind. Now he'd made the decision he wanted it done.

He jogged to the door and took the stairs up to the fourth floor. He was halfway through his living room before he registered the real Christmas tree set up in the corner. Charlotte sat at his dining table wearing a coat, hat and what looked like several sweaters.

In front of her was a brand-new deck of cards.

"You might want to lock that." She nodded toward the door as a smile curled one side of her mouth.

Novak couldn't move. "You're here."

Her smile widened. "I realized how many years I'd spent doing what was expected of me and what made other people happy." Her blue eyes sparkled as they held his. "I decided this year I was going to do what made *me* happy."

The words felt like riches raining down on his head.

"*You* make me happy, Charlotte. You make me feel like the luckiest man alive."

She grinned and started slowly shuffling the playing cards. "That's good. You're going to need lots of luck this time."

Her fingers were still healing. He knew they caused her some pain sometimes as the bone reforged itself. She'd lost some function, but it was slowly returning. Her boss, Quentin Savage, had made it quite clear to FBI administration that there was no way he'd tolerate losing Charlotte from his team, even if she couldn't shoot worth a damn. But Novak felt a whole lot better knowing she could defend herself if necessary. He'd taken her to the gun range so often she was almost as good with her left hand as she had been with her right. Once her injury was fully healed, he'd refocus on getting her back up to speed with that hand too.

He toed off his boots and flipped the deadbolt. Sat and checked his hand. Looked up with one raised brow.

Charlotte's cheeks were a little rosy from all the layers of clothes she was wearing.

"You okay there? Not too hot?" They'd played poker a few times and every time Charlotte had ended up in her underwear before Novak had lost his shirt.

"I'm prepared." There was a glint in her eye.

It took five rounds before she won a hand. He slowly removed his hoodie and was gratified by the annoyed glance she gave his t-shirt.

Another five rounds and she was down to a crimson bra he'd never seen before.

"I don't understand." She ran her hand through her hair. "I'm usually good at cards."

"I told you I was lucky."

"This is beyond luck." She shook her head. "I heard from Kayla yesterday."

"Oh yeah." He knew she was trying to distract him as she shimmied out of her leggings. Matching Christmas underwear was making him sweat.

"She's buying Maple Tree Ranch."

"You're kidding me. Good for her." He laughed. Tom Harrison was in jail awaiting trial. Malcolm Resnick was being held in the same federal facility but had cut a deal to avoid the death penalty before admitting his crimes. The authorities had exhumed Martha Harrison's body and discovered traces of thallium in her body. Resnick had apparently slipped rat poison into his sister's food after she'd asked him to leave Eagle Mountain. She'd caught him stealing from her and Tom. Novak figured if Tom ever got hold of his brother-in-law the other man was dead.

Two individuals had confessed to shooting the wildlife officer and the local deputy. They'd both been charged, and the DOJ appeared satisfied that justice had been served. A few wannabe revolutionaries had been rounded up and were cooling their heels in jail. Conspiracy to kill Federal Agents was not something the government took lightly.

"I call you."

Novak had a full house. Kings and aces.

Charlotte's shoulders sagged. "How? How do you do it?"

Novak couldn't stand another second of having her so

close but not touching her. He stood, drew her to her feet. "I concede."

She laughed as he swept her into his arms and marched into his bedroom.

"I got you a couple of presents." He hadn't had a clue what to get her at first and was worried he'd chosen the wrong thing. "But I can't pick up one of them for a few days."

He laid her on the bed.

"I got you a present too. In fact, I bought you several." Charlotte gazed pointedly at her festive lingerie.

Novak laughed. "And I am very grateful." He spent the next hour showing her exactly how grateful and by the time they were done, they both needed a shower and started over again.

Finally, they sat on his couch drinking beer, admiring the tree she'd dragged inside and set up while he was at work. He played with her hair. "Did you even see your dad?"

"Yeah. I basically said 'Hi' and turned around and caught the next fight home. I did have to use my skills as a negotiator to talk my way onboard, but they were short of air marshals so it all worked out."

He went and grabbed the jewelry box he'd had wrapped in the store. Handed it over and kissed her.

"It's not Christmas yet." But Charlotte was already opening it up. It was a silver charm bracelet she'd admired in the store. She grinned in delight as she started to investigate the charms he'd selected. Entwined hearts. A spinning globe because she wanted to travel. A gun. A shopping cart. A kitten.

She frowned. "Why did you get me a kitten charm? Is that some dubious reference to pussy?"

He choked. "No. Shit, but now I'll never look at that bracelet without having that image in my mind."

She grinned but then frowned again. "So why?"

He kissed her. "You have to wait."

"You got me a kitten?" she almost yelled.

He grimaced. "It's supposed to be a surprise."

"You got me a kitten!" She danced excitedly in a circle.

He grinned. "I know you love pet sitting for friends. I figured maybe it was time for one of your own. Between the two of us we can take care of one cat, surely?"

She straddled his lap and leaned down to kiss him. "Seems like a lot of responsibility."

He ran his hands up her sides. "We're both professionals. We can handle it."

"Why do we have to wait a few days?" she asked, pulling back.

"Because you were away."

"I'm back now. What time does the place shut?"

Novak checked his phone. Smirked. "In a couple of hours. You want to go pick her up now?"

"We have a girl?" Charlotte was already pulling on her clothes.

Novak had hoped a kitten was an appropriate gift, but he was thrilled Charlotte was so happy. They hit the shelter minutes before they closed for the holidays. He'd already purchased everything the kitten would need and had planned to wrap it all before Charlotte got home.

"She's beautiful." Charlotte cooed over the fluffy calico.

"We need to find a family for her brother, and we've homed the entire litter." The woman beamed from behind the desk.

Novak resignedly shook his head as Charlotte filled out

more paperwork.

Once they were ensconced in his truck, he realized they still needed to hit the store. He barely had a loaf of bread at his place.

"Where do you want to spend Christmas? Your place or mine?" he asked.

"I don't care as long as you're there." Her smile was the only gift he needed.

"Let's go to mine first and pick up all the gear I bought for these guys and then head to yours so they can settle in." He motioned to the kittens who were meowing from their travel container.

"I have no food." Charlotte warned him.

Her idea of no food was a full freezer of prepared meals but no fresh salad. His was an almost empty bottle of ketchup.

"I'll go pick up anything we need or we'll order in," he promised.

The kittens meowed, and Charlotte grinned, and Novak finally felt like his life was on the right track. It finally felt like he had everything he'd ever dreamed of.

"I love you, Payne. I love you so much."

"I love you too. I think we should partner up and get our own TV show."

"Blood and Payne does have a nice ring to it."

He felt nervous and cleared his throat. "So what do you say, about partnering up?"

"You mean like living together?"

He wanted a hell of a lot more than just living together, but that would do for a start. "We could look for a bigger place."

She reached over and slid her hand into his. "A house. I

want to get a house with you and our kittens."

He'd live wherever she wanted. In whatever she wanted. He also knew he was going to be ribbed like hell by his teammates for buying Charlotte kittens for Christmas, but he felt happier than he'd felt in years. He had everything he wanted in his life. Everything he needed.

"Merry Christmas, SSA Blood."

"Happy Holidays, Payne."

And just like that, she jolted his heart and made him feel like a worthy member of the human race. Worthy even of a woman like her.

USEFUL ACRONYM DEFINITIONS FOR TONI'S BOOKS

ADA: Assistant District Attorney
AG: Attorney General
ASAC: Assistant Special Agent in Charge
ASC: Assistant Section Chief
ATF: Alcohol, Tobacco, and Firearms
BAU: Behavioral Analysis Unit
BOLO: Be on the Lookout
BORTAC: US Border Patrol Tactical Unit
BUCAR: Bureau Car
CBP: US Customs and Border Patrol
CBT: Cognitive Behavioral Therapy
CIRG: Critical Incident Response Group
CMU: Crisis Management Unit
CN: Crisis Negotiator
CNU: Crisis Negotiation Unit
CO: Commanding Officer
CODIS: Combined DNA Index System
CP: Command Post
CQB: Close-Quarters Battle
DA: District Attorney
DEA: Drug Enforcement Administration
DEVGRU: Naval Special Warfare Development Group
DIA: Defense Intelligence Agency
DHS: Department of Homeland Security
DOB: Date of Birth
DOD: Department of Defense
DOJ: Department of Justice
DS: Diplomatic Security

DSS: US Diplomatic Security Service
DVI: Disaster Victim Identification
EMDR: Eye Movement Desensitization & Reprocessing
EMT: Emergency Medical Technician
ERT: Evidence Response Team
FOA: First-Office Assignment
FBI: Federal Bureau of Investigation
FNG: Fucking New Guy
FO: Field Office
FWO: Federal Wildlife Officer
IC: Incident Commander
IC: Intelligence Community
ICE: US Immigration and Customs Enforcement
HAHO: High Altitude High Opening (parachute jump)
HRT: Hostage Rescue Team
HT: Hostage-Taker
JEH: J. Edgar Hoover Building (FBI Headquarters)
K&R: Kidnap and Ransom
LAPD: Los Angeles Police Department
LEO: Law Enforcement Officer
LZ: Landing Zone
ME: Medical Examiner
MO: Modus Operandi
NAT: New Agent Trainee
NCAVC: National Center for Analysis of Violent Crime
NCIC: National Crime Information Center
NFT: Non-Fungible Token
NOTS: New Operator Training School
NPS: National Park Service
NYFO: New York Field Office
OC: Organized Crime
OCU: Organized Crime Unit
OPR: Office of Professional Responsibility

POTUS: President of the United States
PT: Physiology Technician
PTSD: Post-Traumatic Stress Disorder
RA: Resident Agency
RCMP: Royal Canadian Mounted Police
RSO: Senior Regional Security Officer from the US Diplomatic Service
SA: Special Agent
SAC: Special Agent-in-Charge
SANE: Sexual Assault Nurse Examiners
SAS: Special Air Squadron (British Special Forces unit)
SD: Secure Digital
SIOC: Strategic Information & Operations
SF: Special Forces
SSA: Supervisory Special Agent
SWAT: Special Weapons and Tactics
TC: Tactical Commander
TDY: Temporary Duty Yonder
TEDAC: Terrorist Explosive Device Analytical Center
TOD: Time of Death
UAF: University of Alaska, Fairbanks
UBC: Undocumented Border Crosser
UNSUB: Unknown Subject
USSS: United States Secret Service
ViCAP: Violent Criminal Apprehension Program
VIN: Vehicle Identification Number
WFO: Washington Field Office

COLD JUSTICE WORLD OVERVIEW
All books can be read as standalones

COLD JUSTICE® SERIES
A Cold Dark Place (Book #1)
Cold Pursuit (Book #2)
Cold Light of Day (Book #3)
Cold Fear (Book #4)
Cold in The Shadows (Book #5)
Cold Hearted (Book #6)
Cold Secrets (Book #7)
Cold Malice (Book #8)
A Cold Dark Promise (Book #9~A Wedding Novella)
Cold Blooded (Book #10)

COLD JUSTICE® – THE NEGOTIATORS
Cold & Deadly (Book #1)
Colder Than Sin (Book #2)
Cold Wicked Lies (Book #3)
Cold Cruel Kiss (Book #4)
Cold as Ice (Book #5)

COLD JUSTICE® – MOST WANTED
Cold Silence (Book #1)
Cold Deceit (Book #2)
Cold Snap (Book #3) – Coming soon
Cold Fury (Book #4) – Coming soon

The Cold Justice® series books are also available as **audiobooks**
narrated by Eric Dove, and in various box set compilations.

Check out all Toni's books on her website
(www.toniandersonauthor.com/books-2)

ACKNOWLEDGMENTS

Writing a book is both a solitary endeavor and a group exercise. My thanks go to Kathy Altman who is the best critique partner in the history of the written word. Rachel Grant who beta reads at the expert level. Jodie Griffin who read an early copy and reassured me it didn't suck. More hugs of appreciation go to Rachel Grant (again), Carolyn Crane, and Jenn Stark, for keeping me company online, and being at-the-ready for ofttimes crazy questions and emergency emotional support when self-confidence takes a nose-dive. Thanks also to Leanne Sparks, Amy Gamet, Melinda Leigh and Kendra Elliot, for our weekly virtual hangout that involves alcohol and self-help.

Thanks to my amazing cover designer, Regina Wamba, for her gorgeous artwork, and to my formatter, Paul Salvette, for his hard work. Also, to Jessica at Inkslingers PR for her support. Credit to my editors, Deb Nemeth, Joan Turner at JRT Editing, and proofreader, Alicia Dean. I appreciate the role you all play in making my books coherent.

As always, thanks to my family. My husband and I were expecting to be empty-nesters this year, but instead we have four adults in a house that suddenly seems too small. I'm happy the kids are home. I am grateful for the roof over our heads. I'm counting my blessings, which includes all of my amazing readers. Thank you so much. Thank you, thank you, thank you.

ABOUT THE AUTHOR

Toni Anderson writes gritty, sexy, FBI Romantic Thrillers, and is a *New York Times* and a *USA Today* bestselling author. Her books have won the Daphne du Maurier Award for Excellence in Mystery and Suspense, Readers' Choice, Aspen Gold, Book Buyers' Best, Golden Quill, National Excellence in Story Telling Contest, and National Excellence in Romance Fiction awards. She's been a finalist in both the Vivian Contest and the RITA Award from the Romance Writers of America. Toni's books have been translated into five different languages and over three million copies of her books have been downloaded.

Best known for her Cold Justice® books perhaps it's not surprising to discover Toni lives in one of the most extreme climates on earth—Manitoba, Canada. Formerly a Marine Biologist, Toni still misses the ocean, but is lucky enough to travel for research purposes. In late 2015, she visited FBI Headquarters in Washington DC, including a tour of the Strategic Information and Operations Center. She hopes not to get arrested for her Google searches.

Sign up for Toni Anderson's newsletter:
www.toniandersonauthor.com/newsletter-signup

Like Toni Anderson on Facebook:
facebook.com/toniandersonauthor

Follow on Instagram:
instagram.com/toni_anderson_author

Printed in Great Britain
by Amazon